ANNIHILATION

By Drew Karpyshyn

STAR WARS
Star Wars: Darth Bane: Path of Destruction
Star Wars: Darth Bane: Rule of Two
Star Wars: Darth Bane: Dynasty of Evil
Star Wars: The Old Republic: Revan
Star Wars: The Old Republic: Annihilation

MASS EFFECT
Mass Effect: Revelation
Mass Effect: Ascension
Mass Effect: Retribution

TEMPLE HILL
Baldur's Gate II: Throne of Bhaal

THE CHAOS BORN
Children of Fire
The Scorched Earth
Chaos Unleashed

STAR WARS®

THE OLD REPUBLIC

ANNIHILATION

DREW KARPYSHYN

DEL REY • NEW YORK

Star Wars: The Old Republic: Annihilation is a work of fiction. Names, places, and incidents either are products of the author's imagination or are used fictitiously.

2013 Del Rey Mass Market Edition

Copyright © 2012 by Lucasfilm Ltd. & ® or ™ where indicated. All Rights Reserved. Used Under Authorization.
Excerpt from *Star Wars: Scoundrels* by Timothy Zahn copyright © 2012 by Lucasfilm Ltd. & ® or ™ where indicated. All Rights Reserved. Used Under Authorization.

Published in the United States by Del Rey, an imprint of Random House, a division of Penguin Random House LLC, New York.

DEL REY and the HOUSE colophon are registered trademarks of Penguin Random House LLC.

Originally published in hardcover in the United States by Del Rey, an imprint of Random House, a division of Penguin Random House LLC, in 2012.

This book contains an excerpt from *Star Wars: Scoundrels* by Timothy Zahn. This excerpt has been set for this edition only and may not reflect the final content of the forthcoming edition.

ISBN 978-0-345-52942-8
eBook 978-0-345-53567-2

Printed in the United States of America

www.starwars.com
www.delreybooks.com

9 8 7 6 5 4 3

Del Rey mass market edition: November 2013

To Jennifer, the reason
for everything

ACKNOWLEDGMENTS

Though my name is the one featured on the cover of this book, as with any *Star Wars* novel it couldn't have come together without the contributions of many other people. Theron Shan and Teff'ith were first introduced in *Star Wars: The Old Republic: The Lost Suns* comic series, so I have to thank Alexander Freed and the folks over at Dark Horse Comics for creating such fun and memorable characters. Similarly, Jace Malcolm, Satele Shan, and several other characters featured in *Annihilation* were originally created by the *Star Wars:* The Old Republic team over at BioWare, so I owe them a debt of gratitude as well.

I'd also like to thank everyone over at Del Rey and LucasBooks, particularly my editors, Frank Parisi and Jennifer Heddle. Weaving a new story into a collaborative setting like the *Star Wars* universe is always a delicate proposition, and I couldn't have done it without all their feedback and help.

Finally, I'd like to give a special acknowledgment to all the fans of my writing: Without your support, I wouldn't be where I am today.

THE STAR WARS LEGENDS NOVELS TIMELINE

BEFORE THE REPUBLIC
37,000–25,000 YEARS BEFORE
STAR WARS: A New Hope

c. 25,793 YEARS BEFORE *STAR WARS: A New Hope*

Dawn of the Jedi: Into the Void

OLD REPUBLIC
5000–67 YEARS BEFORE
STAR WARS: A New Hope

Lost Tribe of the Sith: The Collected Stories

3954 YEARS BEFORE *STAR WARS: A New Hope*

The Old Republic: Revan

3650 YEARS BEFORE *STAR WARS: A New Hope*

The Old Republic: Deceived
Red Harvest
The Old Republic: Fatal Alliance
The Old Republic: Annihilation

1032 YEARS BEFORE *STAR WARS: A New Hope*

Knight Errant
Darth Bane: Path of Destruction
Darth Bane: Rule of Two
Darth Bane: Dynasty of Evil

RISE OF THE EMPIRE
67–0 YEARS BEFORE
STAR WARS: A New Hope

67 YEARS BEFORE *STAR WARS: A New Hope*

Darth Plagueis

33 YEARS BEFORE *STAR WARS: A New Hope*

Cloak of Deception
Darth Maul: Shadow Hunter
Maul: Lockdown

32 YEARS BEFORE *STAR WARS: A New Hope*

STAR WARS: EPISODE I
THE PHANTOM MENACE

Rogue Planet
Outbound Flight
The Approaching Storm

---

22 YEARS BEFORE *STAR WARS: A New Hope*

STAR WARS: EPISODE II
ATTACK OF THE CLONES

22–19 YEARS BEFORE *STAR WARS: A New Hope*

STAR WARS: THE CLONE WARS

The Clone Wars: Wild Space
The Clone Wars: No Prisoners

Clone Wars Gambit
  Stealth
  Siege

Republic Commando
  Hard Contact
  Triple Zero
  True Colors
  Order 66

Shatterpoint
The Cestus Deception
MedStar I: Battle Surgeons
MedStar II: Jedi Healer
Jedi Trial
Yoda: Dark Rendezvous
Labyrinth of Evil

19 YEARS BEFORE *STAR WARS: A New Hope*

STAR WARS: EPISODE III
REVENGE OF THE SITH

Kenobi
Dark Lord: The Rise of Darth Vader
Imperial Commando 501st

Coruscant Nights
  Jedi Twilight
  Street of Shadows
  Patterns of Force

The Last Jedi

10 YEARS BEFORE *STAR WARS: A New Hope*

The Han Solo Trilogy
  The Paradise Snare
  The Hutt Gambit
  Rebel Dawn

The Adventures of Lando Calrissian
The Force Unleashed
The Han Solo Adventures
Death Troopers
The Force Unleashed II

REBELLION
0–5 YEARS AFTER
STAR WARS: A New Hope

Death Star
Shadow Games

0

STAR WARS: EPISODE IV
A NEW HOPE

Tales from the Mos Eisley Cantina
Tales from the Empire
Tales from the New Republic
Scoundrels
Allegiance
Choices of One
Honor Among Thieves
Galaxies: The Ruins of Dantooine
Splinter of the Mind's Eye
Razor's Edge

3 YEARS AFTER STAR WARS: A New Hope

STAR WARS: EPISODE V
THE EMPIRE STRIKES BACK

Tales of the Bounty Hunters
Shadows of the Empire

4 YEARS AFTER STAR WARS: A New Hope

STAR WARS: EPISODE VI
THE RETURN OF THE JEDI

Tales from Jabba's Palace

The Bounty Hunter Wars
 The Mandalorian Armor
 Slave Ship
 Hard Merchandise

The Truce at Bakura
Luke Skywalker and the Shadows of
 Mindor

NEW REPUBLIC
5–25 YEARS AFTER
STAR WARS: A New Hope

X-Wing
 Rogue Squadron
 Wedge's Gamble
 The Krytos Trap
 The Bacta War
 Wraith Squadron
 Iron Fist
 Solo Command

The Courtship of Princess Leia
Tatooine Ghost

The Thrawn Trilogy
 Heir to the Empire
 Dark Force Rising
 The Last Command

X-Wing: Isard's Revenge

The Jedi Academy Trilogy
 Jedi Search
 Dark Apprentice
 Champions of the Force

I, Jedi
Children of the Jedi
Darksaber
Planet of Twilight
X-Wing: Starfighters of Adumar
The Crystal Star

The Black Fleet Crisis Trilogy
 Before the Storm
 Shield of Lies
 Tyrant's Test

The New Rebellion

The Corellian Trilogy
 Ambush at Corellia
 Assault at Selonia
 Showdown at Centerpoint

The Hand of Thrawn Duology
 Specter of the Past
 Vision of the Future

Scourge
Survivor's Quest

THE STAR WARS LEGENDS NOVELS TIMELINE

 NEW JEDI ORDER
25–40 YEARS AFTER
STAR WARS: A New Hope

35 *YEARS AFTER STAR WARS: A New Hope*

 LEGACY
40+ YEARS AFTER
STAR WARS: A New Hope

43 *YEARS AFTER STAR WARS: A New Hope*

45 *YEARS AFTER STAR WARS: A New Hope*

DRAMATIS PERSONAE

Theron Shan; Republic Strategic Information Service agent (human male)

Marcus Trant; Director of Republic Strategic Information Service (human male)

Jace Malcom; Supreme Commander of the Republic military (human male)

Satele Shan; Grand Master of the Jedi Order (human female)

Gnost-Dural; Jedi Master (Kel Dor male)

Teff'ith; smuggler for the Old Tion Brotherhood (Twi'lek female)

Gorvich; smuggler for the Old Tion Brotherhood (human male)

Darth Karrid; Sith Lord (Falleen female)

Darth Marr; Sith Lord (human male)

Minister Davidge; Imperial Minister of Logistics (human male)

A long time ago in a galaxy
far, far away. . . .

ANNIHILATION

PROLOGUE

THE AIR inside the cave was cool, but a thin sheen of perspiration coated Satele Shan's skin. The hard, uneven stone dug into her back and shoulders through the blanket she lay on. She shifted and twisted to escape the discomfort, the dim light of glow sticks casting the shadow of her writhing limbs into a grotesque dance on the far wall.

"Try to remain still, Satele."

Master Ngani Zho, the mentor who had brought her to the sanctuary of this cave, spoke softly, but his deep voice still resonated in the close confines of their hidden refuge.

Outside, the galaxy was engulfed by war. The Sith, ancient enemies of the Jedi Order long thought extinct, had returned to threaten the existence of the Republic that had stood for thousands of standard years.

Satele Shan had seen the horrors of this war firsthand, battling with her fellow Jedi alongside the soldiers of the Republic against the enemy hordes. She had seen worlds burn. She had seen friends die. She had suffered more than she ever imagined she could and survived. Yet the pain she experienced now was something entirely different.

There is no emotion, there is peace.

The mantra of the Jedi helped her focus, and she closed her eyes as she tried to draw on the Force to calm herself. But her body refused to obey her mind, and instead of a slow pattern of inhale–exhale, her breath continued to come in ragged, rapid gasps.

The Masters at the Jedi academy had never prepared her for this. How could they?

"Satele! Can you hear me? Are you okay?"

Her eyes snapped open in response to Ngani Zho's voice. Gritting her teeth while another wave of agony washed over her, she could only nod in reply, her fingers clenching his hand as she tried to draw the strength to sustain herself through this ordeal.

"We're almost done, Satele. Just one more push."

The final contraction felt like it was ripping her apart, but she followed her Master's instructions and pushed despite the pain. Satele screamed, and then suddenly the pain was gone. An instant later the loud cries of a child—*her child*—filled the cave.

"It's a boy, Satele," Master Zho said as he cut the umbilical. "You have a son."

Satele had known the child she carried was male for months; she had felt him through the Force as his life grew stronger within her. But hearing the words spoken aloud somehow made this all feel more real. She had brought life into a galaxy overwhelmed with death.

"Here, Satele," Master Zho whispered, holding the infant out to her.

Exhausted, she struggled to find enough strength to reach out with her weary arms. Ngani had wrapped the babe in a swaddling blanket; warm and enveloped as he had been in the womb, he was no longer crying.

Pulling the child close to her chest, she couldn't help but wonder what destiny the Force had chosen for her son. She had no doubt his path would be a difficult one, for in these dark times no path was easy. What role would he play in the fate of the galaxy?

She knew her own role well enough: Satele Shan, hero

of the Republic, paragon of the Jedi Order. Strong in the Force. She was a champion of the light; a symbol; an icon.

The rank and file saw her as the embodiment of everything the Jedi and the Republic stood for. And that was why she had been forced to hide her pregnancy. For the first months it had been simple—the loose-fitting Jedi robes had easily covered the swelling of her belly. But in the later months a more elaborate ruse was necessary.

She couldn't have done it without Master Zho's help. When her condition became impossible to conceal and she had been forced to go into hiding, he had told the Jedi Council and the leaders of the Republic military that he had sent Satele on a vital mission—something he could not speak of for fear of endangering her life. Given Master Zho's impeccable reputation, none had questioned him.

Now, however, the mission was over. It was time for her to return; the Republic had fought too long without their champion. The Sith Empire's relentless advance had gone too far. She could no longer ignore the Republic's need.

"Are you sure about this, Satele? You don't want to reconsider?"

Satele looked down at the baby resting so peacefully in her arms, and realized she would treasure this moment for the rest of her life. Whenever she was scared or alone or consumed by grief, she could draw on the memory of the first time she held her son.

In the early stages of her pregnancy, she'd struggled against her maternal feelings as she'd felt the life growing inside her. She had tried to rationalize her protective instincts as nothing more than a biological imperative—an evolutionary mechanism to ensure the propagation of the species. But as the weeks and months passed, she realized her love for her unborn child was more than just biology and hormones. The emotional bond was real, and her desire to do anything—take any risk or commit any act—to protect her son was almost overwhelming.

She would do everything in her power to protect him—even terrible, violent things. She would put his needs above all others, even if it meant an entire planet must suffer to spare him pain. Given her position and power, this was unacceptable.

"You promised you would take him," Satele said softly, gazing down into the child's wide, wondering eyes.

"I will," Ngani assured her. "If that's still what you want."

"What I want has nothing to do with it," she muttered as she reluctantly handed the child back to her Master. "For the sake of the galaxy, this is what must be."

As he took the child from her arms, the moment of greatest joy she would ever know ended. The child began to whimper, so Ngani stood up and began to cross quickly back and forth across the cave's uneven floor. The movement seemed to settle the child, much to Satele's relief.

"And you're sure you don't want to tell the father?" her Master asked as he paced.

"No. He's a good man, but there is darkness in him."

Ngani nodded, accepting her decision.

"What's his name?" he asked.

Satele was momentarily taken aback. He had never asked her the father's name before, and she had never offered it. Then she realized he was talking about the baby.

"You are going to raise him," she said with a shake of her head. "You should choose his name."

The Jedi Master stopped pacing and fixed her with a glare she remembered from her days as a Padawan.

"You're his mother. His name should come from you."

Satele turned her head to the side and closed her eyes as exhaustion washed over her.

"Theron," she murmured. "His name is Theron."

CHAPTER 1

THERON SHAN walked quickly through the packed streets of Nar Shaddaa's Promenade. His unassuming features—pale skin, brown hair, brown eyes, average build—allowed him to blend easily into the crowd. The cybernetic implants visible around his left eye and right ear were his most distinguishing features, but he wasn't the only one sporting them on Nar Shaddaa, and they typically didn't draw unwanted attention.

The Hutt-controlled moon was a landscape of unfettered urban sprawl, marked by towering skytowers crammed too close together and gaudy, glowing billboards that dominated the horizon as far as the eye could see in every direction. Sometimes called Little Coruscant, it was hard to accept Nar Shaddaa as a true homage to the Republic capital world; in Theron's eyes it was more akin to a grotesque parody.

Coruscant had been designed with an eye to aesthetics: there was a pleasing flow to the cityscape and a consistent and complementary style to the architecture. The city was carefully divided into various districts, making it easy to navigate. The pedestrian walks were crowded but clean, the endless stream of airspeeders overhead stayed within the designated traffic lanes. On Coruscant, there was an unmistakable sense of order and purpose. At times, Theron found it positively stifling.

Here on the Smugglers' Moon, however, it was a glorious free-for-all. Run-down residential buildings were scattered haphazardly among seedy-looking commercial structures; factories abutted restaurants and clubs, with no regard for the toxic clouds of filth spilling out over the patrons. With no traffic rules in force, airspeeders and swoop bikes darted and dived in seemingly random directions, sometimes flying so low the pedestrians ducked and covered their heads.

As Theron turned a corner, he realized someone was following him. He hadn't actually seen anyone on his tail, but he could sense it. He could feel eyes watching him, scoping him out, measuring him as a target.

Master Ngani Zho, the Jedi who'd raised him, would probably have claimed Theron's awareness came through the Force. But despite coming from a long line of famous Jedi, Theron wasn't one of the Order. In fact, he had no special connection to the Force at all.

What he did have was a decade's worth of experience working for Republic Strategic Information Service. He'd been trained to notice minute details; to be hyperaware of his surroundings at all times. And even though his conscious mind was distracted by the details of his coming mission, his subconscious one had instinctively picked up on something that had triggered alarms in his head. He knew better than to ignore them. Careful not to break stride, turn his head, or do anything else that might tip off his pursuer, Theron used his peripheral vision to scan the area.

At street level, everything was a chaotic mishmash of bright, flashing colors. A constant assault from an army of pink, purple, green, and blue signs and billboards provided perfect camouflage for whoever might be following him. Fortunately the intensity of the inescapable neon was muted by the layer of grime that clung to every surface—a reminder of the unchecked pollution in the atmosphere that would eventually transform Nar Shaddaa into an uninhabitable wasteland.

It wasn't easy to pick someone who looked suspicious out from the crowd. The population of the Smugglers' Moon was as varied, unpredictable, and seedy as the surroundings. In the years since the signing of the Treaty of Coruscant, the Hutts had remained staunchly neutral in the ongoing cold war between the Republic and the Sith Empire, making Nar Shaddaa a common gathering place for criminal elements from all corners of the galaxy: Black Sun slavers, Rodian pickpockets, Twi'lek hustlers, Chevin stim dealers. Any and all illicit activities were tolerated on Nar Shaddaa, provided the Hutts got their cut.

Still, there were those too greedy or stupid to cut the Hutts in on their action. When that happened there were consequences. Things got messy.

Is that what this is about? Theron wondered. *Is Morbo on to me? Did he send someone to take me out?*

He passed by the statue of Karragga the Unyielding that dominated the Promenade. Though he'd been to Nar Shaddaa many times, he couldn't help but pause for a second and shake his head in disbelief: a thirty-meter-tall Hutt made of solid gold was too ostentatious to ignore. Shaking his head also gave him a chance to quickly glance from side to side to catch a glimpse of someone darting into a doorway off to his left. He didn't get a good look at whoever it was, but the sudden movement was unnatural enough to stand out.

Someone working alone. Could be a mugger. Or a trained assassin.

Theron was on a tight schedule; it was time to force the action. He turned down a narrow side street, leaving the worst of the crowds—and the relative safety they provided—behind. Off the main thoroughfare there were fewer neon lights and more shadowy corners. If his tail was going to try something, this was the perfect place to make a move.

A slight buzzing of the cybernetic implant in his right ear alerted him to an incoming transmission. There was only one person who knew his private frequency. Theron had to take the call.

"Accept incoming," he whispered. Louder, he said, "Director."

"Theron." The head of Strategic Information Service, as he so often did, sounded annoyed. "Where are you?"

"I'm on vacation," Theron replied. "I put in for some R and R. Remember?"

Theron realized the Director's call could work to his advantage. Whoever was following him would think he was distracted, vulnerable. All he had to do was pretend to be oblivious while listening for his stalker to creep up close, then suddenly turn the tables.

"Vacation, huh?" the Director grumbled in his ear as Theron continued farther into the deserted alley. "That's funny, because I have a report that one of our field agents has been spotted snooping around on Nar Shaddaa."

"Are you keeping tabs on me?"

"What are you doing on Nar Shaddaa?" the Director demanded.

"Maybe I just like the climate."

"Smog clouds and acid rain? Not likely. You're up to something."

Well, right now I'm about to be ambushed in a dark alley, Theron thought.

Out loud, he said, "I'm taking care of some personal business."

"What's Teff'ith mixed up in now?" the Director asked with a sigh.

Even though he couldn't see the man on the other end

of the call, Theron could picture his boss rubbing his temples in exasperation.

"Teff'ith's not a bad kid," Theron insisted. "She just tends to fall in with the wrong crowd."

"Guess that explains how she ended up working with you," the Director grumbled.

Theron had stopped walking, and was standing with one hand up to the cyberlink in his ear, staring straight ahead.

Might as well be wearing a sign that says, come and get me! Time to make your move, whoever you are.

"Ngani Zho saw something special in her," Theron said to the Director.

"I know Master Zho raised you, but by the time he met Teff'ith he was . . . troubled."

You almost said crazy, *didn't you?*

"She has key underworld contacts," Theron explained, "and she knows how to handle herself in a tough spot. We might need a favor from her someday. I'm just looking out for a potential asset."

"What makes you think she'd ever help us? Didn't Teff'ith say she'd kill you if she ever saw you again?"

"Then I'll make sure she doesn't see me."

"I hate to do this, Theron," the Director said with another sigh. "But I'm ordering you to pull out of Nar Shaddaa. It's for your own good."

Theron felt the unmistakable shape of a vibroblade's tip pressing up against his back and a deep voice growled, "Move and you're dead!" in his other ear.

"You worry too much," Theron told the Director, keeping his voice light. "Everything's under control." In a whisper he added, "Disconnect," and the comlink in his ear shut down.

"Get your hands up!" his unseen assailant snarled.

Theron slowly raised his arms in the air, silently cursing himself for letting his assailant get so close.

Never even heard him coming. Was I really that sloppy, or is he that good?

"Lose the piece."

The words were in Basic, but the voice was definitely not human—too deep, too rumbling. The speaker was large, but without turning around there was no way for Theron to pin down what species he was dealing with.

The comlink in his ear buzzed again, but this time Theron ignored the Director's call. He clicked his teeth together twice, temporarily shutting the cybernetics off so he could focus on getting out of the alley alive.

"I said lose the piece!"

The order was accentuated by a jabbing of the blade against Theron's back. Reaching down slowly, Theron slid his blaster pistol from the holster on his hip and let it drop to the ground. He briefly considered making a move; there were a dozen ways he could try to surprise and disarm his opponent. But without knowing exactly who or what he was facing, it was too risky.

Patience. Analyze the situation. Wait for your chance.

"Those are some fancy wrist guards you got. Maybe have a poison dart or a pinpoint blaster built in, right? Lose 'em."

Any hope Theron had of catching his assailant by surprise with the weapons in his customized bracers vanished as he unclipped the metal bands from his forearms and let them fall at his feet.

The fact that his assailant had marked the bracers as potential weapons also meant this wasn't some run-of-the-mill mugger. An Imperial operative would probably recognize the bracers, but it didn't make sense for any of them to be targeting Theron on a Hutt-controlled world . . . especially now that Imperial Intelligence had been officially disbanded. That left only one other likely—and unsettling—option: a bounty hunter or assassin working for Morbo the Hutt.

"Now turn around, real slow."

The pressure of the blade eased as the ambusher took a step back. Theron turned to see a violet-skinned Houk towering over him, his heavyset torso and thick, muscular limbs seeming to fill the entire width of the narrow alley. His froglike features were set in a grim scowl, his eyes fixed intently on his victim.

He was pretty sure the Houk didn't have any backup—he would have noticed if there was more than one person following him. But even if he was acting alone, Theron was no match for the massive brute's raw muscle. Under normal conditions he could make up what he lacked in strength with speed, but in the tight confines of the narrow alley avoiding the deadly vibroblade might be difficult . . . especially if the Houk was trained in close-quarters fighting. Given his choice of weapon, Theron had to assume he was facing a capable and deadly opponent.

"What's your interest in Morbo?" the Houk demanded.

"I have no idea what you're talking about," Theron said, his earlier hypothesis about his ambusher working for the Hutt seemingly confirmed.

"I've seen you scoping out Morbo's place for the past three days," the Houk snarled. "Lie to me again, and I won't ask nicely next time," he added, waving the vibroblade back and forth for emphasis.

The threat didn't bother Theron nearly as much as the realization that he'd been made during his recon trips to Morbo's club.

"Never saw you at Morbo's," Theron admitted. "Didn't think anybody saw me, either."

"I've been trained to know what to look for," the Houk answered.

Trained? Theron wondered. *By whom? Imperial Intelligence?*

As if echoing his own thoughts, the Houk asked, "Who are you working for?"

Theron wasn't about to reveal his connection to SIS, and he suspected another evasive answer would be met with violence.

"Take the shot!" Theron shouted, as if calling out to an unseen accomplice.

The Houk's head turned just a fraction as he reacted to Theron's bluff.

Seizing on the distraction, Theron lashed out with a quick kick to the Houk's midsection. The impact caused no real damage, but it momentarily knocked the big alien off balance, giving Theron more room to operate.

He was already backpedaling in anticipation of the counterattack; even so he barely avoided the expected lunge of his opponent. As he feared, the Houk wasn't just some clumsy brawler—he was quicker than he seemed.

As the Houk moved in, Theron tried to disarm him with a wrist lock, reaching out for the hand that held the blade. The Houk countered by twisting his body and throwing his opposite shoulder into Theron, sending him stumbling back.

Unable to set his feet, Theron was forced on the defensive. The alley was too narrow to dodge from side to side, so his only option was full-scale retreat, backpedaling rapidly as the Houk charged forward, the blade slicing and stabbing the empty air centimeters from Theron's chest. Theron suddenly stopped short and dropped to the ground, rolling into the thick legs of his advancing foe. The move caught the Houk by surprise; he tripped over Theron and tumbled to the ground, the fall knocking the vibroblade from his grasp.

One of the Houk's knobby knees caught Theron in the chin as he fell over him, splitting his lip and making him see stars. Woozy, Theron ignored the pain and leapt to his feet, and with his first step he staggered sideways into the side of the alley before crashing back down to the ground.

A massive hand closed around his ankle as the still-prone Houk tried to drag Theron close enough to finish him off. Theron lashed out with his free leg, smashing his foot twice into the Houk's corpulent face. The vise-like grip slipped just enough for Theron to free himself with a twisting roll, and he scrambled on hands and knees toward where his blaster and bracers lay on the ground.

The Houk struggled back to his feet, but by the time he was upright Theron had seized one of the bracers, slapped it onto his right forearm, and taken aim.

"Toxicity seven," he muttered, squeezing his hand into a tight fist.

A small dart launched from a thin barrel built into the bracer and buried itself in the Houk's chest. The mighty alien went rigid as a powerful electrical charge surged through him. He convulsed for several seconds, and then dropped to the ground, twitching slightly from the aftereffects.

Theron considered what to do with the immobilized but still-conscious Houk as he quickly gathered his gear. It wouldn't take long for the effects of the electrical blast to wear off, but for the next few minutes the Houk was basically helpless. Theron wasn't about to execute a helpless opponent . . . but he wasn't above interrogating him. "Toxicity two," he whispered, firing another dart into the Houk's thigh from point-blank range.

He waited thirty seconds for the mind-clouding drug to take effect before he started asking questions.

"How did you spot me?" he asked. "You said you were trained. By whom?"

The Houk shook his head groggily, struggling to resist the chemicals coursing through his system. In a few minutes they would render him unconscious—Theron needed to get answers before that happened.

"Hey!" Theron snapped, slapping the Houk's meaty cheek. "Who trained you?"

"Republic SIS," the Houk mumbled.

"Republic SIS?" Theron repeated, his mind struggling to accept what he'd just heard.

"Covert surveillance," the groggy Houk confirmed, his tongue loosened by Theron's truth serum. "Watching Morbo. Part of Operation Transom."

SIS has eyes on Morbo. No wonder the Director knew I was here.

Theron had never heard of Transom, but that wasn't unusual. SIS had ongoing missions all across the galaxy, and only the Director and the agents involved would be aware of the details.

Just my luck to stumble into an active SIS mission.

"What are you going to do with me?" the Houk asked, slurring his words and struggling to keep his eyes open as sleep slowly dragged him down.

"Relax, big guy," Theron said. "We're on the same side."

The Director had ordered Theron off Nar Shaddaa; obviously he was worried about him interfering with Transom, whatever it might be. But Teff'ith's life was at stake, and Theron wasn't about to abandon her, even if it meant defying a direct order.

The Houk began to snore loudly, ending any hope Theron had of asking him for more details about Operation Transom.

It has to be in the early stages, Theron reasoned. *They're still just observing the target. If I get in and out quickly, it shouldn't have any significant impact on the mission.*

He knew the Director would never buy that argument

as justification for what he was about to do. But it was always easier to ask forgiveness than permission.

Grabbing hold of the Houk's arms, he dragged the sleeping alien into a corner of the alley, hiding him behind several trash bins. He'd wake up in a couple of hours with a pounding headache, but otherwise unharmed. Plenty of time for Theron to meet with Morbo and bargain for Teff'ith's life.

He set off down the alley at a brisk trot, trying not to think about the fact that he was putting his entire career in jeopardy.

CHAPTER 2

THERON'S LIP started to swell from the blow from the Houk's knee; he felt like he'd been smashed with a swoop rider's helmet. He had a few small medkits tucked into his belt, but it didn't seem worth the effort. The wound was painful, but not debilitating.

Instead, he ran through a simple series of mental exercises Ngani Zho had taught him to soothe the body and mind. It was a trick the Jedi used to help them draw on the Force to heal themselves, but Theron had found that there were benefits even for someone like him.

He acknowledged the pain in his lip, embraced it, then let it slip away from his consciousness. Almost instantly the pain faded, though the damage remained. Good enough until the mission was over and he could get a med droid to fix him up properly.

Winding his way through the back alleys without further incident, he emerged in the corner of a small square in the Red Light District. There were fewer people here than in the Promenade, but it was crowded enough that Theron kept an eye peeled for pickpockets as he crossed the square. A trio of teens on swoop bikes buzzed the crowd, flying the colors of one of the local street gangs. They laughed at the angry shouts of the pedestrians, circling tauntingly just above their heads before zooming off to disappear around the corner.

Theron paid them little heed as he approached his destination: a squat, two-story building on the other side of the square owned by Morbo the Hutt, one of the moon's many local crime lords. In the front of the building was a small casino bar called Morbo's Paradise; in the back was a warehouse for storing whatever illegal goods the Hutt was trafficking, along with Morbo's private office.

The plan was simple: Go into the club, slip a hefty handful of credits to the manager, and ask for a meeting with Morbo. Once inside, Theron would use his powers of persuasion—and the Hutt's greed and self-interest—to convince Morbo to call off the hit on Teff'ith and her crew. Quick, clean, and simple wasn't Theron's usual style, but he wasn't in the mood for any surprises.

The club was more crowded than usual. Probably irrelevant, but Theron couldn't help but notice. After the ambush in the alley, his senses were on high alert. He quickly scanned the club for anyone who seemed out of place—if SIS had assigned the Houk to keep an eye on Morbo, there could be other agents on the case.

He didn't see anyone who specifically grabbed his attention, but he did notice something else unusual. Most of the patrons weren't gambling. They sipped drinks, sitting alone or in pairs at tables and at the bar as if waiting for something. A few openly studied him as he strode toward Rers Shallit, the Neimoidian manager of the club, who was standing in a corner near the back. Behind him a pair of Gamorrean bouncers stood on either side of a door leading to the rooms in the back of the club.

Early in his preliminary investigations, Theron had learned that Rers was Morbo's second in command. The Hutt called the shots; the Neimoidian was in charge of carrying out his orders. Theron had also learned that Rers was dumb enough to take cuts for himself when

Morbo wasn't looking, but smart enough to keep the grifts small and unnoticeable.

Eager at this point to get the mission over with, Theron skipped all pretense.

"I need to speak to Morbo."

"Forget it. Go wait with the others."

The reply caught Theron off guard. He'd expected Rers to say something like, *Nobody speaks to Morbo. Talk to me and I'll pass it along.* Or maybe, *What's in it for me?*

The unexpected response stoked Theron's already burning curiosity; he struggled to stay on script.

"Get me in to see your boss and I'll make it worth your while."

The Neimoidian held him in a withering gaze.

"Morbo runs a clean auction. No sneak peeks at the merchandise. Go sit down before this gets ugly."

The Gamorreans turned to him, their porcine snouts curled in anticipation, revealing their protruding tusks.

"Can't blame a guy for trying," Theron said with a shrug as the pieces clicked into place. The extra patrons at the club weren't gambling because they were here looking to buy. Theron hadn't heard anything about an auction in the three days he'd been on Nar Shaddaa. It must have been set up weeks ago; potential buyers already contacted long before he arrived. And Theron could think of only one reason for all the secrecy.

Morbo's auctioning off captured Republic POWs.

Slavery was legal in the Sith Empire and on Hutt-controlled worlds. The Republic generally turned a blind eye to the Hutt slave trade, but there was one notable exception. Any Hutt who auctioned off captured Republic soldiers inevitably became a target of covert Republic retaliation: privateers seizing cargo in transit, anonymous vandals targeting the Hutt's holdings and warehouses on various planets, customs officials on Core

Worlds conducting numerous "random" inspections on arriving shipments from the Hutt's business partners.

Selling POWs into slavery was bad business, and most Hutts avoided it. But Morbo was greedy, even for his notoriously avaricious species, and a secret auction of Republic prisoners was right up his alley.

Aware that Rers was still watching him, Theron made his way over to an empty table near the entrance and sat down. The Gamorrean bouncers eyed his retreat, snouts sagging in disappointment at the lost chance to pummel a seemingly helpless customer.

He settled into his seat and mulled over his options. Everyone probably assumed he represented a buyer wishing to remain anonymous, and he'd have to play along if he didn't want to raise suspicion. He could wait out the auction, toss out a few lowball bids to play his part, then try to meet with Morbo after to bargain for Teff'ith's life. That would be the most prudent course of action. But the idea of sitting idly by while his fellow soldiers were auctioned off like chattel galled Theron.

What if I'm not the only one not willing to just let this happen? Is this what Operation Transom is about?

Then again, if SIS had learned about Morbo's secret auction, the Director could have thrown together a special op to try to liberate their fellow soldiers.

And I might have just messed the whole thing up by taking out Operation Transom's point man.

Theron's first instinct was to do whatever it took to free the Republic prisoners—if he screwed up the mission, he should be the one to fix it. On the other hand, if Transom was still on, the last thing Theron wanted to get in the way.

There was no way to know which was the right call; not without more information. Unfortunately, contacting SIS wasn't an option. Like all the casinos in the Red Light District, Morbo's club was equipped with top-of-the-line security equipment. Any incoming or outgoing transmissions in a three-block radius would be intercepted and analyzed—a standard precaution to prevent cheaters from communicating with a partner outside the casino who could be using a computer to calculate the odds on the games.

Theron surveyed the crowd, searching again for some sign that SIS had another agent in place posing as a buyer. But nobody stood out from the crowd . . . of course. If they did, the mission would be blown.

Gotta make the call. Sit tight, or get on your feet and get moving.

For Theron, it wasn't hard to reach a decision. Rers and the other patrons had shifted their focus from him to other new arrivals, making it easy for him to get up and slip outside without attracting attention.

In front of the club, he cast a quick glance to make sure nobody was watching, then casually wandered into the side alley and made for the warehouse built onto the back. He didn't need to see inside to picture the scene: armed guards watching over unfortunate prisoners about to be auctioned off.

There was a single durasteel door at the back, a pair of blacked-out windows one story up. He dismissed the door; taking the obvious entrance would give the guards time to react. It was unlikely the windows were alarmed or protected by a security field—the difficulty in getting to them was defense enough. He considered scaling the wall to get to the windows, but he'd be exposed if any of the guards wandered out into the back alley. Better to come at them from above, where he was less likely to get noticed.

Theron wandered back out to the front of the club and merged with the flow of pedestrians wandering the square. He walked halfway down the block, passed three buildings on the same side of the street, then

paused at the entrance of a narrow back lane next to a
three-story building; judging from the signage it was a
combination pawnshop and dance hall. He checked to
see if anyone was watching.

The three hoodlums on swoop bikes he'd seen earlier
streaked overhead again, coming in so low that pedestrians had to duck to avoid getting clipped. They whooped
and yelled before climbing safely out of reach and accelerating into the distance. Theron took advantage of
the distraction and ducked into the alley, sauntering to
the back of the building. He pulled his climbing gloves
from where they had been tucked in at the rear of his
belt, tugged them over his hands, flexed his fingers. He
tested the grip on the side of the building; a million
needle-like nanofibers woven into the fabric of the gloves
caught on the invisible imperfections of the seemingly
smooth surface, giving him purchase.

Moving with the simian dexterity of a Kashyyyk tach,
he scampered up the side of the pawnshop's exterior
wall and onto the roof. He didn't pause to catch his
breath, taking three quick steps and leaping across the
narrow alley separating the pawnshop from the two-
story building beside it. He landed softly, tucking into a
roll to absorb the impact. The alley before the next
building over was slightly wider, and he once again ran
across the roof and jumped across without any hesitation. On the rooftop of the building adjacent to Morbo's
club, he paused and contemplated the nearly ten-meter
gap between them.

*You've made longer jumps before. And if you fall,
you've survived worse.*

Gathering himself, he sprinted toward the edge. Half
a step before he jumped the three joyriding teens whizzed
down the alley in front of him on their swoops, unaware
Theron was leaping across the rooftops just above them.

Distracted, Theron stumbled, his boot slipping on the

uneven surface of the roof as he planted his foot for his final leap. His body's muscle memory reacted instinctively to the sudden loss of balance and momentum by throwing itself forward to offset its shifting center of gravity; Theron was still able to push off the ledge. Halfway across the gap, he realized he wasn't going to make it. He threw his left arm out in a desperate attempt to snag the ledge. The fingertips of his climbing glove grazed against the surface, the nanofibers latching onto the permacrete half a meter below the roof.

His plunge came to an abrupt and jarring halt, nearly wrenching his left shoulder from its socket, and his body twisted so hard he slammed into the building. He grunted in pain as the wind got knocked from his lungs. Supported by his single, aching limb, he dangled in the breeze and struggled to catch his breath.

After several seconds Theron had recovered enough to reach up and slap his right palm against the building, allowing his other arm to bear some of his weight. Ignoring the protest of his left shoulder socket, he hauled himself up and over the ledge and lay on his stomach atop the roof of Morbo's club. Rising to his feet, he tested his shoulder with a quick range of motions. The pain made him grit his teeth, but nothing seemed seriously damaged.

At the same time, Theron listened for any sound indicating that his inelegant arrival had attracted the attention of someone inside the club. Hearing nothing but the noise of the swoop-riding teens fading away into the distance, he dropped into a crouch and scuttled along the rooftop to the edge of the rear wall. From his belt he pulled out a length of thin, flexible wire tipped with a small precision laser cutter and a miniature cam.

Theron flicked the cam on, and the image that fed into its lens was transmitted to a heads-up display embedded in the cybernetic implant in his left eye. Using the cam's relayed image to guide his hand, he carefully lowered the wire over the edge until it was even with the top left corner of one of the blacked-out windows. With a series of whispered commands, Theron cycled the cam through the visible, infrared, and ultraviolet spectrums, searching the various wavelengths for the faint, shimmering glow that would indicate the presence of some type of security field protecting the windows.

He wasn't surprised to find the windows were clean; even Morbo couldn't afford to invest in expensive electronic security fields on every possible point of access.

Theron twisted the base of the wire and the laser activated, melting a tiny hole in the corner of the glass and allowing him to work the cam through for a look inside the warehouse. Scattered crates and shipping containers. In the back corner four Cathar were huddled together on the floor, three males and one female. The prisoners had their hands clasped behind their backs, their heads held high even though their feline features were set in grim resignation. A pair of armed guards, both human, stood watch over them, their slouched stances and disinterested expressions revealing their boredom as they waited for Morbo to start the auction.

Moving the laser in slow circles, Theron melted the circumference of the hole in the window until it was large enough for him to reach his hand through, but hopefully still small enough to escape attention. He retracted the wire, stored it safely in his belt, then carefully lowered himself over the edge until his feet rested on the windowsill.

Using the climbing glove of his left hand to help maintain his balance, he peered through the hole, pinpointing the location of each guard with the automated targeting implant in his left eye. He shifted so he could slip his right hand through the hole in the glass. Though firing blind, his cybernetic augmentations kept him locked onto his targets as he whispered, "Toxicity six," and launched the last two darts from his bracer.

When he peeked back through the hole in the window, he saw that both guards were down and out. The captives on the ground looked around with a confused mixture of fear and hope. Knowing it was unlikely anyone in the casino at the front of the club would hear, Theron turned his head to the side and punched away the rest of the glass with the ball of his fist.

Moving quickly, he squeezed through the window frame and dropped to the ground below, tucking-and-rolling to absorb the impact. He sprang to his feet and raised a finger to his lips. The female Cathar, the senior-ranking member of the group based on her sergeant's stripes, nodded curtly in understanding.

Theron rifled through the pockets of the unconscious guards, finding a small key on the second. Moments later the Cathar were free of their restraints and on their feet. Theron moved to the exit on the far side of the warehouse floor. He made sure the door to the alley wasn't locked, and that opening it wouldn't trigger any alarms, as the Cathar rubbed their wrists to restore circulation.

"Who are you?" the female Cathar asked.

"Republic SIS," Theron said. "We look after our own.

"That door leads to the back alley," he added, pointing to the exit. "Can you make it from here?"

The Cathar nodded as she bent down and retrieved the blaster rifle from the guard at her feet. One of her companions snatched another blaster from the second guard.

"Thank you," she said, before she and the others sped off toward freedom.

Once the Cathar were safely away, he searched the rest of the warehouse until he located the door that led to the private offices between the warehouse in the back of the building and the casino club out front. Theron opened the door carefully, peering through the doorway to discover that the corridor was empty. He guessed Morbo's thugs were probably out front keeping an eye on the prospective buyers waiting for the auction.

The corridor led off in two directions. Standing still, Theron heard the unmistakable murmur of a crowded bar coming from off to his right, so he turned and headed the opposite way. He didn't have to go far before he found what he was looking for: a thick beaded curtain hung across an archway at the end of the hall.

Theron stepped through and came face-to-face with the club's owner. Morbo's private office was a testament to the gluttony, vanity, and avarice of his species. The crime lord's bulk was draped over a luxurious custom-made couch, and the rest of the room was cluttered with opulent gold statues, gaudy paintings, and other garish objets d'art fashioned in the crime lord's own image. Several female Twi'lek servants scurried about the room with downcast eyes as they whisked away the remains of what appeared to be a lavish and exotic feast for a dozen people, but which Theron realized was merely the Hutt's pre-auction meal.

Morbo stared at him with unmistakable disdain. He clearly didn't see Theron as a threat, though his servants had all retreated and were cowering in the far corners of the room.

"*I told Rers no visitors before the auction,*" he growled in Huttese, his voice so deep Theron could feel it trembling through the floor and up into his feet. "*Next auction I should put that useless Neimoidian up for sale.*"

Like all SIS agents, Theron was fluent in Huttese. But the language put a strain on human vocal cords, so he stuck with Basic for his reply.

"I'm not here for the auction."

"*No? Then come back later.*" Morbo's long, thick tongue darted out to lick away a spot of grease rolling down the jowls of his chin. "*I have to show my merchandise in ten minutes.*"

Theron didn't think it was prudent to mention that, because of him, the auction had been postponed indefinitely. "I'll be quick, great and mighty Morbo. What I have to say could be very profitable for you."

The combination of stroking the Hutt's ego and dropping the magic p-word grabbed Morbo's full attention.

"*Speak. It better be worth my time.*"

"I know about the hit on the members of the Old Tion Brotherhood," Theron said, jumping straight to the point.

Morbo laughed, slapping his meaty hands against the rolls of fat covering his chest.

"*You're too late. I hired someone else for that job.*"

"I'm not bidding for the contract. I want you to call it off."

"*Impossible. The Brotherhood smuggled spice through my territory without paying my commission. You should know better.*"

"I'm not with the Brotherhood," Theron assured him. "I represent other interests."

"*Then why do you care?*"

"This isn't a smart business move," Theron continued, evading the question as his mind raced to come up with a convincing argument that wouldn't reveal who he was or whom he worked for. "Going to war with the Brotherhood could be expensive. But call off the hit and I'll find the credits to cover your commission."

"*This isn't about credits,*" Morbo said, his sluglike body quaking with rage. "*Since Zedania took over, the Old Tion Brotherhood has been expanding. Looking for new territory. I need to send her a message—nobody messes with Morbo!"*

"Zedania didn't authorize this mission," Theron explained. "The smugglers are working freelance."

"Then she won't care if I eliminate them."

"One of them works for me," Theron lied. "If you hurt her, I'll care."

"Her," Morbo said with a cunning smile. *"You mean the Twi'lek."*

Theron didn't see much point in trying to deny it. He nodded.

"You say she works for you," Morbo continued, his tail twitching slightly. *"But who are you, exactly?"*

"Someone who wants to see Zedania fail," Theron lied. "I've worked hard to get my contact close to her. If you don't call off this hit, I have to start over."

Morbo chuckled, the rolls of fat quivering with delight. Clearly he relished the idea of a mole inside someone else's criminal organization. His eyes narrowed as he tried to assemble the random bits of truth and fiction from Theron's story together into a single theory.

"You represent a rival looking to take Zedania's place? Another gang looking to bring the Brotherhood down? Law enforcement from the Tion Hegemony?"

"I really can't say."

"It doesn't matter anyway," Morbo said with a regretful sigh. *"Your friends are ready to leave. They're loading the spice onto their ship. My people are already headed to the spaceport. You're too late."*

Theron swore in Old High Gamorrese as he spun on his heel and darted back into the hall. As he ran toward the door leading back to the warehouse he heard angry shouts of surprise coming from the other side; someone had found the downed guards.

He continued past the warehouse door, his legs chewing up the ground in long, quick strides as he continued down the hall and burst through the door leading into the club. The Gamorrean bouncers on either side were too surprised to try to stop him; their job was to keep people from going into the back, not stop someone coming out.

Theron didn't look back as he raced out the door and into the street, heading for the spaceport.

CHAPTER 3

AS HE bobbed and weaved his way through the crowd, Theron realized he'd never get to the spaceport in time on foot. Fortunately, the unmistakable whine of incoming swoop engines gave him an idea.

Dashing into the middle of the square where he'd be most visible, he shook his fist and shouted up at the young gang members who had circled back around to buzz the crowd yet again.

"Take your flying toys and get on home, you little punks!"

As he'd expected, the three riders banked their swoops and came straight at him, drawn by his challenge.

Theron ducked and covered his head as the first swoop buzzed past a couple of meters overhead. The second came even closer. Theron turned and ran toward the cover of the nearest building, throwing quick glances back over his shoulder as he pretended to flee in terror. The third rider took the bait and gave chase, accelerating to cut Theron off before he could get to safety. He came in much lower than the other two, trying to force Theron to prostrate himself on the ground to avoid getting struck by his swoop.

Theron played his part by crouching low as if cowering in fear; then at the last moment he sprang up and grabbed the rider's arm as the swoop narrowly missed him.

Caught by surprise, the young thug was yanked from his seat. Theron held his grip for just an instant, twisting so that the rider fell hard on his backside and not on his unprotected head. The rider rolled across the square as the swoop veered and spun crazily out of control until the internal stabilizers righted it; the swoop's built-in safety protocols detected the rider's absence and brought the vehicle down for a safe landing on the other side of the square.

The crowd processed what had just happened in a stunned silence, broken by the sound of the other two swoops racing away, their riders unaware of their friend's fate. Then everyone erupted in a spontaneous round of applause and cheers.

Theron ignored them and ran over to check on the fallen rider. The young man had rolled over onto his back, where he lay dazed and groaning. Several patches of skin on his bare arms and hands had been scraped raw from his fall, but otherwise he appeared okay.

"Hey, kid—next time, wear a helmet," Theron said, giving him a pat on the cheek.

The teen only groaned in reply, though he did manage to flash an obscene gesture. Theron took that as a sign he was all right.

The sound of the retreating swoop engines changed pitch: the other two thugs were circling back. Theron turned and ran for the fallen rider's swoop, leapt on, and fired up the engine.

As he took off, he hoped the other two would stop to look after their friend instead of giving chase. Glancing back over his shoulder, however, he wasn't surprised to see them close on his tail. Theron punched the accelerator, pushing his ride to full speed as he climbed in altitude, the buildings and streets a blur of colors as he flew past.

In the days before joining the SIS, Theron had carved

out a reputation on the minor-league swoop circuits of Manaan; he doubted the riders in pursuit were a match for his skills. But he was on an unfamiliar machine, racing through streets they knew like the back of their hands. Losing them wasn't going to be easy.

He didn't worry about them taking him down with blasters; swoop bikes were notoriously unstable, and at high speeds even the most experienced riders needed both hands to maintain control. But if they were reckless enough, they could try ramming him with their own swoops to force him into a crash.

"Navigation overlay for current location," he whispered, and the HUD in his left eye implant responded by superimposing a map of the surrounding area over his vision. The blue dot signifying his location was moving too quickly across the map for Theron to look for shortcuts, so he plotted a course through the main thoroughfares. He doubted his pursuers would do the same.

The swoop he took was improperly balanced, and it would take a while for him to get a true feel for the bike. He banked hard around a corner, struggling to hold the line as the swoop tried listing to the left. Throwing his weight in the opposite direction he managed to stay upright, but the awkward move cost him speed.

Glancing back over his shoulder, Theron saw only one gang member in pursuit. Alarms went off in his head, and he focused on the map overlaying his vision. He saw the side alley on the map a split second before it appeared to his left, giving him just enough time to throttle back. The early deceleration allowed Theron to narrowly avoid a collision as the second rider shot out of the alley just in front of him in an attempt to knock him off his swoop. Theron dived down and to the left, the sharp change of direction overstressing the stabilizers on the misbalanced vehicle. Instead of fighting to stay upright, though, he leaned into it and hammered the accelerator, pushing the swoop into a tight barrel roll that took him under the rider who'd cut in front of him.

The kid following wasn't able to mimic Theron's move; the only way he could avoid ramming into his partner was by slamming the emergency brakes, stalling the engine as the other two swoops raced ahead and left him behind.

The spaceport was only a few kilometers away, well outside the territory of the rider's gang. With his friends no longer in the picture, Theron figured his pursuer just needed a little more encouragement to give up the chase. He released the grip of his right hand as he grabbed the blaster on his hip. The swoop bucked and swayed as soon as he let go, but now that he was used to the idiosyncrasies of the machine Theron managed to maintain control long enough to turn and fire a pair of quick shots at his pursuer.

The bolts went nowhere near their target. Flying a swoop bike with one hand was a feat in itself; holding it steady enough to accurately aim was nearly impossible. Regardless, the bolts had the desired effect: the other rider decided he'd had enough and veered off, ending the pursuit.

Theron slowed his vehicle and slapped his blaster back into its holster, struggling to keep the swoop online the entire time. Once he had two hands on the handles again, he took it back up to full speed for the rest of the journey. He arrived at the spaceport less than a minute later, bringing the swoop in for a landing near the main doors leading into the hangar bays where Teff'ith and her crew had docked their ship.

A small crowd was milling around outside the entrance. Curious, Theron tapped an agitated-looking Sullustan on the shoulder.

"What's going on here, friend?"

"*Ugly business,*" the Sullustan replied in his native tongue. "*Hutt business.*"

"Which Hutt? Morbo?" Theron asked in Basic. He had a bad feeling he already knew the answer.

The Sullustan shrugged.

"*Don't know. Armed men show up, tell everyone in Bays Seven through Twelve to clear out. I don't ask questions.*"

The distinctive sound of a heavy repeating blaster rang out from inside the hangar. The crowd collectively flinched and took a few steps back, leaving a clear path for Theron as he ran inside.

TEFF'ITH WAS in the middle of loading crates of tightly packed spice onto the ship when she was suddenly hit with an overpowering sense that something wasn't right. Nothing specific, just a half-imagined tingling in the tips of her lekku. Based on past experience she knew better than to ignore it.

"Something bad coming," she said in her heavily accented Basic, drawing twin blasters that she kept at her sides and scanning the spaceport for anything suspicious.

Gorvich, the human who'd set up the spice deal on Nar Shaddaa, snorted as he finished his preflight inspection of the ship's exterior.

"You've been complaining ever since we landed, Sunshine."

Teff'ith's lip curled up in a sneer. Gorvich had originally given her the nickname because of her yellow skin and "sunny" disposition; she was convinced he kept using it just to annoy her.

She had a nickname for him too: Idiot. Hardly original, but accurate. In her twenty-odd standard years she had worked as security and muscle for low-level scum across the galaxy, trying to scrape out a living on the fringes of so-called decent society. She'd dealt with thieves, killers, slavers, and sociopaths, but nobody brought bile to her throat like Gorvich—not even that SIS agent who'd gotten her mixed up in a crazy suicide mission almost two years ago.

It was tempting to just put Gorvich out of his misery with one clean shot between the eyes, but that would mean walking away from the Old Tion Brotherhood, and Teff'ith wasn't ready to do that. The Brotherhood was growing fast, and Teff'ith was already earning a reputation. If she played her cards right, the next few years could see her moving up the ranks until she was the one calling the shots instead of taking orders from morons.

Frinn—another member of the crew—grunted as he sauntered down the ship's boarding ramp to join them on the loading platform. "Sounds like you're just trying to get out of loading these crates," he said.

Teff'ith ignored him. He was almost as stupid as Gorvich, but he wasn't in charge. She didn't need to convince him of anything.

"Forget the cargo. Gotta go. We leave now."

"Are you crazy, Sunshine? Do you know how much this spice is worth?" said Gorvich.

"Can't spend if you dead."

"Did you know she was this paranoid when you decided to bring her along?" Frinn asked Gorvich, smirking.

"Think Morbo double-crossed us?" Teff'ith asked. "Sent goons to get our cargo?"

Gorvich laughed. "Not likely. Morbo doesn't even know we're here."

Teff'ith's eyes went wide. "What you mean?"

"I'm not cutting that bloated slug in on our deal just because he thinks he owns this district. Figured we'd handle the deal ourselves and make an extra twenty percent."

"Idiot!" Teff'ith spat, barely suppressing the urge to

unleash a volley of bolts into his chest at point-blank range. "Morbo knows! Going to get us killed!"

Gorvich rolled his eyes, but Vebb, the fourth member of their crew, set down the crate he was carrying and joined the conversation.

"Maybe she's right," the Rodian said. "I feel it, too. Something's off."

As soon as he spoke Teff'ith realized what was wrong. The spaceport was always bustling with activity: crews loading or unloading their ships; mechanics making repairs. But instead of the familiar sounds, right now she heard only silence. All the loading docks around their vessel were deserted.

"Down!" she shouted, diving forward, tackling Gorvich, and dragging them both to the ground behind a stack of crates still waiting to be loaded onto the ship.

Vebb followed her lead, his thin, wiry body ducking behind the crate he had just set on the ground. Frinn, however, just stood where he was, staring at them with a look of skeptical bemusement. A second later a heavy repeating blaster echoed through the deserted spaceport and Frinn's body slumped to the ground, his dead eyes open and his face frozen in the same stupid expression.

Teff'ith poked her head up then ducked back down almost instantly behind her makeshift bunker as another volley rang out. From the sound she was able to pick out general points of origin for the shots.

"Two shooters," she said to Gorvich, tilting her head in each direction. "There and there."

Gorvich popped his head up briefly, then ducked back down as the assassins opened fire.

"I can't see 'em."

Teff'ith didn't bother to tell him what a waste of effort his actions were. The far side of the hangar was shrouded in thick shadows and cluttered with heavy machinery for loading and unloading cargo from the incoming ships; the assassins were well protected and well hidden.

"Maybe we can make a break for the ship," Gorvich suggested as he checked the charge on each of his blasters.

She almost let him try, but then realized she'd need his help if she was going to get out of this alive.

"Shooters got the angle on ship. Cut us down if we go for it."

"So what's the plan?"

Teff'ith ran through the possible scenarios in her mind. The shooters had chosen their positions to pen them in and keep them from getting to the safety of the ship, but there was a door in the rear of the hangar she might be able to reach. If she got through the door she could work her way through the adjacent docking bays of the spaceport and try to flank their attackers.

"Slip out the back. Into Bay Seven. Circle around to Bay Nine. Come up behind."

"Sounds risky," Gorvich said, eyeing the open stretch between their current position and the door at the rear of their hangar. "Want me to send Vebb?"

Teff'ith glanced over at the Rodian, still cowering behind the crate. He was a good pilot, but not much use in a fight; he hadn't even drawn his pistol.

"You joking?"

"What if there are more than just two shooters?" Gorvich asked.

Teff'ith was surprised her idiot leader was capable of anticipating a trap, though she had already considered the possibility. If she had been the one planning this ambush, she'd have tried to flush the targets away from the ship and through the door at the rear leading into the adjacent hangar . . . and right into the waiting crosshairs of a third shooter. Bay 7 wasn't in use; the lights were off, and try as she might she couldn't tell if there was someone waiting in the gloom to spring a trap. But she didn't see any other options. Better to just go for it and hope there were only two assassins.

"Cover us," she said, getting her long legs ready for the quick sprint to the door.

Gorvich nodded, then popped up from behind the crates, screaming his fury as he unleashed a wild volley of shots to draw their enemies' fire.

Teff'ith took off, crouching low but moving fast as she broke for the door and the darkness beyond.

THERON RAN through the deserted hangars, heading toward Bay 8, where Teff'ith's crew had docked their ship. He heard another round of blasterfire and took it as a good sign—there wouldn't have been more shots unless Teff'ith and her people were fighting back.

Charging into the middle of the firefight in Bay 8 was too risky even for Theron, so he took a detour through the adjacent hangar. He plunged into the darkness of the unused Bay 7, nearly knocking over a heavily armored figure half hidden in the shadows. A single, thick horn protruded from the center of his bald head, clearly marking him as an Advozse even in the near darkness.

He was standing in the middle of the room with his blaster rifle raised to his shoulder, back toward the entrance Theron had come through, attention focused on the door leading into Teff'ith's hangar. Hearing the pounding steps coming up behind him, the Advozse started to turn toward the new arrival, but Theron was on him before he could react. With a front kick he knocked the blaster rifle from the alien's hands, then threw a quick flurry of punches at his face. However, the assassin wasn't some clumsy street thug; he ducked under the blows and took Theron off his feet with a leg sweep.

Theron rolled out of the way as his foe brought an elbow crashing down on the floor where his head had been an instant before. Still prone, he lashed out with his boot, but the Advozse turned away, and instead of crashing into his jaw it glanced off his shoulder.

The assassin reached to his belt for his backup weapon. Theron was faster, snapping his arm up as he growled, "Toxicity ten," unleashing the only unused weapon still left in his bracer. Unlike the arsenal of incapacitating darts, the single-shot pinpoint laser was lethal at a range of less than three meters. The bright intensity of the needle-thin beam pierced the darkness and struck the Advozse just below the horn protruding from the center of his brow, killing him instantly.

The body toppled forward, momentarily pinning Theron beneath its bulk. Before he had a chance to roll the fallen assassin off him someone else came barreling into the room from the door on the opposite end.

TEFF'ITH HEARD the assassins returning Gorvich's fire as she raced, exposed, across the hangar floor. A pair of bolts ricocheted off the ground beside her as she dived through the open door and into the unlit room beyond, safely out of the line of fire.

She slid across the floor and scrambled to her feet, bracing herself for the deadly impact of a blaster bolt from the possible third assassin waiting in the shadows. But the trap was never sprung, and Teff'ith grinned as she realized they might still get out of this alive.

Assassins didn't want to cut the bounty three ways. Greedy. Stupid.

Eager to make them pay for their mistake, she rushed through the room and out the door on the other side. She never even noticed the two figures—one alive, one dead—lying in the shadows on the floor only a few meters off to the side.

* * *

THERON WATCHED Teff'ith race past, oblivious to his presence. Once she was gone, he rolled out from under the Advozse's corpse and got to his feet. He preferred to disable opponents when possible, but sometimes that wasn't an option. In any case, he wasn't about to shed tears for a hired assassin.

He'd saved Teff'ith from walking into a deadly trap, and he'd done it without giving himself away. But there were other assassins to deal with, and though Teff'ith might have gained the upper hand thanks to his intervention, he wasn't about to leave her fate to chance.

Moving more cautiously and keeping to the shadows, he slipped away in the direction the young Twi'lek had disappeared.

CHAPTER 4

TEFF'ITH EMERGED from the darkness of Bay 7 into the central supply room serving Hangars 7 to 12. Her original plan had been to go through the supply room into Bay 9 and try to come at the assassins from behind. But when her eyes fell on the heavy loader and a damaged fuel core resting in the corner, she had a better idea.

The core was cylindrical in shape, one meter thick and two meters tall, and it weighed over a ton. It wasn't uncommon for ships to make minor repairs while docked at a spaceport, but replacing an engine's fuel core was a major undertaking. It wasn't just the size that made repairs difficult. Residual fuel trapped inside the core was highly flammable. The core was enveloped in thick shield casing, but if the casing was cracked, and the liquid inside exposed to air, it could ignite.

Teff'ith inspected the core. The casing was fully intact; it had probably been replaced because of a blockage in the lines. Reassured the engine core wouldn't unexpectedly explode, she jumped into the loader's operator seat and primed the starter. The compact vehicle's powerful engine coughed, sputtered, and belched out a thick cloud of black smoke before finally catching. The loader had seen better days, but it would be good enough for what she had planned. She could feel the vibrations of the twin treads rumbling over the floor and up through her chair as she maneuvered the loader over to the fuel core.

With a couple of button presses, she manipulated the loading arms so that they grabbed the fuel core at either end and hoisted it into the air, holding it lengthwise. She lowered the arms slightly until the core was level with her seat, allowing her to just barely see over the top of the cylinder toward where she was going. She spun the loader in place, then sent it chugging back through the door she had just entered.

THERON HEARD the loader's engine and quickly ducked into the shadows out of sight as it came chugging past, carrying a discarded starship fuel core. Seeing Teff'ith at the controls, he knew exactly what she was planning and decided it was time for him to make his exit. He waited until the loader disappeared through the door heading back to Bay 7, then he slipped into the supply room and out through one of the bays on the opposite side, confident she could take care of the remaining assassins without any more help from him.

TEFF'ITH SAW Gorvich's eyes grow wide as the loader rumbled through the door at the rear of the hangar. The assassins still hidden on the far side opened fire at the new target, but Teff'ith was careful to keep her head tucked behind the fuel core, and their bolts deflected harmlessly off the cylinder's thick casing. Gorvich took the opportunity to pop up from behind his cover and fire a few token shots at his attackers as Teff'ith steered the loader to where Vebb was hiding.

"Time to go," she shouted over the engine.

She positioned her vehicle to block the assassins from getting a clear shot, allowing the Rodian to scamper over to the ship's loading ramp and disappear into the hold.

As she turned the loader in Gorvich's direction, one of the assassins finally broke cover and moved to a new position to get a shot at Teff'ith. The Twi'lek couldn't make out the species through the helmet and full-body armor, but the figure appeared female.

Finally presented with a target he could see, Gorvich seized the opportunity. His twin blasters struck with deadly precision, dropping the exposed assassin in her tracks before she had taken two steps.

"Nice shot," Teff'ith noted, grudgingly admitting to herself that Gorvich wasn't completely useless.

"Nice ride," Gorvich responded, cocking one eyebrow at the loader.

The lone remaining assassin fired off another round; once again it deflected harmlessly off the massive engine core. The ship's engine behind them roared to life, and the hangar's roof slid slowly open with a loud squeal as Vebb prepared for takeoff.

"Green-skinned scum-sucker better not ditch us," Gorvich spat.

Your style, not his, Teff'ith thought. Out loud she said, "Get to the ship."

Gorvich shook his head.

"I'm not leaving half our shipment behind. Get rid of this last assassin and we can take our time loading up the rest of the spice."

Teff'ith was about to tell him how stupid he was being when she saw something small and round flying through the air toward them.

"Detonator!" she shouted, ducking down low in her seat.

Gorvich dived behind the loader as the detonator exploded. There was a sudden flash of light and sound, and then everything went black.

As her consciousness returned, Teff'ith slowly opened her eyes. She was lying on the ground, covered in a fine powder, and the only sound she heard was a piercing whine. She surveyed the scene around her, struggling to make sense of what had happened.

Much of the detonator's concussive shock wave escaped through the roof, but the blast had still been powerful enough to wreak havoc on the hangar. The crates had been blown to bits, showering the hangar and everything in it in a dusting of spice and splintered chunks of wood. The loader lay on its side beside her, upended by the force of the blast.

The bodies of Frinn and the bounty hunter Gorvich shot had been flung all the way to the rear of the hangar, where they'd landed in twisted heaps. Teff'ith realized the loader had shielded her from the worst of the blast; it was the only reason she'd survived. She wondered if Gorvich had been as lucky as she rose unsteadily to her feet.

Her ears were still ringing and her balance was off kilter; it was all she could do not to topple over. On the far side of the room she saw an armored man crawling on his hands and knees—the assassin who'd tossed the explosive. He was clearly shaken and disoriented, but he was moving slowly toward where his blaster rifle lay on the floor nearby.

Teff'ith grabbed for the pistol at her hip, but the sudden motion was too much in her wobbly state, and she staggered sideways and fell to the ground. Her clumsy movements drew the attention of the assassin as he wrapped his fingers around his weapon.

He drew it up slowly and took aim at Teff'ith. Before he could fire, a single shot came from over her shoulder, striking him in the chest. His armor absorbed the worst of the blow, but the impact sent him sprawling backward and the gun dropped from his hand.

Teff'ith turned to see Vebb coming down the ship's boarding ramp, pistol in hand and a grim look in his eyes as he advanced on his vulnerable opponent.

In a fair fight the pilot wouldn't have stood a chance, but Vebb had been inside the ship when the detonator had gone off—he was the only one not staggering and stumbling around. The assassin sat up and fumbled at his belt, going for his backup weapon as Vebb continued toward him. The Rodian fired three more shots from point-blank range, putting an end to his desperate, clumsy efforts.

He turned to Teff'ith and took hold of her arm, dragging her to her feet.

"Not so fast," she grumbled, swaying unsteadily even with his support.

"Gotta hurry," he told her, his voice sounding distant and hollow.

Teff'ith looked in the direction he was pointing and saw that the ship's core had been badly damaged by the explosion.

"Casing's cracked," he said. "Thing could blow any second."

Teff'ith nodded. With Vebb's help she stumbled over to the waiting ship and half staggered, half crawled up the boarding ramp. To her surprise, Gorvich was already waiting for them in the hold.

"Check her out," Vebb said as he gently lowered her to the floor. Then he punched the button to retract the ramp before racing up to the cockpit.

Gorvich was covered in scrapes and bruises, and he moved with a pronounced limp as he slowly made his way over to the ship's medkit. But otherwise he seemed to be okay; clearly the loader had shielded him from the worst of the blast as well.

Fortune favors fools, Teff'ith thought as the ship took to the air.

There was a deep boom from somewhere far below them as the cracked casing on the engine core gave way. The explosion made the ship buck and lurch, sending

Gorvich tumbling hard to the floor where he landed with a heavy grunt.

"Stupid Rodian can't even fly straight," he muttered as he hauled himself back to his feet.

In her mind's eye Teff'ith could imagine the damage caused by the fuel core's detonation. Bays 7 through 12 would all be out of commission for weeks as crews cleaned up the mess and made structural repairs. The Hutts wouldn't be happy about the lost revenue; they'd be looking for someone to blame. Morbo might end up having to foot the bill—he was the one who organized the hit that went sour. She decided it would be wise to stay far away from Nar Shaddaa for the foreseeable future.

Gorvich sat down gingerly beside her and opened the medkit.

"Show me where it hurts, Sunshine," he said with a lecherous smile.

"Don't need help," she growled, slapping his hand away as he reached out toward her.

"Why are you so mad? We may have left half the spice behind, but it's still a good score."

"Frinn's dead," she reminded him. "Your fault. Should have paid Morbo."

Gorvich shrugged. "Never liked Frinn much. Besides, now we get to split his share. It all worked out for the best."

Teff'ith wasn't so ready to simply dismiss everything that had happened. Now that they were free and clear, she had a strong sense that they weren't seeing all the pieces of the puzzle.

"Missing something," she muttered. "Why only two assassins? Send three, we don't stand a chance."

"We got lucky. Happens sometimes. Try to enjoy it."

"Don't rely on luck. It turns."

"Always doom and gloom with you, isn't it, Sunshine?" Gorvich said, shaking his head as he rose to his feet and made his way to the cockpit.

Alone in the hold, Teff'ith couldn't let it go. She kept playing the fight over and over in her head, trying to understand why Morbo hadn't taken the simple precaution of sending a third assassin to cut off their retreat. The more she struggled with the problem, the more she became convinced she had overlooked something very, very obvious.

THERON WAS already outside the spaceport, milling with the rest of the crowd beyond the doors, when he heard the first explosion. He resisted the urge to rush back inside; he didn't want to draw any unwanted attention to himself, but he couldn't help wondering if something had gone wrong with Teff'ith's plan. When he saw her ship taking off after a short time, he breathed a deep sigh of relief.

The second explosion came an instant later, this one much larger than the first. Cries of dismay welled up from the crowd, most from pilots and captains imagining what damage might have been done to their ships.

"Which hangar are you in?" Theron asked the Sullustan he'd been speaking with earlier.

"*Bay Ten*," he replied glumly in his native tongue. Then his eyes narrowed. "*You ran inside. Why?*"

"Had to check on my cargo," Theron lied. "Make sure everything was safe."

"*You come back out, big explosions,*" the Sullustan continued. "*Suspicious.*"

"Don't try to pin this on me," Theron said defensively. "You said it yourself. Hutt business. You got a problem, talk to them."

The Sullustan continued to glare at Theron for several seconds, then finally turned away.

"*Just worried about my ship.*"

"Me too," Theron said. When he continued, he spoke loud enough for the others in the crowd to hear. "That explosion sounded bad. The Hutts will probably want to shut down the whole spaceport while they make repairs."

"Shut it down?" the Sullustan echoed, the idea suddenly taking root in his head.

"Yeah. They'll probably quarantine the whole area and seize everything inside as evidence while they investigate what happened."

There was a moment of stunned silence as the crowd pondered the implications of his words, then a woman shouted, "No way I'm letting those greedy slugs get their mitts on my ship!"

Her defiant outcry touched off a stampede as everyone tried to get inside at once, pushing and shoving one another out of the way in their haste to grab whatever cargo they could and take off before the Hutts swooped in and closed the spaceport down.

Theron waited a few seconds until the small crowd had completely disappeared into the spaceport. Confident there wouldn't be any witnesses sticking around to give his description to the Hutts and cause trouble for Republic SIS, he sauntered off in the other direction, whistling an old Mantellian tune.

CHAPTER 5

MARCUS TRANT had a lot on his mind. As Director of Republic Strategic Information Service, that wasn't unusual—he was always juggling the day-to-day operations of the Republic's intelligence arm with the political games necessary for any government agency to stay afloat. Unlike some of the Republic's more traditional institutions—the Jedi, or the Galactic Senate, for example—SIS still had to justify its existence at every turn to keep from getting shut down or having its funding slashed by a Senator campaigning for reelection on a platform of "responsible government spending."

Unlike the military, most of what the SIS did was behind the scenes and off the record. Marcus liked to tell his operatives that if they did their job right, nobody would even know what they had done. Unfortunately, that answer didn't fly when facing a budget hearing. The bureaucrats who ultimately decided his organization's fate wanted something to show for the credits they poured into the SIS. They expected the Director to reveal highly classified mission details, ignoring the fact that doing so would jeopardize his people.

Fending off their ridiculous requests was exhausting; things would be much easier with a strong political ally who could vouch for the value of what the SIS did. Someone too powerful and important to be questioned by the politicians and desk-jockeys. Someone like Jace

Malcom, the Supreme Commander of the Republic military. Jace was a highly respected and universally admired war hero; having him in the SIS corner would help get the simpering bureaucrats to back off. The recently appointed Supreme Commander had asked SIS to undertake a special mission. Everything had been going smoothly until Theron got mixed up in it.

The Director hadn't heard from Theron since yesterday, when he'd tersely broken off their conversation about what he was doing on Nar Shaddaa. Since then Theron had disappeared, but not before disabling a fellow SIS agent, causing an industrial accident at one of Nar Shaddaa's spaceports, and unraveling three months of covert surveillance.

Despite all this, the Director was waiting before filing his official report. Theron was one of his best agents; he'd earned the benefit of the doubt. The least Marcus could do was wait to hear his side of the story before ending his career.

The receptionist behind the desk in Jace's waiting room looked up at his arrival, and Marcus was immediately struck by her remarkable green eyes.

"Go right in, Director," she said, flashing him a dazzling smile as she pressed the button to open the office door in the wall behind her. "The Commander's waiting for you."

He passed by the receptionist and into the office beyond, trying to focus on how he could explain what had gone wrong to the Supreme Commander without getting Theron court-martialed.

Jace Malcom was seated behind a desk, studying his computer monitor intently. His skin was lighter than the Director's own ebony hue, though still tanned and weathered—the complexion of a man who had spent most of his life outdoors. Hints of his age showed in the crow's-feet around his eyes and the slight graying at the temples of his dark hair, though it was hard to notice with the short military cut he sported. But his body was still in fighting shape: broad-shouldered and thick-chested, he looked like he could hold his own on the battlefield.

His most notable feature was the gruesome patch-work of scars and melted flesh that covered most of the right side of his face. He'd been wounded by a detonator many years ago at the Battle of Alderaan while serving as the leader of the legendary Havoc Squad special forces unit.

Looking at the scarring, the Director couldn't help thinking of Theron again. It had been Theron's mother—Master Satele Shan, now the Grand Master of the Jedi Order—who'd led the Jedi that fought alongside Havoc Squad that day. Together Satele and Jace fought the Sith Lord Darth Malgus on the battlefield, turning the tide of the conflict. Though Malgus survived the encounter, the Republic won the day and reclaimed Alderaan from the Empire.

"Close the door, Director," Jace said, turning away from the screen. "And take a seat."

Marcus snapped off a curt salute, then settled into the chair across from the Supreme Commander.

"Your message said we had to talk about Transom," Jace said. "I assume something's gone wrong."

"Someone slipped in and freed the prisoners before the auction," the Director explained. "Stole them right out from under Morbo's nose."

"And blew up a spaceport, too," Jace noted.

"And that," Marcus admitted sheepishly.

Transom is Jace's pet project. Should have guessed he'd be following it more closely than usual.

"I thought the plan was to wait until after the auction," Jace pressed. "Get our people back after they left

Nar Shaddaa so Morbo wouldn't know we'd found out about his slave trafficking ring."

"We had a communication breakdown," Marcus said, choosing his words carefully. "Two agents following different agendas got in each other's way. We're still trying to sort out the details."

"Isn't it your job to make sure your agents stay out of each other's way?" the Supreme Commander asked.

The Director's options were clear—tell Jace about Theron defying orders to act on his own, or stay silent and take the blame himself.

"You're right, sir. I accept full responsibility. It won't happen again."

The Supreme Commander didn't reply. Instead, he just stared at Marcus in silence, causing the Director to shift uncomfortably in his seat.

He knows I'm holding something back. Covering for someone.

Eager to get out from under Jace's penetrating gaze, the Director broke the silence.

"I know how important Operation Transom was to you, sir," Marcus said. "And we did manage to rescue Republic soldiers who would otherwise have spent their lives as slaves.

"Maybe what happened on Nar Shaddaa will send a message," he continued. "Make the Hutts think twice before selling off Republic POWs. Remind them that we look after our own."

"Let's hope so," Jace said, his glare softening. "Maybe it's for the best, anyway. Free up resources for something else. Something big."

Something bigger than saving your fellow soldiers from slavery? Marcus silently wondered.

"What are your feelings on the current state of the war effort?" the Supreme Commander asked, seeming to suddenly change topics.

The question was familiar enough; the Director had answered it a hundred different times in various meetings over the years. Usually he would give the answer he thought the listener was looking for to make the meeting go more smoothly. But Jace wasn't like the politicians he usually dealt with, and he decided that being blunt and honest was worth the risk.

"The Empire is reeling. For the first time in decades we have the upper hand. When the Emperor fell, it left a void atop the Sith power structure. Malgus tried to fill it, but when his coup failed and he was killed, the Empire was left without a clear leader to rally them."

After a brief pause he added, "Imperial Intelligence has fallen apart. Without their input, the Imperial military strategy has become ineffective and unfocused. You can't run a war without good intel."

"You don't have to sell me on SIS," Jace told him, a hint of a smile on his lips. "I appreciate what you bring to the table. Believe it or not, I actually read all those reports you send me."

"Sorry, Commander. Guess I'm used to dealing with politicians and bureaucrats."

"I've been studying your analysis of Imperial threats quite closely," Jace continued. "There's one in particular that caught my eye: the *Ascendant Spear*."

Once again Marcus's thoughts returned to Theron. The *Ascendant Spear* was a prototype long-range battle cruiser developed by the brilliant Darth Mekhis as part of a secret Imperial weapons program. Theron, with the help of his mentor Jedi Master Ngani Zho, learned about the program and nearly ended it by killing Darth Mekhis. Of all her deadly creations, only the *Ascendant Spear* still survived.

Zho died on that mission, Marcus thought. *Gave his life to save Teff'ith. That's why Theron feels responsible for her now.*

All the connections to Theron were starting to feel like more than just coincidence. His mother would probably say something about the Force working in mysterious ways, but the Director knew Theron wasn't attuned to the Force. Not like a Jedi.

"Something wrong, Director?"

Marcus shook his head, trying to get out of his own thoughts. "Just thinking about the *Ascendant Spear*."

"Fill me in."

"Most of what we know is theory and conjecture, pieced together from battlefield reports. It's got some kind of revolutionary hyperdrive—probably the fastest ship ever built. Enough firepower to wipe out an entire fleet."

"Your reports estimate the *Ascendant Spear* is responsible for more Republic casualties than the next ten most effective Imperial battle cruisers combined."

"The *Spear* is so much more advanced than any other ship that we still don't know its full capabilities," the Director admitted.

"And what about the commander? Darth Karrid?"

"Darth Malgus's apprentice," the Director said. "She's a Falleen. Used to be on our side. Trained with the Jedi before defecting to the Sith."

"I'm surprised they accepted her," Jace said. "I thought they believed only humans and pure-blooded Sith were worthy of joining their ranks."

"Malgus was different," Marcus explained, before adding, "Karrid's a tactical genius, and she's completely ruthless. Every battle the *Ascendant Spear* has been involved in has been a massacre for our side. If it weren't for Karrid and the *Spear,* we might have already won this war."

Jace nodded, and the Director had the impression that the Supreme Commander already knew all this. It was almost as if Jace had been testing him.

"I'm putting a task force together to take *Ascendant Spear* down," the Supreme Commander said.

Marcus was impressed by the boldness of the plan, but his enthusiasm was tempered by reality. As much as he wanted to voice his support to get in good with Jace, he felt he owed it to the Supreme Commander to be honest.

"SIS has investigated this option before," Marcus said. "We couldn't find a way to make it work."

"This isn't going to be an SIS op," Jace told him. "I want a joint mission with the full cooperation of the military, the Jedi, and SIS."

"SIS is at your disposal," the Director assured him, though inside he was skeptical. Joint missions were great in theory, but in practice they tended to become turf wars as the different agencies fought to take all the credit and shift all the blame.

"I know what you're thinking," Jace said. "But this is too big for anyone to handle alone. The only way to pull this off is to work together."

The Supreme Commander stood and came around from behind the desk, moving quickly. He seized Marcus's shoulders with his massive hands, his steel grip just short of being painful. Leaning forward, he brought his face in close. His unblinking eyes seemed to bore deep into the Director, as if Jace was seeking out the depths of his heart and mind.

"Don't tell me what I want to hear," he insisted. "I believe we can do this, and I need you to believe it, too. Are you with me, Marcus? Really, truly with me?"

"I'm with you, Commander," the Director vowed, his reservations swept away by the Supreme Commander's raw intensity and conviction.

"Good man," Jace said, patting him on the shoulders as he released his grip and stood up. "I knew I could count on you."

He made his way back around to the other side of the
desk and settled back into his chair.

"I'm sending you everything I have on the *Spear* and
Darth Karrid," Jace told him. "Classified reports from
every military engagement the *Spear*'s been involved in,
confidential evaluations prepared by Karrid's trainers
and the Masters at the Jedi academy. Everything. Study
it all in detail and send me a list of agents you'd recommend for this job. I want those dossiers by next week."

"Yes, sir," Marcus said.

"Remember—this is our top priority," Jace said. "The
Ascendant Spear is the single biggest threat to the Republic, our fleets and our citizens. I intend to destroy it,
and I want you to tell me how."

CHAPTER 6

"THIS IS an outrage!" Darth Ravage exclaimed. "Malgus was a traitor who tried to usurp the Emperor's throne! Now you expect us to grant his apprentice a seat on the Dark Council?"

Darth Marr, senior-ranking member of the Dark Council, refused to respond in kind to Ravage's aggressive outburst. Instead, he carefully gauged the reactions of the six other members who had gathered in the meeting chamber deep inside the Emperor's Citadel on Dromund Kaas. Unlike Ravage, they remained calm, though from their expressions it was clear they shared his reservations.

"No one of us can make demands on the others," Marr assured them. "But I will remind you that Darth Karrid turned her back on Malgus when he turned his back on us. And Darth Hadra's untimely demise has left the Sphere of Technology vacant. All I'm asking is that you consider her as a candidate for the position."

"She's a Falleen," Darth Mortis objected. Darth Rictus, the oldest member of the Council, nodded to show he shared Mortis's opinion.

Marr fought back the urge to rail against their bigotry. Malgus had overreached when he tried to proclaim himself the new Emperor, but he was right about one thing: If the Empire wanted to defeat the Republic, they could no longer cling to their overt prejudice against lesser species. Keeping entire worlds subjugated put too great a strain on Imperial military resources; it was far more efficient to try and enlist them as willing allies in the war against the Republic.

But Marr knew arguments would only push the already fragile Dark Council toward a complete schism. Now was not the time for infighting. The Republic had them in retreat across the galaxy; a united front was their only hope of survival. Defense of the Empire was his official Sphere of Influence, so it fell to him to bridge the divides among his fellow Council members.

"Our numbers dwindle," Marr reminded them. "We need allies. Elevating a Falleen to the Council shows other species that there is a place for them in our Empire."

"Perhaps the problem is that the other species have forgotten their proper place," Mortis replied.

"Well played, Mortis," Darth Vowrawn chimed in, letting his words hang in the air for a dramatic moment before adding, "Yet we should not dismiss Darth Karrid so quickly."

Marr had been hoping for Vowrawn's support. A pure-blooded Sith who reveled in the courtly intrigue, sly politics, and unbridled hedonism of the Imperial nobility, he was also responsible for the Production and Logistics Sphere of Influence. He knew numbers better than anyone; the Republic had more soldiers, more resources, and more allies than the Empire, and if the Empire couldn't recruit more worlds to its side it was going to lose.

"Darth Karrid has proven herself quite valuable to our war effort," Vowrawn reminded them all. "Without her our situation would be untenable, rather than just precarious."

Darth Ravage grunted, unconvinced. "You're giving the credit to her, when we all know it should really go to the ship. Any one of us could have her success if we controlled the *Ascendant Spear*."

"And therein lies the problem," Vowrawn continued. "We don't control it. She does. And I doubt she'll hand it over to you just because you ask."

"The ship is part of the equation," Marr admitted. "Darth Mekhis controlled the Technology Sphere when she developed the *Ascendant Spear*. There is some logic in giving the portfolio to the one who now controls the last of her creations."

"Are you scared of her?" Darth Rictus asked, ending his question with a gleeful cackle.

Marr ignored the question, refusing to rise to the old man's bait.

"I'm willing to consider other candidates for the seat," he continued. "If any of you has a worthy suggestion."

"Darth Gravus," Mortis offered, and there was a general murmur of assent from the rest of the group.

Inwardly, Marr cringed. It wasn't that Gravus wasn't suitable for the position. The Dark Lord had proven his worth by successfully undermining the Republic campaign to restore the devastated world of Taris. But Gravus was a link to the old ways. Ambitious and ruthless, he had earned many influential allies in the upper echelons of Imperial society . . . and just as many enemies. Bringing him into the Council would open the door for more infighting as old grudges would be rekindled, and it would do nothing to convince other species to join the Imperial cause. Worst of all, his selection was sure to anger Darth Karrid. Fortunately, Gravus's victory on Taris had been overshadowed when his fleets lost control of the mineral-rich world of Leritor, a costly setback for the Empire.

"Gravus failed to keep the Republic at bay in the Mid Rim," he reminded them.

"He has fallen back to Bothawui to regroup," Mortis

replied. "Soon he will launch a counteroffensive and reclaim Leritor for the Empire."

"If he is successful, then I can see no reason to oppose him as a candidate," Marr grudgingly admitted.

"Then we are all in agreement," Mortis pushed. "Once Leritor is back under Imperial control, Gravus should be given a seat on the Dark Council and control over the Technology Sphere."

Marr spoke quickly, before anyone else could interject. "I said I wouldn't oppose Gravus as a candidate," he said, his voice firm. "He should be considered. As should Karrid. We should take some time to think about both candidates before we make a final decision."

"Once again we are all humbled by your wisdom, Darth Marr," Vowrawn said, his voice hovering on the line between sincerity and mockery. "I propose we adjourn this meeting so we can all ponder this very important decision."

As the members of the Dark Council left the room, Marr could only imagine how Darth Karrid would react when she heard the news. He decided it would be best if he told her himself.

It took less than twenty minutes for Marr's private shuttle to whisk him away from the Citadel to the private landing pad at his personal stronghold on the outskirts of Kaas City. An honor guard of half a dozen Imperial soldiers in full armor stood smartly at attention as he strode down the boarding ramp, and a pair of bowing servants dressed in his personal colors opened the massive doors leading from the landing pad to the interior chambers.

Part domicile, part fortress, the stronghold's halls were busy with household staff and military personnel scurrying to and fro, each tending to their respective duties. They bowed or saluted appropriately as Marr passed, his long strides taking him directly to the communications room.

"Put me in contact with Darth Karrid," he told the officer in charge.

"At once, my Lord," she told him, then barked out a quick series of orders to her three-person staff.

Marr would have preferred to deliver the details of the Dark Council's meeting to Karrid in person, but time was of the essence. He wanted to speak with her before she heard the whispers and rumors of what had happened so he could mitigate her reaction.

"The *Ascendant Spear* has received our signal, Darth Marr," the officer confirmed. "Decryption may take a few seconds."

Marr nodded, knowing there was no possible way any of the other members of the Council—or anyone from the Republic—could overhear what was about to be said. Even if they somehow intercepted the signal he was transmitting, it would be impossible to decode without a black cipher, the Empire's encryption device.

Developed by Imperial Intelligence before the organization collapsed, the black ciphers were the most advanced encryption machines ever devised. Apart from the ones installed on the Empire's fifteen largest capital ships—including the *Ascendant Spear*—there were only two others: one in the office of the Imperial Minister of Logistics, and one in Darth Marr's possession.

The holoimage flickered and materialized before him as the cipher unscrambled the incoming return signal to reveal Darth Karrid. Her bright emerald skin and long black hair—some gathered in a topknot, some flowing down her back—were muted by the blue-tinged holo-signal. She had high, prominent cheekbones, a flawless complexion, and a sharp, well-proportioned nose and chin. But there was a vaguely disconcerting reptilian hint to her exotic features, particularly around her cold, dead eyes. And in Karrid's case the exquisite symmetrical perfection so common to her species was marred by the prominent tattoos and cybernetic implants that completely covered the left side of her face.

"Darth Marr," she said by way of greeting. "I was expecting your call."

From the holo, Marr recognized that she had relayed his incoming signal to the seclusion of her private command pod deep inside the *Ascendant Spear*. The complex network of biomechanical interfaces that allowed Karrid to become one with Darth Mekhis's marvelous warship framed her image: dozens of long, thin wires snaking out from the walls and ceiling and into the back of Karrid's neck and skull.

"Leave us," Marr commanded, and the communications officer and her staff vanished from the room.

"You spoke with the other members of the Dark Council?" Karrid asked once they were alone.

"The ones that matter," Marr said.

"And what was their reaction?"

"They agreed that you are a strong candidate," Marr said, choosing his words carefully. "But there are some who expressed concerns."

"Who?" Karrid demanded, her face twisting in anger. "Ravage? That old fool, Rictus?"

"It doesn't matter," Marr explained. "The Council must reach a consensus to bring in a new member."

"Is it because I'm Falleen?"

"There are other concerns," Marr said, evading the question. "You were Malgus's apprentice for many years; his actions will always color your reputation."

"Malgus was a traitor," Karrid spat out, her bright green skin taking on a reddish hue reflecting her heightened emotional state. "But I have done more to support the Imperial war effort than anyone!"

"Those of us who have dedicated our lives in the service of the Dark Council might disagree," Marr replied coldly.

"I meant no disrespect, Darth Marr," Karrid said, her voice slipping into a seductive purr.

Marr knew her reaction was instinctual; the Falleen had evolved overtly sensual mannerisms as a survival mechanism for the species. Marr was smart enough to recognize and dismiss the subtle feelings of arousal her voice triggered in him, but individuals of most humanoid species found it hard to resist the Falleen charms.

"I have proven my loyalty to the Empire countless times," Karrid continued, pleading her case. "I did not think the Council would simply cast me aside."

"You have not been cast aside," he assured her. "You are still a candidate. But there are others."

"Who?"

Marr hesitated, then decided she would eventually find out anyway. "Darth Gravus."

"Gravus?" she hissed. "So Mortis is behind this; he and Gravus are thick as thieves."

"Mortis supports Gravus," Marr admitted, "but so do many other members of the Council. His work on Taris shows that he would do well in charge of the Technology Sphere."

"The Empire claims to be a meritocracy," Karrid said. "We punish failure and reward success. I have only victories to my name, but Gravus lost Leritor to the Republic. How can the Council prefer him over me?"

"Gravus is planning to recapture Leritor," Marr said. "But even if he succeeds, the decision is not final," he added, hoping to mollify her. "You will both be considered for the position."

"So there is still a chance," Karrid replied, seizing on the thin strand of hope. She brought a delicate hand up to her lips as she contemplated the possibility of victory.

"Assuming he can defeat the Republic fleet over Leritor, most of the Council will probably support Gravus," Marr cautioned, not wanting her to get her hopes too high only to have them dashed.

"And what about you, Marr?" she asked, her voice slipping once more into the seductive purr.

"I would prefer the position go to you," Marr assured her. "In the long run you can be of more value to the Empire than Gravus. But I will not risk tearing the Dark Council apart by challenging the others if they back him."

"So you will not fight for me?"

"We must choose our battles wisely," he reminded her. "Sometimes it is better to be patient."

"I have been patient," she answered, her expression a sensual pout.

"There are other seats on the Council. Other Spheres of Influence that need to be filled. Gravus may be the leading candidate, but you are next in line."

There was a long pause before Karrid nodded her acceptance.

"I understand, Darth Marr. Even though we are allies, I cannot expect you to fight this battle on my behalf."

Marr felt a great sense of relief, though he was careful not to show his reaction. Part of him had feared Karrid might react with blind rage at being passed over. If she turned against the Empire, the *Ascendant Spear* would cripple the Imperial fleet, paving the way for a quick and certain Republic victory in the war.

"Your time will come," Marr assured her. "It is inevitable."

"At least we agree on something," she said with a smile.

CHAPTER 7

THERON PUNCHED the comlink of his small shuttle, opening a hailing frequency with the control tower at one of the hundreds of spaceports on Coruscant's surface.

"This is *Sojourner*, requesting landing clearance."

"Copy that, *Sojourner*. Transmit ship registration for authentication."

"Transmitting."

There was a longer pause than usual on the other end of the comlink before the voice replied, "*Sojourner*, you need to reroute to another spaceport. Sending coordinates now."

Theron didn't bother to protest; he knew what was going on.

Guess I should have called the Director after that mess on Nar Shaddaa.

"Understood," he said, not bothering to look at the new coordinates. He already knew exactly where they would order him to go.

"A security escort is awaiting your arrival," the tower added.

"I bet they are," he answered, disconnecting the call.

As he brought the ship in to land, Theron noticed two men wearing Coruscant Security Force uniforms standing by a waiting speeder. He doubted they were actually part of the official planetwide security force. The Director wouldn't involve a civilian organization unless he had to, and it was common for SIS personnel to adopt the uniforms of local authorities when they were expecting trouble but wanted to avoid drawing extra attention.

"Theron Shan?" one of the men said as he climbed out of his shuttle.

"What if I say no?"

"Don't cause any trouble," the other warned. "The Director's not in the mood."

Theron briefly thought about making a move. It wasn't that he was actually worried about what the Director had planned, but he was eager to test himself against the two agents sent to bring him in. But in the end, he realized he was being foolish. The agents were just following orders; no need to hurt somebody.

"We're all on the same side here," he assured them.

The ride to SIS headquarters was conducted in complete silence. Theron's escorts appeared calm and relaxed, but he could tell they were watching him closely the entire way. Upon landing, they led him into the building, one marching in front of him, the other behind. They didn't break formation until they reached the Director's office.

One of the men reached out and pressed the buzzer on the door. In response it slid open and the Director called out, "I'll take it from here."

Theron gave each of his guards a cheery wave and stepped into the room. As the door slid shut behind him, the Director looked up from behind his desk and shook his head.

"Care to tell me why I shouldn't have you court-martialed for physically assaulting a fellow agent?"

"That Houk came at me first," Theron reminded him. "I was just minding my own business on Nar Shaddaa when he pressed that knife up against my back. How was I supposed to know he was one of ours?"

"A review board might buy that," the Director admitted. "Until they remember the part where I ordered you to get off Nar Shaddaa!"

"I just thought you were being overprotective," Theron protested. "I would have taken you a little more seriously if I'd known you were in the middle of a mission. But you didn't really explain the situation."

"I don't have to explain things!" the Director snapped. "I'm the boss, remember? I give you an order and you follow it."

Theron shifted uncomfortably in his seat.

"At least I managed to rescue the prisoners."

"But you did it in a way that compromised the entire operation. You think this is the first time Morbo's auctioned off our people? We've been watching him for months. Tracking his suppliers and marking his buyers, slowly putting together all the bits and pieces of the entire operation. Operation Transom wasn't about rescuing four Cathar; it was about putting an end to the whole POW slave trade!"

"Come on, Director," Theron replied, raising an incredulous eyebrow. "We both know that would never happen. Even if you shut down everyone Morbo ever dealt with, someone else would just step in to take his place."

"Maybe so," the Director conceded. "But at least we'd slow them down for a while. Make the traffic dry up."

"Morbo and everyone else at that auction thinks the explosion at the spaceport has something to do with selling POWs," Theron countered. "They're not going to start chasing after fresh meat anytime soon."

"I heard there were casualties," the Director said.

"Four dead," Theron admitted. "Three were hired assassins. Kind of asking for it if you go into that line of work. The fourth was a low-level thug working for the Old Tion Brotherhood. I looked into him; he won't be missed."

"So Teff'ith made it out okay?"

"More or less."

"Then I guess it's all worth it in your book." The Director sighed. "Did she have any idea you were there?"

"I don't think so."

"With all the times you've helped her out, she can't be that bright if she hasn't noticed you by now."

Theron smiled. "Maybe I'm just that good."

"I still think you should let her know that she's in your debt. Might make her more likely to help us out down the road."

"That's not how Teff'ith's mind works," Theron said, shaking his head. "She's . . . complicated."

The Director got up from behind his desk and came around to the other side, crossing his arms as he sat on the edge.

"Theron—she's become more trouble than she's worth," the Director told him. "It was bad enough when all you were doing was chewing up your vacation days to help her out. Now it's interfering with ongoing SIS missions. I can't allow that."

"I know you think this is just some crazy obsession," Theron told him. "But down the road this is going to pay off. Sooner or later SIS is going to need her help."

"How do you know that? Is that you talking, or Ngani Zho? You having visions through the Force now?"

The words stung, but Theron wasn't going to back down.

"Master Zho used to tell me that what most people call gut instinct is really just the Force reaching out to us. He said we'd be better off if we listened to it more often. And I have a feeling about Teff'ith."

"And I've got a feeling about you," the Director said. "A bad feeling."

He turned away and went back to sit behind his desk. He took a deep breath and let it out in a long, slow sigh. Then he reached out with his hands and placed them on the top of his desk, fingers spread wide as if bracing himself for what he was about to say.

"Theron—I'm transferring you to the analytics department. Effective immediately."

"Analytics?" Theron exclaimed in disbelief. "You trying to turn me into some kind of number-crunching desk-jockey?"

"I can't just ignore what happened on Nar Shaddaa," the Director said. "You're a good agent, and I want to keep you in the fold, but you have to learn that your actions have consequences.

"Besides," he added, "it's good to have experience in other departments. I think a three-month stretch with analytics will make you a more rounded agent."

"I'm plenty rounded already," Theron said.

"You need a break from fieldwork," the Director insisted. "Since you can't seem to stay out of trouble even when you're supposed to be on vacation, this is the only option I have left."

"I'm not cut out for office work," Theron said. "You've seen my personnel profile."

"Our evaluations say you're highly intelligent, intuitive, and adaptable. I think you'll fit in just fine."

Theron chewed his lip in angry silence before saying, "What if I resign?"

"You won't," the Director countered. "You care too much about the Republic to simply abandon the cause."

"I could go work for the military," he threatened.

"Saluting superior officers? Following orders? Barking out 'Sir, yes, sir' twenty times a day? Right."

"Fine then," Theron said. "I'll just put in for the rest of my vacation time."

"Request denied," the Director answered. "Got a special project in the works, by order of the Republic Supreme Commander. All hands on board. Nothing personal."

Theron sighed and bowed his head in defeat.

"You start tomorrow morning," the Director continued. "Analytics is on the third floor. Do I need to send another escort to make sure you show up?"

"I'll be there," Theron promised. "But I won't be happy about it."

"Give analytics a chance," the Director suggested. "They do important work, and we really are working on a special assignment for Jace Malcom. We're calling it Operation End Game.

"Trust me, Theron," he added. "You want to be a part of this."

CHAPTER 8

SEATED IN the command chair on the bridge of the *Ascendant Spear,* Darth Karrid struggled to keep her contempt at bay as her gaze traced across the two dozen Imperial officers and crew working at their stations all around her. Huddled over consoles and computer screens, their fingers flew over control pads as they reacted to the constant stream of incoming data while the vessel hurled through the empty void of hyperspace. The inefficiency of their clumsy, archaic method of interacting with the ship filled her with disgust.

"Ten minutes until we reach Leritor, my Lord," Moff Lorman said from his seat on the far side of the bridge.

"Be sure to come out of hyperspace beyond the range of the Republic sensors," she cautioned.

It was unlikely Lorman would make such a careless and obvious error; the Moff was a capable officer. But like nearly every Imperial assigned to the *Ascendant Spear* he was an interloper on her ship, an insignificant parasite clinging to the underbelly, and she didn't trust him not to make a mistake that would put her ship in danger.

Darth Mekhis had designed the vessel with numerous automated systems, and the *Spear* required a crew of only three thousand to operate at peak efficiency—less than half of what would typically be assigned to an Imperial capital ship. Karrid had come to accept them as a necessary inconvenience, though there were times, like now, when she resented their presence.

When plugged into the *Spear*'s command pod she had total access to all the vessel's systems and sensors, but the effort of controlling an entire capital ship single-handedly was mentally and physically exhausting. She had no choice but to defer to Moff Lorman and his crew during routine travel and other similarly mundane activities, allowing them to run the vessel using conventional means while she saved her energies for the high intensity of battle.

"When will we send a message to Darth Gravus telling him reinforcements are on the way, my Lord?" Moff Lorman asked.

Karrid rose from her seat. "I will contact Gravus," she said. "After I have taken command of my ship."

She crossed the bridge with quick, purposeful strides, making her way to the turbolift. The doors slid open and she stepped inside, pressing the button that whisked her down past floor after floor until she reached the innermost level of the vessel. She stepped out of the turbolift and made her way down the short corridor leading to a heavily secured door. A retinal scan confirmed her identity, and the door slid open to reveal the *Ascendant Spear*'s true heart.

The circular chamber was nearly thirty meters in diameter, but the inside was empty save for the control console on the perimeter, Karrid's two apprentices—one a male human, the other a female pure-blooded Sith—and the large crystal sphere in the center. The apprentices were sitting cross-legged on the floor on either side of the sphere, meditating to focus their minds in preparation for the coming battle.

"It's time," Karrid said as she approached the sphere.

She placed a hand on the cool exterior, and the sphere parted vertically in the middle, the two halves opening at her touch to reveal the true genius of Darth Mekhis.

The interior of the *Ascendant Spear*'s isolated command pod featured a single chair surrounded by dozens of monitors and screens. A delicate web of interwoven wires was suspended a meter above the chair. A dozen loose strands hung down from the web, each tipped with a long, thin needle.

Lowering herself into the chair, Karrid's fingers tapped at the control panels built into the arms. The pod slowly closed, encasing her in the nearly indestructible glittering cocoon. The fingers of her left hand traced a complex pattern over the control panel, powering up the command pod and causing the web of dangling wires above her head to come to life. Twisting and writhing, they slithered down to wrap themselves around Karrid's face and the back of her skull.

Karrid closed her eyes in eager anticipation, allowing the dark side of the Force to flow through her. Outside the sphere, she sensed her apprentices deep in meditation, opening themselves to her so she could draw on their strength as she took command of the *Spear*.

The wires gently caressed her neck and cheeks with the fine-tipped needles on the end, sending a shiver down the Falleen's spine. Then one of the needles plunged itself into the cybernetic implant at the back of her neck, making her gasp aloud. Another slid into the implant behind her left ear, and two more burrowed into the left side of her skull on either side of her temple. Two connected to her forehead and five more pierced the back of her skull. The final strand of wire slithered across the lid of her still-closed eye before slipping into the tiny aperture of the cybernetic interface implanted in her left cheek.

She opened her eyes, her vision now an amalgamation of what she saw on the screens and monitors as well as everything within range of the ship's sensors. The starfield flickered rapidly into view as the *Ascendant Spear* dropped from hyperspace on the edge of the Yucrales sector, just beyond sensor range of the Imperial and Republic fleets engaged in battle over the skies of Leritor. Though the other ships couldn't detect her presence at this range, the *Spear*'s advanced systems gave Karrid a perfect awareness of what was transpiring.

A combination of her Force abilities and the cybernetic implants relaying data from the *Ascendant Spear*'s long-range scanners enabled Karrid to instantly see that although the battle had just begun, Darth Gravus already had the upper hand.

The Republic had a single capital ship in the fray—the *Mardorus,* a D-class attack cruiser. Over five hundred meters in length, the *Mardorus* had a wide, flat hull covered with a thick layer of armor plating, as if the vessel were hidden under a hump-shaped shell. It was supported by two Hammerheads half its size—easily identifiable by the forward bridges extending perpendicularly above and below the longer main body of the vessel—and three slightly smaller CR-12 corvettes—sleek, narrow ships equipped with battering-ram-shaped bows to run enemy blockades and prominent external afterburners to enhance speed and maneuverability. The fleet was rounded out by half a dozen BT-7 Thunderclap fighters. The latest Republic incarnation in personal attack-craft, the agile Thunderclap resembled a sideways Y, with the cockpit situated in the crook of the two smaller arms.

In contrast, Gravus's personal Dreadnought, *Exemplar,* was almost eight hundred meters in length. The wedge-shaped capital ship was flanked by three claw-shaped C-class destroyers that were nearly as large as the Republic flagship. Each destroyer was supported by a complement of six Interceptors, the Empire's agile, fang-winged answer to the Republic Thunderclap.

Gravus had devised a battle plan that would minimize the risk to his own ship. The destroyers had been deployed to engage the corvettes and Thunderclap fighters, freeing up the quick and nimble Interceptors to continuously strafe the Hammerheads and the heavily armored *Mardorus*. This allowed the *Exemplar* to remain at a safe distance, firing away with its batteries at the Republic vessels with no fear of any return assault. Unfortunately, unless Gravus moved closer to the action he was limited to inflicting minimal damage on the enemy capital ship's deflector shields and reinforced hull. Ultimately the Imperials would prevail, but it would be a battle of attrition.

Karrid had neither the patience nor the temperament for such a strategy. With a flick of her little finger, she opened a hailing channel to the *Exemplar*, accelerating the *Ascendant Spear* toward the other vessels at the same time.

"Darth Gravus, this is Darth Karrid. The *Ascendant Spear* is at your disposal."

Gravus's reply was swift and certain. "Disengage, Karrid! We didn't call for reinforcements. This is my battle to win—not yours!"

Karrid ignored his orders; the *Ascendant Spear*'s engines had already accelerated the ship to 70 percent of maximum sublight speed, bringing them in range of the Republic sensors. The triangular design of the *Spear* was common among Imperial capital ships, but its immense size—more than twice that of any other participant in the battle—was instantly recognizable.

As Karrid had expected, the *Spear*'s arrival drew an immediate response as one of the Republic Hammerheads disengaged and came about to face the new threat. Two of the Thunderclap fighters also veered around, spinning and diving to avoid the destroyer cannons as they sped off to support the Hammerhead.

The Hammerhead's turbolasers opened fire a second later. On a level deep within her subconscious mind, Karrid felt the heat as the *Spear*'s deflectors easily repelled the first volley. An instant later the Thunderclaps swooped in, one from port, the other from starboard. Lacking enough firepower to inflict significant damage on a ship the size of the *Ascendant Spear* beyond point-blank range, the pilots relied on speed and maneuverability to get in close enough to strafe the surface of the larger vessel.

To Karrid they were like annoying insects buzzing in her ear; the only logical response was to slap them out of existence. She focused her mind on the starboard defense turrets, using the *Spear*'s sensors to track the fast-moving Thunderclap before willing the guns to fire. A rapid series of ion blasts hit the fighter in rapid succession, each one striking its target with the unnatural precision made possible only by the perfect fusion of machine and organic.

The Thunderclap exploded in a ball of heat and light, but Karrid barely noticed. She had her sights set fully on the second fighter. The pilot was taking desperate evasive maneuvers, wheeling, spinning, and diving at crazy angles. Against the augmented reactions derived from Karrid's symbiotic link to her ship, he may as well have been standing still. The port turrets fired, and the second Thunderclap disintegrated.

The Hammerhead opened fire again, and Karrid once more had the sensation of distant heat as the deflectors repelled the incoming blasts. The Hammerhead was still too far out to pose any real threat; it had been relying on the fighters to occupy the enemy until it got in close enough to pierce the *Spear*'s shields. Bereft of their escort, they were vulnerable and exposed.

Karrid seized the opportunity, opening fire with the *Ascendant Spear*'s main guns. The blackness of space was illuminated by a blazing barrage of concentrated red energy beams. They ripped through the Hammerhead's deflector shields and shredded the armor-plated hull. Inside, the emergency systems would be overloaded as the vessel's automated systems tried to somehow keep it functional long enough for the crew to evacuate. A second volley from the *Spear* ended that faint hope as the lasers pierced the engine core containment unit, and the Hammerhead vanished in a violent explosion.

Gravus's voice rang out once more, simultaneously echoing in Karrid's ears and in the part of her brain that was linked into the ship's communications systems.

"You think this will turn the Dark Council against me, Karrid?" he sneered. "You could take out every Republic ship in this quadrant, but when it comes time to choose someone to join their ranks, they'll still pick me over a Falleen!"

"You do not grasp the danger you are in, Gravus," she answered coldly. "You could be killed in this battle. I am here to ensure a desirable outcome for the Empire."

The threat was veiled, but like any true Sith her rival immediately understood the sinister implications of her words: only one of them would leave this battle alive.

"Ignore the Republic ships!" Gravus commanded his fleet, forgetting in his panic that the new orders were being transmitted over the same standard Imperial frequency Karrid was using. "Fire on the *Ascendant Spear*! Destroy it at all costs! Do not let it—"

His words were cut off midsentence as Gravus—or someone under his command—had the sense to flip over to an auxiliary communications channel. But Karrid knew words alone wouldn't be enough to justify killing Gravus to the Council; she needed him to make the first move.

The unexpected switch from Republic targets to the *Ascendant Spear* threw the Imperial fleet into disarray.

The Interceptors swarming the *Mardorus* and the Hammerhead abandoned their strafing runs, peeling away to regroup for a coordinated assault on their new target. The destroyers disengaged from the Republic corvettes and Thunderclaps, pulling back as they moved to position themselves between the *Exemplar* and Karrid's retaliation.

The Republic fleet, unaware that they now shared a common enemy with their Imperial foes, seized the advantage. Seven Interceptors were wiped out by the batteries of the Hammerhead and the *Mardorus,* and a steady stream of fire from the corvettes pummeled the retreating destroyers, overloading their deflector shields so that the incoming Thunderclaps were able to inflict heavy damage.

Karrid watched the sudden tactical shift with an intense hunger, instantly aware of the position and shield status of every vessel through the *Spear*'s advanced sensors, the information relayed directly through the pulsing wires of the command pod and into her cybernetic implants. Realizing the Republic vessels were focused on the suddenly vulnerable ships of Gravus's fleet, she sent the *Spear* charging into the heart of the fray.

Neither Gravus nor the Republic commander anticipated her strategy. Capital ships typically stayed at range, knowing their powerful guns could wear down smaller vessels from a safe distance. By moving into range of the fleets Karrid was taking a risk; if they coordinated their efforts they could overwhelm the *Spear*. But Karrid knew the element of surprise would prevent that from happening, and at close proximity the *Spear*'s turbolasers could rip through deflectors and obliterate any of the other vessels in seconds. She started with the *Mardorus*.

As the *Spear* bore down on the Republic ship, the battle descended into chaos. One of the corvettes and two of the Thunderclaps altered course to try to save their flagship; the rest continued their assault on the crippled destroyers. Eight Interceptors swooped back to try to save the destroyers; the rest hurtled toward the *Spear*. The Hammerhead closed on the *Exemplar* as it tried to flee to the farthest edge of the conflict.

The *Mardorus* tried to ward off the *Ascendant Spear*, but before it could bring its guns to bear Karrid opened fire with her entire forward-facing battery. Turbolasers and ion cannons roared, combining in a glorious symphony of destruction, all but vaporizing the *Mardorus* in a matter of seconds.

Karrid relished the kill, sensing the terror of the dying crew through the Force. An instant later she felt a sharp sliver of pain slicing through her, like someone had slid a vibroblade between her shoulders. Gravus had taken the bait, ordering the *Exemplar* to fire on the *Spear*.

The blast penetrated the deflector shields and scorched the exterior hull, damage to the ship registering in Karrid's mind like a wound to her own body. The *Exemplar* was too far away to do any serious harm, but by firing the first shot Gravus had given Karrid the justification she needed to target his ships without having to answer to the Dark Council for destroying an Imperial fleet.

The fighters that had tried to come to the *Mardorus*'s aid swooped by the *Spear*, their strafing run sending a thousand pinpricks up Karrid's arms. She snuffed them out before they could make a second run. The Hammerhead had caught the *Exemplar*, forcing Gravus to focus on the immediate threat and preventing him from firing a second shot at the *Spear*.

One of the damaged destroyers had been finished off by the corvettes, which were now being hard-pressed by a phalanx of Interceptors. The second Interceptor squad was closing in on the *Spear*. Karrid opened fire with her turbolasers, but only managed to hit two of them as the rest continued in undeterred.

Karrid's fingers flickered and danced on the control panel, and the *Spear* banked at an impossible angle, directly into the path of the incoming horde. The *Spear* had the maneuverability of a vessel half its size, and the unexpected change in direction happened too quickly for the Interceptors to react. The tiny fighters were smashed to smithereens against the gargantuan battleship's hull.

The move also brought the front of the *Spear* in line with the surviving destroyers and Interceptors, still locked in battle with the corvettes. Karrid's eyes flickered over the screens of the pod as she descended on the skirmish, the massive capital ship dwarfing the other players.

She tapped the control panel, her fingers a blur as she selected her targets in rapid succession. The Interceptors, too engaged with the Republic vessels to take evasive action, were wiped out in the first volley. The corvettes were next, their deflectors useless against the *Spear*'s point-blank assault. The destroyers, already heavily damaged, were a mere afterthought. Several of the vessels were engulfed by fiery explosions, others rendered lifeless hunks of scrap, their hulls perforated with countless gaping holes. But Karrid didn't have time to relish the carnage as she turned her attention to her final goal.

The remaining Hammerhead was still firing at the *Exemplar*. Locked in close combat with the Republic ship, Gravus had been unable to prepare his vessel for the jump to hyperspace—lowering the shields to make the jump wasn't an option when an enemy was firing at you. There had been a brief window for them both to escape while the *Spear* was wiping out the other ships, but the Republic commander had failed to fully grasp the situation. Instead of mutual flight, he had chosen to continue the battle rather than risk an attempted retreat that would leave him vulnerable to the *Exemplar*. Now it was too late for both of them.

The *Ascendant Spear* closed rapidly on the two remaining ships. Concentrating her turbolasers on the Hammerhead's center, she sliced it cleanly in two. Bodies and debris spilled out from the gutted Republic ship into the cold, dark void of space.

At the same time she sensed a massive energy signature emanating from the *Exemplar*: Gravus was trying to make a last desperate jump to hyperspace. He'd dropped his shields and left his ship vulnerable to attack, but he knew he had no hope of defeating the Empire's most feared weapon if he stayed to fight. Drawing on the automated targeting systems of the *Spear,* Karrid fired a precision strike to disable the *Exemplar*'s hyperdrive, leaving Gravus at her mercy.

A sudden beeping in her ear told her Gravus was trying to open up a hailing channel, but she had no interest in listening to him barter and beg for his life. Instead, she took aim and fired for the last time. The unshielded *Exemplar* exploded into a ball of spectacular blue flame, instantly killing everyone aboard.

Karrid sent the *Spear* in a long slow circle, scanning the wreckage and debris of the entire battle for signs of life, but finding nothing. Satisfied, she contacted the bridge.

"Moff Lorman, prepare to resume command."

"Yes, my Lord," he replied.

Karrid tapped the controls beneath her fingers once more, severing her connection with the *Spear*. She shuddered as the wires retracted, the needles of the biosynthetic interfaces slowly withdrawing from her cybernetic implants. A wave of exhaustion washed over her, along with an overwhelming sense of intense and irreplaceable loss. Each time she broke her connection with the ship it felt like losing a limb.

The crystal sphere slowly opened to reveal her two apprentices still sitting cross-legged on the floor on either side. Their faces were drawn and haggard, their brows covered with sheens of sweat from supporting their Master's exertion. But though they shared her fatigue, only she knew the glory of becoming one with the *Spear,* and only she could understand the emptiness that enveloped her when the connection was broken.

"Tell Moff Lorman to transmit the record of the battle to the Dark Council," she said, her voice weary. "Let them see that Gravus was a traitor to the Empire."

To herself she added, *And let them see what happens to those who get in my way.*

CHAPTER 9

THE ANALYTICS office was a windowless, overcrowded room packed with computer terminals and twenty-three SIS agents gathering, organizing, and analyzing data from the thousands of reports that came in every day.

For the past week the cramped office might as well have been Theron's home as he and the rest of the understaffed team worked double shifts to try to stay on top of everything coming in. However, despite making a sincere effort to contribute, he couldn't shake the feeling that he was wasting his time.

It wasn't that he didn't believe in what analytics was doing; he understood they were a vital component of SIS. But Theron had developed a unique set of specialized skills, almost none of which were applicable to his current position.

It made him want to scream. Twenty times a day a piece of small but unusual information that begged further attention would pass across his desk: a potential lead to what might possibly be a mission critical to the safety of the Republic. Instead of being able to act on these leads he had to write up reports with recommendations on how to proceed, then forward them to his superiors for review, knowing full well that by the time a field agent was assigned to the case the opportunity would probably be lost.

And even when he wasn't in the office, he was still

stuck on Coruscant—probably the safest and most secure planet in the Republic, and the absolute last place Theron wanted to be.

He feared that he was losing his edge, that day after day of boring desk work had dulled his survival instincts. The Director had sentenced him to three months in this prison, and if he served his full time he might never regain them.

If he didn't get out of analytics soon, something bad was bound to happen. Maybe he'd resign in disgust. Go rogue and take off on a mission without SIS approval or support. Or maybe he'd just snap and go on a rampage throughout the analytics office, smashing every monitor and computer station he could before the authorities dragged him away. Or, most terrifying of all, maybe he'd just learn to accept the drudgery of his new post.

The only thing that had kept him sane so far was the few hours each day he was able to work on Operation End Game, Jace Malcom's special project. The *Ascendant Spear* was the last vestige of Darth Mekhis's superweapons research program—one last loose thread from the mission that had cost Ngani Zho his life. Theron had no problem spending his time trying to devise a plan to bring the *Spear* down. What bothered him was the thought that some other agent would be the one to actually put that plan into effect.

He felt a tap on his shoulder as the voice of his supervisor said, "Time to pack it in, Theron."

Surprised, Theron glanced at the chrono on the wall.

"Guess I lost track of time," he said.

Another sign you're losing your edge. The days used to drag on forever; you could feel each individual, agonizing second slipping by. Now you're getting so used to being stuck in the chair you don't even notice when it's time to leave. You're numb.

"Go home and get some sleep," his supervisor ordered. "The reports will still be here tomorrow."

Is that supposed to make me feel better? Theron silently wondered as he stood up and headed back to his apartment.

Once inside, he briefly considered doing some off-the-clock work on Operation End Game—even from home he had access to files with all but the highest level of security clearance. But the drudgery of analytics sapped both his physical and mental energy. All he wanted to do was collapse into bed.

They're grinding you down, bit by bit.

Ignoring the voice inside his head, Theron made his way to the bedroom at the rear of the apartment, stripped off his clothes, flicked off the light, and crawled under the covers. Just as he was on the verge of drifting off, however, he was jarred awake by the chime of an incoming holocall.

"Accept incoming," he muttered groggily, taking a moment to realize the call wasn't coming on his cybernetic implant.

He rolled over and tapped the holocomm on the nightstand beside the bed, propping himself up on his elbow to get a better view. To his surprise, an image of Teff'ith materialized before him, the glow of the holo spreading faintly across the otherwise darkened room.

"Why you in bed?" the Twi'lek asked, arching her eyebrows in surprise. "You sleeping or you with a friend?"

"I'm . . . I'm alone," Theron stammered, his mind spinning as he tried to wrap his head around the situation.

Why is she calling? Where is she calling from? How did she know where I'm staying?

"Didn't think you'd be home," Teff'ith said. "Gonna leave a message."

Theron realized he wasn't the only one taken aback by their unexpected conversation. Knowing Teff'ith was a bit flustered as well helped him regain some of his composure.

"So give me the message."

After a moment's hesitation, Teff'ith took a deep breath then blurted out, "Know you were there on Nar Shaddaa. Don't need you following us. Don't want you following us. Back off or you be sorry!"

"How'd you even get this number?" Theron asked, not bothering to respond to her ultimatum.

"Not so hard," Teff'ith replied. "You think you only one who can find people?"

"So you went to all the trouble of tracking me down just to tell me to leave you alone?"

"Didn't ask for your help," Teff'ith snapped, ignoring his observation. "Don't need it. Take care of ourself."

"Really? Seemed to me if I hadn't stepped in you'd be a rotting corpse in a Nar Shaddaa landfill right about now."

"Think we owe you now?" Teff'ith sneered. "That why you help us?"

"I just happened to be in the area. Thought I'd help you out for old times' sake."

"Liar. Not just Nar Shaddaa, right? You there on Korriban? Belsavis? Ziost?"

"I've never been to Ziost in my life," Theron answered truthfully.

"No more watching," Teff'ith continued. "Stop following us. Got it?"

"Don't worry about it," Theron answered. "I'm staying on Coruscant for a while. Taking some time off from fieldwork. I'm focusing on reports and paperwork now."

Why would you even tell her that? You becoming one of those office drones that complains to anyone who'll listen?

"You behind a desk?" Teff'ith's face broke into a grin. "Funny."

"The choice wasn't really mine," Theron said, his voice betraying more anger than he intended.

"Always got a choice," Teff'ith sniffed. "Sounds like you just a quitter."

"Why do you even care?" Theron demanded.

"Don't," Teff'ith said with a shrug. "Be boring. We don't care. Just leave us alone."

The holo abruptly disconnected, leaving Theron alone in the dark. He rolled over, closed his eyes, and tried to go to sleep. But something Teff'ith had said had lodged itself inside his head, and instead of drifting off into dreamland, he kept circling back to it.

She mentioned Ziost. The Old Tion Brotherhood must have begun moving in there when the Empire started allowing outsiders to visit the world.

The simple fact might seem insignificant, but Theron knew there was a reason he couldn't let it go. His subconscious had latched onto it for some reason; now he had to draw it out.

Ziost. That's the key. Ziost.

In a flash of inspiration, it all came together—Operation End Game. Ignited by the catalyst, the past week of research and analysis fused into the beginnings of a plan to bring down the *Ascendant Spear*.

Theron sprang out of bed, eager to record the details while they were still fresh in his mind.

And with a little luck, this will get me back in the field, too.

DARTH MARR was the last of the assembled Dark Council members to arrive at their secret chamber beneath the Citadel. He'd scheduled the meeting, contacting the others only hours after learning of Darth Gravus's death. But even though he'd summoned them, he still had no idea what he was going to say.

He'd reviewed the official records of the battle over

Leritor, including transcriptions of the communications between Gravus and Karrid in the field reports filed by Moff Lorman.

The Ascendant Spear *dropped out of hyperspace beyond range of the Republic scanners, at which time Darth Karrid informed Darth Gravus of our arrival.*

"Darth Gravus, this is Darth Karrid. The Ascendant Spear *is at your disposal."*

"Disengage, Karrid! We didn't call for reinforcements. This is my battle to win—not yours!"

Darth Karrid disregarded Darth Gravus's request, choosing to aid the Imperial war effort by engaging the enemy fleet. After the Ascendant Spear *disposed of one of the Republic Hammerheads, Darth Gravus and Darth Karrid had the following exchange:*

"You think this will turn the Dark Council against me, Karrid? You could take out every Republic ship in this quadrant, but when it comes time to choose someone to join their ranks, they'll still pick me over a Falleen!"

"You do not grasp the danger yo8u are in, Gravus. You could be killed in this battle. I am here to ensure a desirable outcome for the Empire."

"Ignore the Republic ships! Fire on the Ascendant Spear*! Destroy it at all costs! Do not let it—"*

At this time Gravus switched to an auxiliary communications channel. Shortly after this he fired on the Ascendant Spear *as we continued to engage the Republic fleet. Darth Karrid was forced to destroy Gravus and his fleet to defend her ship and crew.*

The official military review would clearly show Gravus had been in the wrong. However, it was obvious to Marr—just as it would be obvious to everyone on the

Dark Council—that Karrid had intentionally goaded him into firing the first shot.

The fact that Karrid had brazenly defied Marr's instructions and undermined his attempts to unify the Sith by eliminating a rival was disturbing; he was starting to wonder if granting her a seat on the Dark Council would be more trouble than it was worth. His immediate concern, however, was dealing with the fallout from the other Sith Lords assembled in the room.

"Darth Marr," Vowrawn said by way of greeting, "it's impolite to keep us all waiting."

Marr ignored the Sith's sardonic words. "You all know what happened to Gravus," he said, getting straight to the matter at hand. "You all know why we're here."

"It seems Gravus is no longer a viable candidate," Vowrawn said with a coy smile. "Does this mean Karrid is our choice by default?"

"That question must be answered by the entire Dark Council," Marr replied, bracing himself for the outrage and protests of the others.

There was an unexpected silence before the ancient Darth Rictus spoke up.

"Karrid answered the question for us," he proclaimed. "She bested her rival with strength, yet was cunning enough to make it appear she was in the right. These are the traits of a true Sith."

Darth Marr was left momentarily speechless at the unexpected show of support. Given Rictus's many years on the Dark Council, his approval would go a long way toward winning the others over.

"We were willing to give the seat to Gravus if he defeated the Republic at Leritor," Mortis chimed in. "Since Karrid claimed the victory, she deserves the prize."

Marr was even more surprised by Mortis's support. His Sphere of Influence was Laws and Justice. And even though the Empire's version of justice could often be summarized as "might makes right," he had assumed Mortis would be outraged by what Karrid had done.

"Gravus was your candidate," he said, looking for clarification. "You don't want to seek revenge for his death?"

"I thought Gravus was more powerful than Karrid," he replied. "But his death proves otherwise. She issued a challenge, and he accepted by firing on her ship . . . a fatal mistake. It seems I underestimated the Falleen."

"She took bold action," Darth Ravage added. "She saw what she wanted and she seized it. If more of the other Sith Lords beneath us followed her example, the Republic would not have us running like cowards."

Their words momentarily caught Marr by surprise. Though Karrid's actions were perfectly in line with the traditional ways of the Sith, he'd thought it would take longer for the rest of the Dark Council to overcome their inherent prejudice and welcome a member of a lesser species into their ranks.

However, he understood that their willingness to embrace Karrid was still driven by the one trait they all shared—self-preservation. As Dark Lords of the Sith, they understood the power of Karrid's ship, and the opportunity she represented. The *Spear* was vital if they hoped to turn the tide of the galactic war . . . and down the road Karrid could be a powerful ally to use against not only the Republic, but also the other members of the Dark Council.

For now they would invite her in with open arms, each publicly voicing support to try to win her over as they bided their time. Waiting patiently, they would play their political games, trying to twist her allegiance so they could use her and her ship to their own advantage, even as they slowly plotted her destruction. In other words, they would see her as they each saw every other member of the Dark Council: simultaneously a potential ally and a potential enemy.

Marr sighed inwardly. Karrid had not hesitated to wipe out a fellow Dark Lord to advance her own career, even though the loss of Gravus made the Empire more vulnerable to the Republic. He had hoped the Falleen might be more open to his efforts to unify the Sith against a common foe, but she had proven herself to be as much a student of the old ways as all the others.

Despite his best efforts, the culture of backstabbing and infighting still prevailed. The Emperor had kept it under control by virtue of his own unassailable position and power, but in his absence it was eating away at the core of the Empire. And Marr was starting to doubt if he—or any among the great Sith Lords—would be able to stop it.

CHAPTER 10

MARCUS MOVED quickly through the halls of Coruscant's massive Senate Building, heading for Jace Malcom's office in the military wing. Forty standard years ago the Senators would have been horrified if a military officer—even the Supreme Commander of all Republic forces—had an office in the same building. Back then, most politicians had openly called for a massive decrease in the size of the Republic fleet and a reduction in the number of soldiers. The idea of a full-scale galactic war seemed preposterous, and the desire to shrink the scope and budget of the armed forces was virtually unanimous.

Four decades of war against the reemerged Sith Empire had changed things significantly. When the Treaty of Coruscant had been forced on the Republic years ago, some believed a lasting peace with the Empire was possible. But in the last eighteen months the uneasy truce had collapsed, and a return to full-scale hostilities silenced all talk of peace in the halls of the Senate. As the tide of war shifted to the Republic's favor, the idea of ending the Imperial threat once and for all began to gain support.

The Republic's growing military resolve was championed by the newly elected Chancellor Saresh. The former governor of Taris, few had seen her as a candidate for the Republic's highest political position, but she swept to power on a wave of aggressive anti-Imperial sentiment. Unlike others vying to succeed Chancellor Janarus, she hadn't promised to bring the Republic peace; she promised victory.

Within days of her election she enacted all thirty-six wartime provisions listed in the Galactic Constitution, greatly expanding the powers and responsibilities of her office and allowing her to make major political appointments without Senate approval. There had been some behind-the-scenes grumbling at the sudden increase in executive power, but Saresh quickly quieted the dissenters by appointing the wildly popular Jace Malcom as the new Supreme Commander.

The Director had studied Saresh's rapid rise to power carefully; it was impossible not to be impressed by her ambition and her political brilliance. Tapping Jace for Supreme Commander had been a particularly astute move. Nobody would speak out against such a long-serving Republic hero; his selection legitimized every appointment that came after. Saresh had found the perfect candidate to solidify her support, and she'd put the military under the charge of a man who was as eager to wipe out the Republic's Imperial foes as she was.

Not that the Director minded. He also believed crushing the Empire was key to securing the Republic, and he was ready to show how valuable SIS would be to that cause. Operation Transom hadn't ended as planned; Operation End Game was his chance to make up for it.

As he approached Jace's office, Marcus allowed himself a hint of a smile. They'd presented the Supreme Commander with a basic outline of Operation End Game just yesterday, and Jace had already scheduled a meeting to discuss it in more detail. Clearly he'd been impressed.

The Director was more than a little impressed himself. The analytics team had gone above and beyond for this project. They'd managed to pull everything together in just over a week, thanks largely to Theron's contributions.

Marcus had been worried about Theron's potentially disruptive impact when he'd assigned him to the team, though he'd hoped the nature of their research might make the transition from fieldwork easier. Much to the Director's relief, as soon as Theron realized analytics was working on a way to put an end to Darth Mekhis's legacy once and for all, he'd thrown himself into the work.

Maybe he's maturing, Marcus thought.

The Director wasn't normally an optimistic man, but he couldn't help but wonder if things were looking up. If Theron learned to stay out of trouble and Jace could secure SIS's future long-term funding, maybe he wouldn't wake up every morning with a crippling migraine.

"Welcome back, Director," the receptionist greeted him, her features breaking into a smile.

"Did you miss me?" he asked, responding with a grin of his own.

"I count every second of every day that you're not here," she replied, even as she buzzed him in.

As before, Jace Malcom was sitting behind his desk when the Director entered his office.

"I've already started pulling together the resources you requested for Operation End Game," the Supreme Commander told him, jumping right to the point. "You'll have everything you need."

"I'll pass your appreciation on to the analytics team," Marcus replied. "They were pulling double shifts all week to get this done. The overtime took a big chunk out of our budget, but we figured this was worth it."

"I can take a hint," Jace said with a smile, indicating for the Director to take a seat in the chair across from him. "I'll make sure your department gets all the credits you need going forward."

Marcus nodded in thanks as he sat down.

"I was glad to see you calling out the need for the Jedi to be involved in your report," Jace said. "I know some folks don't like working with them."

"They're a valuable resource for the Republic," the Director replied. "We just have to learn to use them properly."

"They offered to have Master Gnost-Dural join our team."

"A good choice," the Director said, recalling the files the Order had sent over to the SIS. "Darth Karrid was Gnost-Dural's apprentice before she decided to study under Malgus."

"I don't think they'd phrase it like that," Jace told him with a wry smile. "They'd probably say she fell to the temptations of the dark side."

Marcus frowned. "You think the Jedi are sending Gnost-Dural so he can try to redeem her?"

"Gnost-Dural's a pragmatist," Jace assured him. "Well, as much as any Jedi can be. He won't do anything that might endanger the mission."

When Marcus didn't reply right away, Jace asked, "Is this going to be a problem for your people?"

"No, sir. Every name on that list I gave you is a professional. Whichever one of my agents you select for the mission will work alongside Gnost-Dural without complaint."

"Actually," Jace said. "I wanted to talk to you about that list."

For some reason, the hairs on the back of Marcus's neck stood up.

"The files were all very impressive. But why wasn't Theron Shan among them?"

For a moment, the Director was too stunned to reply.

SIS kept the identities of their field agents under close wraps. For security reasons, only a handful of people had access to department personnel records, and the Supreme Commander wasn't one of them. The Director had given him a list of six agents who might be suitable for Operation End Game, but that list didn't include Theron.

"You know Theron?" he asked, wondering where the Supreme Commander had come up with the name.

"Only from the analytics report," Jace admitted. "He was listed as the agent who uncovered Darth Mekhis's research."

The Director shook his head, confused. He'd reviewed the report before it was sent to Jace. Theron's name had been redacted from the files—he was certain of it. Someone in analytics must have altered the final report before forwarding it to Jace . . . and Marcus had a pretty good idea who the culprit was.

No wonder Theron was so happy to be working on this report, the Director thought, gritting his teeth as he felt one of his migraines threatening to come on.

Jace picked up on the Director's discomfort.

"Is something wrong? Is Theron Shan no longer with SIS?"

Marcus thought about lying, but he didn't want to risk damaging his relationship with the Supreme Commander if the truth ever came to light. "Theron's still with us."

"Is he a good agent?"

"One of our best," the Director admitted. "But every agent on the list I gave you is just as capable."

"If Theron Shan started this, don't you think he's earned the right to see it through?"

"Theron may not be the best candidate for this particular mission," Marcus replied. "This is a joint operation with the Jedi. He works best on his own."

"The report says he was working with a Jedi when he went after Darth Mekhis. Someone named Ngani Zho."

"That was a unique situation."

Jace arched the eyebrow on the good side of his face in surprise. "You don't think Operation End Game is a unique situation?"

"Theron's methods can sometimes be a bit too . . . stylish," Marcus explained, choosing his words carefully.

"Stylish?"

"He prefers to go through the window instead of a perfectly good door."

"I know the type," Jace said, nodding. "More than a few of them in the military. Get addicted to the adrenaline rush. Always looking for action. Makes them trigger-happy. They get too fond of killing and bloodshed."

"Theron's not like that," the Director assured him, unwilling to sully his agent's reputation, even if he did feel like tossing Theron into a trash compactor at the moment.

"You're obviously concerned about something," Jace continued. "Are you worried he might betray us?"

"His loyalty to the Republic is absolute," the Director said emphatically. "He's just . . . unfocused. He sees something that doesn't sit right with him and he has to get involved, even if it's not part of the mission. He likes to improvise instead of sticking to plans."

"Sounds to me like he's just going above and beyond," the Supreme Commander said. "We could use someone like that for this mission."

Realizing the argument was already lost, the Director held back a sigh as he asked, "Do you want me to send over his file?"

"I doubt there's anything in there you can't tell me now."

"What do you want to know?"

"His name is Shan. Any relation to the Jedi Grand Master?"

"Shan is a very common name. Probably ten million of them on Coruscant alone."

"You didn't answer my question," Jace said, fixing Marcus with a piercing stare.

"Theron's her son," Marcus admitted.

Jace blinked in surprise. "Satele Shan . . . had a son?"

"Only a handful of people know," Marcus explained. "Obviously this is something we want to keep under wraps. The Jedi aren't supposed to have children."

"Who's the father? Another Jedi?"

"I don't know. I don't think even Theron knows."

The Supreme Commander was quiet for a few moments. "I'm guessing Theron isn't attuned to the Force," he said at last. "Otherwise he'd be in the Order instead of SIS."

"True."

"But this could still be good for the mission," Jace said, speaking quickly. "Working with Jedi isn't easy. His relationship with Satele might make it easier to coordinate our efforts with the Order."

"Theron doesn't really have a relationship with Satele," the Director cautioned. "She gave him up at birth. I don't even know if they've ever met."

"I see," Jace said, furrowing his brow. "Seems odd he wouldn't want to get to know her, given that they both serve the Republic."

"Theron's relationship with the Jedi is complicated," the Director explained. "He was raised in secret by Master Ngani Zho, Satele's mentor. Taught him everything the young Padawans learn at the academy—mental discipline, Jedi philosophy. I guess Zho just assumed he would follow in Satele's footsteps when he got older. But the Jedi refused to take him. Turns out he wasn't sensitive to the Force."

"He took after his father," Jace muttered.

"Probably," Marcus agreed. "Kind of made Theron rethink all those lessons he'd learned as a kid."

"Do you think he harbors any resentment toward the Jedi because they rejected him?"

"He respects what the Jedi do for the Republic," Marcus replied. "But he's seen firsthand that they're not perfect. Made him a bit cynical when it comes to some of their more strongly held beliefs."

There was a long silence as the Supreme Commander weighed this new information.

"I want him for this mission," Jace suddenly declared, thumping his hand on the top of his desk for emphasis. "I served with Satele Shan during the war. If Theron has any of his mother in him, he's the perfect man for this job."

"Theron's good," the Director said, making a final halfhearted effort to change the Supreme Chancellor's mind, "but I really think we'd be better off going with one of the agents from my original list."

Jace shook his head. "Theron's the one."

"Yes, sir," the Director replied, though his response lacked any real enthusiasm. "I'll send his file so you can look it over, and I'll let Theron know."

"Don't be so glum, Marcus," Jace said with a grin. "I've got a gut feeling about this kid, and I've learned to trust my gut."

CHAPTER 11

MINISTER DAVIDGE, the Imperial Minister of Logistics, tapped at the console of his computer, flipping through screen after screen of numbers arranged in columns, tables, graphs, and charts.

The entirety of the Empire was represented in those numbers: every citizen, every soldier, every subjugate, and every slave on every world. Every ship in every fleet, as well as all the resources produced across all the systems and sectors under Imperial control, was accounted for in mind-numbing detail and accuracy. The totalitarian rule of the Emperor had led to a very efficient and organized system of inventories and censuses that measured everything under his control. And though he was gone—much to Minister Davidge's relief—the bureaucratic network he'd installed still remained.

The screens and screens of numbers were the lifeblood Davidge needed; without accurate, up-to-date data he couldn't do his job—and in his mind, it was clearly the most important job in the Empire. Logistics, on a meta scale, were the be-all and end-all of the Empire's survival. Resources and manpower dictated supplies and labor, which dictated the potential production and expected consumption of everything.

Without him, the Empire had no plan to guide its course. Without him, the Minister of War wouldn't know how many ships or troops to send to each sector, or which worlds were worth fighting for and which weren't worth the resources to defend. Even the Dark Council's members relied on him to give them a sense of the relative strength of the Empire compared to the Republic.

Unfortunately, the minister lacked hard numbers on the Republic. Ever since the collapse of Imperial Intelligence, data on the enemy had come from estimates, assumptions, and guesswork. It added variance to his equations, and Minister Davidge hated variance. It required him to provide predictions for both high and low ends of the spectrum, doubling his workload as he offered up predictive models tracking the ebb and flow of the galactic war.

Even using the lowest estimates of Republic resources, the truth was inescapable. The tide had turned against the Empire, and if something didn't radically change over the next few years their defeat was inevitable. It was simple math.

The minister finished up his final review of the data, gathered his report, and stood from his desk, stretching to loosen his cramped and tired muscles. He'd been huddled over the chair for nearly twelve hours, but Darth Marr had presented him with a question, and Davidge needed to be sure of the answer before he replied.

Confident in his analysis, he turned and headed to the locked durasteel door in the back of his office. He punched in the sixteen-digit code to unlock it, stepped inside, and sealed the door behind him. He moved quickly over to the communications console in the center of the room and activated the black cipher to send out an encrypted message to Darth Marr.

The Sith Lord answered immediately; clearly he'd been waiting for Davidge's call.

"My Lord," the minister said. "I've reviewed the situation in the Boranall system as you commanded."

"I assumed as much when I saw your call," Marr answered, his voice calm and cold as the grave.

Davidge suppressed an urge to shudder. He didn't like dealing with the Dark Council—the Sith Lords were strange creatures beyond his comprehension. They were driven by emotion and passion rather than logic and careful analysis. They often relied on visions and prophecy gleaned through the Force, allowing some mystical, unquantifiable power to guide their actions rather than the undeniable truth of numbers. And sometimes they stubbornly refused to believe what he tried to tell them—especially when he delivered news they didn't want to hear.

Marr was better than some of the others; he didn't rage and scream at Davidge when he didn't get the answer he sought, like Ravage, and he didn't seem to be eviscerating the minister with his eyes like Mortis. Most important, Marr understood that the minister's projections were not guarantees. Unforeseen variables could alter the equation, rendering the minister's numbers obsolete. But there was still something unsettling about the icy calm with which Marr always addressed him.

"What is your analysis?" Marr pressed, and Davidge realized the Sith had been waiting for him to give his report.

"Uh . . . given the estimated level of Republic-backed resistance and the growing tide of anti-Imperial sentiment among the native population, we should abandon our campaign in the Boranall system."

"There are three habitable worlds in that system," Marr said. "Nearly twenty billion people."

"Y-yes, my Lord. But none of the planets has the abundance of resources necessary to offset the losses we will inevitably sustain if we try to keep the population under Imperial control."

"What's the loss ratio?"

"Extrapolated over six months, there is a net point two percent reduction in total Imperial output if we let the system go."

"And if we try to hold it?"

"Conservative estimates put the loss at point four percent." After a moment he hastily added, "In the worst-case scenario, losses could hit point seven percent."

To some the numbers might sound small, but Davidge knew Marr was wise enough to understand the incredible scope of even two one-hundredths of a percent of the Empire's total resources.

"The cost is high," Marr acknowledged, but then he added, "but the Boranall system is not the only place in the Empire threatening to break away from our control. Crushing this uprising will send a message to other systems."

"Of course, my Lord," Davidge said, though silently he sighed.

He understood Marr's reasoning—expend extra resources on the Boranall system in the hope that it would offset future losses. But in the minister's experience, such a plan rarely worked. Anti-Imperial sentiment would still rise up in other systems, fed and fueled by the Republic and their promises of liberation.

They would never recoup the extra few tenths of a percent it would cost them to hold the system. In Davidge's mind, this is how the Empire would fall—not in some epic battle, but by tiny margins bleeding away. A death of a million microscopic cuts. But he dared not argue with Darth Marr.

"I will arrange to have one of our nearby fleets send reinforcements to the system," the minister said.

"I believe Darth Karrid is still in that sector," Marr said. "The *Ascendant Spear*'s arrival should put a quick end to the uprising."

The minister fought back another sigh. He was all too

familiar with Darth Karrid and her methods. Whenever the *Ascendant Spear* was brought into a conflict, casualties and collateral damage increased exponentially. There was no doubt in his mind that the loss ratio would now push toward the highest of his estimates.

Against his better judgment, the minister decided to speak up.

"I'm still trying to absorb the cost of Darth Karrid's intervention at Leritor. The loss of Gravus's fleet has negatively impacted our projections. In this case, it might be better if you ordered someone else to go."

"Darth Karrid is a member of the Dark Council now," Marr reminded him. "She does not take orders from me. Or from you."

"Forgive me, my Lord. I meant no offense."

"Choose your words more carefully when you contact Darth Karrid to request her assistance in this matter."

Davidge understood numbers better than people, but it was obvious what Marr was hoping to accomplish. It was well known that he had supported the Falleen's candidacy from the beginning, and having the Minister of Logistics personally petition Darth Karrid for aid in the Boranall system would further legitimize her new position. And persuading her to undertake a mission in a remote system would keep her and the *Ascendant Spear* away from the machinations of any other members of the Dark Council who might be looking to recruit her allegiance, at least for a while. It wasn't the first time the minister had been forced to bow to the politics of the Dark Council. At least this time the cost to the Empire was less than it had been on other occasions.

"I understand, my Lord. I will contact her at once."

"Try to be convincing when you ask for her help," Marr warned before disconnecting the signal.

From his reports, the minister knew every potentially significant detail about Boranall and the other worlds in the system: their geography and climate; their citizens and culture; their resources and industry. And he knew exactly how he would present this proposal to Darth Karrid.

He composed a brief message summarizing the situation, running it through the cipher before transmitting it to the *Ascendant Spear* with a highest priority ranking. Despite this, it took almost thirty minutes before he received her reply. The delay was troubling; it hinted that the Falleen, like so many other of the high-ranking Sith Lords, had little regard for the crucial role the Minister of Logistics played in the ongoing galactic war.

Pushing his fears aside, Minister Davidge answered the incoming holo. Darth Karrid's face materialized before him. Each time he saw her, Davidge couldn't help but notice her marred beauty. Her perfect skin had been disfigured by the tattoos on her face that represented her devotion to the ways of the Sith; the cybernetic implants dominating her left side transformed her features into a grotesque mix of flesh and steel.

"I received your message, Minister Davidge," Darth Karrid said, her tone somewhere between annoyance and contempt. "Is this foolishness on Boranall really worthy of the *Ascendant Spear*?"

No, it's not, Davidge thought. *But Marr wants you there.*

Out loud he said, "We have reports of a steady buildup of Republic ships in the region in conjunction with numerous accounts of growing anti-Imperial sentiment among the locals. My projections show that if this potential uprising is not dealt with swiftly, it could have a ripple effect throughout the Empire."

She twisted her face up in a sneer.

"And what made you think this insignificant system was important enough to trouble a member of the Dark Council?"

Knowing Marr would be displeased if Karrid discovered his involvement, the minister instead went with a carefully fabricated justification for contacting her.

"There is a hypermatter research station on Boranall," Davidge told her.

There was some truth to his statement: there was an old hypermatter research station on Boranall, the largest and most heavily populated planet in the similarly named system. But he omitted the fact that it was a useless government boondoggle put in place generations ago by corrupt politicians taking payouts from the wealthy family that owned the research company. The archaic equipment had fallen into disrepair, and the technicians supposedly working there were mostly relatives of influential nobles with no proper training.

"Since you are now overseeing the Technology Sphere of Influence," Davidge continued, blatantly appealing to her ego, "I thought you might want to handle this personally. We can't let the research station fall under Republic control."

Karrid favored him with a coy smile—an expression that at the height of her beauty would have made Davidge's knees buckle with yearning and desire. Now, however, her gruesome visage merely churned his stomach.

"Perhaps Marr is right about you," she purred. "Maybe you are of some use to the Empire after all."

Davidge remained silent.

"You're in luck, Minister," she said after a brief moment of contemplation. "I will set a course for the Boranall system and put an end to the flickers of rebellion."

"I thank you on behalf of the Empire," Davidge replied.

Karrid didn't bother to reply as she terminated the call. Relieved, the minister turned off the cipher, rose from his seat, and walked out of the communications room. He closed the durasteel door behind him, waiting for the single beep that confirmed it was locked and the cipher beyond was secure. Then he returned to his desk and went back to studying his tables, charts, and graphs.

CHAPTER 12

THERON HAD no intention of showing up late for his briefing with the Supreme Commander. The Director was already furious with him for slipping his name into the summary report for Operation End Game; no sense adding fuel to the fire. As a result, he arrived at Jace's office twenty minutes early.

"Take a seat," the receptionist instructed, pointing to one of several chairs against the wall. "The Supreme Commander will see you once everyone is here."

There was nothing in her tone to indicate this was anything but standard protocol, but Theron couldn't help but wonder if the Director had given explicit instructions not to let him in to speak with Jace Malcom unescorted. However, looking at the young woman's bearing—professional, but in no way wary or guarded—convinced him he was just being paranoid. He smiled to himself as he sat down, glad to see his survival skills were operating at full throttle once again. For a field agent, a little paranoia was a good thing: sometimes they really were out to get you.

The Director arrived about fifteen minutes later. He gave a perfunctory nod to Theron, then a warm smile and wink to the receptionist. The young woman blushed and smiled herself as she pretended not to have seen the gesture.

Looks like the Director's looking for wife number three, Theron thought to himself.

"Any advice for this meeting?" Theron asked quietly as his boss took a seat beside him to wait.

"Since when does anything I ever tell you matter?" he replied in a sharp whisper, just low enough to keep the receptionist from hearing. "You just do whatever you want anyway."

"But I get results," Theron reminded him. "That's why you keep me around."

The Director didn't reply, and Theron could tell he was biting his tongue to keep from unleashing a full-blown rant in front of the receptionist.

"Jace is a military man," the Director finally said after regaining his composure. "He likes discipline and order. Pull one of your typical reckless stunts while he's calling the shots and he'll crush you."

"I'll keep that in mind," Theron promised.

They passed the next few minutes in uncomfortable silence until Master Gnost-Dural, their Jedi liaison, arrived. The Kel Dor was slightly taller than Theron, though he appeared thinner—possibly because of his loose-fitting Jedi robe. His rough, ridged skin was a faded hue of yellow-brown. Like all Kel Dor who ventured from the helium-rich atmosphere of their homeworld, his eyes were protected by formfitting goggles and the lower half of his face was partially obscured by a steel breathing mask. The mask covered the fleshy chasm that Kel Dor possessed in place of a nose and mouth, though it left his ten-centimeter-long, downward-protruding tusks exposed.

Given his complexion, the mask, the tusks, and the odd-shaped cranium typical of the species, Master Gnost-Dural's appearance was intimidating and unsettling. But Theron knew the Jedi was one of the most respected and honored Masters in the Order.

He was the Republic's foremost expert on the Sith; he had studied them in detail for many years in his role as keeper of the Jedi Archives. Having reviewed the file the Jedi sent over, however, Theron knew he was more than a mere historian. Gnost-Dural was also an accomplished warrior; he'd been battling the Sith ever since their startling reemergence on the galactic stage, longer than Theron had even been alive.

Theron wondered what the Kel Dor thought of Grand Master Satele Shan. Though there were no records of them serving directly together, he surely knew the head of the Jedi Order personally. He also wondered if Gnost-Dural knew Satele was his mother. Not that Theron really cared either way. Satele's connection to him was purely biological. His lineage had no bearing on who he was or what he had become; the only real parent he'd had was Master Zho.

"Greetings, Director," the alien said, his voice deep and resonant even through his mask. "And to you, Agent Shan."

"Call me Theron."

"As you wish. I knew Master Zho; he spoke of you often. I grieved when I heard of his loss, though I take solace knowing he became one with the Force."

Theron was familiar enough with Jedi philosophy not to take offense at the well-intentioned words. He also made note of the fact that Gnost-Dural mentioned Zho, but not Satele . . . though he might just have been exercising discretion.

"The Supreme Commander will see you now," the young woman said, pressing a button behind her desk that caused the door to swing open. The three men rose as one and entered the room where Jace was waiting. The Supreme Commander sprang to his feet as they entered, coming over quickly to close the door behind them.

"Director. Master Gnost-Dural," he said, nodding at each of them in turn. "Good to finally meet you, Theron."

His words came quickly, as if he was nervous. Theron chalked it up to excitement over the mission.

"I want everyone to speak freely," Malcom continued. "Rank means nothing here—we're all equals in this meeting. If you have something to say, just say it."

"Think you can handle that, Theron?" the Director asked sarcastically.

"I'll try to get over my natural shyness."

"Perhaps we should bring each other up to speed," Master Gnost-Dural suggested. "You can tell me more about Operation End Game, and I can tell you about the *Ascendant Spear*'s commander. She was once my Padawan, though she went by the name of Kana Terrid back then."

"I helped put together the analytics report," Theron reminded them. "I've studied everything that was in the files in detail. I'm more interested in what wasn't in the files."

The Jedi nodded. "Kana showed great promise during her training, though I was always wary of her ambition. She rarely limited herself to the tasks I set her to; she liked to go off on her own. Take risks. Always looking for the next new challenge."

"Sounds familiar," the Director mumbled, but Theron ignored him.

"Instead of trying to change her nature, I sought to guide and direct her natural curiosity. I encouraged her to explore and branch out."

"That doesn't sound familiar," Theron interjected, arching an eyebrow in his boss's direction.

"It may be my fault that she fell to the dark side," Gnost-Dural admitted. "I thought her training had given her the discipline to keep her safe, but perhaps giving her so much freedom was a mistake."

Theron chimed in before the Director could say anything. "Some people are just drawn to the dark side. Forcing her to follow a rigid set of rules might have made her abandon the Jedi Order even sooner."

"She didn't abandon the Jedi Order," Gnost-Dural replied. "Not as you think. I wanted to get one of my people into the Sith; someone to help bring them down from the inside. I was the one who sent her to study under Darth Malgus. I knew it was a risk. If she was discovered she would suffer untold tortures and a gruesome, painful death. Even worse, I knew the temptation of the dark side would test her: Malgus was both powerful and charismatic."

Theron wasn't entirely sure the risk of falling to the dark side was worse than torture and death, but he managed to keep his mouth shut.

"For several years she worked undercover, studying at Malgus's feet while secretly relaying information back to me. Much of what we know about the *Ascendant Spear* came from her initial reports, and her information led to several key Republic victories."

"Let me guess what happened next," Theron said. "The intel kept flowing, but it became less valuable. The information was still accurate, but it wasn't as strategically important."

"She became a double agent," the Kel Dor confirmed. "She was feeding us insignificant scraps on the Empire's plans while relaying critical Republic intel to Darth Malgus.

"Before she abandoned us, we learned that the ship's full potential can only be unlocked by those with a powerful connection to the Force," the Jedi added. "But it also requires special cybernetic implants to interface with the control systems. It is this union of ship and Sith that makes the *Spear* such a formidable weapon.

"I believe Malgus convinced my Padawan to submit to

the surgery for the cybernetic implants so she could take command of the vessel. That was likely the final temptation that lured her over to the dark side."

The Kel Dor's insistence on finding some identifiable reason for Karrid's betrayal didn't sit well with Theron.

"You're not going on this mission to try to redeem your former Padawan, are you?" he asked. "I know you Jedi believe nobody is beyond redemption, but bringing down the *Spear* is going to be hard enough already."

"My actions unleashed Darth Karrid on the galaxy," Gnost-Dural explained. "It is my responsibility to stop her. That is my only concern."

Theron nodded. Taking care of unfinished business was something he could understand.

"In any event, Kana changed her name to Darth Karrid, and I haven't had any contact with her since," Gnost-Dural concluded. "Everything I know about her now comes to me from other sources, like SIS."

"We've just learned that Darth Karrid has recently been given a seat on the Dark Council," the Director chimed in.

"This doesn't change anything," Jace insisted. "It just means taking Karrid and the *Spear* down will have an even greater impact on the Empire. That's why Operation End Game is so important.

"After reviewing all the scenarios analytics offered, we realize we can't stop the *Spear* unless we first get a saboteur on board," the Supreme Commander told Gnost-Dural. "The plan is to have Theron stow away on the ship while it's docked at an Imperial spaceport for crew leave."

"The *Spear* never stays in port for long," Theron added. "Getting a saboteur on board requires preparation and planning. We'd have to know which spaceport Karrid was heading for so we could get there first to set everything up."

"We do have a mole inside Imperial fleet communications," the Director said. "And she can divert copies of any messages being transmitted to or from the *Ascendant Spear* to us. But those messages are coded."

"Then it won't do us any good," Theron noted. "Unless we have a black cipher."

"Hasn't acquiring a black cipher been a Republic priority for months?" Gnost-Dural asked, impressing Theron with his knowledge of something that didn't fall under the Order's typical purview.

"The Empire has taken every precaution to keep that from happening," Jace replied. "On two occasions we even salvaged a damaged cipher from the wreckage of an Imperial capital ship in the hope of repairing or reverse-engineering it.

"Unfortunately, the ciphers are designed with a self-destruct function. When a capital ship goes down, the ciphers automatically burn out their decryption cores. Without a functional core, the cipher is just a worthless metal box."

"So how do you propose we acquire one?" asked Theron.

"The Imperial Minister of Logistics uses one to communicate with capital ships across the galaxy," the Director explained. "It's in his office at the Orbital Defense Command Center on Ziost."

"So we need to break into one of the most heavily guarded buildings on one of the Empire's most critical and well-defended worlds and steal the cipher without setting off the self-destruct sequence?" the Jedi asked, making sure he was clear on the plan.

"It's more complicated than that," Theron said. "If a working cipher goes missing, the Empire will just reprogram all their codes."

Theron knew it wasn't as simple as he was making it sound. The black ciphers had been designed to prevent anyone from tampering with them; they couldn't be reprogrammed in the field. Changing the encryption codes would require the Empire to recall their capital ships so technicians could synchronize the changes on each vessel. It would be costly and time consuming, but it was still a better option than letting the enemy listen in on their classified transmissions.

"But the Empire won't go to the trouble and expense of changing the codes if they don't think the cipher is missing," the Director explained. "We need to break into the minister's office and swap the working cipher's core with one of the burned-out cores from the damaged ciphers we recovered. Make them think the one in the minister's office was somehow damaged, causing it to set off the self-destruct sequence."

"Won't they be suspicious if the cipher is mysteriously damaged?" the Jedi asked.

"Not if they think it was damaged in a terrorist attack," Theron chimed in. "Plenty of Imperial installations on other worlds have been targeted in the past. We switch the cores, then detonate some explosives inside the building. Make it look like local anti-Imperial separatists set off a blast that triggered the cipher's self-destruct sequence."

"Could be heavy civilian casualties if we aren't careful," the Jedi noted.

"We'll do everything we can to minimize collateral damage," Jace promised.

"We'll need the architectural blueprints for the Orbital Defense Command Center," Gnost-Dural added. "Along with a list of all their security protocols. Does SIS have a contact on Ziost we can use?"

"We haven't been able to make any inroads into Ziost yet," the Director admitted.

"I know someone who can help," Theron said. "A

freelancer I worked with before." *The hard part is going to be convincing her to work with me again.*

"Even if Theron's friend helps us out," the Director cautioned, "we're still working on a good cover story to get onto Ziost without drawing attention."

"I can take care of that," Gnost-Dural offered.

Theron raised an eyebrow in surprise.

"SIS aren't the only ones who need to infiltrate Imperial worlds," the Kel Dor explained.

"Then it's settled," Theron said. "So when do we leave?"

He knew they could keep going over the mission backward and forward, hashing out every last detail, but he didn't see the point. Part of what made him a good agent was the ability to think on his feet. Any specifics they came up with now would be pure speculation. It was inevitable things would change during the actual mission, and overplanning would only make it harder to adapt and improvise.

"Give me time to get our cover story in place," Gnost-Dural said. "We can meet at my private hangar in two days. I'll send you the location."

"I'm glad you're both eager to start," Jace said. "But let's not rush into anything."

"You wanted Theron on this op," Marcus said, coming to his agent's defense. "I've learned that when he's ready to go, the best thing is to just get out of his way."

"I can do that," Jace vowed. "Gentlemen, Operation End Game has officially begun. May luck—and the Force—be with you."

Realizing they had been dismissed, Theron, the Director, and Gnost-Dural filed out of the Supreme Commander's office and into the reception area outside.

"You two go on ahead," the Director told them, casting a quick glance over at the receptionist as the office door closed behind them. "I need to speak with this young lady about some paperwork. Coordinating SIS resources with the military . . . gotta make everything official."

Theron suspected that whatever the Director wanted to talk about was decidedly unofficial, but he had enough tact not to say anything as he and Gnost-Dural continued out into the hall alone.

"I'm looking forward to working with you," the Jedi said once they reached a branch in the hall where they would part ways. "And I can assure you that my feelings for my former Padawan won't interfere with our mission."

"That's good to know," Theron said, thinking, *If it comes down to it, will you be able to kill her? Or will you hesitate?*

"I'll see you in two days," Gnost-Dural said, then turned and headed off in the other direction.

As he watched him go, the personal holocomm on Theron's belt started to beep. Curious, he answered the call. To his surprise the Supreme Commander's face materialized before him.

"Theron, I'd like to speak to you again before the mission. Alone. At my private residence."

"Of course, sir," Theron said, too taken aback to think of anything else.

"Good. I'll send you the address. Be there tomorrow night."

The call ended before Theron could ask any questions, leaving him wondering what the Supreme Commander of the Republic could possibly want to discuss.

CHAPTER 13

JACE MALCOM shifted his position, unable to get comfortable on the couch in the living room of his modestly furnished apartment as he waited for Theron to arrive. The Supreme Commander wasn't normally so restless. During his military career he'd spent many hours just sitting and waiting; a soldier's life was long stretches of boredom broken up by brief interludes of intense action. He'd learned long ago how to stay calm and relaxed as the minutes ticked by. But this situation was unlike anything he'd ever dealt with before.

When the buzzer at his door rang, he actually sprang to his feet and paused a moment to collect himself before opening the door.

"Thanks for coming, Theron," he said to the young man on the other side.

"I'm not going to miss a meeting with the Supreme Commander," Theron replied.

"This wasn't an order," Jace assured him. "Just a request."

"Coming from someone in your position, they're basically the same thing."

Jace nodded. He had been an officer in command of others for many years, but his recent promotion to Supreme Commander had taken things to a level he still wasn't quite used to.

"Come in and sit down," he said. "Please," he added, hoping to make it seem like an invitation.

Theron settled into one of the two chairs across from the couch. Jace couldn't help but notice his choice of seat—facing the door, and the farthest position away from where anyone else could sit.

"Nice place you have here, Commander. Kind of expected the walls to be covered with all your medals and commendations."

"They clashed with the drapes," Jace explained. "Can I get you something to drink? I've got a nice Alderaanian vintage if you like wine. Or Corellian Reserve if you prefer brandy."

"No thanks, sir."

"How about some Mandalorian *kri'gee*?"

"Always wanted to try the hard stuff," Theron said. "Sure, I'll take a glass."

Jace made his way over to the liquor cabinet in the corner and poured them both a shot, then brought it over to his guest before taking a seat on the couch facing him. In the light of the apartment he could see that Theron favored his mother's side; he could make out a few faint hints of Satele Shan in the younger man's features, though if he didn't know who his mother was it wouldn't have been noticeable.

"To the Republic?" Theron asked, holding up his glass.

"The Republic," Jace agreed, and they both downed their drinks in a single gulp.

Theron coughed and sputtered for a few seconds—a common reaction in those tasting *kri'gee* for the first time.

"Want another?" Jace asked. "It'll grow on you."

"I'm good," Theron gasped, his face still red from choking on the first glass.

They set their empty glasses on the coffee table between them, and an uncomfortable silence settled over the room. Jace knew Theron was waiting for him to speak, but he honestly didn't know where to begin.

"I served with your mother," he finally said. "On Alderaan. She was a remarkable woman."

He could see a change come over Theron's face—he was suddenly guarded and wary.

"I figured you knew," he said. "Is that why you picked me for this mission?"

"I've seen your service record, Theron. You've earned this."

"You didn't answer my question."

"I wondered if there was some of your mother in you," Jace admitted.

"I don't mean to be rude, Commander, but if you brought me here to ask about Satele you're out of luck. I barely know her."

There was a shortness to Theron's reply. It wasn't exactly anger or bitterness; more like exasperation. As if he'd had or imagined this conversation so many times before that he was simply tired of it.

"So you've never reached out to her? Or she to you?"

Theron shrugged. "Never saw any reason. When I was born, she gave me up to dedicate herself to the Republic. I understand why she did it, and I respect her choice. I chose to serve the Republic, too. That's why I joined SIS. Making her part of my life now would just complicate things for both of us; make both of our jobs harder. I don't see the point."

"You seem pretty sure of this," Jace noted.

"Ngani Zho helped me understand why Satele did what she did. I've come to terms with it. I've moved on."

"But what about your father? Didn't you ever want to ask Satele about him?"

"Master Zho was my father. He raised me. Made me who I am."

The conversation wasn't going as well as Jace had hoped. He was dancing around the real issue, and he realized he was actually afraid. He'd faced death too many times to count, but here he was, too scared to tell Theron why he was really here. Taking a deep breath, the Supreme Commander decided it was time to charge into the breach.

"Theron, I didn't know Satele had a son. I only found out a few days ago when I saw your name in the report and I asked the Director if you were related."

"Kind of wish he'd lied to you," Theron grumbled. "Could have avoided this whole awkward chat."

Jace ignored him and pressed on, determined to get the truth out there.

"He gave me your personnel file. I checked when you were born, confirming what I already suspected. Theron— I believe that I am your father."

There was a long silence before Theron finally spoke.

"I already told you," he said coldly. "Master Zho was my father."

"Theron—you have to believe that I had no idea. When Satele broke off our relationship, I thought it was because of the Jedi Order's ban against emotional attachments. I didn't realize she was pregnant."

Theron stood up suddenly.

"Commander, I'm sorry she lied to you. But this is between you and her. You need to talk to Satele."

"That's the last thing I need right now," Jace replied. "She lied to me. Hid you from me. I'm so mad I wouldn't even know what to say to her."

"But she'd know what to say to you," Theron said sympathetically. "The Jedi always have an explanation."

"Exactly. I'm in no mood to hear her prattle on about peace and controlling your emotions. That's why I came to you."

"I still don't know what you want from me," Theron said, shaking his head. "Why tell me this?"

"Why?" Jace rose to his feet. "You're my son. Doesn't that mean anything to you?"

"No!" Theron snapped, taking a step back. "We're just strangers who happen to share a biological connection."

"That's my point," Jace insisted, resisting the urge to take a step forward. "We don't have to be strangers."

"I don't need someone to take me fishing or teach me how to ride a hoverbike."

"That's not what I meant," Jace said, shaking his head in frustration. "I just want to get to know you better. Maybe we have more in common than you think."

Theron sighed and brought a hand up to rub his temples.

"Your timing on this is really terrible, Commander," he said.

"I could have handled this better," Jace admitted. "I just thought you had a right to know. I'm still trying to figure this all out."

"Fair enough," Theron said, his tone softening. "I've been dealing with Satele's decision my whole life, but you just found out. I guess it's going to take you some time to get a handle on it."

Jace stayed silent, sensing that Theron was heading somewhere.

"I have a lot of respect and admiration for you and what you do," Theron told him. "And maybe we do have a lot in common. We've both dedicated our lives to helping the Republic. Maybe when I get back from Ziost, we can try to get to know each other better."

"Don't worry," Jace assured him. "We can take it slow."

"If we were taking it slow you wouldn't have dropped this bomb on our first visit."

"Sorry about that," Jace said. "I thought you deserved to know before the mission . . . just in case."

The professional soldier in him realized how poorly he had handled the whole situation, though there wasn't much he could do about it now.

"You and Master Gnost-Dural are scheduled to leave tomorrow. Do you need me to postpone the mission for a few days while you process this?"

"Give me a little credit, Commander," Theron replied. "I'm more worried about you. Knowing I'm your son might affect your judgment on Operation End Game."

"You don't get to be Supreme Commander unless you can put personal feelings aside for the greater good of the Republic," Jace replied.

"Glad to hear it."

There was another long, uncomfortable silence before Theron finally said, "I should go. I still have some things to get ready before I leave."

"Right. Of course."

Jace escorted Theron to the door. Just before he left, the young man turned to him.

"We can talk again when I get back."

"Looking forward to it," Jace answered with a smile.

The door slid closed and Jace slowly made his way back over to collapse onto the couch. His heart was pounding and his body felt simultaneously wired and exhausted—the same reaction he had at the end of an intense battle. He closed his eyes to take a short nap and slipped immediately off to sleep—a useful skill most soldiers quickly learned.

Jace lay motionless with his eyes closed on his cot as consciousness slowly returned, floating on a cloud of kolto. He could hear the celebration taking place outside his tent; Havoc Squad had won a great victory today over the Empire. The Republic had been giving ground ever since the Sith had first reappeared and seized Korriban; reclaiming Alderaan was a morale boost the troops desperately needed.

The songs and laughter of the soldiers from outside the tent sounded as if they were coming from a great distance—muted by the drugs that numbed the pain of his disfigured face.

The explosion from the grenade he'd clutched in his hand while tackling Darth Malgus had scarred him for life, but his desperate actions had saved Satele Shan's life . . . just as her unexpected arrival had saved him from execution at the hands of the Sith earlier in the battle.

"How are you feeling?" a gentle voice cooed in his ear, and he opened his eyes to see Satele hovering over him.

"Muddled," Jace said with a smile. "Kolto's making me a bit woozy."

He could feel his burned skin stretching and cracking at the gesture, and he half expected Satele to recoil as he realized what a gruesome sight he must be.

Instead, she returned his smile and reached out to place a soft hand on his bare arm. Her touch sent a shiver along his spine.

"What are you doing here?" he asked her. "On Alderaan, I mean?"

"I had a vision," she told him. "The Force showed me that you would need my help on Alderaan, and I petitioned the Council to send reinforcements."

"Might have to rethink my opinion on that mystical mumbo-jumbo," Jace teased her. "Those Imps were about to make me a full head shorter before you arrived. Guess I owe you one."

"After all the battles we've fought together, I've stopped keeping track of who owes whom," Satele told him. "You know I'll always be there for you, and I know you'll be there for me."

"We make a good team," Jace conceded. "They find Malgus's body yet?"

Satele shook her head. "I'm starting to think he survived the battle."

"You dropped a mountain on him," Jace grunted in disbelief. "How could anyone survive that?"

"He's a powerful Sith Lord. It's possible he used the dark side to survive my final assault. But you should not let that detract from this moment. All of Alderaan is hailing you as a hero this night. If you're up to it I can take you out to enjoy the celebrations."

"I'd rather stay here in my tent . . . alone with you."

Satele tried to dismiss his comment with a laugh, but there was a nervousness in her reaction that Jace could sense even through the fading fugue of the painkillers in his system.

"I'm serious, Satele," he said. "You know how I feel about you. I've felt that way for years, ever since we first met."

"That's the kolto talking," she said, though she sounded unsure.

"The kolto's just giving me the courage to say what I've felt this entire time," Jace insisted, sitting up and clasping her hand between his. "Or maybe it's knowing I was only seconds away from death. Whatever the reason, I can't keep playing this game.

"I can't ignore what's in my heart," he continued, the words coming in a rush, his mind suddenly focused and clear. "And I know you feel something for me, too."

Satele shook her head, but she didn't pull her hand away.

"I am a Jedi. We must unburden ourselves from emotion and passion to find peace."

"What peace can you find when the galaxy is consumed by war?" Jace asked. "Instead of denying what we feel, we should embrace it. Together we are greater than each of us alone. You can't deny it."

"I'm a Jedi," she repeated, though Jace could tell her resolve was weakening.

"There have been Jedi who fell in love," he said. "The Order pretends it never happens, but we both know that isn't true."

Satele was silent for several moments. When she spoke her voice was little more than a whisper.

"I've feared this moment since we first met," she told him.

She leaned in and gave Jace a gentle kiss on the lips, careful not to brush the exposed and tender flesh of his wounds.

Jace woke with a start, nearly spilling himself off his couch.

He hadn't dreamed about Satele for years. He'd thought the memories, and the pain they brought him, had been boxed safely away. Speaking with Theron—speaking with his *son*—had reopened old wounds.

Checking his watch, he saw nearly two hours had passed since Theron had left. That would explain the crick in his neck. The couch was fine for a brief power nap, but it was no place to spend the night.

Grunting like a man decades older, he forced himself to his feet and staggered off to bed, wondering if his nights would now be haunted by the only woman he had ever loved.

BACK IN his apartment, Theron couldn't stop pacing. The conversation with Jace—*with your father*—had affected him more than he wanted to admit. Logically, everything he'd said to Jace was true: Ngani Zho had raised him, and the only real connection he had with the Supreme Commander was some shared DNA.

Emotionally, however, he couldn't simply brush the revelation off. It rekindled long-forgotten feelings of anger and betrayal toward his mother: feelings he thought he'd come to terms with long ago. But when it came to Jace, he wasn't sure what he felt.

He wasn't angry; it wasn't fair to blame the Supreme Commander for what Satele had done. He wasn't feeling happy or excited or relieved: he'd never felt the need to know his biological father before, so it wasn't like some great void in his life had suddenly been filled. Yet even though he couldn't describe it, he was feeling something.

You're not going to figure this out in one night.

Theron stopped pacing and shook his head, trying to regain his focus. Operation End Game had to be his top priority; he couldn't afford to be distracted by this unexpected family drama. He had to put all thoughts of his parents aside and concentrate on the mission.

He took a few deep breaths to regain his composure—a simple trick he'd learned from Ngani Zho.

Your real father.

Ignoring the voice inside his head, he made his way over to the holo-terminal in the center of the room. He'd set up his apartment so that all incoming holocalls were automatically tracked and traced. He pulled up the data from his last call—Teff'ith—and sent off a hailing signal, not bothering to hide the identity tag on the transmission.

If she's dead-set on not talking to me, she'll just ignore the call.

The holo beeped several times before Teff'ith finally answered.

"Told you to leave us alone," she snarled as her image materialized before him.

"You didn't have to pick up."

"Beeping holo's annoying. What you want?"

"I need a favor."

Theron half expected her to cut the call short right there. Instead, she gave an exasperated sigh.

"Knew you were following us for a reason."

"It's a small favor," Theron assured her. "Just need you to make one call."

"To who?" she asked, her eyes narrowing suspiciously.

Theron took it as a good sign that she hadn't said no.

"I have some business on Ziost. I need a contact there who can hold on to an important package for a few days until I come to pick it up. Might also need him to get me a few things. Blueprints. Information. Maybe some explosives. You know anyone like that?"

"Thought you said you weren't following us on Ziost!" she said, her tone dripping with accusation.

Theron held up his hands defensively. "Never set foot on that planet in my life. I only know you were there because you mentioned it on our last call."

Teff'ith's head-tails twitched as she debated whether to believe him or not.

"What this about?" she finally demanded.

"Can't say," Theron replied. "Top secret. But it won't cause any problems for you or the Old Tion Brotherhood."

"Cause problems for the Empire?"

Theron shrugged. "Does that really matter to you?"

"Got a contact who works with the ZLF," Teff'ith said. "Maybe could do it."

Theron had read several reports focusing on the Ziost Liberation Front, a radical separatist group that had vowed to free their homeworld from Imperial control. Relying primarily on violent guerrilla attacks, they targeted both military and civilian targets, making them technically a terrorist organization. The ZLF was too extreme for the Republic to officially support them, but for this mission they were exactly what he needed.

And you won't have to worry about any of them being sympathetic to the Empire.

"That should work," Theron said. "Can you set up a meeting?"

"Never said we'd help you yet," Teff'ith reminded him. "Gotta work out the terms."

"Two hundred credits," Theron opened.

"A thousand," she countered.

"I'm not giving you a thousand credits just to set up a meeting," Theron said with a laugh. "Three hundred—take it or leave it."

Teff'ith chewed her lip for a minute as she considered the offer.

"Four hundred," she said. "In advance. And this makes us even for Nar Shaddaa."

Before Theron could agree she quickly added, "We set this up and you leave us alone from now on. We see you following us again, we kill you."

"Figured that would be part of the deal," he said. "Four hundred credits, in advance, and you'll never see me again."

Satisfied, Teff'ith said, "Okay, we set it up."

CHAPTER 14

THERON WAS impressed with the ship Gnost-Dural had procured for their journey to Ziost. The TZ-6 executive shuttle was one of Corellian Engineering Corporation's most luxurious mass-production vessels; the ship was easily worth five times the value of any craft Theron had ever owned. The name stenciled on the side, PROS-PERITY, seemed particularly apt.

"The Jedi must pay better than I thought," he said, running an appreciative hand along the gleaming hull.

"I'll be playing the part of a wealthy industrialist," Gnost-Dural explained. "It would look unusual if we were traveling in a substandard vessel."

"Hey, you don't need to convince me," Theron said. "I like traveling in style."

Theron took two quick steps up the boarding ramp, eager to check out the interior . . . and just as eager to leave Coruscant behind. He knew from past experience that once the mission was under way, his mind would be too focused to keep brooding over the fact that Jace Malcom was his father.

"So tell me more about our cover story," Theron said, settling into one of the six luxurious reclining passenger seats. The plush cushions momentarily gave way beneath his weight before reshaping themselves to perfectly con-form to every contour of his body.

"I will play the part of Ess Drellid, a wealthy noble

who owns several factories in the Deadalis sector," Gnost-Dural explained. The Jedi chose to remain standing rather than join Theron in one of the adjacent seats.

"You will be my security chief, looking to upgrade weapons and armor for my personal bodyguards; Ziost has a thriving black market for both.

"Everything on board our ship will support this story, just in case customs officials decide to conduct a random search of the vessel."

"What if someone gets suspicious and digs into our backstory?" Theron asked, reluctantly getting to his feet and leaving the comfort of the passenger chair behind.

"My people have seeded the various databases the Empire has access to with documents that will support our story. Short of someone actually traveling to the Deadalis sector to investigate the factories in person, our story will hold up."

"You've got quite the little operation going," Theron said appreciatively. "For a Jedi historian, you make a pretty good spy."

"As I said before, SIS are not the only ones gathering intelligence on our enemy," Gnost-Dural reminded him, following close behind as Theron headed for the cockpit. "But your efforts are focused primarily on the military and the day-to-day operations of the Empire. My people are more interested in those who follow the dark side of the Force: the Sith Lords, the Dark Council, and even the Emperor."

"I heard the Emperor's dead," Theron noted, taking a seat in the copilot's chair.

"That is what many believe," Gnost-Dural said cryptically, settling into the pilot's chair beside him.

"You don't buy that?"

Theron was pleased to discover that, like the passenger seats in the rear of the shuttle, the chairs in the cockpit adjusted themselves to provide maximum comfort and support. That would come in handy for the long flight to Ziost.

"There are many possibilities I have not yet ruled out. The Emperor may be dead. He may be in hiding. Or he may never have existed at all . . . at least not in any true sense of the word."

"Haven't heard that one before," Theron admitted.

"There is some evidence to support the theory that the thousand-year-old Sith Emperor was merely a myth," Gnost-Dural explained while going through a standard preflight check of their vessel.

"It's possible that the Emperor is really just the strongest member of the Dark Council. When he or she dies, the next strongest secretly assumes that role, perpetuating the myth of an eternal, all-powerful being to keep the masses and other Sith Lords in line."

"If that's the case, then why all the rumors that the Emperor is dead?" Theron asked, cross-checking the instruments and readouts. "Why hasn't one of them just stepped into his robes and made a quick public appearance?"

"The Dark Council, like the rest of the Empire, is in flux. There may be disagreement among them as to who should be the next one to assume the Emperor's role.

"Or," the Jedi added, "the rumors could all be true, and the Emperor was actually an ancient being of unfathomable power who has recently disappeared, leaving his followers stumbling in his absence.

"Whatever the truth," Gnost-Dural vowed, "I will one day find out. Knowledge is the key to stopping the Sith."

"I thought taking out the *Ascendant Spear* was the key," Theron joked.

"The *Spear* is the key to defeating the Empire and putting a quick end to the galactic war," Gnost-Dural clarified, raising his voice to be heard as he fired up the ship's engines. "But the Sith are another matter entirely. Even if the Empire falls, the followers of the dark side will continue to exist in hiding.

"That is why I have devoted myself to studying the Sith. I am determined to find a way to cleanse the galaxy of their corrupting influence, putting an end to the eternal struggle between the light and dark sides of the Force."

"Uh . . . okay. Hope that works out for you."

Theron could feel the seat beneath him adjusting as the force of their liftoff pressed him into his chair. The *Prosperity*'s thrust was impressive.

"You mock me," Gnost-Dural said. "Did Master Zho not speak to you of the Force and the battle between the forces of light and darkness?"

"He was more interested in teaching me the skills I needed to survive," Theron replied. "I think he was expecting the instructors at the Jedi academy to fill me in on that kind of stuff," he added. "But when I didn't show an affinity for the Force, they refused to take me."

"The Force manifests itself in many ways," Gnost-Dural assured him. "It flows through all living things. Not being a Jedi doesn't diminish your worth."

"Never said it did," Theron answered, a little more sharply than he intended.

"I need to input our destination into the nav computer," Gnost-Dural said, perhaps sensing it was time to put an end to the conversation.

Theron was all too happy to let the matter drop. In his few weeks at the academy, he'd experienced enough of the unintentional but unmistakable self-righteous superiority of the Jedi to last a lifetime.

Could have been worse, Theron thought. *At least he didn't ask me about my mother.* Once again, Theron wondered if the Kel Dor knew about Satele's secret shame.

The rest of the trip passed in relative silence, both men retreating to inner contemplation as they went through the mundane routines of deep-space travel. Theron actually appreciated the lack of conversation; it gave him time to mentally prepare for the coming mission. By the time they were halfway to Ziost, he'd successfully banished all thoughts of Jace and Satele, leaving his mind clear and focused.

THE CLEARANCE procedures for ships approaching Ziost were far too regulated to actually be efficient, but they passed through the gauntlet of customs and security with little difficulty and were given permission to land. Once the *Prosperity* touched down, the faceless guards tasked with authorizing their presence on the Imperial-controlled world simply asked Gnost-Dural a few routine questions, ran a quick verification of his ship's registration, and made a perfunctory search of the interior before waving them through.

Safely out of earshot, Theron couldn't help but whisper, "If we knew customs was just going to wave us through, we wouldn't have had to ship the decryption core here ahead of time."

"The Empire has ears everywhere," Gnost-Dural cautioned.

Duly chastened, Theron decided to keep any further smart-mouthed comments to himself.

As they made their way from the landing bay to a speeder waiting outside the spaceport to take them to Teff'ith's contact, Theron couldn't help but marvel at the cosmopolitan feel of the crowd. He counted at least a dozen different species from every corner of the galaxy, including sectors where countless Republic soldiers had given their lives to save the local populations from being conquered and enslaved by the Sith.

The scene was even more difficult to fathom when one

considered Ziost's history. The Sith had fled here over twenty thousand years ago when a war of succession reduced Korriban to an uninhabitable wasteland. They adopted Ziost as their new homeworld, and at one time it had even served as the capital of the Sith Empire.

No one from the Republic had ever even officially set foot on Ziost; since its founding it had remained under the absolute control of the xenophobic Sith Empire. Even as recently as a decade ago, the only nonhuman, non-Sith purebloods on the world would have been slaves in chains or cages. Now, however, the planet had been reinvented as the gateway to the Empire: the place where anyone seeking an alternative to dealing with the Republic was welcome to come and do business with the Sith.

While some might see Ziost's newfound openness as proof the Empire had become more tolerant and accepting, Theron wasn't fooled. The Imperials were losing the war; they were desperate. So desperate they were willing to swallow their bigotry to welcome the so-called lesser species with open arms, at least on this one planet.

Theron's thoughts were interrupted by a subtle nudge from Gnost-Dural. The Jedi Master was looking up at a nearby holoscreen running an official news report. The images primarily showed the mangled wreckage of several medium-sized Republic ships—the kind used in hit-and-run attacks on Imperial fleets. The voice of an Imperial shill played over the images of death and destruction.

"A recent attempt by the Republic and anti-Imperial separatists to conquer the loyal citizens of the Boranall system was easily repulsed by the might of the Imperial defenders."

One shot in particular grabbed Theron's attention—two halves of a Republic vessel floating side by side, the hull split cleanly between bow and stern, like a giant saw had sliced it through. He knew of only one ship in the galaxy with laser cannons powerful enough to inflict that kind of damage.

The images changed to show several city blocks on the planetary surface that had been leveled by an orbital bombardment. Most of the buildings were reduced to rubble; those few that still stood had huge chunks torn away to expose the bent and twisted durasteel beams that supported their frames. The streets were impassable, choked with debris and the bodies of innocent civilians.

"Before the arrival of their Imperial saviors, the citizens of Boranall were subjected to a cowardly assault from the Republic fleet orbiting their world."

Theron couldn't help but shake his head in denial at the blatant Imperial propaganda. Orbital bombardment of civilians wasn't something the Republic practiced, and none of the vanquished Republic ships they'd shown had the firepower to wreak that kind of havoc.

The more likely explanation was that the *Spear* had wiped out the Republic ships, then turned its guns on Boranall. Whether Karrid was eliminating resistance on the ground or simply punishing the planet for daring to harbor anti-Imperial separatists didn't matter to Theron—there was no excuse for the kind of slaughter she'd unleashed.

He saw Gnost-Dural stiffen, and he realized the Jedi Master had come to the same conclusions he had. Theron hoped seeing the horrors his former apprentice was capable of might convince Gnost-Dural to abandon his hope that she could be redeemed, though he knew enough about Jedi in general to realize this probably wouldn't change anything.

The two men continued in silence through the spaceport to where Gnost-Dural had arranged to have a speeder waiting for them. Stepping outside, Theron was struck by a cold blast of wind. Shivering, he pulled his cloak tighter around his body. The air was dry and gritty with tiny particles of dirt and dust swept along by the breeze, and he squinted, wishing he had a cover for his face. The Kel Dor, with his goggles and breathing mask, didn't seem bothered by the harsh wind, though Theron took some small satisfaction in seeing him also shivering from the cold.

Fortunately their speeder was as luxurious as their shuttle had been, with a sealed climate-controlled dome to shield them from the elements. Once again Gnost-Dural sat in the pilot's chair and Theron took the seat beside him. Theron wasn't much of a follower, but he was happy to defer to his partner on the little things.

They zipped through the bustling streets of Ziost's market district, their speeder whisking them above the crowds. There were still several hours of daylight, and Theron was clearly able to see the people below them in the light of the world's distant and faded orange sun. Although he only got a brief view from above, the market district had the same vibrant, cosmopolitan feel as the spaceport. As soon as they passed into the neighboring residential district, however, everything changed.

It was still crowded—Ziost was a heavily populated metropolis. But the life and color seemed to vanish in an instant. Everything was drab and gray—the buildings, the streets, and even the clothes of the people in the crowd.

"You can feel the oppression of this place," Gnost-Dural said. "The hopeless despair of the entire city."

Theron nodded, knowing the Jedi wasn't referring to something he sensed through the Force. Under Imperial rule there were harsh penalties for even minor infractions, and it wasn't hard to see the impact. Unlike the chaos of Nar Shaddaa, here there was an orderly, almost rigid flow of traffic, both on the ground and in the air. Pedestrians moved with brisk purpose, heads down, eager to get off the street and back to the anonymous safety of their homes. Speeders stayed in their designated lanes, and nobody dared to go faster than the posted limit. Swoop bikes were nowhere to be found, and if there were gangs on Ziost, Theron imagined they'd be careful to stay well hidden.

It made for good Imperial propaganda; they claimed their worlds were free of all petty crime. But Theron would gladly take a few pickpockets and some graffiti over a sterile, lifeless existence under a completely totalitarian government.

"We're almost there," Gnost-Dural informed him as they left the residential district and passed into an industrial area populated by square, windowless warehouses. "I hope your friend's contact comes through for us."

"Me too."

He brought the speeder down just outside the door of one of the buildings. To Theron's eye it looked exactly like every other structure on the street, but he trusted the Jedi to deliver them to the address Teff'ith had provided.

Bracing themselves against the bitter wind, they rushed from the speeder to the door. It opened as they reached it, and they hurried inside. Beyond the door was a small open-air office and reception area. Four desks were arranged around the room, though none of them was currently occupied. A single door on the far wall led into the warehouse at the back.

"Good to get out of the cold, isn't it?" their host said cheerfully.

He was a middle-aged human. The crown of his bald head was surrounded by a ring of curly brown hair. His face was ruddy, his features plain. His loose-fitting clothes were unremarkable, but Theron could tell they had been selected partly to hide the man's flabby chest and protruding gut.

Unassuming and nonthreatening. The perfect front man for a brutal group like the ZLF.

"Name's Vinn," he said, thrusting out a meaty hand. "You must be Teff'ith's friends."

Theron shook the man's hand but didn't offer his name. Gnost-Dural followed his lead.

"Everything you sent ahead is here, safe and sound," Vinn said, getting right to business. "Got it all safely hidden away back in the warehouse. Even that burned-out computer core.

"Kinda curious as to what you need that for," he added with a chuckle.

"What did you find out about the Orbital Defense Command Center?" Theron said, not bothering to satisfy Vinn's curiosity.

"Got the architectural blueprints right here," he said, pulling out a datapad. "And everything anyone could possibly want to know about the security systems they have in place."

He hesitated for a second, as if debating how much he was willing to share with these strangers based solely on Teff'ith's referral.

"You know," he said, drawing the words out slowly, "if you're looking to cause trouble for the Empire, I have some friends who might be interested in lending a hand."

I bet you do, Theron thought. *But if any of your ZLF brothers get captured, the Imperial interrogators will make them sing. Can't take that risk.*

Out loud he simply said, "We prefer to work alone."

"Understood," Vinn said with a cheery nod. "Just putting it out there."

Theron took the datapad and briefly flicked through the contents.

"Top-of-the-line system; redundant fail-safes," he muttered. "No surprise there. I'm probably going to need some extra high-tech equipment," he continued without looking up. "If I put together a list, can you get me everything I need?"

"That'll cost extra," their chubby host said apologetically.

"We can pay. As long as you deliver the goods."

Vinn's chest puffed up with pride. "Hardware and equipment is my specialty. If somebody manufactures it, I can find it.

"Could take a couple days, though," he added.

"Until then we should try to keep a low profile," Gnost-Dural said. "Stay out of trouble."

You've been talking with the Director, Theron thought.

"Don't worry," he said, holding up the datapad. "I've got plenty to keep me busy."

CHAPTER 15

IN KEEPING with his cover as a wealthy industrialist, Gnost-Dural had rented them a two-bedroom suite on Ziost that was the height of luxury and comfort—nearly twice the size of Theron's apartment on Coruscant. It had taken a good hour to thoroughly sweep the place for bugs and recording devices.

The bed in Theron's room was the most comfortable one he'd ever had the pleasure of sleeping in, but he was never able to get more than a few hours' rest while on a mission. By the time Gnost-Dural emerged from his own quarters, Theron was already hunched over the counter of the breakfast nook, studying the information on the datapad Vinn had given him.

"You're up early," the Jedi remarked.

"I've been thinking about the mission," Theron said, eyes on the screen. "I think we need more than a simple bombing to distract the Empire from what we're really up to. For this feint to work, we need to rattle their cage. Give them something to really worry about."

The Jedi took a seat in the chair across from Theron. "Sounds like you already have something in mind."

"We need to make this look like a failed assassination attempt on the Minister of Logistics," Theron said, finally looking up from the datapad. "Convince the Empire that the cipher was damaged accidentally when the assassins were discovered trying to set up explosives in the minister's office."

"That would certainly give them something else to focus on," Gnost-Dural agreed. "So how do we pull it off?"

"I break into the minister's office and switch the cipher cores. Then I start setting up explosives under his desk. You send an anonymous tip to the Imperials about what's happening so that they charge in and catch me in the act. The explosives go off 'accidentally' during my escape and they think the blast caused the cipher's self-destruct sequence to trigger."

"The second I tip the Imperials off, every guard in that place will be swarming that office from all directions," Gnost-Dural warned. "You won't have a chance."

"Not necessarily," Theron replied. "I've been looking over the security plans. The Orbital Defense Command Center's primary function is to guard against a Republic fleet attacking Ziost. Their biggest fear is that an enemy force will take over the station during a full-scale planetary invasion.

"Because of that, they have an emergency lockdown state that automatically triggers if certain protocols are met that indicate a possible Republic invasion. During lockdown, every floor on the building goes into quarantine to restrict movement of any enemy troops that might have infiltrated the facility.

"Every door and lift in the place is locked and disabled. And the Empire is so worried about being betrayed from within, even the Imperial soldiers inside the building can't open them. There's no way to override the lockdown until a special emergency response unit has swept the building and verified it's clear of hostiles."

"How are we supposed to simulate a Republic invasion of Ziost?" Master Gnost-Dural asked.

"What's the first thing any fleet does when it's trying

to put troops on the ground in a heavily defended enemy city?"

"Knock out the power," Gnost-Dural replied after a moment's consideration. "Leave your enemy fumbling around in the dark."

"Exactly. If there's a citywide blackout, the ODCC's auxiliary generators kick in to keep the place running, and the whole facility goes into lockdown automatically. Even after you tip off the Empire that there's an assassin in the minister's office, they won't be able to send reinforcements in my direction until they restore primary power or the emergency response team finishes its sweep.

"If we hit them at night, when the minister and his staff aren't working, that floor will only have a handful of guards patrolling it. Nothing I can't handle."

"If the whole place is locked down," the Kel Dor asked, "then how are you going to get out?"

"The emergency response team can still use the doors and turbolifts during lockdown—all it takes is an ID badge and a matching retinal scan from one of their officers."

"Do you think Vinn could get his hands on something like that?"

"Maybe, but he already knows more than I like. Give him too many pieces and he might put the whole puzzle together."

"You think he'll betray us?"

"Probably not, but I'd rather not take any chances. The ZLF has its own agenda, and I don't want it getting mixed up in Operation End Game any more than absolutely necessary."

"So how are you going to get the badge and retinal scan?"

"Don't worry," Theron assured him. "I've got it covered."

*   *   *

FROM A table in the back corner of the bar, Theron watched his target closely as he tossed back another drink with his fellow soldiers. The Hammer and Nail was located only a few blocks from the Orbital Defense Command Center, making it a popular hangout for the troops stationed there. It was easy to spot them in the crowd, as they tended to wear their uniforms even when off duty, particularly the officers.

The Empire was a martial society, and there were status and perks given to those of higher rank. The waitress made more frequent trips to tables where the officers gathered; the bartender filled their glasses right to the rim. He'd even seen a handful of civilian patrons and enlisted troops surrender their tables if there weren't empty seats when the officers entered, though the manner in which they slinked away made it seem more like fear than a sign of respect.

Theron had set his sights on a man named Captain Pressik, commander of one of the ODCC's emergency response teams. Tall, blond, and handsome, the broad-shouldered officer carried himself with the privileged air of someone who had grown up being taught he was better than everyone else. Even among the other members of his elite unit, he carried himself with an air of arrogance and superiority.

Theron's investigations had uncovered Pressik's reputation for being a hard drinker when he wasn't on duty. And when he got drunk, he got violent, though he was smart enough to pick his fights with civilians to avoid any consequences that might harm his military career.

Pressik's shift had ended several hours ago; since then he had been here at the bar drinking with a handful of other officers. But while most of them nursed glasses of wine or ale, he was tossing back White Nova doubles with reckless abandon. Not that Theron minded; the more Pressik drank, the easier this would be.

He said something to the others at his table, eliciting a round of ribald laughter. Then he got up and made his way toward the refresher. Theron moved quickly to cut him off, walking with a pronounced drunken stagger. He bumped into the soldier as they both tried to enter the refresher at the same time, using the contact to get in close enough for the scanner in his pocket to read the data encoded on the ID badge prominently displayed on the left breast pocket of Pressik's uniform.

"Sorry," Theron grumbled.

"Watch where you're going!" the man snapped, roughly shoving Theron back with his shoulder and forearm.

"Mind if I go first?" Theron asked, taking a step toward the refresher, stalling to give the scanner the thirty seconds it would take to download the data from Pressik's badge. "Kind of an emergency."

The soldier didn't reply as he squeezed past Theron and into the refresher, the door whooshing shut behind him.

Theron remained standing just outside the door, considering his options. He knew the scanner hadn't had enough time to finish the job. And the holorecorder in the implant of his left eye hadn't captured a clear enough shot of Pressik's face to duplicate his retinal scan. He had no choice but to try again.

The refresher opened a few moments later and Pressik stepped out, giving Theron a dangerous glare when he saw him still waiting by the door.

"What's your problem, Subjugate?" he said, using the Imperial term for those without citizen status.

The implication in the word was clear: Here on Ziost, you have no rank. You have no rights. Back down.

"I was here first," Theron said, slurring his words and

leaning forward as if he were having trouble keeping his balance. "You cut the line."

From the corner of his eye, Theron noticed the patrons at the nearby tables scooping up their drinks and rapidly retreating to a safe distance.

Pressik's lip curled up into a snarl of contempt as he fixed his piercing blue eyes on the maggot in front of him.

Perfect, Theron thought. *Give me a nice clear shot of those pretty little peepers.*

To Theron's surprise, Pressik turned away after a few seconds.

"Sit down, Subjugate," he said.

Theron wasn't sure why Pressik was backing down. Maybe he'd seen something in Theron's eyes that made him realize this wasn't the typical cowering victim he was used to bullying. Maybe his superiors, fed up with his off-duty altercations, had taken him to task and warned him to keep his temper in check.

One thing Theron was sure about, however—he still needed more time for the scanner to do its job.

"You're the Suj-u-grate," Theron spat out, fumbling over the word in his feigned drunken stupor. He reached out and shoved Pressik in the back as he walked away.

Pressik wheeled on him, his right hand balled into a fist. He dropped low as he threw a powerful uppercut into Theron's midsection. Theron saw it coming—it was a clumsy brawler's punch. But he resisted his natural instincts to block or evade the attack. Staying in character as an inebriated civilian, all he could do was brace himself as the blow landed.

The air whooshed out of him and his knees buckled. He staggered forward and wrapped his arms around Pressik in a bear hug, using the other man to support his weight so he could stay on his feet . . . and to keep him from stepping back and out of the scanner's limited range.

"Get off me!" Pressik shouted, struggling to shake him off.

Theron grappled awkwardly with the bigger man, managing to tie up his arms and buying himself a brief respite from further punishment. The other officers rushed in from the far side of the bar to join the fray.

Just a few more seconds, Theron thought, still holding on to Pressik for all he was worth.

He felt the hands of the other soldiers seizing him as they tried to pry him loose from their friend. Someone was raining blows down on his neck and shoulders from behind.

Four on one, Theron thought as he twisted and turned, doing his best to absorb the beating. *The kind of odds the Empire just loves.*

They managed to haul Theron off Pressik just as he felt the scanner in his pocket vibrating to signify the download was complete. As Pressik stumbled backward, Theron went limp and collapsed to the floor.

"Get him on his feet!" Pressik shouted, and two of his companions grabbed Theron under his armpits and yanked him to his feet.

And now the big finale, Theron thought as Pressik wound up and launched a haymaker at his jaw.

Everything went white as stars exploded in Theron's vision. When the men holding him up let go, he dropped to the floor, semiconscious. He tried to keep from blacking out as someone grabbed his ankles and dragged him facedown to the door, his cheek scraping roughly across the dirty, sticky floor.

His head was still spinning as they lifted him up into the air, rocked him back and forth a few times to gather momentum, then tossed him out onto the street. He landed awkwardly on his shoulder, re-aggravating the injury he'd sustained during his last job on Nar Shaddaa.

Somehow he rolled onto his side, just in time to receive a hard kick from Pressik right in the ribs. The soldier leaned over and spit on him, then—laughing—he and his friends turned and headed back into the bar.

Theron lay curled up in the fetal position on the street, evaluating his injuries. The inside of his lip was cut where Pressik's punch had mashed it against his teeth, filling his mouth with blood. As he spit it out, he could feel a gap with his tongue where one of his teeth had been knocked out. The side of his face that had scraped along the floor was raw and stinging, and a sharp pain every time he inhaled was probably a sign of a cracked rib.

Could have been worse, he thought, slowing his breathing and running through some basic mental exercises to help him deal with the worst of the pain. *They could have curb-stomped me right into the nearest medcenter. Or the morgue.*

After a few minutes, Theron gingerly got to his feet and made his way slowly down the street toward the room he shared with Gnost-Dural, careful to keep up a lurching, drunken gait in case anyone was watching him.

"ARE YOU sure you're up for this, Theron?" Gnost-Dural asked.

"I'm fine," Theron said, trying not to wince as he strapped on the backpack carrying the burned-out cipher core and all his other supplies.

Three days had passed since he'd been pummeled at the bar. His face was still bruised and his ribs and shoulder were still tender, but the injuries weren't worth delaying the mission over.

He was wearing a black bodysuit and balaclava to conceal his face. Gnost-Dural's outfit was more elaborate—a loose-fitting black robe with a heavy hood and a fabric mask to obscure his alien features. Theron made one last run through his mental checklist, making sure everything had been taken care of.

"You'd better get going," Theron told his Jedi companion once he had finished his final cross-check. "Give me thirty minutes to get in position before you kill the lights, and another ninety before you tip off the Empire. That should give me plenty of time to switch the cipher cores and get the explosives ready before they sound the alarm."

Master Gnost-Dural nodded. "I'll be waiting for you at the rendezvous site when you're done inside the ODCC," he said. Just before Theron slipped out the door Gnost-Dural added, "May the Force be with you."

CHAPTER 16

ZIOST'S ICY, unrelenting wind buffeted Theron's body as he huddled on the roof's edge of the building across the street from the Orbital Defense Command Center. He had on his night goggles and had already anchored the tripod of his grappling gun securely. He'd even carefully selected his target—a spot just below the surveillance cams mounted on the side of the windowless ODCC building. Now he was just waiting for Gnost-Dural to do his part.

The citywide blackout would temporarily disable the surveillance cams, but it would only take a few seconds for the auxiliary generators to ramp up and get them working again. Theron would have to act fast if he didn't want to be seen breaking in; his adrenaline was pumping, his mind focused and alert, his muscles poised to spring into action. But he couldn't do anything until Gnost-Dural knocked out the power.

This is why I like to work alone, he thought, crouching lower to the rooftop as another blast of wind whipped across the surface.

He trusted the Jedi, and his role in the mission was simple enough. But in the back of his mind he couldn't help but wonder if his partner was up to the task.

Guess I'll know in a few minutes. Either the lights go out and the mission is a go, or I lose my fingers to a serious case of frostbite.

* * *

UNLIKE REPUBLIC worlds where electricity was supplied by private companies, Ziost's main power station was a government-controlled facility under military supervision. To defend it against orbital strikes, it had been built into a reinforced bunker twenty meters below the surface of the planet. The only entrance was a heavily defended turbolift, making it virtually impossible for someone to get inside without being seen.

Fortunately, Master Gnost-Dural didn't have to get into the main station to wreak havoc with Ziost's power supply. The electricity generated in the heavily defended facility had to be dispersed across the entire city through a network of substations and transformers, which divided and subdivided to feed the millions of users plugged into the electrical grid. And though the network was designed with redundancies to reroute power in the event of damaged lines or substations, it was a logistical impossibility to fully guarantee uninterrupted service. That was why places like the ODCC had their own emergency generators.

Vinn had provided them with blueprints for the electrical grid, allowing them to identify the three key junction points that needed to be taken out to kill the power supply for their target. By planting explosives at each location and detonating them simultaneously, they could cause a massive blackout that would take hours to restore.

The first two locations were both small auxiliary substations; neither one was guarded, and it was a simple matter for the Jedi to plant the detonite charges and set the timers. The third location, however, was one of the city's five primary substations. It would have been prohibitively expensive for the Empire to replicate the near-impregnable defenses of the main power station at each of the substations, but it did take some precautions.

The small building was surrounded by a three-meter-high, electrified chain-link fence. There were half a dozen guards stationed at the facility; every twenty minutes they took turns circling the perimeter in pairs while the others sat inside the substation's tiny break room playing sabacc and trying to stay warm.

Gnost-Dural could have easily used his lightsaber to slice through the fence and dispatched all six of the soldiers before they could call for help. But the iconic weapon of the Jedi left distinctive marks on both flesh and steel. Leaving behind evidence pointing to a Jedi's involvement would blow apart the cover story that this was the work of a local anti-Imperial resistance group. Instead, he hid in the shadows and waited for the two guards on patrol to pass, then raced up to the fence. Using a pair of insulated wire cutters, he snipped open a hole just large enough for him to slip through without touching the deadly fence, then he raced up to the side of the building.

Heading in the same clockwise direction as the patrolling guards, he circled the perimeter until he reached the building's only entrance. Instead of the modern automatic security doors that slid open with the touch of a button, the building was fitted with an archaic metal plate that swung open on its hinges when the handle was turned.

Pressing himself against the side of the door, the Jedi carefully turned the handle and eased it open a few centimeters. Light spilled out into the dark night, along with the conversation and laughter of the guards in the break room just on the other side. Crouching down, he rolled a small canister along the ground and into the room before pulling the door shut.

Calling on the Force he warped, twisted, and snapped the handle off. A second later there were cries of alarm from inside as black, noxious smoke billowed out from the imperfectly sealed edges of the door. He heard running feet, followed by the sound of someone frantically struggling with the door's handle on the other side, unaware it had been disabled. There was a loud bang as someone threw their body at the door, then a woman shouted "Stand clear!"

Three blaster bolts pierced the door in rapid succession, ripping finger-sized holes in the steel. Then there was a loud thump as someone kicked at the door, once again to no avail. By this time the two guards on patrol had heard the commotion. Still playing the part of an anti-Imperial terrorist, Gnost-Dural crouched on one knee, drew his blaster, and shot the first one as he came racing around the corner, killing him instantly.

As he always did, the Jedi felt a twinge of sorrow at taking another's life. But decades of war against a brutal and relentless foe had forced Gnost-Dural, like so many others in the Order, to come to grips with the moral ambiguity of killing an enemy in the pursuit of a peace that would save the lives of trillions.

The partner of the guard whom Gnost-Dural shot managed to duck back behind the cover of the building's edge. Gnost-Dural stood up and reached out with the Force, using it to pick the surviving soldier up and pull her out into the open. She flew several meters through the air before landing on the exposed ground; Gnost-Dural shot her before she could even get to her feet.

Turning back to the door, he placed a thin strip of detonite along the edge, retreated to a safe distance, then set it off. The blast blew the damaged door open. It took several seconds for the poison gas from the detonator to clear the room and reveal the bodies of the four guards just inside the door. Gnost-Dural was reminded of the value of the Jedi teachings. Had the soldiers stayed calm during his attack, they could have retreated into the small control room in the back of the building to escape the smoke. But fear had clouded their minds, and in their panic they had congregated around the only exit to the outside world, dooming themselves.

The Jedi stepped over the fallen soldiers and crossed the room to the door at the rear. It was locked, but another strip of detonite gave him access to the control room beyond. He set the explosives, syncing the timer to go off in three minutes—the exact same time as the charges at the other two locations. Then he turned and left the building, slipped through the hole he'd cut in the perimeter fence, and headed toward the rendezvous point where Theron would meet up with him later.

THERON DIDN'T hear the explosions from the substations, but he knew exactly when they happened. Everything in an area of six square blocks went instantly and completely dark; a second later his night-vision goggles adjusted to the lack of illumination, allowing him to see everything through a hazy green filter.

He fired his grappling gun, the three-pronged harpoon embedding itself in the permacrete side of the Orbital Defense Command Center five meters below the height of the roof Theron was perched on. He clipped a sliding pulley and handle onto the line and leapt off the edge, letting gravity pull him down the zip line.

It took only a few seconds until he reached the end of the line. Clamping down on the pulley he slowed his descent to keep from smashing into the side of the ODCC. He made sure the pulley was latched on to the end of the grappling hook protruding from the wall, then released the line.

The thin wire shot away from him, retracted at an incredible speed by the recoiling springs in the grappling gun anchored on the roof across the street. A second later the auxiliary generators kicked in and the ODCC emergency lights illuminated the night. He heard the soft whir of the surveillance cams sticking out from the side of the building a few meters above him as they resumed their automated pan-and-scan search of the surrounding area. But the cams weren't positioned to look straight down; he was safe.

Forced to dangle by one hand from the grappling hook's pulley, he used his free arm to pull out a small tube of inert plasma gel. Squeezing the tube, he covered a one-meter-by-one-meter square on the side of the building with the pasty-white substance. Then he tucked the half-empty tube back into his belt and brought out a small rod tipped with a pair of electrical prongs.

He waited a few seconds for the gel to set, then pressed the prongs into the gel on the wall and pulled the trigger. The rod hummed as it discharged a powerful current, catalyzing the inert plasma suspended in the paste.

Theron turned his head to the side and closed his eyes as the substance began to smolder and spark. When he opened his eyes a few seconds later, the gel had burned a hole clean through the permacrete wall.

Still hanging from the grappling hook, Theron hauled himself up so he could swing his legs through the hole before letting go. The effort aggravated his injured left shoulder, but it was more annoyance than inconvenience.

He found himself in an empty office on the third floor of the ODCC. Theron slung the backpack off his shoulder and onto the ground. The soft glow of the building's emergency lights made his night goggles unnecessary, so he stashed them in the pack, then peeled off the outer layer of his clothes. Underneath the black bodysuit he wore an exact replica of an emergency response team's captain's uniform, complete with an encoded ID badge like the one he'd scanned in the bar. From inside the backpack he pulled out a heavy assault rifle—more firepower than he probably needed, but it would fit the story of a militant terrorist group. He stuffed the discarded outer clothes into the pack before hoisting it up onto his back again.

From the architectural diagrams Vinn had provided, he knew he was on the same floor as the minister's office, though he was on the opposite side of the facility. Unfortunately, his access point had been limited by the surrounding buildings; there weren't any structures tall enough on the other side of the ODCC for him to get high enough to use the zip line. With the facility still in lockdown, however, he didn't have to worry about any guards patrolling the area.

The door leading from the office and out into the hall was locked; he could tell by the blinking red light above the small access panel on the side. As he approached, the panel began to blink yellow as the security system automatically scanned his badge. He leaned forward, bringing his eyes only a few centimeters away from the panel to let it scan the contact lenses he'd slipped in before the mission. The lenses didn't affect his vision, but they mimicked the retinal pattern of Captain Pressik.

The light above the panel switched from yellow to green and the door slid open. Theron poked his head into the hall, looking both left and right but seeing no one. He stepped into the hall and moved quickly to the door at the far end that would lead him into the adjacent wing.

Once again he let the system read his badge and scan his eyes, and the door's status changed from red to yellow to green before it slid open. On the other side were two guards sitting casually on the floor of the hall, idly passing the time as they waited for the lockdown to end.

They glanced up in surprise as Theron stepped through the door. Seeing his captain's uniform, their first instinct was to scramble to their feet and stand at attention. But even though Theron was dressed like an officer, there were too many other things that didn't add up. The lockdown was only a few minutes old; it was too soon for the emergency response team to already be on the third floor. Plus, he should have been coming from the other direction—working his way up from the main floor and the front entrance. Finally, Imperial officers carried blasters, not backpacks and assault rifles.

All of this passed through their heads in a fraction of a second, and though they were already reaching for their weapons as they started to stand, the momentary delay gave Theron time to mow them down.

As he stood over the bodies of the two soldiers, Theron knew he'd have to be more cautious from this point forward. At some point this pair would be expected to check in, and when they didn't the other guards would know something was wrong. It was also possible someone had heard the sound of the shots, and though the lockdown kept them from investigating they'd be alert and on guard from this point on. He wasn't going to come through any more doors to find his enemies lounging on the floor.

The corridor he was in took a ninety-degree turn to his right before coming up against another sealed door. This time Theron was more careful, crouching low to the side of the door as he slipped his backpack off and set his assault rifle on the floor beside him. He dug around until he found what he wanted—a pair of detonators—then leaned in and let the scanner read his retinal signature.

As the door slid open Theron pressed himself against the wall, taking cover behind the edge of the doorjamb. He poked his head out just enough to see down the corridor, then pulled it back as the waiting guards unleashed a volley of blaster bolts in his direction.

There were three this time, strategically spread out at various points along the hall. Theron pressed the small button on the first detonator to prime it, then tossed it down the corridor with a flick of his wrist, careful to keep from exposing himself to the enemy's line of fire.

Even before the inevitable explosion, he was already priming the second detonator. The first blast went off and Theron made his move. He wanted to get this one all the way down to the far end of the hall, so he had to lean out to get enough leverage for the throw, momentarily leaving himself open.

As he did so he saw one of the guards lying on the floor, a casualty of the first blast. The other two had been far enough down the hall to survive, but the explosion had left them distracted and disoriented, and neither one was able to get off a clean shot in the brief second Theron was exposed.

In the aftermath of the second detonator's explosion, Theron scooped up his assault rifle and peeked around the edge of the doorjamb. Another soldier was down, and the third was reeling from the explosions. He fired at Theron, but his shots flew high and wide. Theron remained calm as he took careful aim and dropped his foe with a short burst.

He threw the backpack on once more and continued down the hall, counting the doors on his left. When he reached the third one, he stopped and went through the necessary routine to unlock it. He stepped into the minister's office then sealed the door behind him, just in case.

The office was large—ten meters by ten in Theron's estimation. A number of comfortable-looking chairs were arranged around a small, circular meeting table near the front. In the back was a massive desk made of dark brown wood. Intricate designs had been carved into the front and sides, and the heavy legs were sculpted into ornate, sweeping curves. Theron had expected to find propaganda posters or a self-portrait of the minister, but the walls were surprisingly empty.

According to Vinn's blueprints, the minister's private communications room was through an exit in the back—the most logical place to store the black cipher. But as Theron stared at the massive durasteel door at the rear of the office, he realized Vinn's blueprints hadn't shown everything.

He approached the security panel of the locked door and quickly determined that a simple badge and retinal scan weren't going to get him in this time. There was a numbered keypad beside the door, and Theron guessed only the minister himself knew the access code.

Theron quickly reviewed his options. He still had some plasma gel left, but not enough to burn through the heavy steel door. He had his slicing equipment; he could probably crack the code, but that would take time he didn't have. And even if he managed to get lucky and crack the code quickly, it was possible the door wouldn't even open until the lockdown was over.

"This is going to be a problem," Theron muttered.

CHAPTER 17

MASTER GNOST-DURAL didn't need a chrono to know it was time to send the anonymous tip; being attuned to the Force made his internal clock as accurate as any manufactured timepiece.

He punched a button on the holocomm belted to his waist to scramble the signal, which would distort the image and make it harder to trace. Then he sent a transmission to the Imperial garrison next to the Orbital Defense Command Center.

Because of the scrambler, when they answered the signal was a mess of static-snow, flickering low-res images and bad audio.

"Imperial Garrison Three Forty-Three." He could just barely make out a woman's voice over the crackles and hiss. "Check your holo settings," she advised. "We're getting strong interference."

"The minister's life is in danger," Gnost-Dural said. "They're setting explosives in his office."

"Who are you?" the voice on the other end demanded sharply. "How did you get this frequency?"

"I'm a friend of the Empire," the Jedi lied. "If you hurry you can stop them." Abruptly, he ended the call.

Even if the woman on the other end suspected the call was a hoax, they couldn't afford to ignore it . . . not with the citywide blackout.

"Your friends are on their way, Theron," Gnost-Dural whispered to himself. "I hope you're ready for them."

THERON RACED down the hall outside Minister Davidge's office, heading for the stairwell with the assault rifle clutched in one hand, and the pack with the damaged cipher core inside still strapped to his back.

The pack was much lighter now that he'd finished planting the explosives and setting the timer in Minister Davidge's office, but he was behind schedule. Thanks to Gnost-Dural's anonymous tip, it wouldn't be long before the emergency response team converged on the third floor to try to catch the would-be assassins in the act.

If everything had gone according to plan, he would already have the cipher core and all he'd have to do was get far enough away from the office to be clear of the blast radius. When the team showed up the detonite would go off "accidentally," and he'd slip away in the ensuing chaos.

Unfortunately, the durasteel security door between him and the comm room had thrown a kink into his plans. Theron had stared at it for several minutes, his mind desperately trying to figure out a solution. He couldn't open it, and he couldn't go through it. But, he realized, he could still go around it.

The walls of the minister's communications room were probably reinforced with the same durasteel as the door, but the ceiling would have to be made from more conventional building materials to allow the minister to transmit and receive signals from the room.

Theron didn't have enough plasma gel left to eat through the durasteel, but if he got into the office directly above the room, he could make a hole in the floor and drop down.

As he raced toward the stairwell, he saw the status light shift from red to yellow, even though he was still too far away for the scanner to read his badge. By the time it switched to green he had realized what was happening, and as the door slid open he dropped to the ground in a tumbling roll, bracing himself for the collision with the man on the other side.

The Imperial soldier was bent over and leaning forward so the retinal scanner could confirm his identity, the other five members of his team huddled close behind him, alert and ready. Two were watching the stairs above and below, guarding against an enemy ambush. The other three had their weapons trained on the hall, ready to fire on any available target the instant the door opened. But their weapons and their focus were at chest height; they hadn't expected someone to come rolling in like a human wrecking ball.

In the split second before their collision, Theron recognized the man on the other side of the door—his old friend Captain Pressik. Theron plowed into his knees, sending them both crashing to the ground. In the tight confines of the stairwell the momentum of their flailing bodies had a domino effect on the other guards, and the entire team was sent sprawling. The one farthest back from the door tumbled down the stairwell, while the others were knocked from their feet in a pile of thrashing limbs.

Theron's impact jammed his sore shoulder, and the pain made him lose his grip on his assault rifle. Despite this, he was still the first to regain his feet. Pressik's eyes opened wide in recognition as he saw who was responsible for the carnage.

As Pressik reached for the pistol on his hip, Theron delivered a hard kick to his jaw, stunning him. Then he scooped up his assault rifle from the ground and sprang backward into the hall.

One of the other soldiers had managed to collect himself enough to fire off a wild shot with his own weapon.

The bolt whizzed by Theron's ear as he slapped at the panel, shutting the door with a sharp *whoosh*. He heard the ricochet of a second shot deflect off the door panel as he turned and sprinted back toward the minister's office. He managed to duck inside just as the stairwell door opened again and a barrage of bolts whisked down the corridor.

Theron slung the backpack off his shoulders so it wouldn't impede his movement. Staying low to the floor, he poked his head around the corner to return fire. Knowing he'd present too tempting a target if he took the time to aim, he squeezed off a burst of wild shots, hoping to get lucky.

He didn't hear any cries of pain, but he also didn't hear the sound of feet charging down the hall toward him. He may not have hit his target, but at least he'd made them think twice about coming after him. Unfortunately, they had him pinned down and they knew it. The hallway was filled with a steady barrage of blaster bolts—suppressing fire to keep Theron from getting off a return shot.

He reached into the backpack and pulled out a small reflective mirror. Carefully, he angled it so he could see down the hall without exposing himself to the endless rain of enemy shots. What he saw didn't fill him with encouragement.

Captain Pressik was back on his feet; he and other members of his team were crouched low and advancing down the hall, pressing themselves up against opposite walls of the corridor. The others were positioned several meters behind them, weapons trained on the office door, ready to unleash with their assault rifles if Theron exposed himself again.

Theron realized his situation was hopeless. If he still had his detonators he might be able to toss one down the hall. Even though leaning around the corner to make the throw would be the last thing he ever did, at least he'd take a few of the Imperial scum with him.

Actually, Theron realized, *I can take them all with me.*

He scrambled over to the explosives by the minister's desk, knowing he could set off the entire charge just by pulling out the wrong wire on the timer. With the amount of detonite he'd used, the blast would take out the entire team . . . and reduce him to ashes and dust.

He took a deep breath, readying himself for a martyr's death. He knew the men outside were getting close; in a few more seconds it would all be over.

Guess Jace and I aren't going to get to know each other better after all.

The sound of a single assault rifle echoed down the hall. A second later it was joined by screams of pain and surprise, and then the sound of several weapons firing. But to Theron's surprise, the bolts weren't ricocheting off the floor and walls around the still-open door of the minister's office.

He scrambled over to the door and poked his head around the corner, his weapon ready. Two of Pressik's men were down; the captain and the others had turned their attention to a figure firing at them from the shadows just beyond the door leading to the stairwell. Seizing his chance, Theron opened up with his own weapon. In a matter of seconds the deadly cross fire had mowed the trapped Imperials down.

"It's me," the voice of Master Gnost-Dural called out, careful not to use any names. "Are you hurt?"

"I'm okay," Theron called back, stepping out into the hall.

A second later the Jedi emerged from the darkness of the stairwell. In the glow of the emergency lights, Theron could see that he was still wearing his disguise, his features carefully hidden by his robe and hood. But over the fabric that concealed his face he wore a monocle-like lens, and pinned to the front of his robe was an ID badge identical to the one on Theron's uniform.

"Seal that door," Theron said.

The Kel Dor leaned in close enough for the retinal scanner to read the holoimage off his monocle, then hit the button to close the door when the status light turned green.

"Any reason you didn't tell me you made copies of the badge and retinal image for yourself?" Theron asked.

"You seemed to think the mission would be easier if you went alone," Gnost-Dural told him. "I didn't see the point in arguing."

"So you were planning to show up the whole time?" Theron asked. "What, did the Force give you a vision that I was going to need some help?"

"It doesn't work that way," the Kel Dor said, missing the fact that Theron was joking. "When you were late arriving at the rendezvous point I feared something had gone wrong. Fortunately, you left the grappling gun set up on the building across the street. I was able to use it to follow your path and get inside."

"Well . . . thanks," Theron said. "I owe you one."

"The Jedi don't keep track of such things," he replied, and Theron wondered if the Kel Dor was trying to be funny.

"It won't be long before they send another emergency response team to this floor," Gnost-Dural continued. "We need to get out of here."

"One problem," Theron said. "Follow me."

He led the Jedi into the minister's office and showed him the durasteel door.

"So . . . any chance you can use the Force to just rip that thing open for me?"

"Some of the great Masters of legend might have had that kind of power, but such a feat is beyond me."

"I was afraid you'd say that. Okay, new plan. I need

to get to the fourth floor, but like you said: there could be another emergency response team coming up the stairwell at any moment. I know that durasteel door's too thick for your lightsaber to cut through it, but I'll bet you can slice a hole in the ceiling of this office for me to crawl through, right?"

"I could, but it would leave a very distinctive mark."

"Don't worry about that," Theron told him. "When that detonite blows all that's going to be left of this office are splinters and ash."

The Jedi nodded. He pulled out the hilt of his lightsaber and ignited the blade. Reaching up, he slowly carved a perfect circle in the ceiling above them. Tiles, plaster, and a shower of insulation came tumbling down.

"Imperial reinforcements are coming," Gnost-Dural said. "I can sense them."

"How close?"

"Close. I'll hold them off to buy you some time."

Theron nodded and scooped his backpack off the floor, tossing it up and through the hole in the ceiling. Then he jumped up, his fingers wrapping around the lip as he pulled himself up and into the fourth floor office above them, grunting with the effort and the burst of pain that flared up in his injured shoulder.

The minister's office was larger than the one he was now standing in. After slinging his backpack over his good shoulder, he had to go out to the hall and into the office next door before he was standing above the communications room.

He pulled out the igniter rod and the tube of plasma gel, using the last of it to melt a hole in the ceiling as he heard the sound of blasterfire rising up from the floor below. Knowing Gnost-Dural wouldn't be able to keep the Imperial reinforcements at bay for long, he dropped down into the communications room.

The black cipher was sitting on the communications

console in the center of the room. Extracting the core without triggering the self-destruct sequence was a delicate process—one wrong move and the entire mission became nothing but a waste of time and resources. Fortunately, Theron had practiced the procedure hundreds of times on the damaged ciphers the Republic had recovered. When he started, it had taken him almost ten minutes. But with each attempt he got faster and faster, cutting his time to under a minute.

No need to try for a personal record, he reminded himself as his nimble fingers worked their magic.

Ninety seconds later, the prize was his. He wrapped it in a protective layer of microweave fabric and pulled out a hard-sided protective case from his backpack. He opened it up and removed the damaged core, slapping it into the cipher. Then he placed the working core into the protective case, snapped it shut, and stuffed it in his backpack.

"It's time to go." Gnost-Dural's voice came from above him. Looking up, he saw the Jedi peering down at him through the hole in the communications room ceiling.

Theron jumped up and grabbed Gnost-Dural's offered hand, allowing the Jedi to help haul him up so he didn't have to put any further strain on his aching shoulder. The wounded joint had gone from sore to outright painful, but Theron pushed all thoughts of it aside.

"What happened to the reinforcements?" he asked.

"I was unable to keep them from advancing into the room," the Jedi told him. "Once they were in close quarters, I had no choice but to use my lightsaber."

"It's okay," Theron told him. "The blast will cover up the evidence. The timer's ticking—we need to get clear."

"How much time do we have?"

Theron checked his chronometer.

"Sixty seconds—run!"

Theron led the way, his mind tracing the optimal escape route from his memory of the ODCC's architectural diagrams.

It took them ten seconds to reach the fourth-floor stairwell and use the badge/retinal scan combo to open the door. Ten more to head up two flights to the sixth floor and over to the emergency roof access. Ten more to race to the far side of the roof.

There Theron realized one of them wasn't going to make it.

"I packed an emergency chute into my backpack," he said, struggling to take it off so he could hand it to Gnost-Dural. "Take a running leap off the edge and pull this cord to deploy."

"Don't be foolish," the Jedi told him. "The Force will protect me."

And with that, he disappeared over the edge. Theron blinked in surprise, then scrambled to get the backpack securely on again.

His chrono beeped, warning him he only had five seconds until detonation. He took three running steps toward the edge and jumped, pulling the cord to deploy the chute as the building erupted behind him. A wave of hot air propelled from the blast seized his parachute, launching him high in the air and sending him spinning and tumbling out of control. The guide wires tangled together, partially collapsing the chute. Instead of floating gently to the ground, he began to pick up speed, his legs and arms flailing as he tried to control his rapid descent.

Ten meters above the ground the wires suddenly untangled, and the fabric canopy unfurled wide over him. It slowed his fall, but Theron was still coming in hard. He braced his legs together and flexed his knees as he hit the ground, absorbing the crushing landing with the big muscles of his lower body and core while simultaneously trying to roll with the impact. His teeth slammed together and he felt a sharp pain shooting through his ankles and all the way up to the crown of his head as his body crumpled from the force of the landing.

The roll wasn't much better, as he came down on his already damaged shoulder, causing his arm to pop out of the socket. He would have cried out in pain if all the wind hadn't been knocked from his body, leaving him gasping for breath.

He lay there for a few seconds, amazed that he was alive. He forced himself to his feet just as Gnost-Dural emerged from the darkness of the night to check on him. Seeing that the Jedi was limping badly after his six-story fall gave him a small bit of satisfaction.

"Guess we both had a rougher landing than expected," Theron said, shouting to be heard above the wailing sirens that now filled the night.

"Let me help you," Gnost-Dural said, noticing Theron's left arm dangling uselessly at his side.

Theron nodded, then braced himself as the Jedi took hold of his arm by the wrist and elbow. With a quick twist and pull, he popped the shoulder back into the joint. Theron let out a loud scream. Fortunately the wailing sirens would drown out the sound so that it wouldn't give away their position to any nearby Imperials.

"Emergency crews are responding to the blast," Gnost-Dural said. "We need to get out of here. Can you walk?"

Theron nodded and the two men limped away into the shadows, leaning on each other for support.

CHAPTER 18

MINISTER DAVIDGE found it difficult to focus on his work. In part it was relocating to a temporary office on the west side of the Orbital Defense Command Center—an unavoidable circumstance considering that his old office and a dozen others on the eastern wing of the building had been reduced to rubble the night before last.

The extra guards posted outside his door—and inside his door, and following him even when he went home at night—didn't help, though he understood the reason behind the extra security.

Most troubling of all, however, was the fact that he had personally been targeted for assassination. He'd always considered himself a mere cog in the Imperial machine—a key cog, to be sure, but not one who would ever garner that kind of attention. The Sith Lords and Grand Moffs were the face of the Empire; he was just the man who kept the shuttles running on time. He always believed he was protected by his anonymity; he wasn't really part of the war—he was just an analyst crunching numbers.

That comforting illusion had been blown to pieces just as surely as everything in his office. While he might not bear any particular ill will to the enemies of the Empire, the attempt on his life made him understand that they hated and despised him. It was unsettling. Disturbing. And it made dealing with the entire unpleasant business extremely stressful.

He'd reviewed the latest report from the Imperial investigators multiple times; looking over the facts that had been gathered over the last thirty-six hours again and again as he tried to make sense of the whole affair . . . and prepared to give his own report to Darth Marr.

The communications room they had set up for him in his temporary office lacked the durasteel door of his original office; it was separated from the rest of the room by a simple sliding door. But it still gave him the privacy he needed. More important, it also had a black cipher to make sure nobody could listen in on his most sensitive communications.

He activated the cipher and waited for the holo of Darth Marr to materialize as he received and decoded the incoming call with his own cipher.

"I didn't expect to have to wait a day and a half to get a status report from you, Minister Davidge," Marr said to open their conversation.

"I didn't want to contact you until I was certain the conversation would be secure," he explained.

The cipher in his old office had been destroyed, and there was only one other on Ziost—an inactive spare that had been stored in the maximum-security underground vault beneath the ODCC. With everything else that was going on, it had taken some time before the engineers had hooked it up to the communications equipment in his new office.

"Cautious as ever," Marr noted, though Davidge couldn't tell if it was meant as a compliment, an insult, or simply an offhand remark.

"I have the details of the report, my Lord," he said.

"I assumed as much when you called me."

Realizing he was testing Marr's patience, the minister dived right into it.

"None of the suspected terrorists were captured," he said, opening with the bad news. "We believe there may have been as many as six involved, but our surveillance cams were only able to capture one of them."

"I assume you have authorities looking for this person?"

"He—or possibly she—was covered head-to-toe in heavy clothing. Even the face was obscured by a hood and mask."

"So we have no leads," Marr said.

"We know the Ziost Liberation Front was behind it," the minister told him. "They've claimed responsibility."

"What about our security protocols? How did they fail so completely?"

"Actually, my Lord, they didn't. The protocols were designed to keep enemy forces from taking control of the ODCC, not to prevent an attempted assassination. Even with all the damage, orbital defense systems were never compromised or in danger of being disrupted."

"What of the cipher in your office? Was it compromised?"

"We recovered the cipher from the wreckage," the minister told him. "The blast severely damaged it and triggered the core's self-destruct sequence, but at least it's accounted for."

In the minister's mind, this was the best news of all. Had they been unable to find the cipher in the debris and ashes, they would have had to change the cipher codes. Recalling all the capital ships equipped with a black cipher to be reprogrammed and synchronized would have reduced Imperial efficiency by almost a full percent for the quarter—a loss ratio the minister didn't even like to contemplate.

"So what is your recommendation going forward?" Marr wanted to know.

"The overall impact of this terrorist attack on the Imperial war effort is negligible," the minister assured him. "Resources and personnel amount to a loss ratio of less than a one-thousandth of one percent. I've already requisitioned troops to replace those who died during the attack, and repairs on the damaged section of the ODCC are under way."

"So you propose we should simply continue on exactly as before?"

"I've ordered security for all the Imperial ministers to be increased," Davidge admitted. "Again, the overall impact on the Empire is almost too small to calculate. Even at my highest estimates—"

Marr held up a hand to cut him off.

"Spare me the specifics. There's no need to justify your personal protection detail. The Dark Council is well aware of the value you and the other ministers contribute to the Empire."

The compliment should have made Davidge feel good. Instead, it only reinforced his recent epiphany that he was not an anonymous bean-counter. The implications of the Dark Council understanding his importance to the Empire were even more terrifying than the attempt on his life. The Sith Lords didn't ignore things of value. They fought to control them . . . or destroy them if they belonged to someone else.

"Thank you, my Lord. It's good to know I'm appreciated."

"I think this attack should signal a shift in our policy," Marr told him.

"What sort of change?"

"When this war began, we were the aggressors. Now we keep giving ground to the Republic."

"It's not a matter of choice, my Lord. It's a question of

resources. The Republic has more ships in their fleet and more soldiers in their army."

"Retreat makes us look weak. Vulnerable," Marr continued, as if he hadn't heard Davidge. "It emboldens groups like the ZLF. Makes them dare to plot the assassination of top Imperial officials."

"This was one incident, my Lord. But overall we have not seen a statistically relevant increase in anti-Imperial activities."

"You understand numbers, Minister. I understand the minds of our followers and our enemies. This attack heralds a shift in attitude that we cannot ignore.

"We need to push forward on several fronts. Reclaim some of the worlds we have lost to the Republic. Attack new worlds that have never before trembled before the might of Imperial power."

Davidge groaned inside. There was no point in arguing with Marr's orders, but the minister knew launching new campaigns of conquest against the Republic would increase the quarter's loss ratio.

"I am sending a list of possible targets for analysis. Find where we can reap the most reward for our efforts," Marr told him.

"Of course, my Lord," Davidge replied. "You know what is best for the Empire."

"I recommend we use Moff Nezzor," Marr said. "You don't seem to have him doing anything vital at the moment."

That's because he's an unprofessional, bloodthirsty sociopath with no regard for the lives of the enemy or his own soldiers.

"I will be sure to choose targets from your list that will take best advantage of Moff Nezzor's unique talents," Davidge said aloud, though the idea caused bile to bubble up in his throat.

"I know you will," Marr told him. "That's why I find you so useful."

"**THE FIRST** stage of the plan was a complete success," Jace told the three fellow conspirators who had gathered in his office for the debriefing. "I think we should celebrate with a drink!"

"I agree," the Director said. "Master Gnost-Dural—we have some Dorin pleech."

"A gracious offer, but I will decline."

"Suit yourself," the Director said with a shrug. "Theron, what's your preference?"

"I don't have any *kri'gee* here in the office," Jace said with a smile. "But I've got some of that Corellian Reserve I told you about."

"Sounds good," Theron replied.

It had been five days since he and Gnost-Dural had leapt off the edge of the exploding ODCC building. They'd spent the first three of those days waiting on Ziost after local authorities closed all the spaceports and temporarily barred any civilian ships from landing on or leaving the planet.

Not that Theron had minded at the time. He spent the days convalescing while Gnost-Dural made some discreet inquiries into the Imperial investigations. Fortunately, the ZLF had been all too happy to claim responsibility for the attack. Even though they'd actually had nothing to do with it, its members were eager to take the credit for striking a blow against the hated Empire.

With the Imperials focused on hunting down the ZLF members responsible, it was simple enough for Theron and Gnost-Dural to leave once the spaceports reopened.

Bad luck for any members who get caught, though, Theron had thought at the time. But the fate of a small group of radical anti-Imperials on Ziost wasn't something he could afford to worry about.

After leaving Ziost, they'd returned directly to Coruscant to deliver the cipher core to Jace, who had promptly turned it over to the Director and SIS. Now, two days later, Theron and his partner were in the Supreme Commander's office, being waited on by two of the most important men in the Republic.

"We've already intercepted several key Imperial transmissions," the Director said, bringing Theron's drink over to him once Jace was done pouring it. "It appears they're ramping up their military presence in several contested sectors."

Theron took a sip of his drink before speaking, savoring the warm, sweet liquid as it traced its way down his throat.

"If SIS is careful, we could use the intel to our advantage without the Empire ever suspecting we're listening in on their encrypted messages."

"Sounds risky," Jace warned. "We're closer to stopping the *Ascendant Spear* than we've ever been. I'm not going to let it slip through our fingers because we got greedy."

"SIS knows how to be discreet," the Director assured him. "Give the analytics team access to those transmissions. Let us run our scenarios. I'm sure we'll find something we can exploit without tipping anyone off."

Jace was still reluctant.

"What do you think, Master Gnost-Dural?"

"A tool is of no use if you never pick it up," the Jedi told him.

Master Zho couldn't have said it better himself, Theron thought, raising a glass to his dearly departed friend before taking another sip of the delicious brandy.

"I promise we won't act on anything without your approval," the Director added.

"Looks like I'm outnumbered," Jace said with a smile.

"Just be careful. And don't forget what we're really looking for.

"We've moved into phase two of our plan," he declared. "We monitor the Imperial transmissions and wait for the *Spear* to send word that it's coming into port."

He turned to Theron. "Once it's docked, you slip on board, slice into the *Spear*'s systems, program a dormant virus to disrupt the ship's hyperdrive and defenses, and get off the ship before it returns to duty."

"Sounds easy when you say it," Theron said.

"Can't be any harder than stealing the cipher," the Director noted.

"Once everything's in place, we track the *Spear*'s movements and set an ambush," Jace continued. "Hit her with everything we've got. During the battle, we send a signal to activate the dormant virus and we take Darth Karrid and her ship down."

"SIS is still trying to pull together the necessary resources," the Director cautioned.

"The *Spear* will dock at a military space station, not some civilian spaceport. We'll need an Imperial military shuttle, proper IDs, uniforms, clearance papers . . . it's proving more difficult than we thought."

"Perhaps Theron's contact can help us again," Gnost-Dural suggested.

"The Old Tion Brotherhood has been smuggling contraband onto Imperial space stations for years," Theron agreed. "They know every trick in the book to get past security."

"Getting Teff'ith to set up a meeting on Ziost is one thing," the Director cautioned. "But I don't like you bringing her into an active role in this mission."

"Why not?" Jace wanted to know. "Can't we trust her?"

"Yes," Theron said, even as the Director answered, "No."

Jace looked back and forth between them, but neither man was willing to back down.

"I've got this covered," Theron assured the Supreme Commander. "Compared to getting the cipher, this job's a piece of cake."

"You had help getting the cipher," the Director reminded him.

"I'm willing to accompany Theron again when he goes to meet his contact," Gnost-Dural offered.

Before Theron could object, Jace spoke up.

"Then it's settled. We let Theron and Master Gnost-Dural reach out to this Teff'ith person."

"I'll have SIS keep working on getting what we need," the Director said. "Just in case Theron's contact doesn't pan out."

"Let's take the *Prosperity* again," Theron said to the Jedi, ignoring the Director's lack of confidence. "Might as well travel in comfort."

"We can leave tomorrow," the Jedi agreed.

The Supreme Commander raised his glass in the air.

"To the Republic!"

Theron and the Director echoed his toast, and all three men downed what was left in their glasses.

With the meeting over Theron, Gnost-Dural, and the Director left Jace's office. The young woman behind the reception desk nodded pleasantly at the first two, then gave the Director a glare so filled with venomous rage it actually made Theron shiver.

"Uh, you two go on ahead," the Director whispered. "I need to schedule some other appointments with the Supreme Commander."

Maybe she's not going to be his third wife after all, Theron thought as he and Gnost-Dural continued down the hall.

"Theron," the Jedi said once they were out of earshot of the others. "I have a message for you. From Grand Master Satele Shan."

"Oh?" Theron said, trying to appear nonchalant. Once again he wondered if the Jedi knew about their relationship.

"She wishes to speak with you tonight. In her private chambers."

"Did she say why?"

"No. She only asked that you not mention this to the Supreme Commander."

Great, Theron thought. *Mom and Dad are fighting. Isn't it fun being part of a family?*

"Not sure if I'll have time," Theron said. "Some things I need to take care of before we leave tomorrow."

"I understand," Gnost-Dural said. "But if you change your mind, Grand Master Shan will be expecting you."

CHAPTER 19

THE LAST time Theron had spoken with Satele had been on Tython. That meeting had been his idea; he'd snuck into her private quarters to tell her about Ngani Zho's death. Zho had been her Master and her mentor, and she deserved to hear the news in person, not over a holo or in some report.

At the time, he'd pretended not to know she was his mother, and she made no mention of recognizing him as her son. But he had the sense they both knew the truth, though neither was willing to acknowledge it. This time would be different, Theron decided. He was tired of playing games.

Well, most games. Despite being invited, he was still breaking into her apartment. Part of it was the challenge—he just wanted to prove he could do it. But he also didn't want others to figure out that he and Satele were related. Shan was a common surname, but it was unusual for an SIS field agent to meet in person with the Grand Master of the Jedi Order. It wasn't like he was being followed, but on the slim chance someone saw him at her door he didn't want anyone to start making connections. Theron was convinced his life would get a lot more complicated if their relationship went public.

Probably bad for her, too, Theron assured himself. *Doing her a favor by breaking in.*

The Jedi still officially condemned the emotional attachments of marriage and children. If people found out Satele had a son, they'd think she was a hypocrite.

If they knew she spent her whole life acting as if I didn't even exist, Theron wondered, *would that make things better or worse?*

Disabling the building's perimeter sensors and scaling the wall took only a few minutes, and it gave Theron a chance to work out his injured shoulder. He'd been favoring it for the past five days; it was time to see how it was healing.

By the time he swung his legs over the railing of her third-floor balcony, he was satisfied that he'd make a full recovery. His shoulder was a little tired, but otherwise felt good. Another week and it would be back to 100 percent.

The sliding glass doors leading from the balcony and into the apartment were wide open, despite the chill of the night air. Clearly, Satele was expecting him.

As he stepped into the apartment, she rose from the chair she had been sitting in.

She was wearing the simple brown robes of a Jedi, her hood thrown back. Her shoulder-length hair was brown with some faint silver-gray highlights that gave her a regal air. Theron didn't see much family resemblance in their features, but he wasn't looking that hard. Her skin was surprisingly smooth and clear; though she was close to sixty, she looked at least two decades younger.

Is that because the Force flows through her, or is it just good genes?

"Thank you for coming," she said. "Please come in and close the door."

Theron complied, sliding the patio doors shut as his eyes took in his surroundings. The apartment was fully furnished and decorated—nothing overly lavish or opulent, but it was obvious more than a few credits had been spent.

"I thought the Jedi didn't believe in material goods."

"The apartment was furnished when I moved in," Satele said. "And it's important to make visitors feel comfortable. Do you really think less of me because I'm not living in an empty hut with nothing to my name but the clothes on my back and a meditation mat?"

"That's how Master Zho lived most of his life," Theron said.

"He was never Grand Master. He enjoyed a simpler existence. I have certain expectations and obligations that I must meet, even if they go against what I would choose for myself."

"You wanted to see me," Theron said, changing the subject. After a brief pause he added a sarcastic, "Mother."

"You have every right to be angry with me," Satele replied, her voice calm but also tinged with sorrow. "I don't expect you to fully understand why I had to give you up, but you should know it was the most difficult thing I have ever done."

"Is that why you wanted to see me?" Theron asked. "To tell me you made a mistake?"

"I didn't say that," she replied. "As hard as it was, giving you up was the right choice. I would do it again."

Theron sighed. "I understand better than you think," he said, his voice softening. "I'm not angry at you. I respect what you did. You made a sacrifice for the sake of the Republic."

"And for you, Theron," Satele said, coming toward him and placing a hand on his arm. "I knew Ngani Zho would raise you well. You were better off with him than me."

Theron didn't shrug her hand away, though he stiffened uncomfortably at her touch. Sensing this, she pulled back, though her serene expression never changed.

"When I see what you've become," she continued, "I

know I made the right decision. Ngani Zho would be proud of you, Theron. I'm proud of you."

"I don't need your approval," Theron said, though he was careful to keep any venom from coloring his words.

"Of course not," she said, turning away and walking back to the center of the room before turning to face him again. "But you have it anyway."

"Was there anything else you wanted to say?" Theron asked. "Master Gnost-Dural and I are leaving tomorrow morning."

"I know you've been working with Jace Malcom."

"You mean my father?"

"I suppose it was inevitable that he would find out," she said. "Perhaps I should have told him sooner."

"That's between you and him," Theron insisted. "I'm happy with my life. I'm comfortable with who I am. None of this matters to me."

"But it matters to Jace," she said. "You may not hold any bitterness in your heart toward me, but I fear he does."

"I can see how that might be a problem," Theron said. "For the Republic, I mean."

He didn't need a report from analytics to understand that anything that might negatively affect the relationship between the leader of the Jedi and the Supreme Commander of all Republic forces was a potential cause for concern.

"Jace is a good soldier," Satele assured him. "He will not put his personal feelings ahead of his duty and responsibilities. We have that in common."

"Really? I thought that might be the reason you never told him about me. You didn't think he'd be able to handle the emotional burden of a child."

"It wasn't that," she said, speaking slowly. "I've known Jace for many years. We fought side by side, and we truly cared for each other. But as the war continued,

I felt something change in him. I feared he would fall to the dark side."

Theron actually laughed out loud. "You were afraid Jace Malcom, the Supreme Commander, would betray the Republic?"

"Of course not," she replied, a hint of frustration poking through her calm exterior. "Jace will always be loyal to the Republic. But you do not have to follow the Sith to be an agent of the dark side. Jace is a good man, but the war has left its mark on him. There is so much anger and bitterness inside him. So much hate."

"Hate leads to the dark side," Theron said, getting the words out before she could. "Ngani Zho taught me all the Jedi platitudes," he added.

"You mock, but there is truth in our teachings," she chided him.

"Wow—you sound just like my mother," Theron joked.

"Jace fights this war out of revenge," she continued, trying to make him see the urgency of her warning. "It clouds his judgment. It can make him do terrible things if he believes they are necessary to save the Republic."

"That doesn't sound so wrong to me," Theron answered. "Sometimes the ends justify the means."

"The dark side is insidious," she warned. "Hate will transform you into the very evil that you are fighting so hard against.

"I know Master Zho taught you this lesson," she added softly.

"He taught me a lot of things," Theron shot back, his blood suddenly boiling. "Back when he thought I was going to be a Jedi. But I'm not a Jedi, and neither is my father."

It was clear to him now what was going on. Satele was afraid Jace was going to somehow corrupt him, and she was determined to save her son by sharing her glorious wisdom. Her condescending arrogance encapsulated everything that was wrong with the Jedi.

"Light side, dark side—these are just empty words," he continued, his voice rising to a shout. "There are only two sides I care about: us and them. Republic or Empire!"

"It was not my intention to upset you," she said.

"Of course not," Theron replied. "That would mean I was showing some emotion. And we all know there is no emotion, only peace. Right?"

He waited for Satele to offer another prepackaged Jedi mantra in response, but the Grand Master caught him off guard.

"Theron, I know you don't want me as part of your life," she said, seemingly abandoning their argument midstream and changing topics. "I respect your choice. But you know where to find me if you ever need my help. Reach out to me and I will be there. I promise."

"Don't hold your breath," Theron said. "Are we done here?"

"I have said my piece," she told him.

Theron turned his back on her and marched over to the balcony doors. He yanked them open and climbed over the railing, relieved to leave Satele and her insipid Jedi philosophy behind.

SATELE WATCHED Theron go, hoping she hadn't done more harm than good.

The meeting had been a constant battle between the logical part of her mind and the powerful feelings she had felt welling up inside her. She hadn't expected to be so profoundly affected merely from speaking with Theron; even though he was her biological son, she barely knew him. He wasn't part of her life anymore, not in any real sense. And yet it had taken all her training to deny the emotions that threatened to overwhelm her.

The Jedi restriction against family attachments made more sense to her now than ever. She couldn't even fathom how much harder it would have been to remain calm and focused if she had raised Theron herself. All of her feelings would have been magnified a thousandfold, making it impossible not to respond to his anger with her own.

Even now, several minutes after he was gone, she could still feel the effects of their confrontation. Her heart was beating far too rapidly in response to the adrenaline that had flooded her system.

"There is no emotion, there is peace," she whispered, seeking solace in the same words Theron had thrown in her face.

She had hoped that being raised by Ngani Zho, her old Master, would have prepared Theron to better understand and appreciate her fears about Jace. And it was possible he might still heed her warning. Satele suspected her son's anger was more a product of the emotional stress of confronting his mother than a response to her actual arguments. Once he calmed down, there was still a chance he would see her point.

Or maybe he just has too much of his father in him.

Maybe meeting Theron was a mistake. Maybe she had made things worse. Maybe she was wrong to speak with Theron behind his father's back.

Because of their history, she tried to keep her relationship with Jace strictly professional. By focusing exclusively on their duties to the Republic, they avoided dredging up painful memories and feelings. But maybe denying their past wasn't always the answer.

Maybe it was time to talk to Jace, not as Grand Master to Supreme Commander, but as a man and woman who had once shared a deep and powerful love.

Satele shook her head. She was restless and unsettled, unable to find a proper sense of calm and balance. She sensed long-denied memories creeping around the edges of her consciousness, awakened by Theron's presence. Instead of pushing them away as she had so often done in the past, she closed her eyes and sat down cross-legged on the floor, opening herself to them. Painful as they were, she needed to accept and acknowledge their existence if she hoped to focus and still her racing thoughts.

Jace's command tent was a buzz of activity, with soldiers rushing in and out, delivering status reports to the newly promoted general and relaying his orders to his troops. He was standing over a small table, looking over a map of the battlefield covered with red and blue markers indicating the respective position of enemy and allied troops,

"General Malcom," Satele said as she entered the tent and approached the table, "I need to speak with you. Alone."

She could have waited until evening fell; most nights Jace still managed to slip away and see her in private. But what she had to say couldn't wait.

So far they had managed to keep their love—and their six-month affair—secret. Approaching him in the open lacked discretion, but it wasn't unheard of for a Republic general and a Jedi Master to discuss strategy in private, so her request wasn't likely to raise any suspicions.

"You heard Master Shan," Jace barked. "Clear out."

The soldiers in the tent, along with the half dozen officers who served as his advisers in the field, moved with typical military precision and efficiency, emptying the tent in a matter of seconds.

"What is it, Satele?" Jace asked, dropping the formal address he'd used in front of the others.

She heard the worry and concern in his tone. She hadn't told him she was pregnant yet. She'd only sensed the days-old life growing inside her because of her powerful connection with the Force; it would be months before her body began to show any physical signs of her condition.

Jace must have read something in her expression— after six months of sharing their most intimate moments, it was difficult to hide anything from each other. But Satele hadn't come to tell him about the pregnancy. Not yet. There was something else she had to deal with first.

"I've heard you're sending troops up into the mountains to search for the Imperials who fled the battle."

Jace nodded. "Some of them surrendered when we broke their ranks, but most of them are trying to make their way over to the spaceports near Gell Mattar so they can escape offworld."

"Let them go," Satele said. "You don't need to hunt them down like animals."

"If they surrender to the patrols, we won't do them any harm."

"They don't know that," Satele reminded him. "They will fight out of fear for their lives, and your people will have no choice but to fight back. Call off the patrols and many lives will be spared."

"I'm not going to let enemy soldiers get away and go back to the Empire just so we can face them in another battle on some other world!" he protested.

"How many of them will actually return to the Empire?" Satele countered. "Most of them will slink off to other worlds and disappear into civilian life."

"I disagree," he said. "And it's my decision, not yours."

"This decision is guided by anger and hate," Satele warned him.

"Of course it is!" Jace shouted. *"You've seen what they're capable of. You've seen the death and horror they've unleashed on innocent worlds. We're supposed to hate them! They're the enemy!"*

There was a sudden silence, the fury of his words momentarily shocking them both into silence. Then Jace came around from behind his table and placed his hands on Satele's shoulders.

"I'm sorry, Satele. I didn't mean that the way it sounded. But I can't do what you do. I can't just brush away all the pain the Empire has caused."

"Revenge won't ease that pain, Jace."

"When the war first started, I used to keep a list of every friend I'd seen die in battle," Jace told her. *"I'd recite their names each night before I went to sleep, trying to remember their faces. Clinging to their memories.*

"As the war dragged on, the list grew longer. After a few years it was too long for me to recite each night. Then it became too long for me to even remember them all. Hundreds and hundreds of good men and women, their lives taken by the Empire.

"And every Imperial soldier that isn't captured or killed is someone who might add another name to that list," Jace continued. *"That's why I have to send out my patrols. That's why we have to hunt the enemy down like animals. I owe it to the names on that list."*

Satele remained silent as he spoke, but his words filled her with horror and dread. She knew Jace was loyal, but she'd never imagined his loyalty to his fallen friends would be the catalyst for so much anger.

"Killing Imperials can't bring back the people on the list," she told him.

"Killing Imperials is how we win this war," he told

her. "And winning the war is the only way to stop adding names to my list."

"This is a dangerous path, Jace. You're taking the love for your friends and turning it into something dark and twisted. Something that will drive you to evil."

"We don't see things the same way," Jace explained. "I'm not a Jedi."

"What if something happens to me?" Satele wondered. "What happens if one day you add my name to your list?" Silently she added: Or your child's?

Jace's expression was grim. "I'd rain destruction down on the Empire," he said quietly. "I'd destroy their cities and burn their worlds."

"That's not what I would want."

"I know," Jace answered. "But I can't help who I am." After a few seconds he added, "And I don't think we're really that different. If something happened to me, I don't believe you could pretend it didn't matter. I think in your grief and anger you'd lash out at the Empire, too."

"That's not the Jedi way," she said, but even as she spoke the words she wondered if Jace was right.

How could she not hate the Empire if they took away the man she loved? How could she not hate them if they had the blood of her unborn child on their hands?

"I'm . . . I'm not a soldier," she said, her voice uncertain as she took a step back from him. "I'm a Jedi."

"It's okay, Satele," Jace said, stepping toward her and extending his hand.

She turned and rushed from the tent, ignoring him as he called out for her to wait. She fled beyond the perimeter of the camp and into the cover of the night's darkness, where she finally stopped and collapsed on the ground. Her breath was coming in ragged gasps *that quickly turned into hitching sobs as she was drowned in a flood of powerful emotions. The tears came next, and she didn't try to stop them.*

She cried for several minutes before slowly collecting herself. The flow of tears dried up and her sobs became a soothing rhythm of inhale–exhale.

She recognized that part of her reaction was due to the hormones coursing through her pregnant body, and some of it was due to her still struggling to accept the fact that she was going to have a child. But that couldn't explain everything away.

She had sensed the hate and darkness inside Jace before, though it had taken the impending birth of their child to make her confront him about it. What she hadn't realized was that the same potential for hate and anger lurked inside her, as well.

Her feelings for Jace were too strong. If something happened to him, she feared all her Jedi training wouldn't be able to save her from seeking vengeance against the Empire. With her child, she knew, it would be even worse.

"This path leads to the dark side," she said, and in that moment of clarity Satele knew what she had to do.

Satele opened her eyes as the memories faded away. They still hurt, even three decades later. As much as she wanted to believe she could master and control her emotions, when it came to Theron and Jace she had to recognize that it simply wasn't possible. They would always evoke a powerful reaction in her; it was a weakness she had to acknowledge.

If she were to confront Jace about his potentially harmful influence on their son, it would only make things worse. Like Theron, he would react to her interference with anger, and she would inevitably respond in kind. Better not to get involved any further.

She had cut them out of her life for a reason: it was the only way she could fully serve the Republic. She had sacrificed her chance to have a family and an ordinary life when she chose the Order, and—hard as it was—she couldn't go back on that decision now.

CHAPTER 20

GNOST-DURAL WAS already waiting for him when Theron arrived at the shuttle. He expected him to ask if he had spoken with Satele, but the Kel Dor didn't bring it up.

"So where do we go to meet this contact of yours?"

"Jigani Port," Theron said. "On Desevro."

Tracking Teff'ith down hadn't been hard; the SIS had a well-established network of informants at all the major spaceports that weren't under Imperial control. Getting information on the movements of people passing through the ports in the Hutt worlds or non-affiliated sectors like the Tion Hegemony was a routine procedure, provided the target wasn't taking unusual steps to conceal his or her identity.

The purpose of the network wasn't really to allow Theron to get regular updates on a small-time criminal working for the Old Tion Brotherhood, but he wasn't the only agent who used SIS resources to track individuals for non-official reasons. The Director normally turned a blind eye to these minor violations if the agents didn't overly abuse the system, though now that Teff'ith could actually be useful to the Republic there was no reason to worry about being discreet.

As the Jedi punched in the coordinates to the *Prosperity*'s nav computer, Theron's mind kept drifting back to his meeting with Satele and her warnings about Jace. It wasn't like him to lose his composure. Satele hadn't done or said anything that didn't fit with what he expected from a Jedi Master. It really shouldn't have set him off like it did.

"Prepare for liftoff," Gnost-Dural said.

Theron understood that in the grand scheme of things, the Jedi were good to have around—the Republic wouldn't have survived without them. And though there may be differences between how they perceived the war against the Empire and how the rest of the Republic viewed it, in the end they were all on the same side. So why had he lashed out so intensely at Satele? Was it because, as Grand Master, all the stereotypical Jedi traits he found most irritating were amplified in her? Or was it just because she was his mother?

Their shuttle took to the sky, breaking Coruscant's atmosphere a few seconds later. Once it was clear of the planet's orbital flight lanes, Gnost-Dural flipped the switch and they made the jump to hyperspace. As the starfield through the cockpit window became a blur of white, Theron decided he might as well pass the time by finding out if his partner shared Satele's opinions about the Supreme Commander.

"I met with Grand Master Shan," he said.

"Good," Gnost-Dural replied. "I trust the meeting went well?"

Theron still didn't know if the Kel Dor knew Satele was his mother, so he decided not to bring it up.

"She has some concerns about Jace Malcom. She's worried he's driven by hate and vengeance. She's afraid he might slip over to the dark side."

"Grand Master Shan knows him better than I do," Gnost-Dural admitted. "They served together many times. It's possible she saw something in him that troubled her."

"You don't sound too worried about it."

"It's a common fear in our Order when we work with the military," Gnost-Dural explained. "Jedi are not soldiers; we do not approach war with the same mentality. Times of galactic strife and suffering will inevitably force the Republic into a struggle between the darkness and the light. As Jedi, it is our role to try to keep the Republic on the proper path.

"At times, this can lead to tension and conflict, particularly when dealing with someone as strong-willed as Jace Malcom. But it does not mean we are not all working to achieve the same goals."

"Sounds pretty reasonable when you say it like that," said Theron.

"I'm surprised Grand Master Shan didn't explain this to you herself."

"Maybe she tried," Theron admitted, "but the words she used didn't really get through."

"Sometimes personalities clash. Even the Grand Master is not the right teacher for every student," Gnost-Dural noted.

Theron bristled momentarily at the implication that he was learning at Gnost-Dural's feet, but he quickly brushed his irritation aside. The Kel Dor hadn't meant anything by his words; it was just that odd way Jedi had of speaking that made normal folks feel like they were being condescending.

Maybe half the problem is you, he chided himself. *Gotta stop being so sensitive.*

He yawned, suddenly aware of how tired he was. He hadn't slept well after his meeting with Satele.

"I'm going to grab forty winks," he said. "Wake me when we get to Desevro."

THE CUSTOMS authorities at Jigani Port weren't anything like Imperial security on Ziost. They didn't require clearance papers or approvals or even an official ship registration. All they wanted was someone to pay the fifty-credit docking fee and a hundred-credit deposit on the hangar.

Theron paid them out of his own pocket, not bothering to get a receipt so he could apply for reimbursement later. He wasn't sure how much of this mission was coming out of the SIS budget, but considering the Jedi had supplied the ship he didn't mind footing the bill for parking.

"Where to now?" Gnost-Dural asked Theron as he paid the customs official.

"If I know Teff'ith, she'll be hanging around the dirtiest, nastiest, most dangerous spot to get a drink in this place."

"That'd be the Crooked Finger," the customs agent answered. "Not sure it's your kind of place, fellas," he said, glancing up at the Jedi's luxury shuttle. "Want me to arrange a security escort?"

It wasn't difficult to understand his concern. Gnost-Dural was wearing nondescript robes rather than his Jedi garb, and his lightsaber was tucked out of sight. Theron had donned his custom bracers, with a full complement of toxin darts and a recharged pinpoint laser. But not everyone would realize they were more than just a stylish choice of wardrobe, and the single blaster on his hip looked woefully underpowered for the kind of people they were bound to run into wandering Jigani Port's seedier dives.

"We can handle ourselves," Theron assured him. "Just point us in the right direction."

When they reached the Crooked Finger, it was everything Theron had expected: dimly lit to hide the dirt and grime, and overflowing with a motley assortment of heavily armed thugs and criminals. Music from a slightly out-of-time live band spilled out the door, along with the clamor of the patrons shouting to be heard above the music.

A pair of large Nikto sitting by the door sprang up as they entered, barring their way.

"Cover charge to get in," the bigger of the two said. "Fifty credits each."

Theron highly doubted they actually worked for the bar, but he didn't see the point in starting something. Before he could dig out any more credits, though, Gnost-Dural intervened.

"No cover for us," he said, waving his hand in front of him in an almost hypnotic gesture. "We're friends of the owner."

"Guess we can let you through," the smaller Nikto answered as he and his friend stepped to the side. "Seeing as how you know the owner."

Once they were inside, Theron leaned in close enough for Gnost-Dural to hear him above the music and the general din of the crowd.

"Do you know how much easier my life would be if I could learn that trick?" he said. "Best thing about being a Jedi, if you ask me."

"It doesn't work on everyone," Gnost-Dural reminded him. "Only those with weak minds. Nikto are particularly susceptible."

They made their way through the maze of tables and chairs, Theron's eyes scanning the bar for a yellow-skinned Twi'lek. He spotted her sitting at a table in the back corner with a scrawny-looking Rodian.

Theron had expected her to be sitting alone; Teff'ith didn't normally make friends.

"There she is," he told his companion. "Better let me do the talking."

As they drew near, he could see that the Rodian was talking animatedly with Teff'ith. He couldn't make out the words, but the Rodian's lips were moving, his ears were twitching, and his hands gesticulated wildly. Teff'ith, on the other hand, was barely paying attention. She looked bored, or maybe drunk, sitting slumped forward in her seat with her hands folded in her lap beneath the table.

"Hello, Teff'ith," Theron said when they reached the table. "Mind if we sit down?"

Her disaffected posture vanished as she whipped a blaster up from under the table; clearly she'd had it in her lap the entire time. The Rodian's eyes opened wide, then went back to normal once he realized she wasn't pointing the pistol at him.

"Saw you across the room," Teff'ith said to Theron. "Too crowded to shoot until you got close."

Despite her words, Theron knew she had no intention of actually pulling the trigger. Not unless he gave her a reason to.

"You get to the count of three to walk away," she said, her oddly accented Basic still as impossible to place as Theron remembered.

"There's no need for the pistol," Gnost-Dural said, his hand making the same slow wave he'd used on the Nikto at the door. "We're all friends here."

A strange look crossed over Teff'ith's face and the tip of her blaster dipped momentarily, only to pop back up and take dead aim at Theron's midsection.

"Not friends. One."

"I'm not here checking up on you," Theron reassured her. "I'm just here to talk business."

"Not interested. Deal was you leave us alone. Two."

"The job pays well," Theron continued. "If you can handle it."

"Maybe we should listen to him," the Rodian chimed in.

Teff'ith glared at him, before turning her gaze back to Theron.

"Vebb convinced us," she said, placing the blaster flat on the table. "You sit. You talk. We listen. Then we shoot you."

Theron and Gnost-Dural settled into the two open seats at the table.

"Ugly-head got a name?" Teff'ith asked, nodding at the Kel Dor.

"Gnost-Dural," he answered, not even slightly offended by the insult.

"Master Gnost-Dural," Theron clarified. "He's a Jedi. Like Master Zho."

"Zho not like other Jedi," Teff'ith grunted, and Theron couldn't argue with that.

"Your assistance on Ziost was quite helpful," the Kel Dor said, trying to get on her good side.

"You cutting deals with outsiders behind Gorvich's back?" Vebb said, shaking his head. "That's bad business, Teff."

Teff'ith shot Gnost-Dural an angry glare before turning her attention back to Theron.

"You said you got another job?"

"Everyone knows the Brotherhood smuggles contraband onto the Imperial space stations," Theron said, speaking quickly. "You've got the contacts, you've got the clearance codes, and you've got the ships."

"We know what we got. You got a point?"

"I want you to help us get onto one of the space stations."

"Which one?"

"We don't really know yet. It's going to be sort of a last-minute thing when it happens."

Teff'ith shook her head. "Can't help."

"What are you talking about, Teff?" the Rodian exclaimed. "Gorvich can pull this off no problem."

"Shut up, Vebb," Teff'ith growled. Turning to Theron she said, "Too dangerous. Another crazy mission." Nodding in Gnost-Dural's direction she added, "Another crazy Jedi."

"Come on, Teff'ith. You won't even have to be involved. Just set up another meeting with someone who can help us out."

"Already set up meeting for you," she said. "One per customer."

"Don't do it for me, then," Theron said, reaching for one last card to play. "Do it because it's the right thing. Do it because Ngani Zho would have wanted you to help us. It's the least you can do for him, now that he's gone."

"Zho's debt's nontransferable," she said, but Theron could see her resolve softening at the mention of their old friend. Teff'ith hadn't been around Zho for long, but he knew they'd formed a powerful bond. His mentor had that effect on people.

"I'll throw in enough credits to choke a bantha," Theron offered.

"Okay," she finally agreed. "We take you to Gorvich, but that's it. Then you disappear. For real this time."

"Of course," Theron promised her. "I wouldn't have it any other way."

CHAPTER 21

HUDDLED WITH Gnost-Dural in the back of the air-speeder taking them from Jigani Port to the nearby city of Maslovar, Theron was convinced they would drop out of the sky at any moment. The constant high-pitched whine of the engine made conversation impossible, and every few minutes the pilot had to drop them to a height of only a few meters above Desevro's swampy surface to keep the repulsorlift from overheating. The stabilizers weren't much better, and each time a gust of wind hit them the speeder threatened to flip over.

The flight lasted only twenty minutes, but by the time they touched down in the center of the city Theron's stomach was trying to crawl up and out of his throat.

"Best hotel in Maslovar!" their pilot proclaimed as his passengers climbed out of the backseat.

Looking at the dilapidated building before them, Theron was convinced there had to be a better option. But he wasn't eager to get back on the speeder anytime soon.

Maybe it won't be as bad as it looks, he silently hoped as they collected their bags and headed inside.

Teff'ith had agreed to set up a meeting with Gorvich three days from now. Theron wasn't happy about the delay, but she insisted it would take some time to pull together everything they'd need to get past Imperial security on whichever space station ended up being their destination. Until then, there was nothing for Theron and Gnost-Dural to do but wait.

They'd asked Teff'ith to recommend a place to stay; seeing where she'd sent them made it clear she still wasn't happy about working with him.

"We need a room," Theron said at the check-in desk. "Three nights. Two beds."

The woman behind the counter didn't speak as she punched at the buttons on her console. Eventually she produced a pair of keycards.

"Sixty credits per night. Pay up front."

Theron slid the credits across the counter, and she handed him the keycards. "Level six. Top floor. Turbolift is broken."

Theron prepared himself for the worst as he entered the room, and he wasn't disappointed. An unidentifiable but distinctly unpleasant odor wafted out to meet them as the door slid open, and Theron was certain he heard the scuttling of vermin running for cover as he flicked on the lights.

"There is no comfort, only filth," he mumbled.

"We could return to the shuttle," Gnost-Dural suggested. "There are sleeping quarters, a shower, and a refresher on board."

"I think the floor of the shuttle would be more comfortable than this place," Theron agreed. "But I need a few minutes before I can handle another speeder ride like the last one."

"You and Teff'ith have an interesting relationship," Gnost-Dural said.

"It's not really a relationship," Theron explained. "She's just one of my contacts."

"She is clearly more than that," Gnost-Dural countered.

"Ngani Zho saw something in her. He took her under

his wing. I guess I feel responsible for her now that he's gone."

"Do you have feelings for her?"

Theron laughed. "Not like you're implying. She's more like a kid sister. Annoying, always getting into trouble, but you know there's good buried somewhere deep inside."

"It must be buried very deep," the Jedi noted, "for her to send you to a place like this."

"She's not going to double-cross us," Theron assured him.

"Because of her respect for Master Zho?"

"It's not just that. She's got honor.

"She could have abandoned me on Darth Mekhis's flagship. Could have taken my shuttle and left me to die there when it self-destructed. But she didn't. She waited while the whole place was collapsing around her. Gave me time to get back to the shuttle."

"No wonder she's hostile," the Jedi said. "She saved your life, and now you come and ask her for another favor. You are the one in debt to her."

Before Theron could reply, the cybernetic implant in his right ear buzzed.

"Hold on," he said to Gnost-Dural, holding up a hand for silence. "Incoming call from the Director."

He whispered, "Accept incoming," before saying more loudly, "Director—any news?"

"The bird is coming back to the nest," the Director said. "The one in the manax tree."

From the analytics report, Theron knew there were just a handful of Imperial space stations large enough to accommodate a vessel the size of the *Spear*. Only one was located in a system starting with the same letter as *manax*—Reaver Station in the Marranis system on the Outer Rim.

"Copy. What's the timetable?"

"Landing tomorrow. Should splash around in the birdbath for two days before flying south for the winter."

"Got it. Anything else?"

"Nothing relevant," the Director said after a brief pause. "Good luck," he added, ending the call before Theron could ask any more questions.

"Disconnect," Theron whispered as the static of the open channel hissed softly in his ear.

He waited for the comlink to click off before telling Gnost-Dural, "The *Spear*'s docking at Reaver Station to give the crew two days of R and R."

"When?"

"Tomorrow. By the time we meet with Teff'ith's contact they'll already be back on active duty."

"It might be weeks—maybe even months—before the *Spear* docks again," Gnost-Dural warned.

"We need to convince Gorvich to move a little faster," Theron agreed.

Theron didn't believe it was possible, but the speeder that took them back to Jigani Port was in even worse shape than the previous one. But his stomach wasn't lurching when they touched down this time; he was too focused on the mission.

Returning to the Crooked Finger, they found Teff'ith and her Rodian friend still sitting at the same table where they had left them an hour earlier.

"Didn't like the hotel?" Teff'ith asked when she saw them approaching.

"Change of plans," Theron said. "We need to see Gorvich today. Right now."

The Twi'lek shook her head. "Impossible. Three days, remember?"

"I'm not playing around, Teff'ith."

Something in his voice made her take notice, and she let out a long sigh.

"We take you to Gorvich. Follow us."

* * *

THE INSTANT Gorvich opened the door to his apartment, Theron disliked him. He was dressed in expensive, overly fashionable clothes—dark, tailor-fit slacks and a patterned shirt made from expensive Saava silk. He was wearing several ostentatious rings, and a thick gold chain dangled from his neck. His hair was blond, his features average, but there was something distasteful about his look—an expression on his face and the way he carried himself—that elicited a powerful sense of revulsion. When he opened his mouth to speak, he did nothing to offset the first impression, his voice arrogant, mocking, and self-obsessed all at the same time.

"Hey, Sunshine," he said to Teff'ith by way of greeting, flashing her a lecherous grin that made Theron want to pop him in the nose. "These the big spenders you told me about?"

"Gorvich, Theron," Teff'ith said, making her introduction as brief as possible. "You two talk. We're done."

Gorvich laughed. "Sunshine hasn't succumbed to my charms yet, but she'll come around. They all do. I have a special relationship with the ladies."

"Keep talking," Teff'ith said, tapping the handle of her blaster. "Make it so you never have a special relationship ever again."

He responded with a wink and another laugh before turning his attention to Theron.

"Come on in. Let's talk business."

The three of them followed him into the living room. Though the apartment was small, it was well furnished. Theron noticed that all the pieces appeared new, and they seemed more suited for a much larger place.

He's getting a little taste of success, Theron thought. *Figures he'll be moving on to bigger and better things in the near future.*

Gorvich settled himself into an oversized easy chair,

but didn't invite his guests to sit. Instead, he left them standing awkwardly in the center of the room.

Trying to make us feel uncomfortable. Inferior. Like we're servants waiting on him.

"Heard you need to get aboard an Imperial space station," Gorvich began. "Going to have to throw together clearance papers for the whole lot of them since you don't know which one you want to visit. Gotta charge you extra for that."

"We know where we're going now," Theron told him. "Reaver Station."

"Still gotta charge you extra, I'm afraid," Gorvich said with an affected shrug. "Started the paperwork when Teff'ith first called."

"Fine. Whatever," Theron said, knowing he didn't have time to argue. "But we need to leave today or the deal's off."

"You must be inhaling some of your Kel Dor buddy's atmosphere. That stuff will rot your brain. No way I can pull it all together today."

"It's today or not at all," Theron insisted.

"Do you know how complicated this is? We need uniforms. IDs. Clearance papers. An Imperial shuttle."

"The Old Tion Brotherhood moves thousands of credits' worth of contraband spice and stims through Imperial space stations every week," Theron said. "You telling me you don't have that stuff on hand and ready to go?"

"I might be able to scramble something up in a few hours," Gorvich admitted. "But I'm going to have to charge you a premium for short notice."

"Not a problem," Theron assured him, though he wasn't sure that was true. They had a lockbox stuffed with thirty thousand credits hidden away in a secret security compartment on Gnost-Dural's shuttle, but Gorvich had all the leverage and he knew it. It was possible he might come up with a ridiculous price they couldn't meet with the funds on hand. And authorizing more credits from SIS would take time . . . not to mention, a transfer of that size to any account on a gang-ridden planet like Desevro was bound to attract all kinds of attention from anyone involved in the transaction.

Theron decided not to bring this up, however. Better to negotiate the deal, then try to convince Gorvich to settle on a lower price once he'd already done the work to get everything ready.

"You know I can't do anything for your friend there," Gorvich told them. "Ain't no Kel Dor in the Imp army. He'll stick out like a sore thumb."

"I will stay out of sight on the shuttle," Gnost-Dural assured him. "I assume the kind of clearances you procure will allow us to avoid a search of our vessel."

"We have a couple of security folks we pay to look the other way."

"So, do we have a deal?" Theron wanted to know.

"You don't know my price yet."

"Just name it."

"Forty thousand credits."

"Done," Theron said with no hesitation, relying on his partner to be smart enough to play along. Fortunately Gnost-Dural didn't show any reaction.

Two hours later they were in Gorvich's private hangar while he walked them through the Imperial shuttle he'd procured. Teff'ith was still hanging around, though she hadn't said more than two words the entire time.

"Standard Imperial fleet issue," Gorvich said, pointing to a uniform draped over the pilot's chair. "Made you a corporal. Any rank higher than that starts to attract too much attention. You know who to salute and when? You mess that up and people are going to notice."

"I think I can handle it," Theron said. This wouldn't

be the first time he'd gone undercover as an enemy combatant.

"Got your clearance codes programmed into the ship's computer. All you have to do is send them when they ask for verification. They'll have you dock over on C wing. We've got an understanding with security there. Shouldn't give you any trouble. After that, you're on your own."

Gorvich scratched at the stubble on his chin and squinted one eye at Theron.

"Teff'ith never did say why you were going there. You ain't sellin' nothing, are you? Because the Brotherhood won't be too happy if you cut them out."

The way you tried to cut Morbo out of your deal on Nar Shaddaa? Theron thought.

"Got a cousin stationed on one of the capital ships," Theron said aloud. "Docking at Reaver Station. He's done with the war. Wants me to come get him out."

"Desertion and dereliction of duty," Gorvich said with a nod. "That I can understand."

"Anything else we need to know?" Theron asked.

"Guess not. Just hand over the credits and you're on your way."

"They're on our ship," Theron said.

"Great," Gorvich said, rubbing his hands together in excitement. "Let's go get 'em."

When they reached the *Prosperity*'s hangar, Gorvich let out a long whistle of appreciation.

"Nice ride," Teff'ith grudgingly admitted.

"Wait here," Theron said as he tapped in the code to open the boarding ramp, then climbed up and into the shuttle.

Gnost-Dural didn't bother to come with him; Theron was glad to see the Jedi had no problem letting him take the lead when it was appropriate. Even better, he knew his partner had his back if something should go wrong, as it had at the ODCC on Ziost.

He opened the hidden security panel and dragged out the lockbox, then carried it back down the boarding ramp and set it at Gorvich's feet and opened it.

"Isn't that a pretty sight, Sunshine?" Gorvich said.

"Just hand over our cut," Teff'ith replied.

"Give me a minute to count it. Make sure your friends aren't pulling a fast one."

"About that," Theron said. "There's only thirty thousand credits there. That's all we've got."

"So go get more," Gorvich growled.

"We don't have time," Theron told him. "Not sure I'd trust anyone around here with that kind of transaction anyway."

Theron was watching the other man closely, ready in case he went for his weapon. Shooting Gorvich might mess up the plan—the corrupt guards on Reaver Station could be friends of his—but he wasn't going to let Gorvich get the drop on him. In the back of his mind, he wondered whose side Teff'ith would be on if things got ugly.

"We agreed on forty," Gorvich reminded him.

"I'm good for it," Theron assured him. "Thirty now and ten when we get back."

"I'm not convinced you're going to make it back," Gorvich said. "I need enough credits to cover the cost of the shuttle in case you mess up and the Imps don't let you leave."

There was no way the simple Imperial supply shuttle Gorvich was lending them was worth anything above twenty thousand credits, but Theron wasn't going to argue the point.

"Tell you what," he said. "We get back, we'll give you another twenty instead of ten."

Gorvich was silent as he considered the offer.

"Good money, Gorvich," Teff'ith chimed in. "Easy money."

"Okay, here's the deal," he finally said. "Thirty up front. Twenty when you get back. And you leave me the command codes to your shuttle as collateral."

"The *Prosperity*'s worth at least fifty thousand credits on its own!" Theron protested. *Not to mention Gnost-Dural might have sensitive information on board.*

"Good incentive to come back," Gorvich said. "Wouldn't want you to 'rescue your cousin' and then take off somewhere."

From his tone it was clear he didn't buy Theron's cover story.

Theron glanced over at Gnost-Dural, who gave him a slight nod.

"Okay, we have a deal."

"Let me throw in one last wrinkle," Gorvich said with a grin. "You take Teff'ith with you."

"What?" the Twi'lek exclaimed. "Why?"

"Not sure what these two are really up to," Gorvich said, "but I want someone to keep an eye on them. Make sure they don't do anything that's going to cause trouble for the Brotherhood."

"So *you* go," Teff'ith spat.

"Sounds a little too risky for me. Besides, you're the one who brokered this deal. You're the one vouching for these two."

"Just wanted the credits," Teff'ith protested.

Gorvich shrugged. "That's the deal, Sunshine. You go with them or we cancel the whole thing."

Teff'ith glared at Theron, then over at Gorvich.

"Want a higher cut. Hazard pay."

"Sure thing, Sunshine," Gorvich said. "I'll throw in an extra three thousand when you get back . . . if you get back."

She turned on Theron. "You dragging us on another suicide mission?"

He shook his head. "Quick in and out," he promised. "A couple of hours and you're heading back. Easy money."

"Spend the credits before we get back," she warned Gorvich, "and you wake up missing a finger."

"Sounds like we have a deal," he said with a smile.

CHAPTER 22

COMPARED WITH the *Prosperity*, the interior of the Imperial supply shuttle was cramped and uncomfortable. It had seating for four, but because most of the rear was occupied by the cargo hold, the chairs were jammed two by two in the cockpit with hardly any legroom.

When Theron tried to sit in the pilot's seat, Teff'ith pushed him aside.

"You sit in back," she ordered.

Knowing she was still fuming over being forced to accompany them on the mission, he didn't bother to argue. Gnost-Dural took a seat in the copilot's chair beside Teff'ith without comment.

At least this Imperial uniform's a good fit, Theron thought as he squeezed into the seat behind Teff'ith.

But though it was the right size, he knew from past undercover experience that the cheap material of the cuffs and collar would still end up chafing his skin.

Just one more reason nobody should ever enlist with the Empire.

A few minutes later they were on their way to Reaver Station, a journey that would take roughly ten hours at the shuttle's top hyperspace speed. Theron would have been fine passing the journey in silence, but Gnost-Dural seemed to have other ideas.

"Your friend Gorvich is an unpleasant man," he said to Teff'ith.

"Gorvich is no friend. Just work for him. Pay's good."

"So that's your driving motivation in life?" the Kel Dor asked. "Material wealth?"

"Tell Ugly-face not to get all Jedi-preachy," Teff'ith said over her shoulder to Theron.

"Sorry," Theron replied. "Jedi can't help trying to save someone they think is in need of moral guidance. It's like a compulsion with them."

"Don't need saving," Teff'ith said to Gnost-Dural.

"You don't mind spending your life surrounded by people like Gorvich?"

"Just a stepping-stone. Won't be there forever. Moving up the Brotherhood ranks."

"And when you do, you'll find those in charge are even more selfish, brutal, and vicious than Gorvich," the Jedi assured her.

"Why we really going to Reaver Station?" Teff'ith asked, changing the subject.

"To rid the galaxy of a great evil," Gnost-Dural replied.

Teff'ith snorted.

"Gorvich is plenty evil. Should rid the galaxy of him."

"If you hate him so much," Theron asked from the back, "why'd you save him on Nar Shaddaa?"

"Don't leave partners behind. Even scum like Gorvich. Part of being a team."

The next few minutes passed in silence before she returned to her earlier line of inquiry.

"What's going down at Reaver Station? Need to know if things get ugly."

"Don't worry," Theron assured her. "You just need to drop me off and wait inside the shuttle with Master Gnost-Dural for a few hours while I take care of some business. That's it. Easy."

"Too easy," Teff'ith replied. "Not your style."

"Maybe I've changed."

Another snort from Teff'ith ended all conversation until they reached their destination, and Theron allowed himself to slip into a light meditative trance—yet another useful trick he'd learned from Ngani Zho—to rest up and ready himself for what lay ahead.

When they finally dropped from hyperspace, they had a clear view of Reaver Station; the massive spaceport was the size of a small moon. Struggling to look over Teff'ith's shoulder, Theron could make out an enormous capital ship docked on the far side—the *Ascendant Spear*.

"Go ahead and open a hailing frequency," Theron said, then added, "Better let me do the talking."

Teff'ith clicked the transmit button on the shuttle's control panel, but she didn't give him a chance to speak.

"Reaver Station, this is Imperial shuttle TK-37059 requesting permission to dock," she said, her heavily accented Basic disappearing as her voice slipped into the precise, clipped cadence common to citizens of the Empire.

"Copy, TK-37059. Ready for clearance codes."

"Transmitting codes now," she said before clicking off the comm channel.

"You've done this before," Gnost-Dural remarked, clearly as impressed and surprised as Theron. "Your accent is impeccable."

"Easy to fake Imp fancy talk," she said, brushing away the compliment.

The console beeped, and she pressed the button to reopen the channel.

"TK-37059, you have clearance to land," the voice on the other end said. "Proceed to Hangar Fourteen in D wing."

"Copy, Reaver Station," Teff'ith replied, then clicked off the channel a second time.

"I thought Gorvich said we were supposed to land in C wing," Theron said.

"Usually do," Teff'ith answered.

"So why the change?"

"Maybe Gorvich sold us out. Want to turn back?"

"No," Theron said after a quick deliberation. "Go ahead and dock."

Teff'ith brought the shuttle into the open hangar bay for a landing and the air-lock doors closed behind them. A pair of guards—both human, both male—emerged from a door leading into the station, but they didn't act as if they were expecting anything out of the ordinary.

"Wait here," Theron told the other two. "But be ready to bug out if something goes off the rails."

Exiting the shuttle, he approached the two guards, trying to appear casual even as his mind was racing. There wasn't an ambush waiting for them, so Gorvich hadn't betrayed them. But if these guards weren't on the take, they might want to inspect the shuttle, and Theron couldn't let that happen.

"Gorvich didn't say anything about sending a fresh face on this run," one of the guards said.

Theron let out a sigh of relief.

"He told me we were supposed to dock in C wing," Theron said, warming up to the part of a small-time thug working for the Old Tion Brotherhood. "Had me worried."

"C wing's reserved for that giant capital ship you saw on your way in. Had to shift some stuff around."

"Could've given us a heads-up," Theron said.

"Told Gorvich," the guard replied. "Guess he didn't pass it on."

"Guess he wanted to make the new guy sweat," the other guard said with a laugh.

"Where's your friend?" the first one asked. "The one with that sexy voice?"

"Staying on the shuttle," Theron said. "Keeping an eye on the cargo."

"Yeah? What's the haul this time? Stims? Spice? Banned holovids?"

"Is this part of hazing the new guy?" Theron asked. "Gorvich tell you to waste my time with all these questions?"

"Just trying to be friendly," one of the guards said. "Maybe you can leave us a little free sample when you go."

"I think we're done here," Theron said. "We keep chatting and someone's going to get suspicious."

"Fine," the first guard said, finally taking the hint. "We got other shuttles coming in, anyway."

"Just keep your head down and don't do anything stupid, rookie," the second warned him. "You get caught, we don't know you."

Theron waited for the guards to leave before returning to the shuttle.

"Everything's good," he said, giving a quick status update. "Sit tight. Everything goes smooth and I'll be back in a few hours."

"May the Force be with you, Theron," Gnost-Dural said.

"Don't mess up," Teff'ith said, offering her own words of support.

Theron left the shuttle and exited the hangar, making his way onto Reaver Station, marveling at the size and scope.

The Empire understood the need to let military personnel enjoy a break from their daily routine, but unlike the Republic it was paranoid about soldiers deserting whenever they landed on a world. To offset this, they'd designed Reaver Station to have all the amenities anyone would expect in a planetary port city, giving the soldiers a place to relax, but leaving them no other option but to return to their ship when their leave was over. Spread out over the station's four levels was a wide assortment of shops, bars, restaurants, holotheaters, casinos, sport courts, and clubs, all packed with men and women eager to cut loose before returning to the drudgery and discipline of their assigned posts on their respective ships.

Theron's plan was simple enough—sneak onto the *Ascendant Spear* while it was docked, slice into the computer systems, and plant the dormant virus. Next, he'd rig up the communications protocols to receive a special Republic transmission that would trigger the virus when the time was right. Then he'd slip off the ship, head back to the shuttle, and get off the station with no one the wiser.

The fact that Reaver Station was a secure military facility would only make things easier. The only people on board either served in the military or had special authorization to be here. Because of that, security on the ships actually docked at the station was bound to be lax. For a vessel the size of the *Spear,* there'd be a constant stream of men and women coming and going—heading out into the station for some fun, then stumbling back to their bunks on the ship to rest for a few hours before heading out again. At most, they'd have to flash a boarding ID to the guards stationed at the hangar's entrance—a nod to the fact that nobody would be able to remember the names and faces of every person who was stationed on the ship.

All Theron had to do was borrow a boarding ID from someone too drunk or preoccupied to notice it was missing so he could forge a copy. But first he had to figure out where the crew members of the *Ascendant Spear* were gathered.

The bonds among those who served together on a ship were strong, and most personnel on leave tended to hang out with the same people they worked beside day after day. They would congregate in the same general area of the station, their sheer numbers driving away most of those on the station who served on smaller vessels.

He made his way toward an information booth located near the hangar bays.

"Welcome to Reaver Station, Corporal," the woman behind the desk said.

Her voice was chipper and she had a wide smile plastered across her face, but there was something in her eyes that made Theron think her cheerfulness was just a façade—the result of Imperial training to boost the morale of the men and women arriving for a few precious days of R&R.

"Just got in on a supply run," Theron said. "First time here. Looking for a good place to grab some grub."

"Normally I'd suggest the Golden Galley," she said. "Great food, good prices, and you can have them take it right off your payroll if you're a little short of credits. But you don't want to go there today."

"Why not?" Theron asked, feigning ignorance.

"Had a full capital ship arrive earlier today. They hit that place like a fefze swarm."

"I'm not in a rush," Theron said. "Care to tell me how to get there?"

Following the woman's directions eventually brought Theron to his destination. The woman at the information booth's description of a deadly fefze swarm was accurate—the restaurant and every other establishment around it were overflowing with men and women in uniform. They spilled out into the streets, forming haphazard queues to wait outside the doors of any spot that served food or drink.

Theron slowly made his way through the crowd, searching for an easy target that could provide him with a boarding ID. Many of the bars he passed were projecting the feed from the official Imperial news holo where the crowd outside could watch as a way to keep the people in line from becoming too impatient and unruly.

It was hard to hear the newscasters over the din of the crowd, but the sharp trill indicating a breaking story caught Theron's attention. He stopped and turned his head up to hear the latest Imperial propaganda.

"The Empire scored a major victory just hours ago with a surprise assault on the Republic agriworld of Ruan."

A cheer rose up from the crowd, but Theron was too shocked to join in. Ruan was a major producer of food for Coruscant and several other ecumenopolis worlds. It was also deep inside Republic space—a planet most considered well beyond the reach of the Empire.

"Enemy casualties are estimated in the thousands, as an Imperial fleet under the command of Moff Nezzor unleashed an orbital bombardment that devastated production facilities on the surface."

And killed thousands of innocent civilians in the process.

"The Republic fleet in the area was destroyed, with enemy reinforcements arriving too late to affect the outcome of the battle. An official press release from the office of the Minister of War reads as follows:

" 'Moff Nezzor's resounding victory at Ruan demonstrates the strength of the Empire and exposes the vulnerability of the Republic. Those who say our enemy has gained the upper hand in the galactic war must clearly recognize this day as proof that the Empire is stronger than it has ever been. The Republic is unable to defend its own worlds and her citizens tremble before the might of the Imperial fleet. Their defeat and eventual surrender is inevitable. All hail the Immortal Emperor.' "

Theron turned away from the holo, ignoring the raucous celebrations of those around him. As bad as the attack itself had been, what it represented was far worse. The holo claimed capital ships had been involved in the attack; that meant the orders should have been transmitted using the black cipher. SIS should have known the attack was coming, but somehow the Republic was caught completely unprepared. It didn't make any sense.

Unless our cipher isn't working anymore.

The realization made Theron feel physically ill. He needed to speak to the Director. He needed to know what had gone wrong. If there was a leak in SIS analytics, they might have to scrap the entire mission.

Abandoning the still-cheering crowd around the Golden Galley, he ran back to the hangar where they had docked and scrambled up and into the shuttle.

"Why you back so soon?" Teff'ith demanded as Theron burst in on them.

"Something's wrong," he said, addressing Gnost-Dural. "I need to speak with the Director. Or Jace. Maybe both of them."

"Impossible," the Jedi said. "We don't have a secure channel."

Theron rushed up to the cockpit. He quickly surveyed the hangar through the window until he spotted a communications terminal in the corner.

"I can slice into the Imperial comm channels," he said. "Piggyback our signal on the station's secure network. Scramble it with a basic SIS encryption and bounce it through half a dozen relays so nobody knows where it's originating from.

"Should buy us a minute or two of secure time."

"Sounds risky," Teff'ith said.

"We don't have any choice," Theron insisted, still speaking to Gnost-Dural.

"Do what you have to do," the Jedi said.

Theron exited the shuttle and raced over to the comm

terminal, pulling his custom-designed slicer spike from the hip pocket of his uniform. The spike was small, about twice the size and thickness of a pen, with a small interface cable extending several centimeters from the bottom. He plugged the cable into one of the terminal's access ports and turned the spike on. A second later the spike's short-range signal synced up with Theron's cybernetic implants, allowing him to interface directly with Reaver Station's communications network.

His fingers flew over the keyboard as the spike relayed streams of data to his implants. It only took a minute for him to burrow his way through the various levels of electronic security and gain unrestricted access to the network's core operating system. It took several more minutes to set up the encryption and the complicated system of relay jumps, but it was a necessary precaution. He'd use them to buy a few minutes of secure transmission before the station's automated network systems responded to the unauthorized intrusion and shut them down.

He raced back over to the shuttle and climbed inside.

"Got it," he said as he settled into the pilot's seat. Gnost-Dural and Teff'ith crowded in on either side of him.

Theron switched the shuttle's transmitter on, keying it to the same frequency as the terminal in the hangar. He had to work fast, so he fired off an emergency priority signal to SIS, knowing protocols would relay it immediately to the Director wherever he was.

A few seconds later the Director's voice came through the ship's speaker; adding video to the signal would only have made things more complicated.

"Theron—what's wrong?"

"You heard about the attack on Ruan?"

"Of course," the Director said. "I'm in a debriefing with the Supreme Commander right now."

"Is everything all right, Theron?" Jace's voice chimed in. "Where are you calling from?"

"Reaver Station."

"Are you insane?" the Director sputtered.

"It's okay. The signal's secure. For now."

"You can't know that," the Director insisted. "What if the—"

"I don't have much time," Theron said, cutting him off. "I think the mission's been compromised."

"Why?" Jace demanded.

"The Empire should have used the black ciphers to transmit the orders to the capital ships. We should have known about the attack."

There was a moment of silence on the other end of the line before Jace said, "We knew."

"You . . . you knew?" Theron said, his mind struggling to grasp what he was hearing. "Why weren't we better prepared? Why didn't you do anything?"

"We sent medical supplies, food, and emergency volunteers," Jace replied.

"What about the reinforcements? Why were they too far away to get there in time? We should have scrambled one of our fleets."

"We couldn't," Jace said. "The risk of tipping off the Empire was too great. If they found a fleet waiting for them on Ruan, they'd know we were intercepting their cipher transmissions."

Horror slowly dawned on Theron as he realized what Jace was saying.

"You knew the Empire would wipe out our ships at Ruan. You knew they'd bombard the planet. Thousands of civilians are dead, and you did nothing to help them!"

"I had no choice," Jace said, his voice cold. "If we don't stop the *Ascendant Spear*, we don't stop this war. You're worried about thousands of innocent lives, but I'm worried about millions."

Theron didn't say anything. He sat in the pilot's chair, speechless as Satele's warning ran through his mind:

Jace fights this war out of revenge. It clouds his judgment. It can make him do terrible things if he believes they are necessary to save the Republic.

"Theron?" Jace said from the other end of the transmission. "Theron, are you still there?"

"We're here," Gnost-Dural spoke up.

"You have to see the big picture, Theron," Jace said, "We have to wait for our chance to stop the *Spear*. No matter how horrific these attacks may be."

"Attacks?" Theron said, snapping out of his daze. "Ruan wasn't the only one?"

"Theron," the Director's voice snapped. "Your job is to get on board the *Spear*! This doesn't concern you."

"Where will they strike next?" Theron demanded, ignoring the Director. "Jace—where?"

"Duro," the Supreme Commander said with a heavy sigh. "They're going to hit the shipyards in thirty-six standard hours."

Duro was a heavily industrialized and densely populated world. Though the planet itself was too polluted to support life, billions lived in the orbital cities above it. An Imperial attack on Duro would have minimal long-term strategic value for the Empire, but the casualties for the Republic were almost too catastrophic to fathom.

"You have to stop them," Theron said. "Set an ambush. Take out the Imperial fleet the second they enter the system."

"That's not going to happen," Jace told him. "The *Spear* isn't going to be involved in the attack."

"We're increasing Republic patrols in the sector," the Director added, "but if we scale them up too fast the Empire will grow suspicious."

"Theron, sometimes sacrifices have to be made," Jace said.

"But you have to draw the line somewhere!"

"The Empire won't. So neither can we."

Satele was right about you, Theron thought, remembering her final argument: *Hate will transform you into the very evil that you are fighting so hard against.*

"There's nothing you can do to stop this, Theron," the Director told him. "So do your duty. Complete your mission. The Republic is counting on you."

The transmission abruptly ended, though Theron wasn't sure if they had cut him off or if the Reaver's automated security systems had finally unraveled his tricks and disconnected the signal.

CHAPTER 23

THERON STOOD up from the pilot's seat slowly, his body and mind numb.

"Theron," Gnost-Dural asked, "are you okay?"

"The Director was right," Theron replied. "There's nothing we can do. An Imperial fleet is going to hit Duro, and we can't stop it."

"Call back," Teff'ith suggested. "Tell them you quit."

"There may be another way," Gnost-Dural said. "If the *Spear* was part of the Imperial fleet attacking Duro, Jace would be willing to set up an ambush."

"But it's not," Theron said, his mind unable to follow where the Jedi was heading. "The *Spear* will still be here when Duro is attacked."

"Maybe not. Can you send off another message?"

Theron shook his head. "Used every trick in my bag to pull that off. The network security programs automatically adjust and adapt to slicer attacks. They'll be able to lock me out almost instantly if I try it again. Probably even trace the location to this hangar."

"Then we need someone to deliver it." Gnost-Dural turned to Teff'ith. "We need your help."

"Not trying anything to get us killed," she warned.

"All you have to do is deliver a message," he told her. "Tell Jace Malcom that the *Ascendant Spear* will be at Duro."

"She'll never be able to get a message to the Republic

Supreme Commander," Theron said, suddenly under-standing where Gnost-Dural was headed. "But I know who can—Satele!"

"I should have thought of her myself," the Jedi agreed.

"Go to the Jedi enclave on Coruscant," he said to Teff'ith, speaking quickly. "Ask for Grand Master Satele Shan. Tell her everything that happened here."

"We fly Imperial shuttle to Coruscant, we get blown from the sky!" Teff'ith protested.

"Go back to Jigani Port and take my shuttle," Gnost-Dural said. "It's faster anyway."

"We leave, you two going to be stuck on Reaver Station," Teff'ith reminded them.

From her tone Theron wasn't sure if she was worried about them, or sarcastically pointing out something obvious she thought they were foolishly forgetting.

"Theron and I can look after ourselves," the Jedi as-sured her.

"Tell the authorities that I sent you," Theron said. "Grand Master Shan will listen if you mention my name."

"Grand Master Shan," Teff'ith said, her eyes narrow-ing suspiciously as she put two and two together. "Theron Shan. You related?"

"She's my mother," Theron said, the situation too ur-gent for him to even care whether Gnost-Dural already knew.

He expected Teff'ith to make some kind of comment, maybe ask why he wasn't a Jedi. But all she said was, "What's in it for us?"

"Another ten thousand credits," Theron promised. "And a get-out-of-jail-free card if you're ever arrested in Republic space."

"Deal."

Gnost-Dural turned his attention back to Theron. "You still need to get on the *Spear*. If you don't sabotage the systems, Karrid will be able to escape the Republic ambush."

"I'm on it," Theron said. "What about you?"

"I'm going to convince my old apprentice to take her ship to Duro."

Pulling the hood of his cloak up over his head to obscure his features, the Jedi slipped out of the shuttle and took off, moving with the supernatural speed of one driven by the Force. Theron watched him until he vanished through the hangar door, leaving him and Teff'ith alone.

"Can I trust you on this?" he asked the Twi'lek. "Millions of innocent lives are at stake."

"Ten thousand credits to deliver one message? Stupid not to do it."

"Good. Tell Satele Shan everything that happened here. She has to convince Jace to send the Republic fleet to Duro."

Theron wondered what the Director or Jace would say once they learned that a Twi'lek enforcer for the Old Tion Brotherhood now knew all the critical details of their top-secret mission. He'd probably get court-martialed, and rightfully so. But he trusted Teff'ith. More important, he didn't have any other options. Not if he wanted to keep Duro from being the site of one of the war's bloodiest massacres.

He started to leave the ship, then paused to say one last thing to Teff'ith. "Remember," he warned her. "Double-cross us and you don't get paid."

"Got it," she said, her lekku flicking in annoyance. "Said stupid not to do it. We not stupid."

GNOST-DURAL WAS little more than a blur of motion and movement as he raced through the corridors of Reaver Station. The Imperial soldiers he flew past reacted with a mix of surprise, curiosity, and alarm, but he came and went so fast none of them fully realized what had happened. Left in his wake, they exchanged a few puzzled glances with their friends, then laughed off the odd but seemingly harmless encounter as their minds convinced them that the person who'd just run by couldn't possibly have been moving that fast.

He didn't know exactly where he was going, but he let the Force guide him. When they'd first arrived at Reaver Station, he had gently reached out with his mind until he sensed his former Padawan. Now he was using her familiar presence—shrouded in the dark side, but still unmistakable after so many years—as a beacon to guide him to her.

At the same time, he was careful to mask his own presence so as not to warn her of his coming. As he drew closer it would be impossible to completely hide himself from her awareness should she suddenly choose to focus her thoughts on finding him, but there was no reason she would do so. Not until he was so close that it no longer mattered.

As he drew near the *Ascendant Spear*'s hangar, he slowed his pace. There were more people here, men and women returning from or heading out on shore leave. But none of the off-duty soldiers paid him any special heed. Those coming back to the ship were tired and inebriated, and those leaving were too eager to begin their leave to pay close enough attention to the hooded figure's hidden features to realize he wasn't human.

That changed when he reached the two guards on duty at one of the many boarding ramps leading from the hangar floor into the *Spear* itself.

"Who are you?" one demanded, stepping in his path.

She moved with a sure confidence that Gnost-Dural recognized all too well; he knew there would be little chance of using the Force to persuade her to let him pass. Should it be necessary, he was ready to resort to violence to get inside, but he thought there might still be another way.

He threw back his hood, revealing his alien features. He took deep, slow breaths through his mask, which gave off a deep, angry hiss in response as he tilted his head back slightly to make his tusks more prominent.

"My name is Darth Malitiae," he said, dropping his already baritone voice a full octave lower. "I have business with Darth Karrid."

The guard hesitated but held her ground, and he realized she would need more convincing. The Kel Dor extended his hand while simultaneously reaching out with the Force to apply a faint pressure on her windpipe.

She threw her hands up to her throat and her eyes went wide with terror as her air supply was cut off. After a few moments he released his hold, causing her to collapse to her knees as she took in deep, desperate gulps of oxygen.

"When a superior wants to pass," he snarled, "you would be wise to step aside."

"Forgive me, my Lord," the guard gasped as she crawled out of his way. Keeping her eyes carefully averted to the ground, she said, "I will inform Darth Karrid of your arrival."

"Darth Karrid is expecting me. I refuse to wait so my presence can be announced by some groveling worm," he sneered as he brushed past her.

The second guard made no move to stop him. Instead, he cowered off to one side, trying very hard not to be noticed.

The Jedi moved quickly up the boarding ramp and into the *Spear,* not certain how long the ruse would work. Though the guards hadn't dared to stop him, once he was gone they would almost surely inform someone on board the ship of their honored guest's arrival. It wouldn't take long after that for someone to realize something was wrong and order security to hunt down the intruder.

Still guided by the power of the Force emanating from Darth Karrid, he made his way deeper and deeper into the ship. He could feel evil and corruption enveloping him, growing steadily stronger during his descent, and he knew it wasn't because of his former Padawan's presence. When Darth Mekhis had created the *Ascendant Spear*, she'd used a combination of experimental technology and Sith alchemy to imbue the ship itself with the energies of the dark side. By the time Gnost-Dural stepped into the turbolift that would take him to the black heart of the vessel, the Jedi was feeling physically nauseated from the effects. But he also sensed he was nearing his goal.

As he dropped into the very bowels of the ship, the claustrophobic feeling of the dark side pressing in on him from all sides was so strong that he almost didn't sense the soldiers waiting in the corridor just beyond the turbolift's doors. At the last possible instant, the Force granted him a sudden premonition of the lethal trap. Pulling his green-bladed lightsaber from his belt he dropped to the ground, pressing himself facedown flat on the floor as the turbolift came to a stop on the *Spear*'s lowest level.

The guards' blaster bolts shredded the turbolift's doors as they slid open, ricocheting over Gnost-Dural's head as they carved an arc at waist height. The Jedi responded by lashing out with the Force, hurling the four heavily armored soldiers several meters back down the corridor. Before they even hit the ground he had sprung to his feet, charging toward them as he threw his lightsaber sidearm. The spinning blade struck the nearest of his foes, slicing through the chest plate of his battle armor and into the vulnerable flesh beneath.

The surviving three guards didn't try to regain their

feet, instead firing wildly at him from where they lay sprawled on the floor. The Kel Dor angled his charge toward the side wall, leaping and planting a foot halfway up the surface to give him leverage for a high, twisting spin that scraped the ceiling, his arms tucked in close to his chest and his horizontal body perfectly parallel to the floor.

The unexpected move again caught the soldiers off guard, their bolts whizzing beneath him. He landed on his feet amid his still-prone adversaries, his lightsaber flying back into his hand as he recalled it with the Force. He turned sideways, narrowly dodging fire from the closest soldier while a pair of quick flicks with his lightsaber deflected the bolts from the other two harmlessly off to either side.

The hard heel of his boot slammed down on the helmeted head of the man at his feet. At the same time he used the Force to pick up the other two and send them crashing into the ceiling before letting them drop back down to the floor. Momentarily stunned, all three were defenseless against the quick series of cuts and thrusts from his lightsaber that finished them off.

Knowing reinforcements wouldn't be far behind, he raced down the hall and burst through the door at the end, coming face-to-face with Darth Karrid and her two apprentices.

They were standing in a large, circular chamber: his former Padawan in the center, a male human on her right and a female pure-blooded Sith on her left. Behind Karrid he could see a large crystal sphere, and on the side wall he saw a small control console. Otherwise the room was empty.

All three of his adversaries wore black armor and sported the fierce facial tattoos so common in those who followed the dark side. Their lightsabers were drawn and ready, the shimmering blades casting a crimson glow over the dimly lit room. Clearly they were expecting him, though whether they had sensed his presence through the Force or had simply been warned by the guards outside, he couldn't say.

"I knew you would come for me one day, Gnost-Dural," Karrid said, her lips curling into a smile of anticipation. "But even you should know better than to challenge me here on my own ship."

"A Jedi pursues the dark side, no matter where it tries to hide," he answered.

"Noble and foolish as ever," she mocked. "You have no idea of how powerful I've become.

"Malgus showed me the true power," she said, her voice slowly rising with each word. "He led me down the path to greatness. He revealed the secrets you dared not face!

"He taught me to embrace all the things the Jedi fear!" she shouted, her voice echoing off the circular chamber's walls. "Now I will use them to destroy you and every follower you have brought onto my ship!"

"I have come alone," Gnost-Dural replied, remaining calm in the face of her growing anger. "It was my decision to send you to Darth Malgus. I started you on this path; no one else is to blame."

"How quaint," she said with a sneer. "I thought you'd led a strike team here to kill me, but you just want to save your Padawan from the perils of the dark side."

"I will purge the galaxy of the evil I unleashed upon it," he said, his voice betraying nothing beyond firm resolution. "Whether this ends in redemption or death is your decision, not mine."

Karrid casually twirled her lightsaber, carving long, lazy circles in the air as her apprentices fanned out to either side, slowly moving into position to flank the Jedi.

"I heard tales of your great prowess in battle while I was on Tython," she told him. "But during all my years as a Padawan I never saw any evidence of it. I'm curious to see how badly your reputation has been exaggerated."

Gnost-Dural sensed Imperial reinforcements drawing near. Spinning back to the door behind him, he thrust his lightsaber into the access panel on the wall, sending up a shower of sparks as he fried the circuits, sealing the door so nobody else could enter the room.

He wheeled back to face Karrid and her apprentices and slowly circled to his left, keeping his back against the wall as he tried to gauge the strength of his opponents.

"You've given yourself over to the *Ascendant Spear*," Gnost-Dural warned his former Padawan, holding his own weapon steady in front of him, two hands on the hilt in a classic defensive posture. "It has consumed your thoughts and training. In learning to master this ship, your other skills have atrophied."

"That is why I don't intend to face you alone," Karrid said.

A slight nod of the Falleen's head sent her apprentices rushing forward, and Master Gnost-Dural braced to meet their charge.

CHAPTER 24

THERON HAD no idea what Gnost-Dural was planning, but he knew he had to get on the *Ascendant Spear* quickly. Instead of heading back to the Golden Galley where he might hope to steal a boarding pass, he headed for the hangar where the ship had docked.

The scene was one of chaos—hundreds of crew members milled around the hangar, clearly agitated. Six guards stood with weapons drawn, lined up at the base of each of the half dozen ramps leading into the ship, blocking the way.

Theron slipped into the crowd, studying the guards. He quickly realized they weren't allowing anyone to leave the vessel. Anyone trying to board was subject to a lengthy interrogation and inspection of their ID before being allowed to pass; the delay was causing a steady increase in the crowd waiting impatiently to be allowed back on.

Whatever Gnost-Dural had done had caused security to clamp down hard.

"What's going on?" Theron asked a tall woman beside him.

"Your guess is as good as mine," she answered, clearly annoyed and not entirely sober. "I just want to get back to my bunk."

There were angry murmurs in the crowd, and a handful of people actually pushed through to verbally con-

front the guards at the base of the boarding ramps—
something that would never have happened a year ago.
Imperial citizens were raised in a military culture that
trained them to respect authority. But the traditional
discipline of the Imperial troops had been frayed by their
recent setbacks in the war. And with hundreds of tired
and drunk crew members coming back from R&R, tem-
pers were high.

An idea struck Theron. It was crazy, impulsive, and
risky . . . in other words, just his style.

He worked his way through the crowd, heading out of
the hangar and back into Reaver Station. He remembered passing by a small security post: a room where the
soldiers responsible for inspecting the incoming vessels
could pass the time while they waited for arrivals. With
C wing shut down to other traffic because of the *Spear*'s
presence, the guard post was unstaffed.

Theron paused at the door, glancing around quickly,
and made sure nobody in the crowd of people passing
by was paying any attention to him; they were too
wrapped up in their own thoughts and conversations, or
focused on meeting up with friends to enjoy their brief
time on the station away from whatever vessel they
served on.

He pulled the slicer spike from his pocket, concealing
it in his palm as he clipped it into the access panel on the
wall. He was careful to stand straight and tall, his shoulders back and his head held high as he quickly sliced
through the locked door; hunching over and other fur-
tive behavior would draw far more attention from the
people walking by than someone who clearly looked
like he had every right to be there.

The door slid open and Theron stepped confidently
into the small room beyond before closing it behind
him. The guard post was crowded—four chairs packed
in around a large control console, with vidscreens dis-

playing the various hangars across the station: EMPTY; PENDING ARRIVAL; SECURITY CHECK IN PROGRESS; CLEARED TO BOARD. Every hangar in C wing was set to the same status: INACTIVE.

Because hangar security needed to know the number and size of incoming vessels so they could properly handle inspections, the guard post had access to Reaver Station's external scanners and the early-warning beacons. The beacons were the first line of defense, strategically placed to detect incoming vessels long before they actually reached Reaver Station.

It didn't take long for Theron to slice into the system. The scanners currently showed a few dozen Imperial vessels in the sector, arriving, departing, or waiting for clearance from the central tower to land.

He quickly verified that Teff'ith was gone; the status display of the hangar where they had docked now read EMPTY. Satisfied, he made a small adjustment to one of the settings on his slicer spike, then began to feed a steady stream of false data into the system.

Several dozen vessels ranging in size from single-pilot fighters all the way up to full capital ships suddenly materialized on the scanners, popping into existence near the early-warning beacons. The data mimicked the effect of a large, well-coordinated fleet dropping from hyperspace all at once on the farthest edges of the sector. A few seconds later alarms began to ring out through Reaver Station warning of the simulated Republic attack.

THE SIZZLE and hum of clashing blades echoed off the walls of the cavernous chamber as Karrid's apprentices engaged Gnost-Dural. Their attacks were basic variations on the Makashi style, a precise and economical lightsaber form designed for maximum results with minimal movement by stressing jabs and thrusts.

Their skills were raw; like Karrid much of their training had focused on developing the unique abilities required to help their Master command the *Ascendant Spear*. They were still able to call on the fury of the dark side to move with astonishing strength and speed, but they hadn't mastered the subtle art of allowing the Force to guide their blades. They were wielding the weapon instead of allowing it to become an extension of themselves.

Nevertheless they were relentless in their attacks, and there were two of them. Gnost-Dural was forced onto the defensive to ward off their attacks, occasionally slipping in quick maneuvers drawn from the more aggressive Ataru form to keep them off balance.

Darth Karrid merely observed the battle at first, keeping a safe distance from the deadly blade of her former Master while his focus and energies were drained by her apprentices.

Realizing he would eventually wear down if he allowed the battle to become a duel of attrition, the Kel Dor countered with Djem So, the fifth of the seven recognized lightsaber forms. Concentrating his counterattacks exclusively on the physically smaller female Sith, he unleashed a series of savage blows, driving her into a stumbling retreat.

For an instant he was left completely exposed to her human companion, but the unexpected ferocity of Gnost-Dural's sudden switch in tactics caught him unprepared. He hesitated a fraction of a second before thrusting forward, giving the Jedi enough time to leap aside, even as his Sith opponent tripped over her own backpedaling feet and fell to the floor.

Gnost-Dural lunged forward to deliver a coup de grâce, but his momentum was suddenly reversed and he found himself sailing backward as Darth Karrid hit him with a powerful Force push. He was able to roll into a back somersault as he hit the ground and spring back to his feet, but his brief advantage was lost.

The two apprentices closed on him again, cutting him off before he could even think about charging toward Karrid. As they approached, he sensed the Imperial reinforcements in the hall outside, scrambling to restore power to the sealed door so they could join the fray.

Knowing he was running out of time, Gnost-Dural switched tactics again. He thrust out with a powerful Force wave, sweeping them both off their feet. But before he could finish off his prone opponents Karrid unleashed a blast of crackling dark side energy in his direction. Gnost-Dural leapt clear, the deadly blue lightning scorching the floor where he had been standing an instant before.

He threw his lightsaber in Karrid's direction, sending it end-over-end on a direct line with his target. The Falleen parried the attack with her own blade, though she was forced to retreat a step to absorb the impact. Gnost-Dural was already in motion, charging past her apprentices before they could scramble to their feet. His lightsaber flew back into his outstretched palm as he fell on Karrid.

He had trained her in Niman, the sixth and most balanced form of lightsaber combat. Malgus might have taught her other styles, but faced with Gnost-Dural's furious assault she instinctively fell back into the one she had learned before all others. Niman lent itself well to the Jedi ways, eschewing naked aggression for balance and economy of movement that relied on focus and precision. As a Sith Lord who drew her strength from channeling the raw emotional fury of the dark side, the style compromised Karrid's abilities. The effect was minimal, but it was more than enough for Gnost-Dural to exploit.

He used a quick shove with the Force to send her off balance and brought his lightsaber in high to strike at her shoulder. When she raised her own blade to block the blow, he dropped low and took her feet out from under her with a sweep of his leg.

Karrid toppled over, but the Jedi was forced to turn his back on her to engage the female Sith as she leapt to Karrid's aid. They exchanged a quick series of blows— plenty of time for Karrid to regain her feet. Instead of attempting to finish Gnost-Dural off by attacking from his flank, however, she retreated from the melee, putting the preservation of her own life above the opportunity to finish off her opponent.

The male apprentice joined in a second later, and Gnost-Dural switched to the defensive Soresu form. He could sense fatigue seeping into his muscles: the toll of the battle was wearing him down, fractionally slowing his blade and leaving him more vulnerable to the Force attacks of his enemies. An instant later the door *whoosh*ed open and a dozen Imperial guards spilled into the room.

Karrid held up a hand to indicate they should hold their fire.

"The outcome is inevitable," Karrid called out to him as he fought off the twin attacks of her apprentices. "I sense your exhaustion. Throw down your weapon and I will let you beg for mercy."

Gnost-Dural hadn't expected to win the battle. From the moment he decided to board the *Ascendant Spear*, he'd known defeating Karrid was a near impossibility. But he wasn't about to surrender and grovel at her feet— if for no other reason than that if he did, she would be suspicious and his true plan would never work.

"I didn't come here seeking victory," he said.

Karrid's head tilted to the side as she searched for the meaning behind his words. Failing to grasp it, she turned to the soldiers arrayed just inside the door.

"I want him alive," she told the captain.

Gnost-Dural used the last of his dwindling strength to call on the Force for a final desperate leap that sent him hurtling over the apprentices' heads toward his former Padawan.

The attack was doomed to failure; there were a dozen ways Karrid could have avoided or repelled the attack. But she didn't even have to react as the soldiers opened fire with a dozen blasters all set to stun. The bolts knocked the Jedi from the air and sent him slamming hard to the ground. His lightsaber fell from his paralyzed fingers, the blade extinguished as the hilt clattered to the floor.

As he lay there facedown struggling to cling to consciousness, Karrid strode over and picked up his lightsaber, tucking it into her belt like a hunter claiming a trophy from a prized kill. She rolled him over onto his back with her boot, then crouched down to peer into his masked face.

"You knew you couldn't win this battle," she said. "So why did you really come here?"

Gnost-Dural had no intention of answering her question, but even if he had his voice would have been drowned out by the sounds of an alarm ringing through the ship.

Karrid snapped her head in the direction of the guard captain, who was listening intently to a message coming over the receiver in his ear.

"Reaver Station is under attack!" he blurted out. "A Republic fleet has been detected in the sector. ETA sixteen minutes!"

"Activate our shields," Karrid answered, concerned but not panicked. "Recall all crew to their posts. We leave dock in twelve minutes. Anyone not on board will be left behind and face a full court-martial."

As the captain relayed her commands to the person on

the other end of the transmission, Karrid turned back to look down at Gnost-Dural.

"Was this your plan? Sacrifice yourself so the Republic could catch us in port and unprepared? Or is there more to your scheme?"

Gnost-Dural stayed silent, the edges of his vision growing dim as the blackness closed in, the blaring alarms growing fainter and more distant.

Just before he finally lost consciousness, he heard Karrid say, "This is another battle you cannot win. The Imperial interrogators will make you tell me everything."

REAVER STATION was in chaos. The alarms echoing through the station were quickly matched by alarms from every ship docked in the hangars as the central tower spread word of the Republic fleet closing in.

Men and women sprinted back to their vessels, scrambling to get to their battle stations before the enemy arrived. Theron didn't know how long it would take for his ruse to be discovered, but he knew he had to act fast.

He ran from the guard post, joining the stampede of soldiers bearing down on the hangar where the *Ascendant Spear* was docked. As he burst into the bay, he was swept up in the crowd and carried toward the ramps. The guards keeping the crew from boarding the ship were gone, either recalled onto the *Spear* or overwhelmed by the sudden crush of people scrambling to get to their posts.

Theron continued to let the crowd carry him along, heading up the ramp and into the vessel. Once aboard, the crowd thinned quickly as people broke off in different directions, heading to their assigned stations.

Theron did his best to look like he knew where he was going, though in truth he had no idea. He'd only had time to plan out how he'd get himself on the ship. Now that he was aboard he needed to figure out something new, and it was hard to concentrate due to the incessant clang of the *Spear*'s warning klaxon.

It wasn't unheard of for new crew members to get lost when first assigned to a ship as large as the *Ascendant Spear*, and there were diagrams of the ship's basic layout posted at several places along the bulkheads. He stopped to check one, quickly memorizing the layout before choosing his destination. He needed somewhere with access to the ship's main systems so he could slice in and plant the virus, but it had to be isolated enough for him to work in private.

His eyes fell on the engine room near the rear of the ship. Separated from the rest of the vessel by a heavily shielded bulkhead to guard against explosions and radioactive discharges, it was accessible only through a single maintenance hatch.

Moving with a new sense of purpose, he worked his way through the ship toward the turbolift leading down to the vessel's lowest level. He encountered fewer and fewer people as he went, and by the time he reached the lift he was alone.

Before he could press the button to call it, the doors slid open to reveal a short, heavyset woman in a major's uniform.

"Corporal!" she snapped on seeing Theron waiting for the elevator. "Where do you think you're going?"

"Shorry, shir," Theron said, slurring his words and snapping off a sloppy salute. He squinted one eye closed as he swayed unsteadily on his feet. "Gotta get to my posht."

"This lift is reserved!" she barked, her voice even louder than the incessant alarms. "Authorized personnel only!"

"Alarmsh woke me up," Theron mumbled. "Gotta get to en-ger . . . en-ger . . . en-ger-reering."

"You're drunk!" she spat, her voice filled with disgust. "Are you scheduled for duty?"

"Oh-nine-hundred," he replied.

"That's not for another six hours," she said with an exasperated shake of her head. "Go back and sleep it off in your bunk."

"Shure thing, shir," Theron said, fumbling out another clumsy salute.

He turned and staggered off in the opposite direction, down the corridor and around the corner. Once he was out of sight he dropped the act and moved quickly down the passage, taking a series of twists and turns that eventually doubled him back to the turbolift.

Peering around the corner, he made sure the major was gone before making a dash for the lift. He waited impatiently for the doors to open, then slipped inside and punched the button for G Deck, hoping he wouldn't run into anyone else.

Luck was with him. He didn't see anybody as he made his way from the elevator to the engine room's access hatch. Unlike the automated doors controlled by access panels, this was an old durasteel hinge model, opened by turning a heavy wheel in the center of the hatch.

The wheel was stiff from lack of use, and despite his best efforts Theron couldn't budge it. He realized the maintenance crew probably used a wrench to gain the necessary leverage, but all he had was his pistol. He looked around the empty corridor, trying to find something else he could use. Seeing nothing, he shrugged and pulled the blaster from the holster on his hip, jamming it into the spokes of the door's wheel.

Grabbing the pistol's grip with one hand and the barrel with the other he pulled for all he was worth. The veins on his neck bulged as his muscles strained. Just as he thought he was going to pass out from the effort, the wheel let loose with a groan and moved a quarter turn.

Theron adjusted his grip on the pistol and pulled
again. The wheel moved more easily this time; another
quarter turn. He regripped for a third time and pulled.
The wheel completed its revolution and the door popped
open with a loud clang.

Standing motionless, he waited to see if anyone would
respond to the noise, but all he heard was the clanging
alarm. When he removed the pistol from the spokes of
the wheel he noticed that the barrel had been bent. The
weapon was useless.

Out of habit he slapped it into his leg holster, then
stepped in through the hatch, pulling the heavy durasteel
door closed behind him. He turned the wheel on the inside a quarter turn—enough to keep the hatch from
popping open, but not so far he'd have to struggle to
open it when he was ready to get out.

He was standing on a narrow metal walkway that
ran the full forty-meter length of the engine room. To his
left was a reinforced bulkhead, to his right the *Spear*'s
massive hyperdrive and the enormous ion engines that
propelled the ship when it moved at sublight speeds.
The walls and ceiling were covered with a maze of pipes,
tubes, cords, and wires running among hundreds of
seemingly randomly placed electrical boxes, fuse panels,
and computer chip relays.

In addition to the alarms he could still hear and feel
through the vibrations in the walkway, there was a
steady, low-pitched hum coming from the ion engines.
The air in the engine room was twenty degrees warmer
than the corridor he had just come in from, and it
smelled of ozone and burning plastic.

*If the heat doesn't make me pass out, the fumes just
might.*

There were no control panels down here in the bowels
of the ship, but Theron knew he could slice the *Spear* by
tapping directly into the main system. All he had to do

was figure out which of the hundreds of wires and relays connected the engine room to the primary command console on the bridge.

Shouldn't take more than a few hours, right?

To his relief, the clanging alarms finally stopped. The blessed silence was broken by two long blasts from a distant horn, and the ground shifted under his feet as the *Ascendant Spear* disengaged from Reaver Station.

Guess you're not leaving anytime soon, he thought. *Might as well get to work.*

CHAPTER 25

THE IMPERIAL shuttle's ten-hour journey from Reaver Station back to Jigani Port gave Teff'ith plenty of time to think about her deal with Theron. She wasn't entirely sure what had happened, but the basic details were clear—Theron and the weird-looking Jedi were trying something crazy and foolish, and if she didn't deliver her message to Grand Master Satele Shan a lot of people were going to die.

She tried to tell herself she didn't really care what happened to a bunch of people she'd never met, but during the long flight her mind kept conjuring up images of orbital cities in ruins, the bodies of men, women, and children scattered among the wreckage. She'd seen plenty of pictures of death and destruction on the holovids and never given them a second thought, but this was different. Those people were already dead; there was no point worrying about them. The ones on Duro were still alive.

No profit for us in letting them die, she thought, reminding herself why she was really doing this. Theron had promised her a big fat payday when this was all over, and it wasn't like she was taking any real risk. Agreeing to the job had actually gotten her off Reaver Station before the Jedi and Theron pulled off whatever crazy stunt they were planning.

Only risk is if Theron doesn't make it, she thought. She realized the thought of him dying on Reaver Station actually bothered her more than thinking of all the nameless victims on Duro. Try as she might, she couldn't convince herself it was entirely because he wouldn't be able to pay her.

She slept for a few hours, letting the shuttle's autopilot navigate through hyperspace. She dreamed of Ngani Zho, the crazy old Jedi who'd thrown himself in front of a blaster bolt meant for her, sacrificing his life for her own. But she didn't dream of their time together or his death; in her dreams it was like the old man had never left.

Teff'ith was on the Imperial shuttle, heading back to Jigani Port. Ngani Zho was sitting in the seat beside her. His scraggly gray hair and bushy eyebrows were wild and disheveled—looking at him, it wouldn't be hard to imagine he had never owned a comb in his life. He wore an old Jedi robe, wrinkled and stained, with the hood thrown back. There were several charred holes in his chest where the blasters had ripped through him, but his blue eyes were sharp and bright.

"I expected better from you, Teff'ith," he said. "You think I gave my life up just so you could keep on working for the Black Sun?"

"Pft. Work for Old Tion Brotherhood now."

"That's not the point."

"Big things ahead for us."

"At least we agree on that."

"Why did you save us?"

A beep from the autopilot alerting her that they were preparing to drop out of hyperspace startled her awake before the man in her dream could give her an answer.

"Stupid Jedi," Teff'ith muttered as she switched the shuttle over to manual control.

She dropped from hyperspace in the Desevro system, charted a course for the shuttle to bring her into Jigani Port, then opened a holochannel.

"Welcome back, Sunshine!" Gorvich said once the holo was connected. "Quick turnaround. I guess everything must have gone real smooth."

"Not smooth. Left Jedi and Theron at Reaver Station."

Gorvich chuckled. "Sounds like a good story. Lay it on me."

"Not over comm channels. Meet us at Jedi's fancy shuttle. You move it?"

"Nah, it's still in the hangar at Jigani Port. How long till you get there?"

"Thirty minutes," she said, flicking off the holo so she wouldn't have to deal with Gorvich for one second longer than absolutely necessary.

By the time she arrived at the hangar where the *Prosperity* was parked, Gorvich was already waiting for her.

"Okay, Sunshine. We're here. So what's the deal? Why'd you ditch the others?"

She hesitated, choosing her words carefully. She wanted to tell Gorvich as little about what had happened as possible. If he knew Theron had offered her ten thousand credits, he'd want a cut.

"Didn't ditch them. Told us to go. Need us to deliver a message."

"I don't follow," Gorvich said, scratching his head. "You going back to pick them up later?"

"Not part of the plan."

"So how are they going to get off Reaver Station?"

Teff'ith shrugged. "Never told us. Just said take shuttle. Go deliver message."

Gorvich shook his head. "I knew they were up to

something funny. This won't come back later and bite me when I'm not looking, will it?"

"You be fine," the Twi'lek assured him.

Gorvich crossed his arms and stared at Teff'ith, his eyes staying above the neck for a change.

"I know you're keeping something from me, Sunshine. But I'll let it slide since you set this whole deal up."

"Still owe us our cut," she reminded him.

"Don't worry, I got the credits stashed away somewhere safe." Gorvich laughed—a mean, spiteful sound. "Guess we aren't going to get those bonus credits your friend promised, though."

"Might still make it off Reaver Station," Teff'ith said, a little more defensively than she intended.

"I'm just going to assume he's not coming back," Gorvich said. "Good thing we took this shuttle for collateral. Already got a couple of buyers lined up."

Seeing Teff'ith's scowl, he added, "Hey, I didn't think any of you was going to make it back."

"Why you sent us with them? Want to keep all the credits for yourself?"

"Water under the bridge, Sunshine," he said with an indifferent shrug. "Now that you're back I'm happy to share."

"Can't sell shuttle," she told him, already tiring of the conversation. "Need it to deliver message."

"Whoa, hold on a second. What are you talking about? You think I'm going to just let you take off in my collateral?" Gorvich's eyes narrowed. "How do I know you and your friends aren't trying to pull a fast one? You say they're still on Reaver Station, but for all I know you dropped them off at some luxury resort. Then they send you back here to get the *Prosperity* so you can all meet up later and get out of paying me the rest of the credits I was promised!"

"Idiot," Teff'ith said with a shake of her head, turning away from him and heading toward the shuttle.

"One more step and I ventilate your pretty little skull, Sunshine."

She turned around slowly to see Gorvich had drawn his blaster and was pointing it right at her.

"Saved your life on Nar Shaddaa," she hissed.

"That's why I didn't shoot you in the back," he admitted. "But I don't like being played. So stop holding out and tell me what's really going on."

Teff'ith bit her lip, trying to find a way to talk herself out of this without having to cut Gorvich in on her side deal. In the end, she couldn't do it.

"Theron offered ten thousand credits to deliver message to Coruscant. Gotta take fancy shuttle to get there in time."

"Ten thousand credits, huh?" Gorvich lowered his blaster, though he didn't put it away.

"Cut you in for three," Teff'ith said.

"Hold on a second, Sunshine," he said, holding up his free hand. "You really believe you're going to get ten thousand credits just to deliver a message to Coruscant? You're dreaming."

"Deal's good," she insisted, not wanting to get into the details.

"You don't think Coruscant customs has access to the *Prosperity*'s records? They'll toss you in jail for theft the second you touch down."

Teff'ith hadn't considered that. Hopefully she'd be able to convince the authorities that she really did have an urgent message for Grand Master Satele Shan.

"Hah, didn't think of that, did you?" Gorvich gloated, recognizing the reason for her silence. "See, that's why you need me around watching out for you."

"Worth the risk," Teff'ith argued. "Ten thousand credits too good to pass up."

"If he pays you. He already owes us another twenty on credit. And remember how he renegotiated the original deal? He says ten now, but when it comes time to pay who knows how much he'll actually be willing to fork over. Maybe zero."

"Won't be zero," Teff'ith grumbled.

"Even if he comes through with the ten he promised and the twenty he already owes us, I've got a better deal for you," Gorvich said. "Forget about the message. We sell the *Prosperity* and split the profit. We both come out way ahead in that game."

Teff'ith wasn't surprised by Gorvich's plan; he was a despicable man with no honor. But he knew how to turn a profit. And everything he'd said about Theron was true—Theron *had* reneged on the original deal. And even if she delivered the message and he didn't double-cross her, there was a good chance whatever crazy plan he was trying to pull off wouldn't work. If he was killed or captured by the Sith, she could kiss her credits good-bye.

"Well, Sunshine, what's it going to be?"

"How much we get for the shuttle?"

"Fifty thousand, easy. Plus I've still got your cut of the thirty I stashed away."

If she tried to help Theron, Gorvich might just shoot her where she stood. Even if she tricked or overpowered him, her days with the Old Tion Brotherhood would be over. And there was a good chance she might not get paid anyway.

Or she could abandon Theron, keep working with Gorvich, and continue climbing the ranks of the Brotherhood while making an easy forty thousand credits.

"Good money, Sunshine," Gorvich prodded. "Enough to ease any guilt about betraying a friend."

And how long till you betray us?

Teff'ith sprang into action, hoping to catch Gorvich

off guard as he waited for her answer. He was standing three steps away from her, his gun still pointed casually at the ground. Her first step was free. On her second his eyes went wide with the realization of what was happening. On the third he was bringing the gun up, but he only got it halfway before she knocked it out of his hand with a spinning back kick. She followed it up with a jumping front kick, swinging her foot as hard as she could and catching him right between the legs. Gorvich collapsed on the ground, curled up in the fetal position, groaning softly.

Teff'ith scooped up his fallen pistol, pointed it at him, then decided not to pull the trigger. Instead, she tucked it into her belt and raced over to the shuttle. She punched in the access code and the *Prosperity*'s boarding ramp descended with a soft hiss from the pressurized cabin. She ran up it, turning to glance back at Gorvich.

He was still on the floor, but he was crawling toward the ship. He met her eye with a hate-filled gaze. Something in that look made Teff'ith realize he wasn't done yet. Reacting on pure instinct, she threw herself back and to the side, grabbing one of the boarding ramp's struts to keep from falling off. At the same time, Gorvich's hand flickered, dropping to the sharpened blade he kept strapped to his thigh and hurling it in her direction with a single, well-practiced motion almost too quick for the eye to follow.

The blade buried itself deep in Teff'ith's shoulder, almost knocking her off the boarding ramp. Using the strut for leverage, she hauled herself into the ship and hit the button to close the boarding ramp behind her, acutely aware that if she hadn't tried to get out of the way the blade now protruding from her shoulder would have buried itself deep in her back. Ignoring her injury, she rushed to the cockpit, fired up the engine, sent the signal to open the hangar doors, and took to the air.

Back on the ground Gorvich crawled over to the control panel and hauled himself up, slamming the button to close the hangar doors with his fist.

Teff'ith saw the hangar doors stop at halfway open, then slowly start to close again. She gritted her teeth, yanked back hard on the control stick to send the ship hurtling forward, and braced for impact.

The *Prosperity*'s hull, like everything else about the vessel, was top-of-the-line. The multiple layers of durasteel plating and the reinforced frame struck the hangar's doors and wrenched them off their hinges, sending them flying as the thrusters powered the ship on through and up into the sky.

Climbing toward the upper atmosphere, Teff'ith felt a subtle shimmy in the shuttle's formerly velvet-smooth ride, but checking the ship's instrument panel showed no significant damage. A few minutes later she was far enough away from the planet's gravitational field to engage the hyperspace drive and activate the advanced autopilot to take her to Coruscant.

Only then did she tend to her wounded shoulder, digging out the medkit from beneath the pilot's seat. She inspected the blade, making sure she wouldn't bleed out if she pulled it free. Fortunately it had struck muscle and bone rather than a major artery, and she was able to remove it without any real difficulty . . . though doing so made her tilt her head back and scream.

Blocking out the pain, she treated and dressed the wound with the efficiency of one all too familiar with administering back-alley medicine. She inspected her work one final time before taking a pair of kolto-filled hypodermics and jabbing them into her thigh.

The pain disappeared almost instantly, and she felt a pleasant warmth spreading through her. She shifted in her seat and the chair responded by automatically adjusting itself to her new position, enveloping her in luxurious comfort.

She turned her head to the side and saw Ngani Zho once again sitting in the seat beside her.

"I'm proud of you, my girl. For sparing Gorvich, and for making the right choice."

"Now maybe stupid Jedi leave us alone," she murmured, her words trailing off into a soft snore.

"I HAVE the latest casualty estimates for tomorrow's attack on Duro," the Director said.

"Do you really think I want to see them?" Jace asked. The Supreme Commander was slumped in the chair behind his desk, his hand clutching an empty glass. He leaned forward and grabbed the long neck of the half-full bottle in front of him and refilled his drink for what Marcus guessed wasn't the first time this evening.

"The extra patrols you're sending help. Not much, but a little."

"We save a few hundred," Jace grunted bitterly. "But we still sacrifice thousands."

"We could try to come up with an excuse to have an actual fleet orbiting the planet," the Director suggested. "Make up some honor to give to one of Duro's citizens. Have the ships there as part of the celebration."

"Imagine you're the Imperial Minister of Logistics," Jace said, his words clear despite the alcohol he'd consumed. "What would you think if you found a ceremonial fleet stationed at Duro when you launched your surprise attack? Would you believe it was just coincidence?"

The Director sighed. "No. I'd think the cipher codes had been compromised."

Jace raised his drink in a silent toast to his honesty, then downed it in a single gulp.

"Grab yourself a glass," he said, nodding over to the bar in the corner as he refilled his own.

The Director did just that before sitting in one of the chairs on the opposite side of the Supreme Commander's desk. Jace held the bottle up and Marcus extended his glass.

"You think Theron's going to follow through on the mission?" Jace asked as he poured.

Marcus drained half his drink before answering, "He's my best agent."

"You used to say he was 'one of the best,' " Jace noted.

"I upgraded him after he brought back the black cipher."

"What about Gnost-Dural? He's a Jedi." Jace emptied his glass again. "They're not always great at following orders that don't fit their understanding of the universe."

"I think he's smart enough to understand why we had to do this. And aborting the mission doesn't help Duro."

"So you think they'll go forward?"

"I think so. They both care too much about the Republic to let this go off the rails."

"And after this is over—after we bring down the *Spear* and finally put an end to this blasted war—you think Theron will ever forgive me?"

The Director didn't answer; instead he just drained what was left of his drink.

"Do you support my decision?" Jace wanted to know.

"I do," Marcus said. "It's the right call. Don't know if I could have made it, though. And I don't know how either of us is supposed to live with it."

Jace grabbed the bottle and refilled their glasses.

"Making a decision like this is brutal," the Supreme Commander agreed. "But living with it is worse."

CHAPTER 26

HUNCHED OVER one of the many computer relay panels in the *Ascendant Spear*'s engine room, Theron wiped the sweat away from his brow before it ran down and stung his eyes. With the help of his slicer spike, he tapped into the panel and ran a diagnostic search to map out the various systems it was connected to.

Theron had been hiding in the engine room ever since the *Spear* left Reaver Station. He had no way to get off the vessel until it docked again short of stealing an escape pod, which would trigger an emergency alarm and get him blasted out of existence. Fortunately, the hours he'd been stuck on the narrow walkway in the sweltering, reeking engine room had actually proved beneficial. Realizing he wasn't going anywhere soon, Theron had spent his time trying to get a better understanding of the vessel's inner workings.

Mapping each relay individually was a simple but time-consuming process—one he'd already repeated over a dozen times. But the grueling work was the key to piecing together a complete picture of the *Spear*'s control systems. There was no single central network connecting everything; each system was controlled independently, linked to several different relays that could allow functionality to be rerouted through multiple pathways if something went wrong.

His exploration of the engine room was proving to be

simultaneously exhausting, fascinating, and disheartening. The complexity of the ship was mind boggling. It was the crowning achievement of Darth Mekhis's experimental weapons program. SIS had long suspected that there was some kind of link between the vessel itself and whoever was in command; Mekhis had specialized in combining biology and cybernetics. But the full scope of the symbiotic relationship went far beyond anything they had theorized.

Whenever Theron sliced into a computer terminal, his cybernetic implants allowed him to interface directly with the network. But there was still a wall of separation, a clear distinction between user and device. Mekhis had found a way to tear down that wall; when Karrid was in command of the *Spear* the ship became part of her . . . or maybe she became part of the ship. They were inseparable. The connection gave her the ability to read and react almost instantly during a battle, the *Spear*'s sensors relaying information directly into her awareness, then responding immediately to her commands.

It also gave her a heightened awareness of everything that was happening with the vessel's systems while she was linked to the ship. Theron would have to be extremely cautious with anything he did, taking extra care to use a light touch so Karrid wouldn't sense his presence. And he realized the original plan of planting a dormant virus probably wouldn't work.

Even if Karrid didn't notice the intrusion, the *Spear* had multiple layers of safeguards and redundancies that would quickly isolate and disable the virus, the relays cutting off the malware as they rerouted the damaged functions through a new path.

The only hope of effectively sabotaging the vessel was for Theron to be actively slicing the system while the *Spear* was in battle, shifting and switching his electronic attacks to stay a step ahead of the vessel's security protocols. The dilemma of how he was supposed to actually get off the ship if he was actively sabotaging it in the middle of a battle was something he tried not to worry about for the moment.

On the plus side, the *Spear*'s unique design allowed Theron's own cybernetic implants to operate at peak efficiency while he was plugged into the ship, giving him a level of access unlike anything he'd experienced before. He'd already managed to patch into the ship's internal communications, allowing the implant in his ear to receive all their transmissions.

"Red Patrol checking in," a voice chimed in his ear. "E Deck is clear. Proceeding to F Deck."

Theron sighed and disconnected his slicer spike from the panel. He stood up straight, stretching to ease a crick in his back.

Tapping into the comm systems had allowed him to follow the progress of the security patrols Karrid had dispatched once she realized the Republic fleet hadn't really existed. Theron had been tracking them closely as they systematically worked their way through each level of the vessel wing by wing. He hated to interrupt his work, but it was time to move if he didn't want to be discovered.

He went to the durasteel maintenance hatch and slowly turned the wheel to open it. There was a sharp clink as the hatch popped free, and a soft squeak from the hinges as it swung open. Theron poked his head out into the corridor, not expecting to see anyone but also not willing to take any chances. His only weapon was the blaster he had tucked in the holster of his uniform, but he had no intention of firing it after bending the barrel prying open the engine room's security hatch.

Fortunately the hall was deserted, so he climbed out and closed the hatch behind him, trying not to make any noise. He worked his way down the hall, listening intently for the footsteps of anyone approaching. It wasn't likely he would run into anybody; G Deck consisted primarily of the engine room and, way on the opposite end, the *Spear*'s private command chamber. Apart from the security sweep, nobody had any reason to be on the level. Even Karrid wouldn't venture down unless the *Spear* was about to go into battle.

Two turbolifts—one near the engine room at the stern, the other near the command chamber at the bow—were the only ways to access the lowest level of the ship. Theron knew the security patrols worked from stern to bow, so he carefully made his way toward the stern, away from the lift he had taken when he first boarded the vessel.

Because of the size and irregular shape of the ion and hypermatter drives, the two sides of G Deck weren't connected by a single straight corridor. The hall twisted and turned. At each bend, Theron paused and peeked around the corner, knowing if he was discovered he would have a hard time explaining his presence. After several minutes of careful skulking, he finally reached the turbolift near the front of the vessel. The hall continued another thirty meters before finally terminating in a large, sealed door.

Theron knew the *Spear*'s command chamber lay beyond, but he resisted the urge to go investigate. The engine room was where he could do the most damage; no point in risking exposure by snooping around just to satisfy his curiosity. He hit the panel on the turbolift, contemplating his next move as he waited for it to arrive. In his ear he could hear the progress of the security team as they reported back each time they cleared another section of the deck above him.

Theron considered heading up to the crew quarters on C Deck. He could look for an untended cabin where he could switch his grubby uniform for fresh clothes, leaving him less likely to draw attention if he needed to move around the ship. He might even get a chance to swap his blaster for one that worked. But whoever's uniform and weapon he borrowed was likely to notice if one or the other was missing, and that could reinforce suspicions about a stowaway on board. The last thing he needed to worry about was another round of security sweeps.

When the turbolift arrived, he realized he'd have more luck going to the laundry on E Deck. He could also try to sneak something to eat from the nearby food prep areas in the galley kitchens, and his sweaty, shoddy appearance was less likely to draw attention among crew who spent their days working around steam-belching laundry machines, smoking ovens, and splattering pots and cauldrons. Hitting the button, he took several deep breaths to get into character, mentally throwing together a number of potential excuses and explanations in case anyone caught him helping himself to a uniform or stealing some extra food.

Stepping off the lift, he saw he didn't have to worry. E Deck was a hub of frenetic activity, the men and women assigned to the military's essential but often forgotten service roles rushing back and forth with the energy and focus of a highly trained special ops team. Too absorbed in their own tasks to worry about a junior officer wandering through, none of them paid Theron any attention. In his earpiece he heard another update from the security team; by Theron's estimate they were halfway done with their sweep through F Deck.

Making his way into the laundry, Theron snagged a pair of pants and a top that looked as if they would fit and tucked them under his arm. Careful not to act suspicious, he made his way over to a hidden corner by one of the washing machines, ducked behind it, and stripped off his grimy clothes. Once he had the new uniform on he was pleasantly surprised to see he had been promoted to captain. Given the harsh penalties for insubordination in the Empire, it was unlikely anyone below his rank would want to draw attention to themselves by confronting him.

If I could find a Grand Moff's outfit I might just be able to walk onto the bridge and take command.

Though it was only a joke, the thought gave Theron pause. If he could somehow get his hands on some explosives, say from the armory, he could plant them in the engine room and wreak significant damage. As quickly as the idea came to mind, however, he dismissed it. Security around the armory would be much tighter than what he faced here, and even an officer requisitioning several kilograms of explosives was bound to raise questions he couldn't answer.

Sticking with his original plan, he made his way into the kitchens, dumping his soiled uniform into a hamper half full of dirty laundry. As he'd hoped, the enlisted men and women did their best to avoid making eye contact with him as he marched past, his chest puffed out with what he hoped was the appropriate level of Imperial arrogance and privilege.

In the kitchen he resisted the urge to go after the hot food being prepared for the crew's next meal, despite his grumbling stomach. Instead, he made his way into the storage lockers in the back and grabbed a pair of ration packs. A young man in cook's garb gave him a curious look, but when Theron narrowed his eyes at the soldier, his gaze snapped down to the floor. Without saying anything, Theron marched out with his prize and back into the hall.

Another update in his ear informed him the security team had completed the sweep of F Deck and was moving on. Theron made his way back out into the hall and headed down the length of the ship toward the turbolift at the stern. As he reached it he heard another update from the security team.

"Engine room is clear. Moving on."

He called the turbolift, stepped inside, and thumbed the button for G Deck to complete his circuitous route and return him to where he started.

The corridor was empty as he stepped off the lift; the security patrol had already moved on to the other side of the ship. The wheel on the access hatch turned easier this time, loosened up by its recent use.

Back inside the engine room, he stripped off the captain's uniform, carefully folding it and setting it in the metal walkway just inside the hatch, along with his bent pistol, his slicer spike, and one of the ration packs he'd stolen. He took a few minutes to consume the contents of the second ration pack. By the time he was done eating he was already covered in sweat. He'd hoped the heat would be more bearable wearing only his underwear and boots. It wasn't, but at least his new uniform wouldn't end up covered in dirt and sweat stains.

Retrieving his slicer spike, he returned to the arduous task of learning everything he possibly could about the *Ascendant Spear*.

A JOLT of excruciating pain jarred Gnost-Dural back to consciousness. It felt as if he were being cooked alive from the inside. His eyes popped open wide, adding to his suffering. Someone had removed his protective goggles, and the oxygen-rich atmosphere of the ship felt like acid on his pupils. Squeezing his tortured eyes shut, he let loose a scream, the sound muffled by his breathing mask.

"He's awake," he heard Darth Karrid say, and the burning agony suddenly stopped.

Though still unable to open his eyes, the Kel Dor was

able to take stock of his surroundings. He was lying on a hard platform or table set at a forty-five-degree angle, his wrists and ankles tightly shackled so that he was spread-eagled against the surface. His robe and most of his clothes had been stripped away, leaving him almost naked.

In addition to Karrid, there were others in the room with him. He recognized the presence of the female Sith apprentice, though he couldn't sense Karrid's male follower anywhere close by. And there were two others. He couldn't feel the dark side emanating from them so he assumed they were not Sith but rather Imperial soldiers: guards, or specially trained interrogators. He heard footsteps approaching, then the sound of Darth Karrid's voice, much closer than before.

"We know the attack on Reaver Station was staged," she said, her voice filled with an icy calm. "But I don't understand why. What was the purpose of setting off a false alarm?"

The Jedi didn't know what she was talking about, but he suspected Theron had something to do with it. Whatever his partner had been up to, he hoped it had worked—if Theron hadn't successfully planted the virus in the *Spear*'s systems, Gnost-Dural's plan was doomed to fail.

"Hit him again," Darth Karrid said, tired of waiting for him to answer her question.

This time his body felt not heat, but a strange kind of internalized pressure. His lungs and stomach expanded, as if rapidly filling up with air; his arteries and veins engorged with blood; his arms and legs swelled with fluid, the restraints on his wrists and ankles biting hard into his swelling flesh.

His eyes bulged against his lids and every organ in his body felt stretched and distended, ready to burst or tear apart. Gnost-Dural screamed again through his mask.

The pain was unlike anything he had ever felt before, the experience uniquely horrifying . . . and then suddenly it was gone. Gnost-Dural's body went limp, like a partially deflated balloon. A second later he began to tremble, every muscle quivering involuntarily. The spasm lasted for several seconds before he was finally able to calm his mind and regain control of his physical body.

"Darth Mekhis was a true genius," Karrid said with obvious admiration. "She understood that the normal methods of torture had little value against those who can draw upon the Force to sustain them. But even a Jedi Master is helpless against her remarkable machine.

"It attacks the mind and the spirit," she explained, "but leaves the body intact. Any imaginable horror can be inflicted simply by stimulating the receptors of the brain. The pain will feel completely real, but the flesh is unharmed."

Gnost-Dural understood the grim implications of what she was saying. Conventional torture would eventually surpass the limits of physical endurance; beyond a certain point the subject would perish. But with Mekhis's infernal machine, no matter how much a victim suffered, the agony would never end.

Dwelling on the endless horror is another part of the torture, the Jedi reminded himself. *Stay calm. Focus on what you need to do.*

When he'd first regained consciousness, Gnost-Dural had no sense of how long he had been out. Despite Karrid's torture, however, he felt his perception of time and space—an awareness born of being closely attuned to the universal power of the Force—returning. A little more than ten hours had passed since the confrontation in Karrid's inner sanctum; the attack on Duro was still too far away. He needed to hold out for several more hours if his plan was going to work.

"You cannot break me," he said, his voice cracking from the strain he had already been put through.

"We both know I can," Karrid whispered from just beside him, running her long fingers seductively along the rough skin of the Kel Dor's cheek. "But I don't have to. I know you weren't acting alone. A security sweep of the ship captured your friends. If you want to spare them this suffering, you will tell me what I want to know."

Gnost-Dural had to admire the ploy, but he knew she was bluffing. It was possible Theron was somewhere on the ship—he hoped it was true—but he trusted his partner was skilled enough to avoid any kind of security patrol. And Theron was working alone. Karrid had said "friends," plural, as if there were more than one.

"I know you're lying," he told her. "Because I came alone."

Karrid pulled her hand away from his face in frustration.

"Again," she said.

This time it felt like a million long, thin needles were impaling every centimeter of his body. They punctured his flesh clean through, sliding through skin, muscle, sinew, and bone before sliding out the other side. They pierced his internal organs; his eyes; even his skull, stabbing into his brain.

He fought against it, trying to summon the Force to ease his suffering. He opened his mouth to recite the Jedi Code to focus his mind and energy, but instead of the soothing words all that emerged was another endless scream.

The needles vanished, disappearing instantly just like the heat and the pressure. And once again, there had been no real harm done to his body, though the memories of the pain lingered.

"The Republic attack on Reaver Station wasn't real,"

Darth Karrid said, her voice finally betraying a hint of her impatience. "So what was the point of a false alarm? Is a real invasion coming next? One we will dismiss because we think it's just another equipment malfunction?"

"Yes," Gnost-Dural croaked. "That's it. You figured it out."

"Or was it a ploy to cause confusion?" Karrid continued, ignoring his obviously false confession. "A distraction so your allies already on the Reaver Station could set some kind of trap? Something that will be waiting for us if we return to port?"

"The dark side has made you paranoid," the Jedi whispered. "It blinds you to the truth. Reject the teachings of the Sith and you will have clarity and understanding."

"Clarity comes through suffering," Karrid told him. "You will learn that lesson soon enough."

He heard footsteps as she walked away from him, then heard her speaking to someone else—probably her pure-blooded Sith apprentice.

"Stay here with the interrogators. Watch the Jedi. Do not underestimate him, and beware of trickery through the Force."

"As you wish, Master," a female voice replied.

"We will speak again when I return," Karrid called out to him. "After a few hours on the table has made you more cooperative."

Gnost-Dural wasn't aware of her leaving as the interrogators turned on the machine and his world became pain.

IN THE hall beyond the interrogation room, Karrid paused long enough to savor her former Master's screams before continuing on. Her security sweeps hadn't turned up any other stowaways, though she hadn't expected them to. Sneaking onto her ship was a mission doomed to failure, as evidenced by Gnost-Dural's capture. She felt it was far more likely his presence was a feint; a suicidal sacrifice to draw her attention away from the real threat.

She'd hoped the Kel Dor would break easily, but she hadn't really expected that, either. Even Darth Mekhis's wondrous device would need time to wear down a Jedi Master. But eventually he would tell her everything she wanted to know: who he was working with; how he had known to find her on Reaver Station; why they had staged the false Republic attack. Until then, she was going to keep the *Ascendant Spear* out on deep patrol, safely away from whatever plot the Republic had cobbled together to destroy her. But that wasn't the only precaution she was taking.

She took the turbolift to A Deck, where the highest-ranking officers had their private quarters. There she found the newest additions to her crew ready and waiting for her arrival.

Lord Quux was a red-skinned pureblood; Lord Ordez was a dark-skinned human. They had come to Reaver Station to swear fealty to the newest member of the Dark Council, though Karrid had initially been reluctant to welcome them aboard her vessel for fear they might one day be tempted to try to take it from her.

However, Gnost-Dural's attack had made her reconsider her position. Now that she was on the Dark Council, she had to expect there would be other attempts on her life—if not by the Jedi, then by rivals within the Empire. Realizing it might be wise to keep a pair of well-trained warriors by her side at all times, she'd sent a shuttle to the station to retrieve them.

"I trust your accommodations are to your liking?"

"Exquisite," Lord Quux replied, while Lord Ordez only bowed his head to show he approved.

"Come with me," she told them. "We must begin your training."

"Training, Darth Karrid?" Lord Quux asked.

"If you want to serve me, you must learn to serve my ship as well," she told them. "I promise you'll find the experience . . . rewarding."

CHAPTER 27

THE KNIFE wound on Teff'ith's shoulder barely bothered her as she worked the *Prosperity*'s controls, bringing the shuttle out of hyperspace just beyond the mass shadow cast by Coruscant's gravity well.

The capital world of the Republic loomed before her in all its glory, a city world with almost a trillion people on the surface. The four moons orbiting the planet were almost lost among the artificial satellites swirling around it. Massive mirror stations collected and redirected light and heat from Coruscant's sun to the poles, transforming every square centimeter of the surface into livable land. Ponderous habitation spheres slowly circled the world, swelling the official population by another hundred billion. And giant space stations directed the endless stream of thousands of ships arriving and departing.

Teff'ith just stared out the window of the cockpit. It had been almost two years since she'd last been here . . . not since her first run-in with Theron. She'd forgotten how overwhelming the galaxy's most densely populated planet could be when seen from above. The incessant beep of the shuttle's comlink finally snapped her out of her fog, and she reached out to open the channel.

"*Prosperity,* do you read?" a man's voice crackled out. "This is Coruscant flight control station 473. *Prosperity,* please acknowledge."

"This is *Prosperity,*" Teff'ith answered, realizing the

shuttle's autotransponder must have transmitted the registration directly to the nearest space station for clearance upon her arrival. "What's wrong?"

"Been trying to hail you for almost two full minutes. Might want to check your comm equipment."

"Roger," Teff'ith replied, not certain what else to say. She knew how to smuggle a ship onto Coruscant, but she had no idea what the protocols were for a legal landing on the surface.

"You looking for surface clearance?" the man asked her after a few seconds of silence.

"Roger," Teff'ith agreed.

Another few seconds passed before the man asked, "Do you have your destination?" He was clearly getting annoyed.

"The Jedi," Teff'ith blurted out. "Grand Master Satele."

There was a long pause on the other end before the man replied, "You are cleared for landing at Diplomatic Spaceport 27-B. Transmitting coordinates now."

"Roger," Teff'ith said again.

"Over and out."

Relieved to put an end to the awkward conversation, Teff'ith turned the ship over to the autopilot, allowing it to chart its own course down to the surface. She was surprised she didn't have to wait in some kind of queue or touch down at one of the orbital space stations for some kind of verification before landing. But then she remembered whose shuttle she was flying, and she realized she had probably been given some kind of special priority service.

The shuttle plunged down into Coruscant's atmosphere, the autopilot falling into the nearest officially designated flight path as it sped her rapidly to the surface. The ship rattled slightly as it came in, a result of the damage it had sustained crashing through the doors of the hangar during her escape from Jigani Port. But Teff'ith barely noticed, her attention focused on the unimaginable crush of buildings, speeders, and people on the surface.

Coruscant truly was a wonder of the galaxy. There were other worlds with endless cityscapes, like the Hutt-controlled moon of Nar Shaddaa, but none of them rivaled the Republic capital. The tallest, grandest buildings on the Hutt world would have been dwarfed by even the smallest of Coruscant's skytowers. The general feel of Nar Shaddaa was one of claustrophobia: cramped and crowded. The effect of Coruscant was almost the exact opposite—the towers reaching up forever into the sky and the endless streams of traffic stretching off to disappear over the horizon made the world appear even larger and grander than it actually was.

The autopilot chimed softly, indicating she was nearing her destination. Teff'ith switched over to manual control when she saw the spaceport below her. She didn't trust autopilots to bring a ship down smoothly at the best of times, and she feared the *Prosperity*'s damaged hull might throw its precisely calibrated systems off.

Diplomatic Spaceport 27-B was an arrangement of half a dozen circular landing pads in a circle atop a very large, flat-roofed building. In the center of the landing pads was a small structure that Teff'ith guessed housed a turbolift leading to the building's interior, along with a handful of security personnel. A pair of small airspeeders were parked in one corner of the room, with enough space to accommodate several more.

The shuttle touched down with a slight thump, and Teff'ith killed the engines. She saw two men in official-looking uniforms—one carrying a blaster rifle, the other armed with a pistol—striding out of the central structure toward her vessel, confirming that at least half of her hypothesis was right.

Just like Gorvich said. Coming to arrest us.

She briefly considered firing up the shuttle again and taking off, but she'd come too far to turn back now. Hopefully the guards would be willing to listen to reason.

As she came down the boarding ramp the two men were waiting patiently. She took it as a good sign that neither one had bothered to ready his weapon, yet.

"Miss, is there anyone else on your shuttle?" the one with the pistol asked.

Teff'ith shook her head. She could see the guards exchange a knowing glance, and she saw their muscles tense up slightly.

"Is this your shuttle, miss?" the second wanted to know.

"Not ours. Belongs to Jedi. Gnost-Dural."

"And where is Master Gnost-Dural, miss?"

Had the guards tried to bully or intimidate her she would have had no trouble dealing with them. But she found this unrelenting politeness, with its thinly veiled undercurrent of suspicion, strangely alarming.

"Gnost-Dural not here. Gave shuttle to us. We have urgent message for Grand Master Satele Shan."

"Who's 'we,' miss?" the one with the pistol asked. "I thought you said you were alone."

Teff'ith rolled her eyes. "We is me. Nobody else. Just *me*." She put an unduly heavy emphasis on the final pronoun.

"Do you have any identification, miss?"

"We—*I*—got no time for stupid questions," she snapped, her composure finally slipping. "Got to see Grand Master Shan right now."

The guards looked at each other, then back at her.

"If you have a message for her you can give it to us. We'll make sure she gets it."

Teff'ith shook her head. "Gotta be in person. Now!"

The guards must have exchanged some kind of unspoken signal, because suddenly they both had their weapons trained on her.

"Miss, please remove your blaster and set it on the ground. Slowly."

Teff'ith did as instructed.

"Miss, you need to come with us."

"We go with you," Teff'ith said, trying to sound calm instead of like some raving lunatic. "But you send message to Grand Master Shan. Tell her Theron sent us."

While the guard with the blaster rifle kept his weapon pointed at her, the other holstered his pistol and came over to collect her weapon from the ground. Then he gave her a quick pat-down, careful to avoid the wound on her shoulder. To her surprise, he didn't slap a pair of stun cuffs on her, only took her by the elbow and led her inside the small structure in the middle of the spaceport, his partner following behind with his weapon still at the ready. It was clear they didn't trust her, but since she'd arrived in a Jedi Master's shuttle they were hesitant to treat her like a common criminal.

As Teff'ith suspected, there was a turbolift at the rear of the structure, along with two chairs and a holo-terminal. The only door was the one they had just entered, though there were two small windows on each of the side walls.

"Sit down, miss," the guard at her elbow said.

Still hoping she could reason with them, she did as instructed.

"Send a message to Grand Master Shan," she reminded him. "You promised us."

"Just try to remain calm, miss. We'll get this sorted out."

"Nothing to sort," she said, rising up from her chair. "Call Shan!"

The guard with the blaster rifle took a step back,

weapon raised, as the other came forward and grabbed her elbow again.

"We'll put a request in through the proper channels," he said, hoping to calm her while trying to guide her back into the chair. "Just sit down and relax. Someone is on the way."

Teff'ith let her shoulders slump and bowed her head as she started to lower herself into her seat. Thinking she was resigned to her fate, the guard at her elbow relaxed his grip.

Instead of sitting down, Teff'ith spun free, yanking the pistol from his holster with one hand as she slid around behind him, using his body to shield her from the guard with the blaster rifle. At the same time she grabbed his wrist with her other hand, twisting his arm up and behind his back while jamming the pistol against the side of his neck.

It happened in the blink of an eye; the other guard didn't even have time to cry out in surprise before Teff'ith had his partner at her mercy.

"Let him go!" he said, raising his blaster rifle.

Teff'ith twisted her human shield's arm up even farther behind him. He grunted in pain as she peered at the other man from over his shoulder.

"You go outside. Close the door. Come back in, friend dies!"

The guard hesitated, and Teff'ith pressed her pistol even harder into her captive's neck.

"Listen to her!" he pleaded. "Do what she says!"

Keeping his weapon high, the other guard slowly backed up until he was outside the small building. He waited a moment, then ducked to the side and out of Teff'ith's line of fire. She braced, fearing he would pop back around the corner to take a shot at her. But instead the door slid shut as he hit the access panel on the outer wall.

Teff'ith shoved her captive in the back, sending him stumbling away from her. She raised the blaster and fired, frying the panel by the turbolift and causing the man to let out a sharp yelp as he dropped to the floor.

Backing away to the far corner of the room, Teff'ith said, "Get up. Use holo. Call Grand Master Shan."

"I . . . I don't know how to reach her," he said. "I don't have that kind of authority."

"Call your boss. Call boss's boss. Get Shan on the holo or you die."

"Okay," he said, getting to his feet. "Okay, I'll try."

Teff'ith had no idea if her plan would work. She knew in the Empire they'd rather let a hostage die than disturb a Sith Lord with this kind of request. She hoped things were different in the Republic.

In the five minutes it took the guard to run his request up a chain of superiors, explaining his situation each time, three speeders came in to land on the roof outside, each carrying four more armed security personnel.

Teff'ith kept one eye on the guard at the holo while the other darted back and forth to the windows at the gathering array of firepower, wondering how long she had until they tried to storm the building.

Just as she was about to give up hope of ending this without bloodshed, the man at the holo said, "I got her! She's here!"

Teff'ith glanced over to see a woman's face on the holo. She had no idea what Grand Master Shan looked like, though she thought she could see a faint resemblance in the face to Theron.

"In the corner," she said, motioning with the gun. "Face down. You move, I shoot."

"There's no need for violence," the woman on the holo said as the guard complied with her instructions. "Let's try to stay calm."

"Tried that," Teff'ith told her, keeping the weapon

trained on the guard in the corner. "Nobody listened. Violence only way to get results."

"I'm here now," the woman said, obviously trying to soothe her. "I'm listening."

"You Grand Master Satele Shan?"

"I am."

"Message from Theron. Needs your help. Sent me to tell you."

From the expression on the woman's face, Teff'ith knew Satele was who she claimed to be. She also knew Satele had no doubt that she was telling the truth.

"What happened? What's wrong?"

"Not here," Teff'ith said, shaking her head. "Too many ears. Somewhere private."

"Do you want to come to me?" Satele asked. "Or should I come to you?"

Teff'ith glanced out the window to see more than twenty armed guards waiting on the roof outside.

"You come here. We not going anywhere."

Thirty seconds after ending her holo call with Satele, Teff'ith saw the guards outside pulling back and lowering their weapons, though none of them left. Five minutes later another airspeeder touched down, this one carrying a single figure in a brown robe.

Ignoring the armed guards, she jumped from her speeder and walked quickly toward where Teff'ith was holed up. As she drew closer, the Twi'lek recognized her as the woman from the holo call. She paused at the door.

"It's Grand Master Satele Shan," she said.

"Get up," Teff'ith said to the man still lying on the ground. "Open the door."

He did as instructed. Satele glanced from the guard, to Teff'ith, then back to the guard before stepping inside.

"Go," she said to the guard. "And take the rest of your CSF friends with you. This is Jedi business."

The man looked back at Teff'ith, then bolted for freedom when she nodded.

Satele closed the door behind him, sealing the two of them alone in the room.

"You don't need that pistol anymore," she said.

Teff'ith glanced down at her hand, surprised to realize she was still holding the blaster. She quickly set it on the chair beside her.

"You said Theron sent you," the Jedi said. "He needs my help."

"Gnost-Dural, too. Tried to tell guards. Wouldn't listen."

"Tell me everything," Satele said. "Starting with your name."

CHAPTER 28

THERON POPPED the salt tablets and downed the last of the water from his second ration kit, hoping it would be enough to keep his body hydrated and his muscles from cramping for a few more hours in the sweltering engine room.

He was nearly finished mapping the *Ascendant Spear*'s control systems; he had only a handful of relays left to go. And as he had become more and more familiar with the systems, he'd started writing preprogrammed subroutines to disrupt the ship's operations: one to disable the hyperdrive; another to take down the shields; a third to throw off the targeting systems of the laser cannons. He saved each subroutine as he created it in his cybernetic implant, storing them electronically for later reference, much the way he might memorize a list of names or numbers using his organic memory. Later, he'd be able to call them up and deploy them in rapid succession against Karrid and her ship, giving the Republic fleet a fighting chance when they faced off against the *Spear* over Duro.

There was just one problem with his plan: so far he had heard nothing about the *Spear* making preparations to go to Duro. Master Gnost-Dural had assured Theron he'd convince Karrid to go there, but Theron had no way to know if his friend was alive or dead. He'd been listening to the commands issued to and from the vessel's bridge ever since he'd sliced into the comm channels, but so far he hadn't heard a word about the Jedi, and the only orders Karrid had given the *Spear* were to stay out in deep space until they knew more about the feigned attack on Reaver Station.

His slicer spike pinged, notifying him that it had finished mapping the current relay. Theron disconnected it and scanned the data, the information transmitted wirelessly from the spike to the implant in his left eye, superimposing the image over his normal vision.

He recognized a familiar pattern from a previous relay—one that indicated a holding cell, complete with security cams providing live images. The previous cell Theron had stumbled across had been empty. He'd tapped into the cams hoping to see Gnost-Dural, only to be faced with an empty room. He hadn't thought to look for another holding cell, however. Reattaching the slicer spike to the relay, he established a connection with the security cams, projecting the image onto his visual overlay. This time he found what he was looking for.

Gnost-Dural was alive, strapped to some kind of table. His robe and most of his clothes had been stripped away; even on the low-quality image there was no mistaking the Kel Dor's exposed body.

Theron carefully used his link with the cam to have it pan slowly around the room. The Jedi was not alone. In addition to a pair of Imperial soldiers, there was also a female Sith pureblood in the room watching over him. From her black robes and facial tattoos it wasn't hard to assume she was a follower of the dark side. She was probably Darth Karrid's apprentice, tasked with making sure the prisoner didn't escape.

Moving the cam back to its original position, Theron cut the feed. He had no idea if the Sith would be able to sense him spying on them through the Force, but he didn't want to take any chances. Besides, he'd seen all he needed to see.

His mind quickly ran through his options. He could try to help the Jedi escape, but was that what Gnost-Dural wanted? He'd told Theron he was going to convince Darth Karrid to go to Duro; was getting captured part of the plan? Did he know his former Padawan well enough to think he could manipulate her into going to Duro by allowing her to interrogate him? It was a tactic SIS had used in the past, though the success rate wasn't high. Sometimes the target saw through the ruse and refused to take the bait. Other times they simply killed their prisoner before the false information could be fed to them.

There was no way to know if getting caught was actually a calculated gamble by his partner or if something had simply gone terribly wrong with his original plan. But if something had gone wrong, Theron realized there wasn't much he could do to help. He might be able to overpower the guards or the Sith individually, but he doubted he could handle all of them together. And even if he did, breaking Gnost-Dural from his prison would only alert Karrid that her old Master wasn't the only one who had infiltrated the *Spear*. The entire ship would go into lockdown until they were both found.

Most important of all, rescuing Gnost-Dural did nothing to address the problem of getting the *Spear* to Duro in the next twelve hours. If getting captured was part of his plan, rescuing him would ruin everything. If it wasn't, they were doomed anyway. Hard as it was, Theron had to leave Gnost-Dural in enemy hands, trusting that his partner knew what he was doing.

Trying not to think about what the Imperials would do to the Kel Dor, he returned to his work, attaching the slicer spike to the next relay. But it was impossible to push the Jedi completely from his mind. If Gnost-Dural was going to do something to deliver Karrid and the *Spear* into the hands of the Republic, he had to do it soon. Time was running out.

THIS TIME Gnost-Dural's torment was cold. Not the cold of bitter wind or a frozen world, but the black chill of the grave. He could feel his flesh rot and decay, his skin growing taut, his bones becoming hollow and brittle before crumbling into dust.

When the suffering abruptly and mercifully ended, Gnost-Dural's mind teetered on the brink of madness, shattered by hours upon hours of unspeakable torments. Even as he sought refuge in an ocean of dementia and delusion, some small part of him fought to cling to the last threads of his sanity.

Had the Sith ordered another immediate bout of torture, he would have succumbed, sinking into the depths of lunacy. Instead, she commanded the interrogators to halt, perhaps sensing how close he was to being lost forever and knowing the punishments Darth Karrid would inflict if she failed to uncover his secrets.

"Are you ready to talk now, Jedi?" she asked.

Still struggling to sort reality from the crazed pain hallucinations creeping around the edges of his mind, Gnost-Dural could only whisper, "No more. No more."

"You can end this," the Sith told him. "Tell Darth Karrid what she wants to know and your suffering will be over."

"I will talk," he promised. "No more . . . I will talk . . . no more . . . I will talk . . . no more . . ."

Turning away from the babbling Kel Dor, the apprentice said, "Inform Darth Karrid that the prisoner is ready for her."

BY THE time Darth Karrid arrived a few minutes later, Gnost-Dural had regained much of his composure, though he was careful to keep playing the part of a broken victim. Given his current state, it was an easy role to slip into.

"No more . . . I will talk," he mumbled as he heard Karrid's familiar footsteps approach. "I will talk."

"I told you I would break you," the Falleen whispered in his ear. "Now that you have tasted the power of the dark side, you can understand why I left the Jedi to follow Malgus."

"I will talk," the Jedi answered. "No more . . . I will talk."

"Why did you come aboard my vessel?" Karrid asked. "Why face me and my apprentices? Why enter a battle you knew you couldn't win?"

"A distraction," Gnost-Dural breathed. "Keep you away."

"Away? Away from what?"

"Duro. The attack on Duro."

"How do you know about that?"

Though blind without his protective goggles, he knew Karrid was watching him closely. Studying him; analyzing his words to see if he was lying. The best way to keep her from recognizing his deception was to blend fact and fiction; seed his lies with bits of truth.

"The black cipher. We cracked the codes."

He could sense Karrid suddenly stand up straight, shocked by the news.

"That's how we found you," Gnost-Dural continued. "We intercepted a message that you were going to Reaver Station."

"How long have you had the cipher?" she demanded, crouching down beside him again.

"Since Ziost."

He didn't need to say any more for her to know what he was talking about. And the less he said, the harder it would be for her to get a read on him.

"You came to the station, you attacked me on my ship, you staged a false Republic invasion fleet . . . all to make sure we didn't go to Duro?"

"We were afraid of you," Gnost-Dural said, feeding her ego. "The Republic is setting an ambush at Duro. But we can't spare enough ships to bring down the *Spear*. You would turn the battle against us."

"My ship was never part of the fleet heading to Duro," Karrid said, and he heard the suspicion in her voice.

"You are on the Dark Council. You choose your own path," Gnost-Dural explained, remembering how headstrong she had been as his Padawan as he played even further to her pride. "We feared you would defy the will of the Minister of War and come to Duro to claim your share of the glory."

"Then why are you telling me this now?" Karrid asks. "Are you hoping I will show you mercy?"

Gnost-Dural tried to laugh, but all that came out was a hollow, haunted rasping of breath.

"My plan worked," he said, offering the final piece of bait. "It's too late. We're too far away. You'll never get to Duro in time for the battle."

Now it was Karrid's turn to laugh.

"You're wrong, *Master,*" she sneered. "You have no idea how fast my ship really is. When the Republic springs their trap at Duro, we will be there!"

Karrid stood up and headed for the door.

"Watch him," she said. "No more torture. I want him alive and sane so he can witness our destruction of Duro and the Republic fleet."

"Should we send a message to warn Moff Nezzor about the ambush?" her apprentice asked.

"The Republic has broken the cipher codes," Karrid snapped. "Sending the message now will only let them know we're coming. They might even abandon their plan. Better to sacrifice a few of our own ships than to let the Republic fleet escape."

"Forgive me, Master," the apprentice replied. "There is so much I still have to learn."

"Tell Moff Lorman to set a course for Duro, maximum speed," she ordered before leaving the room.

I've done all I can, Theron, the old Jedi thought. *Now it's up to you.*

DEEP IN the bowels of the engine room Theron finally heard the orders he'd been waiting for coming from the bridge.

"Set a course for Duro."

A klaxon rang out three times across the ship, the signal for the crew to prepare for the jump to hyperspace. A moment later the hyperdrive core began to howl as it ramped up to full power.

He did it! Somehow, Master Gnost-Dural did it!

Theron redoubled his efforts, knowing he had to finish mapping the relays if the ambush was going to stand any chance of taking down the *Ascendant Spear* . . . assuming there actually was an ambush.

Gnost-Dural had done his job, and Theron was busy doing his. But none of it would matter if Teff'ith and Satele couldn't convince Jace to send a Republic fleet to Duro.

CHAPTER 29

"NO!" JACE said, slamming his fist down on the back of the couch he was standing by. "This is insane!"

Satele's call had woken him in the middle of the night. When she told him she was coming over right away to see him, he'd still been too bleary from the shots he'd shared with Marcus earlier to ask any questions or protest. Not that he would have refused her request. He and Satele had spoken many times since she'd ended their relationship—given their respective roles in the Republic and the Jedi Order it was inevitable. But their meetings had always been official, held in offices or meeting rooms. She'd never come to his apartment before, so he knew whatever business she had was urgent; the Grand Master of the Jedi Order was not a woman prone to overreaction.

By the time she'd showed up at his door, Jace's mind was right enough to guess what this was about—somehow she'd found out about Theron, the *Spear*, and the impending attack on Duro that was now less than ten hours away. He expected she would try to talk him out of his plan. What he hadn't expected was the scruffy-looking Twi'lek street thug who accompanied the Grand Master, nor the wild story she told.

"Do you know how many laws and regulations Theron violated by roping you into this?" he shouted at her.

Satele and the Twi'lek were standing side by side in the middle of his living room, a united front opposing him.

"Theron could be court-martialed," Jace continued, stepping around from behind the couch and moving toward them as his voice got louder and louder. "Arrested. This is bordering on treason!"

"You shout at him, not me!" Teff'ith snapped back, holding her ground and refusing to be intimidated by his bluster.

"None of that matters now," Satele told him. "Theron and Master Gnost-Dural will bring the *Ascendant Spear* to Duro. You need to be there waiting for them."

"You don't know that," Jace said. "You just met this Twi'lek. For all we know, she's an Imperial agent leading us into some kind of trap."

"I can sense the truth in her words," Satele assured him.

Jace snorted. "And you couldn't possibly be wrong, because no Jedi in history has ever been betrayed by someone close to them. You Jedi may see more than the rest of us, but you don't see nearly as much as you think."

"Sometimes we are blind when it comes to those close to us," Satele admitted. "But I'm right about this," she added with the resolute calm Jace had found so infuriating when they were together. "We can trust Teff'ith."

"Even if she's on our side, we still don't know if the *Spear* will actually show up at Duro. She can't even tell us what Theron and Gnost-Dural were planning."

"Was no plan," Teff'ith explained. "Making it up as they go."

"That's even worse!" Jace shouted, turning away from them to stalk around the living room. "You can't just improvise your way through something like this."

"Don't underestimate Master Gnost-Dural," Satele cautioned. "Darth Karrid was his apprentice for many years. He knows her mind and personality better than she does."

"Then why didn't he know she was going to defect to the Sith?" Jace challenged.

"We knew the risk. But we decided it was worth it to get someone close to Malgus," Satele said. "Gnost-Dural will find a way to make Darth Karrid bring the *Spear* to Duro."

"I wish I had your confidence," Jace said, shaking his head. "But even if he does get her to send the *Spear,* we can't face it at full power. Theron was supposed to sabotage the ship, but we have no idea what he's done. Even if he manages to plant the virus in the *Spear*'s systems, we don't have any way to activate it without knowing what frequency to transmit the code on."

"Theron will find a way," Satele assured him. "Maybe he'll trigger the virus himself."

"And maybe he won't. If I send a fleet to Duro and the *Spear* shows up at full power, we'll be slaughtered along with the civilians on the planet."

"Send two fleets!" Teff'ith blurted. "Send five. Send ten! Even the *Spear* can't win then."

"We don't have enough ships in the sector," Jace said. "And even if we did, sending orders to have everyone converge on Duro at the same time would tip the Empire off. They'd know we were there, and they'd call off the attack."

"At least Duro would be spared," Satele chimed in.

"Duro is irrelevant," Jace said. "This is about stopping the *Spear*. It's about winning the war."

"The Republic doesn't win if we don't protect our people," Satele told him. "We are not the Empire. You used to understand the difference."

Jace bristled at her words. "Is that why you left me? Is that why you didn't tell me Theron was our son?"

He heard a slight gasp from Teff'ith as she reacted to

the revelation, but he ignored the Twi'lek, his attention focused on Grand Master Shan.

"I saw the war change you," Satele said. "I saw you heading down a path I could not follow. I tried to help you, but I realized I was only being dragged down with you."

"So you abandoned me."

"I thought our feelings for each other were making things worse. I was afraid if you knew you had a son, your desire to protect him at any cost would take you even farther down that dark path."

"Is that how you really see me?" Jace asked. "As some kind of monster?"

Satele shook her head.

"I do not always agree with your decisions, but I know you are a good man. Hate and anger are part of you, but they have not consumed you."

The Jedi sighed. "I used to believe that was because of what I had done. Turning away from you, hiding your son from you—I used to tell myself these actions saved you from yourself."

"And what do you think now?"

Satele hesitated, her eyes shifting to the floor momentarily as if she couldn't bear to meet Jace's gaze.

Is she ashamed? Jace wondered.

"Now I do not know," she said.

She looked up at him again, struggling to maintain the reserve appropriate for a Jedi Grand Master. But Jace knew her well enough to see what was beneath her stoic mask: regret, uncertainty, self-doubt.

"Maybe I was wrong to hide Theron from you. Maybe I made things worse."

There was a long silence, finally broken by Teff'ith. "Jedi Grand Master mom, Supreme Commander dad. Now we get why Theron's so messed up. So you sending a fleet, or what?"

When Jace didn't answer, Satele spoke up.

"You can't let Duro be sacked," she told him. "I know you, Jace. You'll never be able to live with yourself. It will destroy you."

"It's worth it if holding back our fleet means we still have a chance to take down the *Spear*," he said stubbornly.

"If you send the fleet and the *Ascendant Spear* isn't there, you save Duro," Satele said, trying to reason with him. "If you don't send a fleet, and Karrid is there, then you lose both Duro and your best chance of taking down the *Spear*."

"Easy choice," Teff'ith agreed.

"You're forgetting the third option," Jace told them. "We send a fleet, the *Spear* is there, but Theron fails in his mission. Then we lose everything—our chance at the *Spear*, Duro, and our fleet. You're asking me to risk all this on blind faith that Theron will succeed. The Supreme Commander doesn't have the luxury of blind faith."

"It's not blind faith," Satele assured him. "It's faith in Theron. Faith in our son."

Jace stared down at the floor, clenching and unclenching his hands. He knew what he *wanted* to do, but this was the most important decision he'd ever make. He couldn't afford to be wrong.

"I don't suppose you've had some kind of vision?" he said to Satele. "Something telling us what we should do?"

"The Force has not shown me what will happen," Satele admitted. "The future is always in motion."

"Could've just lied," Teff'ith mumbled.

"Trust your heart," Satele told him.

"Not a very Jedi thing to say," Jace said.

"You're not a Jedi," she reminded him.

The Supreme Commander took a deep breath, then slowly let it out. He'd been fighting the Sith for forty years: fighting for the Republic, fighting for the men and women who went into battle beside him, fighting for the future of the entire galaxy. But now that he knew he had a son, he had something else worth fighting for. Theron was counting on him, and he wasn't going to let him down.

"I'll send the fleet," he said. "Now get out of my apartment so I can change—I need to be on my flagship within the hour or we won't get there in time."

"You leading the fleet?" Teff'ith asked, clearly surprised.

"If Darth Karrid doesn't show, then Chancellor Saresh is going to demand my resignation for botching this mission anyway. Might as well go out in a blaze of glory."

"I'm coming, too," Satele declared.

"Forget it," Jace replied. "We're not risking both the Supreme Commander and the Grand Master of the Jedi Order on the same mission."

"We serve the Republic," she reminded him, "and this mission is critical to the war effort. If there's even a chance I could help, I need to be there.

"And the Order is strong enough to survive my loss if something happens," she assured him. "Just as the military can survive yours."

"Good luck," Teff'ith said.

"You're coming, too," Jace told her.

"What? Why us?"

"I'm risking everything on your story, but I'm still the Supreme Commander of the Republic military. I still have responsibilities. If it turns out you're actually an Imperial spy setting us up, letting you go would make things even worse. So I'm not letting you out of my sight until all this is over, just in case."

"Theron better mess up the *Spear* real good," Teff'ith grumbled. "Don't wanna get blown to bits."

"You're not the only one," Jace agreed.

* * *

THE HOWLING of the hyperdrive made it hard to concentrate, but Theron was still able to tap into the *Spear*'s navigation systems to get a sense of where they were. At first he thought there was no way they'd get to Duro in time, but the ship was moving at speeds he was having trouble believing. He checked and double-checked the data, wondering if there was an error somewhere. He'd studied the hyperdrive systems, and it shouldn't have been possible for them to be moving this fast. Not without some external power source boosting the system.

Darth Karrid.

Tracking their progress backward, he realized the ship's velocity had jumped when the systems for her personal command pod engaged. The engines were actually drawing more power from her, the symbiotic link between Sith and ship channeling dark side energies through Karrid to augment the *Spear*'s abilities.

With a sinking feeling he realized that even with all the time he'd spent mapping the networks and studying the ship, he still didn't have any real concept of the *Ascendant Spear*'s full potential. Darth Karrid's ship might be too formidable a foe for the Republic fleet. Theron hoped the Republic's chance for victory wasn't already lost.

CHAPTER 30

ENCASED WITHIN the crystal sphere of her command pod, Darth Karrid could feel the power of the *Ascendant Spear* coursing through the wires attached to the implants in her neck, face, and skull. The wires twitched and twisted like they were alive, pulsing with energy and matching the rhythm of her racing heart as it sent blood rushing through her veins.

Her excitement was more than the anticipation of the coming battle. Guiding the ship through the extra-dimensional landscape of hyperspace was exhilarating, a thrill beyond any other mental or physical pleasure. She had transcended her shell of flesh and bone, becoming one with the *Ascendant Spear* as planets and stars flew past her on all sides, sensed rather than seen, vanishing from her awareness in seconds as they were left trillions of kilometers behind her.

She could feel the presence of her apprentice and his two new companions outside the confines of the pod as she fed off them to enhance and augment her connection to the dark side . . . and to the ship. Yet she realized that, eager as she was to get to Duro, she had to pace herself. Her second apprentice was still watching guard over Gnost-Dural, and though Lord Quux and Lord Ordez were strong, they were still not used to the unique strain of supporting her while she controlled the *Spear*. She had to be careful not to exhaust them before the battle.

The ship slowed ever so slightly in response to her unspoken directive, allowing her to conserve her strength as they continued to hurtle to their destination.

MOFF NEZZOR, commander of the Imperial capital ship *Extempus*, relished the moments before leading his fleet into battle. The attack on the agriworld Ruan had been a glorious victory, but it would pale compared with the devastation he planned to unleash against Duro.

As with the previous attack on an unsuspecting, lightly defended Republic world, the plan was elegant in its simplicity. Hit the Duro shipyards to cripple production, bombard the orbiting cities to inflict maximum damage and casualties, then retreat before Republic reinforcements in the sector could respond to the threat.

Nezzor approved of this recent shift in Imperial tactics. While some—like Davidge, the prissy Minister of Logistics—might argue that the Empire gained little tangible benefit from an attack on Duro, the Grand Moff understood the psychological value of striking soft targets with the primary purpose of massacre and mayhem. And personally, he much preferred an unopposed run against a heavily populated civilian world to a lengthy engagement against Republic defenders over a resource-rich planet with high long-term strategic value.

"Two minutes to Duro, Moff Nezzor," the navigator seated on the other side of the bridge informed him.

"Ready a general comm channel," Nezzor commanded, eager to begin issuing orders to direct his fleet's assault the instant they dropped from hyperspace.

"Aye-aye, sir."

A smile crept across Nezzor's thin, cracked lips.

He felt the familiar surge of deceleration, and the starfield outside the bridge's viewing window transformed from solid white to the starfield of realspace. They arrived on the edges of the Duro system, far enough from the sun's gravity well but still only a few minutes from the world itself. But instead of seeing the eponymous planet and its orbiting cities in the distance, helpless and at their mercy, Moff Nezzor found himself facing an entire Republic fleet stretched out before him, arrayed for battle.

Impossible! he thought, shouting out "Full shields!" even as the enemy opened fire.

JACE MALCOM kept his eyes carefully focused on the battle monitors on board the bridge of the *Aegis* in the moments before the battle began.

From the intercepted cipher transmissions, he knew the Empire was sending a fleet designed for a cowardly hit-and-run assault: Moff Nezzor's capital ship *Extempus*, a *Delta*-class carrier with a full complement of two dozen Interceptors, two Dreadnoughts, and three destroyers.

On the Republic side, Jace had called in all military vessels in the sector: three capital ships, including the *Aegis,* four Hammerheads, six corvettes, and four support squads of eight Thunderclap fighters. The Empire was outgunned by a greater than three-to-one margin, but Jace wasn't taking any chances. If the *Ascendant Spear* was with them the Empire had the edge.

He had already given the commanders of the other capital ships the order to concentrate their fire exclusively on the *Spear* the instant it dropped from hyperspace, hoping to inflict some significant damage before Karrid could activate her shields. At the same time, the rest of his fleet would focus on the *Extempus* and the remaining Imperials.

The monitor began to flash with Imperial vessels blinking into existence on the scanner as they dropped out of hyperspace. The Hammerheads and corvettes opened fire on the enemy, but per Jace's orders the capital ships held off, waiting for the *Spear*.

The *Extempus* suffered several direct hits before its shields came up, giving it a momentary reprieve. A destroyer exploded as a lucky shot from one of the corvettes ruptured the hypermatter core. The other destroyers, the Dreadnoughts, and the carrier managed to escape significant damage in the initial assault.

Jace continued to stare at the screen, trying to will the *Ascendant Spear* to materialize. The Thunderclaps dived into the fray, two squadrons swarming the *Extempus* while the other two each went for one of the Dreadnoughts. The corvettes descended on the carrier, trying to disable it before it was able to deploy the Interceptors in its hold.

"Supreme Commander Jace," Admiral Gorwin radioed from one of the other capital ships. "No sign of the *Ascendant Spear*. Permission to engage other targets."

"Permission granted," Jace growled, his hands gripping the arms of his command chair so hard his knuckles turned white.

He turned to where Satele and Teff'ith were standing in a corner of the bridge.

"Darth Karrid is coming," the Jedi assured him.

"We can't wait any longer," Jace replied. "Not if we want to minimize Republic casualties."

He turned to the comm terminal that connected him to the other sections of the ship. "Concentrate fire on the *Extempus*. Make Nezzor pay for what he did to Ruan."

THE BRIDGE of the *Extempus* was dark, lit only by the dim illumination of emergency lighting and the glow of the panels from the consoles that lined the perimeter.

"We just lost the *Dravilla*," his first officer informed him.

Outside the viewing window, Moff Nezzor could see the doomed destroyer as it was engulfed in a series of explosions.

"Shield status," he demanded.

"Under twenty percent."

Nezzor had come expecting a slaughter. He'd found one, but there was no denying he was on the wrong side. Even without the advantage of surprise, the Republic force he was facing would have crushed his fleet.

But if he was going to die, it wouldn't be while attempting a retreat.

"Set a course for the nearest orbital city," he ordered. "Full speed ahead."

The helmsman hesitated before a lifetime of Imperial training compelled him to obey the suicide order. "Aye-aye, sir."

If this was Nezzor's final battle, he was going to take as many Republic lives with him as possible.

JACE SAW the *Extempus* change course and accelerate, though it took him a few seconds to realize what Nezzor was planning.

"All ships, concentrate full fire on the *Extempus*!" he shouted, transmitting his orders across the entire Republic fleet. "They're trying to crash into the cities!"

Following his command, the entire Republic fleet—minus six fighters that were lost during the battle—disengaged from their targets and turned toward the Imperial flagship. Seeing the opportunity, the rest of the Imperial fleet began a full retreat in the opposite direction, desperately trying to put enough distance between them and the Republic ships to safely activate their hyperdrives and escape with their lives.

KARRID BRACED herself for a moment of disorientation as the *Ascendant Spear* dropped out of hyperspace in the Duro system. Though it only took a fraction of a second for the sensors to adjust to the physical laws and dimensions of realspace and come back online, in her state of heightened acuity the delay felt like an eternity. The instant her hyperspace-induced blindness passed, however, she was able to pinpoint the location of every ship across the entire battlefield.

The *Spear* had appeared well beyond the edges of the Duro system, rather than where she expected the Republic ambush would engage Nezzor's fleet. The lifeless remains of several Imperial vessels floated silently in the distance. Beyond them, a single vessel—Nezzor's *Extempus*—was racing toward Duro itself, with Republic ships giving chase. The surviving remnants of the Imperial fleet—a Dreadnought, a destroyer, and a handful of Interceptors—were headed in the opposite direction, toward Karrid and the edges of the system. Facing overwhelming odds, they'd chosen to abandon their commander and flee the battle.

Karrid's fingers tapped lightly at the control pad on the arm of her chair, sending signals shooting up the wires linked into her cybernetic implants and off to the ship itself. The *Ascendant Spear* responded to her commands by targeting the approaching Imperial vessels as they lowered their shields in preparation for the jump to hyperspace, never suspecting one of their own would fire at them. The *Spear*'s ion cannons tore into the defenseless ships, blasting them into cosmic dust as a reward for their cowardice.

The *Spear* changed course as Karrid sent it accelerating toward the Republic vessels. Still too far away for even her incomparable weapons, she targeted the enemy flagship and prepared to fire as soon as she got into range.

THERON HAD felt the *Spear* drop from hyperspace, the screaming drive core mercifully winding down as it did.

When the ship's sensors came online, he was already plugged in, lurking in the corners of the network just beyond Karrid's consciousness.

Even though he was receiving data in real time, he was still caught off guard when she fired on the advancing Imperial vessels. Not that he would have done anything to stop her even if he'd been expecting it. But the speed and precision with which she dispatched her targets reinforced his earlier fears that the *Spear* was going to win the battle, despite his best efforts.

He pushed the negative thoughts from his mind as Karrid advanced on the Republic fleet in the distance. His link to the ship gave Theron a rough idea of the Republic numbers, but the data was coming too quickly for him to fully process it. Not that it mattered—his attention needed to be focused on the internal workings of the *Spear* if he had any hope of slowing Karrid down.

As the targeting systems came online, Theron used his slicer spike to upload one of his virus subroutines, praying it would work.

NEZZOR'S DESPERATE suicide run never had a chance, but that didn't keep Jace from cursing under his breath as the Republic fleet bombarded the Imperial flagship. When the *Extempus*'s shields went down, exhausted by the constant barrage of enemy fire, he pumped his fist. A second later he stood up and let out a primal victory roar as a series of explosions tore the vessel apart, eliminating the threat.

"Darth Karrid is here!" Satele suddenly declared, abruptly ending his celebration.

Jace slammed himself back into his chair, his eyes flicking back and forth over the screen depicting the battlefield.

"Where? I don't see it!"

A second later a ship appeared on the very edge of

scanner range, and he didn't need the helmsman's confirmation to know it was the *Ascendant Spear*.

"Never in doubt," he heard Teff'ith say, though it sounded more like she was speaking to herself.

"All ships, prepare for battle," he barked out. "We do whatever it takes to bring the *Spear* down!"

The ships in the fleet turned away from the smoking wreckage of the *Extempus*, carving a wide arc as they circled around to head in the opposite direction. The *Spear* was closing on them fast, though it was still too far away to engage.

"Look at the size of that beast!" the helmsman gasped as the sensors threw up the enemy vessel's dimensions on his readout.

"Shields up. Prepare to fire the second we come in range," Jace ordered, knowing full well the *Spear*'s guns would be able to tear them apart long before they ever got close enough to retaliate.

Come on, Theron. Don't let us down!

"Sir!" the helmsman warned. "Enemy fire incoming!"

"Brace for impact!" Jace shouted as his screen showed the incoming ion blasts.

He prayed the shields would hold, but to his surprise the blast flew high and wide.

"She missed," the helmsman said, shocked. "Flat-out missed us!"

"Target in range," the gunner told him.

Jace bared his teeth in a fierce grin.

"Hit her back with everything we've got!"

DARTH KARRID saw her shot miss its mark, but it took her a second to wrap her mind around what had happened. The target hadn't taken any evasive maneuvers, or deflected the attack with shields . . . she had just missed.

She ran a quick diagnostic check of her targeting

array, only to find it was entirely miscalibrated. It only took her a few seconds to correct the mistake, but in that time the Republic vessels had come close enough to bring their own weapons to bear.

Sensing the incoming fire, she redirected energy from the aft shields to reinforce the deflectors facing the advancing fleet. The incoming blasts were deflected harmlessly, and Karrid took aim for a second time, only to see her shot go wide yet again. As the Republic ships launched a second volley, Karrid reran the diagnostics on the targeting array, isolated another error, and adjusted for it.

An instant before the second round of incoming Republic fire hit, the aft shields suddenly surged to full capacity, draining all power from the forward deflectors. Instead of being easily repelled, the laser bolts and ion blasts smashed into the *Spear*'s hull, making Karrid cry out in pain. The damage was significant, and she tapped frantically at the control pad to reroute the affected systems through new relays and restore optimal efficiency, starting with the deflector shields.

The Republic ships were fanning out as they drew closer, looking to surround her vessel so they could attack from all sides. Karrid engaged the sublight thrusters and veered sharply to starboard, tilting the nose of the *Spear* down at a forty-five-degree angle and accelerating far too quickly for the Republic vessels to keep up. She dived down and away, buying time to fix her malfunctioning systems.

She saw the Republic vessels trying vainly to pursue her, and then suddenly they were gone as the entire external sensor network went down. Completely blind to what lay outside her vessel, Karrid momentarily panicked, her arms flailing wildly and her head thrashing violently from side to side. The sensation of the wires connecting her to her ship slapping against her face and shoulders snapped her back to her senses, and in that instant she felt him.

An intruder. An interloper. A saboteur on her ship, slicing into her private network.

The violation enraged her. Bellowing out a roar, Karrid threw herself into the task of finding and destroying the enemy within. Her fury energized her, fueling the fires of the dark side that burned within her and her ship. Outside the crystal sphere of her command pod she felt Lord Quux and Lord Ordez nearly break from the increased strain, though her apprentice never wavered. But as close as they came to failing her, they somehow managed to stay in their meditative trance, allowing Karrid to draw on their power to push herself and the *Spear* far beyond their previous limits.

Within seconds she had rerouted all primary battle systems to new pathways, sealing off the old ones to isolate any potential viruses and keep them from spreading. The sensors came back online, as did the shields and her targeting array. Now that she knew the slicer was there, she was able to sense his next attack, disable it before it could take effect, and trace it back to its source.

"Security to the engine room," she hissed into the pod's comlink. She realized the slicer could probably hear her, but there was nothing she could do about it.

The slicer tried to disrupt another system, but now that she knew where the attacks were coming from it was easy to keep them from doing any real harm. With the internal threat neutralized, she turned her attention back to the battle just in time to throw up her shields to ward off another attack. Her evasive maneuver had separated her from the Republic fleet, but they were closing in once again. She took aim at the closest vessel—one of the Hammerheads—and fired.

* * *

WHEN THE *Ascendant Spear* suddenly veered away from the fleet and took off in an unexpected direction, Jace knew they had Karrid on the run.

"She's vulnerable," he said. "Finish her off. Now!"

Every ship in the Republic fleet scrambled to intercept the enemy vessel on its new course. Emboldened by the misfiring guns and the failing shields, they came in hard and fast, looking to put a quick end to the battle. The *Aegis* fired again, as did many of the other vessels, targeting the same location where they had pierced the shields and punctured the *Spear*'s hull in their previous attack.

Rather than inflicting even more damage, the entirety of their attacks was deflected away. The guns of the *Spear* opened fire again, but this time instead of sailing wide they scored a direct hit on one of the Hammerheads. The combined power of the precisely aimed ion cannons and turbolasers ripped through the shields and shredded the Hammerhead, crippling the ship with a single devastating attack.

"Pull back!" Jace ordered, realizing their advantage had been lost. "Pull back and regroup!"

One of the corvettes was lost as the Republic fleet aborted its headlong charge, snuffed out by the *Spear*'s defense turrets when it got too close. Another blast from the ion cannons rocked the *Aegis* as it tried to retreat to a safe distance, sending Teff'ith and Satele sprawling to the ground and nearly knocking Jace out of his command seat.

"Damage report!"

"Shields took the worst of it. No critical systems hit. We've lost power to Sector Four. Medical teams are on their way."

"Shields?"

"Down to seventy percent."

Shields drained 30 percent from a single attack? Jace marveled.

An instant later he was hit with the sobering realization that they didn't stand a chance. War raged across the entire galaxy; the Republic had brought in only as many ships as were in the vicinity. "Call for reinforcements," he said, knowing it would be hours before any ships stationed in other parts of the galaxy could reach them. "Take evasive action," he ordered the rest of his fleet. "Keep your distance."

Even if they couldn't beat the *Spear,* they could at least try to drag the battle out as long as possible to give Theron and Gnost-Dural a chance to pull off a miracle.

CHAPTER 31

THERON RAN back and forth along the engine room's narrow walkways, racing from relay to relay as he uploaded his virus subroutines. The first few worked perfectly, sending the *Spear*'s shots wide, dropping the shields, and disabling the sensors. Then Karrid had figured it out.

He tried desperately to find new vulnerabilities to exploit, but each time he did it only took two or three seconds for her to counteract his efforts. Still plugged into the ship's comm system and scanners, he heard her send security down to the engine room, and he let out a strangled cry of frustration when she destroyed the Hammerhead.

She's too good. Too fast. Too smart. This isn't going to work.

But she was also in the middle of fighting an entire Republic fleet. Her focus was on the weapons and shields; sensors and communications: all the things the *Spear* needed to survive the battle. She still hadn't realized that he'd disabled the turbolifts leading down to G Deck to buy himself more time.

She's on G Deck, too. The far side.

If he couldn't stop Karrid remotely by slicing into the *Spear*'s systems, maybe he could stop her face-to-face. After all, he'd stopped Darth Mekhis.

That was different. You caught her off guard. Tricked

her. Karrid's going to be ready. And she might not be alone. You're going to need help.

Even if Karrid didn't realize he'd knocked out the turbolifts, he only had a couple more minutes before the ship's automated repair systems got them working again. He'd have to work fast.

Grabbing his slicer spike, he tapped into the relay controlling Gnost-Dural's holding cell. Karrid was still focused on protecting the critical battle systems, and he was able to worm his way inside.

GNOST-DURAL HAD spent the hours since Darth Karrid's last visit in quiet, reflective meditation. As per the Sith Lord's instructions, the interrogators had spared him more torture with Mekhis's infernal machine. The respite had allowed the Jedi to calm and focus his mind, subtly drawing on the Force to refresh and restore his ravaged body and spirit.

The power of the dark side all around him was impossible to ignore; it seeped from the very walls of the *Ascendant Spear,* a twisted creation of a brilliant but diseased mind. Yet even here, surrounded by darkness, the power of the light shone through. The Force flowed through all living things, and there were several thousand crew on the ship. Most of them were ordinary men and women, soldiers for the Empire because of birth and upbringing, not because of some inherent evil.

Careful not to do anything that might draw the attention of the pure-blooded apprentice he sensed in the room with him, Gnost-Dural drew upon the Force to grant him a picture of his surroundings. The first thing he sensed was the battle raging outside the ship; the Republic fleet had come to Duro! But it didn't take him long to realize they were overmatched, and he knew if he didn't do something the battle would be lost.

He turned his heightened perception inward, allowing

him to construct a highly detailed picture of his holding cell. The interrogators were seated in chairs on the far side of the medium-sized room, next to the panel that could unleash unbearable horrors on their prisoner with a simple touch of a button. They were both male, and both carried pistols at their sides. His protective goggles, Jedi robe, and other clothes had been discarded in the back corner of the room, tossed aside once he had been stripped down and strapped to the table.

In the opposite corner of the room was the Sith apprentice, sitting cross-legged on the floor. She was turning the hilt of a lightsaber over and over in her hands, as if somehow drawn to it. Gnost-Dural recognized the weapon he had forged while still a Padawan on Coruscant. She had witnessed his lightsaber skills during their battle; now it seemed she was intent on finding some explanation in his weapon. Gnost-Dural sensed and sympathized with her confusion: she had been raised to believe the power of the dark side dwarfed that of the light, and she was unable to convince herself that a Jedi could so easily have bested her in combat without some kind of inherent advantage.

"I could teach you how to use that," he said.

Startled, she glanced up at the prisoner, taking a moment to realize he was drawing on the Force to "see" her.

"I know how to use a lightsaber," she said defensively.

"I could teach you how to use it properly," he explained. "Not as a clumsy weapon guided by hate and anger, but as an extension of yourself that protects and defends those in need."

The interrogators glanced over, their curiosity piqued by the exchange. Noticing them, the Sith stood up, suddenly self-conscious about sitting on the floor as if subservient to them.

"Karrid warned me to watch for your tricks," she said.

"This is no trick. Karrid is afraid of me—you sensed it. But I am not afraid of her."

"Because you are stronger?" she sneered.

"Because the light side teaches us not to be afraid. Don't you want to live free of fear? And anger? And hate?"

For a second Gnost-Dural felt a connection with her, and he thought he might reach her. Then a wall of blackness fell between them, and the connection was gone.

"Your friends are dying out there," she said, her voice filled with spite and venom. "Can you feel it? Darth Karrid and her ship are tearing them apart. I should be at her side for this victory to share in the glory, but instead I'm here watching over you!"

"Then go," Gnost-Dural said. "I'm not the one keeping you."

One of the interrogators laughed, and the Sith silenced him with an icy glare.

"I don't need you or your weapon," she said to Gnost-Dural, tossing his lightsaber into the corner of the room with the rest of his discarded property. Then she crossed her arms and stood with her back to the door, staring at him defiantly.

The Jedi sighed, knowing the opportunity was lost. But before hope could slip away completely, the shackles on his wrists and ankles sprang open with a sharp click, dropping him to the floor.

Theron!

Gnost-Dural reacted with the superior reflexes and blinding speed of a true Jedi Master, already in motion before the others even realized something had gone wrong. He landed on his feet, his lightsaber flying from the corner and into the outstretched palm of his right hand, the blade springing to life with a sharp hiss. At the same time his protective goggles flew up into his left hand and he yanked them into place.

One of the interrogators slammed his hand on the button to activate the machine, but with the prisoner already free of his restraints nothing happened. His partner reacted with more sense, pulling his pistol. Darth Karrid's apprentice made the wisest choice of all. She turned and fled out the door.

The guard with the pistol fired, but Gnost-Dural batted the blaster bolt aside. He saw the second guard reaching forward to hit the alarm, and knocked him back with a powerful Force push. Two quick steps closed the distance between them in the small room, and he ended both their lives with a pair of clean, efficient cuts of his glowing blade. Then he raced from the room in pursuit of Karrid's apprentice, ignoring his Jedi robe and clothes still lying in the back corner of the room.

He saw her disappear around a corner at the end of a twenty-meter hall, and he gave chase. She was waiting for him as he rounded the corner, her own lightsaber drawn. She tried to impale him, hoping his momentum as he came barreling around the corner would carry him right onto the deadly tip of her outstretched blade. But Gnost-Dural twisted to the side; her thrust only traced a thin line across the topmost layer of skin of his bared chest. Ignoring the smell of his own charred flesh, he retaliated by driving an elbow into the Sith's jaw, sending her stumbling back.

She threw up her lightsaber in a defensive stance to hold him off, but one-on-one she was no match for the Kel Dor. He came at her with a flurry of intense strikes drawn from Juyo, the highly aggressive seventh form of lightsaber combat designed specifically to overwhelm a lone opponent in a one-on-one duel. The chaotic patterns and haphazard sequences picked apart the Sith's defenses in a matter of seconds, the battle ending with

Master Gnost-Dural plunging his lightsaber through her chest and out the other side, impaling her as she had originally tried to do to him.

As her corpse toppled to the floor, Gnost-Dural was already on the move, headed directly for the *Spear*'s control room to face Darth Karrid yet again.

THERON HAD no idea if his plot to free Gnost-Dural had worked or not. Just as he finished slicing into the holding cell's systems and released the Jedi's restraints, Darth Karrid shut him out, rerouting the pathway through another relay.

Realizing she would soon do the same with the turbolift, he decided to get moving or he'd end up trapped in the engine room. Grabbing his slicer spike and tucking it into the top of his boot, he dashed over to the captain's uniform he'd carefully folded and set on the floor. He considered then quickly rejected the idea of spending the time to pull it on; a stolen uniform wasn't going to fool the security teams converging on his location.

Grabbing the pistol with the bent barrel just in case, he turned the wheel and pushed open the maintenance hatch. The corridor outside was blessedly cool; he actually shivered as the climate-controlled air washed over his sweat-soaked body.

The sound of the nearby turbolift as it cranked into operation set him in motion. He had reached the first bend in the passage leading to the far side of G Deck when he heard the door open.

Glancing back, he saw several heavily armored security guards step out. Fortunately, it took them a moment to notice the man in his briefs running away from them at the far end of the hall. Theron had just enough time to dart around the corner as blaster bolts struck the ground and wall beside him, missing him by the narrowest of margins.

Theron didn't think he'd have any trouble staying ahead of the Imps in their heavy armor. But after half a dozen more running steps he pulled up lame and cried out in pain, hopping on one foot as his left calf seized. Despite his efforts to stay hydrated during his time in the sweltering engine room, his body was rebelling. The muscle had cramped up, a brutal contraction so tight it felt as if it was going to rip itself apart. Any movement of his toes or ankle caused bolts of fire to shoot up through his body, and trying to put any weight on it almost made him pass out.

Suddenly the soldiers in the armor didn't seem that slow. Bracing himself with his left hand against the wall, he hopped down the corridor on his good foot, teeth clenched against the agony emanating from his knotted muscle. He heard the heavy footsteps of his pursuers closing in, and he half turned to fire off three quick shots back down the hall.

He didn't bother to aim; his blaster's warped barrel would have made it impossible to guess where the bolts were headed. All he wanted to do was send a warning to his pursuers, hopefully slowing them down. The pistol made strange sounds as he fired. Instead of the familiar sharp, reverberating twang, the shots sounded almost wet, with a lower pitch. With the bolts impeded by the warped barrel, the blaster's power pack wasn't able to fully discharge the intense energy buildup generated with each shot. He could feel the heat radiating out from the power pack in his hand, and he knew he couldn't keep shooting without risking a power pack overload and a deadly explosion of superheated gas.

On the bright side, the cramp was fading as he rounded another corner, and he was able to carefully put weight on his left foot again, though he still wasn't able to run at full speed. He pressed onward, hobbling along and hoping the security team behind him was the only one he had to worry about. If there was another team coming down the lift near Karrid's command chamber he'd be trapped between them with no hope of escape. To his relief, when he rounded the final turn he saw the long corridor leading to the entrance of the command chamber stretched out before him, totally empty. He shambled down the hall, but just as he passed the turbolift the door flew open.

Theron tried to wheel around and deliver a spinning kick to the first guard coming through the door, but as he planted his left leg and tried to push off for leverage, the calf seized up again. His leg caved beneath him, and instead of pulling off a dazzling martial arts move that left his opponent incapacitated, he ended up in a sweaty pile on the floor.

"Theron!" a familiar voice said, and he looked up to see Gnost-Dural standing over him, lightsaber in hand.

"Thought you were another security patrol," Theron grunted through the pain as the Jedi extended a hand to help him up.

"I ran into them on my way to the lift," the Jedi replied, his voice grim. In a lighter tone he added, "Why are you in your underwear?"

"Didn't want you to feel awkward," Theron said, nodding at the Kel Dor's own near nakedness as he leaned on him for support.

He stepped gingerly on his cramping leg and winced in pain. Before the Jedi could ask about it, a pair of guards from the pursuing security patrol poked their heads around the corner and fired. The Jedi stepped in front of Theron and batted away the blaster bolts before using the Force to hurl the guards back around the corner. From the grunts and groans it was clear they had slammed into the other members of the team hard enough to inflict real damage.

"Come on," Gnost-Dural said, using one hand to help

hold Theron upright while the other kept a firm grip on his lightsaber.

Together they staggered the last twenty meters to the sealed door ahead of them. Theron dropped to a knee to relieve the pressure on his injured leg, pulled the slicer spike from his boot, and set to work on the door.

At the same time, Gnost-Dural hurled his lightsaber down the hall, striking down a guard who'd dared to peek around the corner.

"I can't hold them off forever, Theron," he said. "And reinforcements are on the way."

As if summoned by his words, the turbolift door slid open again, spilling out another half dozen armored Imperial soldiers.

"Got it," Theron said, yanking his spike free and crawling forward on his hands and knees as the door slid open.

Gnost-Dural was right behind him, and as the guards in the hall opened fire, the two men rolled for cover on either side of the door's interior. With the bolts ricocheting off the floor, the Jedi reached up and jammed his lightsaber into the access panel on the wall, sending off a shower of sparks as the door slammed shut.

To Theron's surprise, the room was empty except for a control panel along the periphery, a large, opaque crystal sphere in the center, and three figures with facial tattoos and black robes sitting cross-legged on the floor around the sphere. Two were human males—one younger with white skin, the other older with dark skin. The third was a male red-skinned Sith pureblood. Their eyes were closed and they appeared to be lost deep in meditation.

Gnost-Dural sprang to his feet and hurled his lightsaber, but he wasn't aiming at any of the figures on the floor. The whirling blade flew over their heads and ricocheted off the crystal sphere before returning to the Jedi's hand, leaving no mark on the surface.

Simultaneously, the eyes of all three figures on the floor snapped open and they sprang to their feet, their weapons flaring to life. Instead of conventional weapons, the Sith held a pair of slightly shorter purple blades, one in each hand, while the dark-skinned man wielded a long, double-bladed lightsaber that seemed to shift between crimson and black.

"I see you've got some new friends," Gnost-Dural said to the apprentice he had faced before.

When he didn't reply, the Jedi said to Theron, "Let me deal with them. You find a way to get inside Karrid's command pod and stop her from destroying the Republic fleet!"

CHAPTER 32

DARTH KARRID had to admire the Republic fleet commander. Realizing they couldn't exchange blows with the *Ascendant Spear,* they'd switched tactics, scattering to harry her from a distance while employing a series of hit-and-run attacks and feints to frustrate her and extend the battle.

The defensive strategy gave them no hope of inflicting any actual damage against the *Spear,* but it prevented Karrid from wiping them all out in a single glorious attack. Instead, she was forced to hunt down each ship one by one. She began with one of the capital ships, turning the *Spear* on an intercept course as her target used a series of random and unexpected changes of direction to try to evade her. The other vessels in the Republic fleet tried to distract her from her goal, firing at her flanks while keeping to what seemed a safe distance.

But with the *Spear* there was no safe distance. Even as she closed on the first capital ship, choosing one of the three at random, she was able to target one of the corvettes swooping in on her starboard side. The *Spear*'s guns roared as the corvette tried to veer off at the last second, but the ion cannons were able to penetrate the shields, ravaging the hull and knocking out all power other than emergency life support.

Instead of changing course to finish off the now helpless corvette, Karrid continued to bear down on the capital ship, relentlessly pursuing it as she hammered away with her turbolasers, rapidly draining what remained of their shields in preparation for the coup de grâce.

The other two capital ships converged on her, guns blazing. Even the *Spear*'s deflectors couldn't hold up for long against their coordinated assault, and Karrid was forced to break off from her original prey . . . but not before unleashing a final volley that crippled the engines.

She changed course and accelerated, circling up and away from the other two capital ships before coming around to face them. The vessels wisely broke off in opposite directions, so she chose one at random and resumed her pursuit, knowing this one wouldn't be saved by an untimely intervention of the others . . . not with one of them forced to limp along at a fraction of its top speed.

Before she could engage the second capital ship, however, she felt a sudden drop in power, and the *Spear* slowed noticeably. It took her a moment to recognize what had happened, and then she realized she could no longer sense Quux, Ordez, and her apprentice. Something had broken them out of their meditative trance, forcing Karrid to rely only on her own power to control the vessel.

Briefly turning her focus from the battlefield to her immediate surroundings, she sensed a battle raging in the command chamber outside her impervious crystal sphere. Gnost-Dural had escaped and come for her. Karrid returned her attention to the battle, confident her new followers would be more than a match for the Jedi. And though it was more difficult trying to control the *Spear* alone, she had done it before.

At the same time, she sensed another intrusion attempt from the saboteur—this one coming from the control console outside her command pod. She batted away the clumsy attempt, knowing he would try again—one more distraction to further slow her down. Though it would now take longer to finish off the Republic fleet, Karrid knew that victory was still inevitable.

JACE HAD tasted defeat before, but never as bitter as this. Though the battle would drag on, he already knew it was over. Republic casualties were mounting; he'd lost several support vessels, and one of his capital ships was barely mobile. Now Karrid was coming after the *Aegis*.

The *Spear* was closing in on them, though more slowly than before. He didn't know if Karrid was being cautious, or if she was merely toying with them, but it didn't matter. Her ship was still too fast and maneuverable for them to outrun. And with only one capital ship still able to come to his aid, there wouldn't be enough of a threat to force her to break off her attack.

"Enemy coming in range," the helmsman noted.

Jace realized he meant they were now in the *Spear*'s range . . . they were still too far away for the *Aegis* to fight back.

"Divert all available power to the deflectors," he said, knowing it would only buy them a few more minutes. "Shut down everything except life support and sensors. Even the weapons systems."

The bridge suddenly went dark, lit only by the glow of the screens.

"Going to end bad?" Teff'ith asked from somewhere in the blackness.

"Very bad," Jace answered.

GNOST-DURAL RUSHED his three opponents, hoping to put a quick end to the battle. His blade flickered and danced as his body went into a series of spins and leaps. Karrid's apprentice—the one he'd fought before—

retreated, but the two newcomers met his assault head-on, driving him back with their aggressive counter-attacks.

Realizing he wasn't just facing raw apprentices this time, the Jedi switched back to a more defensive strategy as his enemies pressed forward. The Sith's twin purple blades came at him from all angles, a high slash from the right; a low cut from the left; a pair of diagonal chops. The human's massive double-bladed lightsaber was more direct, crashing down in a repetitive series of overhand strikes as he tried to bludgeon his way through Gnost-Dural's guard.

The Jedi Master met and repelled each and every attack, holding his ground behind a near-impenetrable wall of defense. Even with the apprentice joining the fray, he didn't waver—the Soresu style, when performed perfectly, could keep numerous attackers with a variety of styles at bay indefinitely . . . or at least until exhaustion and fatigue forced Gnost-Dural to make a mistake.

That was the great drawback of Soresu: it demanded a passive role—it could delay defeat, but it couldn't bring victory. And at three against one, his enemies would not need long to wear him down. Fortunately, despite the impressive individual skill possessed by two of his three opponents, his foes were not attacking him as a group. They lacked unity of purpose. They didn't time or coordinate their attacks, occasionally even getting in one another's way.

Gnost-Dural was able to exploit this single flaw to his advantage, drawing both of his more skilled opponents in at the same time by dipping his right shoulder and letting his blade slip a fraction too far forward as he parried one of his third foe's clumsy thrusts.

Both seized the chance to come at him hard, looking to exploit the perceived vulnerability, allowing Gnost-Dural to spin quickly away in the opposite direction.

Suddenly bereft of their shared target, the two Sith were forced to pull back and abort their attacks to keep from getting tangled up with each other, momentarily leaving the apprentice at Gnost-Dural's mercy.

He wasted no time in disposing of his lesser opponent. The apprentice blocked two overhand strikes, but then overreached when the Kel Dor feinted a third, leaving himself vulnerable down low. The Jedi turned his wrist and spun to his left, reversing the direction of his blade too quickly for the apprentice to recover, and removed him from the battle with a deep slash across the midsection that nearly severed the young man in two.

The entire sequence had taken less than a second, but even so Gnost-Dural barely turned back in time to ward off the next wave of attacks from the two more dangerous warriors. Once again he fell into the precise, efficient moves of Soresu to battle them to a standstill. But he could already feel fatigue creeping in, the intensity of the combat wearing him down despite the sustaining power of the Force.

THERON WORKED furiously at the command console along the edge of the room, knowing his slicer spike wouldn't last much longer before burning out. He'd overclocked to 150 percent capacity as he burrowed into the digital labyrinth, looking for a way to get inside Karrid's invulnerable crystal sphere.

This was different from slicing the relays in the engine room. The console was linked directly to Karrid's command pod, an emergency override her apprentices could use to get her out if something ever went wrong—say, if the vessel suffered major damage while she was at the controls, leaving her comatose and trapped inside the crystal sphere. But every time Theron tried to activate the emergency override, Karrid thwarted his efforts. She wasn't three steps ahead of him this time;

without the support of her meditating followers she had slowed down to Theron's level. But she had home-field advantage; she knew the inner workings of her ship better than he ever would.

Theron kept trying, waging digital war with her, painfully aware that time was running out. Gnost-Dural couldn't hold off her lightsaber-wielding bodyguards much longer; the security personnel in the hall were using a plasma torch to carve through the disabled door, and outside the *Spear* was picking off the Republic ships one by one.

He cursed as Karrid booted him from the system, forcing him to start all over.

"SHIELDS DOWN to ten percent," the helmsman said as another volley slammed into the *Aegis,* causing it to buck and heave.

Jace knew they'd already taken heavy damage; the only reason the alarms weren't blaring through the ship was because he'd diverted power from the emergency response systems to the deflectors. With their shields down to critical levels, one more hit was all it would take to finish them off.

"I'm sorry, Jace," Satele said, emerging from the darkness to place a hand on his shoulder.

He reached up and covered her hand with his thick, callused fingers.

"At least we fought the good fight," he replied, squeezing Satele's hand as they braced for the end.

THERON REALIZED what he was doing wrong. He was trying to gain control of the pod's emergency override— basically trying to pull control of a vital system out of Karrid's grasp. But he didn't need to control the emergency override to trigger it.

Instead of trying to take control of the system, he

flooded it with a rush of false data. Critical damage reports from all sectors of the vessel poured in, the catastrophic failure of the entire ship setting off the emergency evacuation alarms.

At the same time he heard a loud hiss as the airtight crystal sphere popped open. Darth Karrid was seated in a chair in the middle, surrounded by a writhing mass of loose, dangling wires that only seconds before had linked her to the ship.

The Falleen's eyes went wide and she screamed as the connection was broken—a keening wail of loss and suffering. Seeing Theron, she rose from her seat, pulled her lightsaber, and slowly advanced on him with murder in her eyes.

"STATUS REPORT!" Moff Lorman shouted as the evacuation alarms rang out on the bridge of the *Ascendant Spear*.

"Has to be a system malfunction, sir!" one of the crew said. "According to this, we're all dead."

"Darth Karrid has relinquished control of the vessel," someone else informed him.

The Moff hesitated, knowing his next decision could forever alter the course of his career . . . and possibly cost him his life. Darth Karrid had never turned control of the *Spear* over to him during battle. Not once. If she was incapacitated, then he clearly needed to step in. But it was hard to imagine how something like that could have happened.

What if she hadn't relinquished control? What if this was just another malfunction? Or some kind of ploy to trick the Republic? If he tried to take control of the ship against her wishes, she'd have him skinned alive.

"Sir? Do you want to take command?"

"No," he said. "Not yet. Not until we know what's going on."

* * *

IN THE darkness that enveloped the bridge of the *Aegis,* every second spent waiting for the *Spear*'s final attack felt like an eternity. Satele had turned her hand on Jace's shoulder so she could grip him more tightly—Jace felt her squeezing as hard as she could. He didn't mind; at least in their final moments they had each other.

Several more eternities ticked by. Then Teff'ith said, "Not dead yet."

No, Jace thought. *But we should be. Unless . . .*

"This is our chance! Transfer all power to the forward guns! All ships fire at will! Fire at will!"

AS THE *Ascendant Spear* heaved and shook under the relentless Republic assault, Moff Lorman realized the alarms ringing out were no longer due to a malfunction in the system. His reluctance to take command of the *Spear* had left it vulnerable, and the Republic fleet had seized the moment.

All around him people were shouting, relaying damage reports from all decks. He had no idea if Darth Karrid was still alive, but he wasn't going to hesitate a second time.

"Abandon ship!" he shouted, thumbing the button to transmit his orders to the entire crew. "By order of Moff Lorman, abandon ship!"

Then he jumped from his chair and joined the rush of men and women racing from the bridge toward the nearest escape pods.

CHAPTER 33

IN ALL her years learning the ways of the dark side, Karrid had never felt a rage like this. The alarms pealing through the ship only added to her fury; to her they were like the cries of her own child. The worm crawling away from her in his underwear had caused this. The maggot had violated her ship, his intrusion corrupting the *Spear*. He had befouled Darth Mekhis's perfect creation. He had torn her away from her second self, severing the bond that made her whole. For that, she wasn't going to just kill him. She wasn't even going to capture him and strap him to the interrogation machine. She was going to hack him apart piece by piece, listening to him scream and beg for mercy as she hewed off his limbs one by one before gutting him and leaving him writhing in agony on the floor.

THERON DIDN'T bother calling out to Gnost-Dural for help as Karrid slowly advanced on him; the Jedi already had his hands full. He didn't try to reason with his assailant, either—he could see the madness in her eyes.

She threw her lightsaber and Theron rolled out of the way, grabbing his damaged blaster from where it rested on the floor beside him as he did so. The blade cleaved the control panel he'd used to slice into the *Spear* and force her from her pod, and he realized she hadn't been aiming at him—she was just destroying the thing he'd used against her.

The lightsaber flew back to her hand and she turned to Theron, who was still lying on the floor. He raised his blaster and pointed it at her, a hollow gesture considering he couldn't fire it again without causing the overloaded power pack to explode.

She took another step forward, raising her blade to hurl it again, and this time Theron knew he was going to be the target. Just as the blade was released from her hand, the entire ship was rocked, knocking Karrid off balance and disrupting her aim by a few precious centimeters. The deadly blade carved a furrow in the floor just beside Theron's right hand.

The room shook again, and Theron heard the distant sound of an explosion, audible even over the clanging alarms. It was followed quickly by several more detonations, and the entire vessel began to shake and shudder as the Republic fleet rained fire down upon them. Karrid screamed and wheeled away from Theron, racing back to her command pod so she could retake control and save her precious ship. She threw herself into the seat, the dangling wires coming to life, their tips burrowing into the implants of her flesh.

Theron squeezed the trigger on his defective blaster. No bolts came out, but the power pack shrieked and squealed in protest. He hurled the blaster in Karrid's direction. It landed short and skittered across the floor, sliding up against the base of her command chair as the two halves of the sphere snapped shut.

Even through the impervious crystal, the explosion was loud enough to make his ears ring. It was impossible to see through the opaque crystal to witness the gruesome carnage inside, but Theron didn't necessarily think that was a bad thing. As much as he wanted to defeat Darth Karrid, he had no desire to see her splattered all over the command pod's walls.

But though their Master was dead, her apprentices fought on.

MASTER GNOST-DURAL saw Darth Karrid leave her pod and head toward Theron, but he wasn't able to break away from his duel with the two Sith Lords. As fatigue had whittled away the Jedi's speed and concentration, he had stopped being able to stand his ground. The relentless pressure of his opponents had slowly driven him backward until they had him against the wall.

Despite what was happening all around them, their battle had raged on unabated. With single-minded focus his enemies ignored the alarms as they began to ring out. The explosions that rocked the ship and made the entire room shake had given them no pause. But the blast from inside Karrid's command pod was so near and so loud it actually snapped the attention of all three combatants away from their duel.

Over the loudspeaker a voice rose above the alarms, giving the order to abandon ship. Gnost-Dural knew the Imperial soldiers outside trying to cut through the door would heed the call, but he wasn't so sure about the two Sith in the room.

"You can stay and finish me off as this ship crumbles around us," the Kel Dor said, gasping for breath. "Or we can call this a draw and make a break for the escape pods."

The pureblood raised his purple blades as if ready to continue the fight, but he quickly changed his mind when his partner turned and raced toward the exit. A powerful blast of the Force sent the jammed door panel hurtling out into the now empty hall beyond. A second later they were gone, disappearing down the hall.

Another explosion caused the *Spear* to start listing

over to its side. The artificial gravity systems should have reacted and automatically recalibrated themselves. But the damage inflicted by the Republic fleet must have been too great, and suddenly Gnost-Dural found himself slipping down the tilted floor. He slid out the door and into the corridor, joined a second later by Theron. The Jedi Master used the Force to keep himself from slamming into the wall; the SIS agent wasn't so lucky.

"I think we've overstayed our welcome," Theron said.

"Lead the way," the Jedi offered.

The ship slowly continued to tip, and soon the side wall served as their floor. They reached the turbolift without seeing any sign of the two Sith Lords, or any of the soldiers they had run into earlier.

"Looks like we're the last ones at the party," Theron said as the lift doors opened and they awkwardly crawled inside. "Better remember to turn out the lights."

"I think the Republic is doing that for us," the Jedi answered as another series of explosions capsized the *Spear* completely and the turbolift shuddered to a halt.

FROM ON board the bridge of the *Aegis,* Jace watched the mass exodus of nearly a thousand escape pods as the Imperials fled the *Ascendant Spear*. By his order, the fleet was still firing on Karrid's ship. He thought about calling off the assault; he had no idea if his son—and Master Gnost-Dural—were still aboard. But the risk of a final retaliation, even as the vessel lay dying, was too great. As Supreme Commander of the Republic forces, he couldn't jeopardize the lives of everyone aboard the ships under his command for the sake of a single person— not even his own son.

He tried to reassure himself by arguing that he didn't actually have any proof Theron had been on the ship during the battle, but given everything that had taken place it was likely. Hopefully he had some way of getting off alive, though from what he knew of his son, not having a pre-planned evacuation strategy wouldn't have stopped him.

The escape pods continued to deploy, shooting off in a hundred different directions. It would be impossible to track them all down . . . though it wouldn't be hard to turn the guns of the fleet against them and wipe virtually all of them out.

"Just letting them all go?" Teff'ith asked.

"What do you care?" Jace snapped.

"Don't," the Twi'lek said with a shrug. "Just surprised. Thought you hated Imps."

Lacking hyperdrives, the range of the pods was limited; most would end up landing on Duro's orbital cities, where authorities would take them into custody. Some would head in the opposite direction, trying to make it to the system's less populated worlds. There they would hole up, relying on the transponders to lead an Imperial recovery team to their location for rescue, but the number who would actually make it back to the Empire was minimal.

Besides, Jace thought, *Theron might be on one of them.*

He glanced over at Satele and saw that her eyes were staring off into the distance at nothing in particular. He recognized the look; she was reaching out with the Force to try to find Theron and Gnost-Dural.

"Are they out there?"

"I don't know," she said at last, bowing her head in defeat. "The dark side energies of the *Spear* make it difficult to see. Perhaps if we had a special bond . . ." She trailed off.

"Don't worry," Teff'ith said. "Theron's tough. Just better remember to pay us when it's over."

Despite her seemingly cavalier attitude, even Jace could tell she was as troubled as the rest of them.

* * *

THERON HAD left his slicer spike behind in the control console of Karrid's inner sanctum; at the time retrieving it had taken a backseat to avoiding getting chopped in half by her flying lightsaber. Without it, however, he was unable to slice into the turbolift to try to restart it. Forced to rely on cruder methods, he kicked the wall twice and a deep groan came up from the shaft below— or maybe now it was above. Slowly, the lift started moving again.

"I'm surprised that worked," the Jedi remarked.

"Me and this ship have a bit of a history now," Theron said with a wink.

When they reached D Deck the lift doors opened several centimeters, then stopped. Theron kicked the wall again, but nothing happened.

"Can you, uh, you know?" Theron asked his companion, twiddling his fingers in the air.

"Using the Force is more taxing than you think," the Jedi told him. "Grab on." Gnost-Dural took hold of the edge of one of the doors, Theron the other. Grunting and straining, they managed to make enough room to squeeze through. The corridor beyond was dark—even the emergency lighting had failed. As they climbed out onto the floor—what had been the ceiling before the *Spear* capsized—the Jedi ignited his green blade to light their way. The ship shuddered again, and they heard a deep boom—distinctly different from the sound of the explosions caused by the Republic bombardment.

"Engine room," Theron said. "Cooling systems must have shut down."

He knew Gnost-Dural didn't need him to explain what would happen when the hypermatter containment unit overheated—the resulting explosion would vaporize the entire ship. Scrambling down the hall, they reached the escape pod bays.

"Empty," Theron muttered as they passed the first bay. "Empty. Empty. Empty. Ah—there it is!

"Karrid's private escape pod," Theron said with a smile. "Figured nobody would be dumb enough to grab it."

They piled in as the ship began to shake even more violently than before. Theron slammed the button to seal the pod doors and Gnost-Dural punched the controls to jettison them out into space.

Theron looked back at the dying *Spear* through the rear viewport as they floated away. The ship erupted in a fireworks display of explosions, each one seemingly brighter and larger than the last. And then the vessel was consumed in a brilliant white flash, punctuated by the rapidly expanding ring of glowing energy that characterized a massive hypermatter explosion.

AN OPPRESSIVE silence hovered over the bridge of the *Aegis*. The sound of fingers tapping at control consoles and the soft electronic beeps from the workstations only emphasized the complete lack of conversation.

It's been too long, Jace thought. *Nobody on board could have survived that last explosion.*

He glanced over at Satele, but she didn't return his gaze. She was standing with her eyes closed and her hands clasped in front of her chest. Jace had no way of knowing if she was still trying to use the Force to find Theron, or if she was just trying to hold herself together.

"Signal coming in from one of the escape pods, sir!"

The crewman's voice shattered the silence. Startled, Jace let out a breath he didn't even know he was holding.

"Patch it through," the Supreme Commander ordered, his heart pounding with a mixture of hope and dread.

"Hey, *Aegis*," Theron's voice came over the speaker.

"Any chance me and my Jedi friend here can hitch a ride?"

FIVE MINUTES later Jace, Satele, and Teff'ith were down in the docking bay—along with another twenty members of the *Aegis* crew—as the escape pod door popped open. Master Gnost-Dural came out first, followed by Theron. Everyone assembled broke into a round of spontaneous applause and cheers. Jace joined in, slapping his big hands heartily together as an unexpected wave of pride and joy he hadn't felt in years rushed through him. It was all he could do to keep from charging forward and embracing both of the heroes in a fierce bear hug.

"Welcome back," he said, snapping off a sharp salute instead.

"Looks like everyone showed up to say hi," Theron said, his eyes shifting from the crowd, to Jace, to Teff'ith, and finally to Satele. "And I do mean everyone."

"The Republic owes you a debt it can never repay," Satele said, and Jace could tell she was also struggling to stay reserved in front of the rest of the assembled troops.

It was the irrepressible Twi'lek who finally said what they were all thinking but didn't have the courage to bring up.

"You know you both naked, right?"

EPILOGUE

JACE TRIED to project an outward display of authoritarian calm as he sat in the chair behind his desk, but inside his stomach was churning.

This is crazy. You've done a million debriefs. This is no different.

But it was different, simply because of who was involved.

Satele and Master Gnost-Dural were already there, seated in two of the four chairs that had been set up on the other side of Jace's desk. The other two seats were empty, reserved for the Director and, of course, Theron. Three days had passed since the victory at Duro. In that time, Jace hadn't spoken to either Satele or Theron, apart from a few words as he presented Theron, Gnost-Dural, and Teff'ith with the Cross of Glory, the Republic's highest honor, at a semi-private ceremony attended by several dozen dignitaries and officials. From the other side of the door he heard his receptionist's cheerful, high-pitched laugh; a few seconds later the door opened and Marcus stepped in, closing it behind them.

"Where's Theron?" Jace asked.

"He said he couldn't make it," the Director said, clearly uncomfortable. "He's given me his report. We can contact him after the debrief if we have any follow-up questions."

Jace was stunned. Blowing off the debriefing wasn't an

official act of insubordination; technically Theron answered to the Director, not Jace. Marcus could have ordered him to come, of course, but that would have been entirely counterproductive. Still, Jace had been hoping to see him.

"Okay then," he said, covering his disappointment with gruff professionalism. "Let's begin."

The debrief didn't take nearly as long as Jace would have expected for an assignment of this nature and complexity. He could have blustered about how the entire mission was put in jeopardy because Theron and Gnost-Dural failed to follow orders, but it would have been just for show. Everyone in the room knew the truth, and Jace trusted Satele and Marcus to know best how to handle their people going forward. Instead, they stuck to facts and analysis, and the whole thing was over in less than an hour.

As everyone rose to leave, Jace said, "Grand Master Satele, can you stay a moment?"

Gnost-Dural and the Director left quickly, closing the door behind them without being asked.

"You aren't the only one who was hoping Theron would be here," Satele said once they were alone.

"Is it that obvious?" he asked, coming out from behind his desk to try to pace out some of his frustration.

"It is to me," Satele said, standing motionless as she watched him go back and forth. "But I can understand why he wouldn't be in the mood for a family reunion."

"Do you think he still blames me?"

"You did the right thing. You brought the fleet to Duro."

"Does that make up for letting the Empire attack Ruan?"

"We can't always fix our mistakes," she told him. "We can only learn from them."

Jace frowned—as usual, he didn't find the typical Jedi

wisdom particularly helpful. He stopped pacing and turned to Satele, standing right in front of her.

"How do I make this right?"

Satele shook her head. "You know him as well as I do."

"That's the problem," he said. "I want to get to know him better."

"Then wait for him to come to you," she said.

"That doesn't seem to be working too well for you," Jace pointed out.

"The circumstances of your relationship with our son are different from mine," Satele noted, and Jace sensed a deep regret behind her words.

"Don't you ever want to go and talk to him?"

"There are a lot of things we want that we cannot have," she answered, her expression unreadable. "It's the burden of leadership."

She reached out and placed a tender hand on his shoulder. She left it there for a long moment, then pulled away and turned to go.

"Good-bye, Supreme Commander."

"Good-bye, Grand Master," he replied.

When she was gone, he sat down at his desk and fired up his workstation, determined to lose himself in the endless mountain of reports that always seemed to need his attention. To his surprise, he saw there was a private holorecording waiting for him.

"Sorry I missed the debrief, Commander," Theron said to him when he opened the message. "Something I needed to take care of. But maybe later we can go get that drink we talked about. Give us a chance to just . . . I don't know . . . talk, I guess."

Jace flicked off the message as it ended with a small, contented smile.

HIDDEN IN the shadows in the back corner of Teff'ith's hotel room, Theron watched the Twi'lek pack, listening with amusement to her grumbling complaints as she rummaged through the room in search of anything worth stealing.

"Stupid Republic gives us a stupid medal! Can't spend medal. Not even worth it to melt down."

"Looking for something?" he asked, stepping into view.

As if by magic, her blaster suddenly appeared in her hand.

"How'd you get in?"

"Believe it or not, these high-class hotels don't actually have great security."

Teff'ith lowered her blaster, but shot him a dirty look. "Never paid us," she accused.

"Got your credits right here," Theron said, pointing to a bag in the corner where he'd been standing.

"Actual credits? Not a Republic chip?"

"Ten thousand actual credits. I didn't think a Republic credit chip would have much value where you're going."

"Ten thousand?" she protested. "What about credits Gorvich stole from us?"

"That's between you and him," Theron said with a shrug.

"Knew we couldn't trust you," Teff'ith said with a scowl as she went over and picked up the bag.

"I might be able to come up with a couple thousand more if you stick around," he offered.

"Not staying," she said, dumping the credits onto the hotel room bed so she could count them. "Hate it here. Too shiny."

I know what you mean, Theron thought. Out loud he asked, "So what's your plan?"

"Don't know. Figure it out. Can't go back to Old Tion Brotherhood thanks to you."

"I bet the Director could find a position for you with SIS as a field agent."

"Pass," she said, scooping up the credits and stuffing them back into the bag. "Not interested in filing reports for a boss behind a desk. We only work for ourselves."

She slung the bag over her shoulder and headed toward the door. Before leaving, she turned back to Theron.

"No more spying on us," she said, waggling a finger in his direction. "Don't need you watching over our shoulder like big brother."

Theron watched her go, not saying anything until the door had closed behind her.

"You might not need me watching over your shoulder, but I'll be there anyway," he vowed softly. "That's what family does."

READ ON FOR AN EXCERPT FROM

STAR WARS: SCOUNDRELS

BY TIMOTHY ZAHN

PUBLISHED BY DEL REY BOOKS

THE STARLINES collapsed into stars, and the Imperial Star Destroyer *Dominator* had arrived. Standing on the command walkway, his hands clasped stiffly behind his back, Captain Worhven glared at the misty planet floating in the blackness directly ahead and wondered what in blazes he and his ship were doing here.

For these were not good times. The Emperor's sudden dissolution of the Imperial Senate had sent dangerous swells of uncertainty throughout the galaxy, which played into the hands of radical groups like the so-called Rebel Alliance. At the same time, criminal organizations like Black Sun and the Hutt syndicates openly flouted the law, buying and selling spice, stolen merchandise, and local and regional officials alike.

Even worse, Palpatine's brand-new toy, the weapon that was supposed to finally convince both insurgents and lawbreakers that the Empire was deadly serious about taking them down, had inexplicably been destroyed at Yavin. Worhven still hadn't heard an official explanation for that incident.

Evil times indeed. And evil times called for a strong and massive response. The minute the word came in from Yavin, Imperial Center should have ordered a full Fleet deployment, concentrating its efforts on the most important, the most insubordinate, and the most jittery systems. It was the classic response to crisis, a method that dated back thousands of years, and by all rights and logic the *Dominator* should have been at the forefront of any such deployment.

Instead, Worhven and his ship had been pressed into mule cart duty.

"Ah—Captain," a cheery voice boomed behind him.

Worhven took a deep, calming breath. "Lord d'Ashewl," he replied, making sure to keep his back to the other while he forced his expression into something more politically proper for the occasion.

It was well he'd started rearranging his face when he did. Barely five seconds later d'Ashewl came to a stop beside him, right up at his side instead of stopping the two steps back that Worhven demanded of even senior officers until he gestured them forward.

But that was hardly a surprise. What would a fat, stupid, accidentally rich member of Imperial Center's upper court know of ship's protocol?

A rhetorical question. The answer, of course, was nothing.

But if d'Ashewl didn't understand basic courtesy, Worhven did. And he would treat his guest with the proper respect. Even if it killed him. "My lord," he said politely, turning to face the other. "I trust you slept well."

"I did," d'Ashewl said, his eyes on the planet ahead. "So that's Wukkar out there, is it?"

"Yes, my lord," Worhven said, resisting the urge to wonder aloud if d'Ashewl thought the *Dominator* might have somehow drifted off course during ship's night. "As per your orders."

"Yes, yes, of course," d'Ashewl said, craning his neck a little. "It's just so hard to tell from this distance. Most worlds out there look distressingly alike."

"Yes, my lord," Worhven repeated, again resisting the words that so badly wanted to come out. That was the

kind of comment made only by the inexperienced or blatantly stupid. With d'Ashewl, it was probably a toss-up.

"But if you say it's Wukkar, then I believe it," d'Ashewl
continued. "Have you compiled the list of incoming
yachts that I asked for?"

Worhven suppressed a sigh. Not just mule cart duty,
but handmaiden duty as well. "The comm officer has
it," he said, turning his head and gesturing toward the
starboard crew pit. Out of the corner of his eye he saw
now that he and d'Ashewl weren't alone: d'Ashewl's
young manservant, Dayja, had accompanied his superior and was standing a respectful half dozen steps back
along the walkway.

At least one of the pair knew something about proper
protocol.

"Excellent, excellent," d'Ashewl said, rubbing his hands
together. "There's a wager afoot, Captain, as to which
of our group will arrive first and which will arrive last.
Thanks to you and your magnificent ship, I stand to win
a great deal of money."

Worhven felt his lip twist. A ludicrous and pointless
wager, to match the *Dominator*'s ludicrous and pointless errand. It was nice to know that in a universe on the
edge of going mad, there was still ironic symmetry to be
found.

"You'll have your man relay the data to my floater,"
d'Ashewl continued. "My man and I shall leave as soon
as the *Dominator* reaches orbit." He cocked his head.
"Your orders *were* to remain in the region in the event
that I needed further transport, were they not?"

The captain allowed his hands, safely out of d'Ashewl's
sight at his sides, to curl into frustrated fists. "Yes, my
lord."

"Good," d'Ashewl said cheerfully. "Lord Toorfi has
been known to suddenly change his mind on where the
games are to continue, and if he does, I need to be ready

to once again beat him to the new destination. You'll be no more than three hours away at all times, correct?"

"Yes, my lord," Worhven said. Fat, stupid, and a cheat besides. Clearly, all the others involved in this vague high-stakes gaming tournament had arrived at Wukkar via their own ships. Only d'Ashewl had had the supreme gall to talk someone on Imperial Center into letting him borrow an Imperial Star Destroyer for the occasion.

"But for now, all I need is for your men to prepare to launch my floater," d'Ashewl continued. "After that, you may take the rest of the day off. Perhaps the rest of the month as well. One never knows how long old men's stamina and credits will last, eh?"

Without waiting for a reply—which was just as well, because Worhven didn't have any that he was willing to share—the rotund man turned and waddled back along the walkway toward the aft bridge. Dayja waited until he'd passed, then dropped into step the prescribed three paces behind him.

Worhven watched until the pair had passed beneath the archway and into the aft bridge turbolift, just to make sure they were truly gone. Then, unclenching his teeth, he turned to the comm officer. "Signal Hangar Command," he ordered. "Our passenger is ready to leave."

He threw a final glower at the aft bridge. Take the day off, indeed. Enough condescending idiocy like that from the Empire's ruling class, and Worhven would be sorely tempted to join the Rebellion himself. "And tell them to make it quick," he added. "I don't want Lord d'Ashewl or his ship aboard a single millisecond longer than necessary."

"I SHOULD probably have you whipped," d'Ashewl commented absently.

Dayja half turned in the floater's command chair to look over his shoulder. "Excuse me?" he asked.

"I said I should probably have you whipped," d'Ashewl repeated, gazing at his datapad as he lazed comfortably on the luxurious couch in the lounge just behind the cockpit.

"Any particular reason?"

"Not really," d'Ashewl said. "But it's becoming the big thing among the upper echelon of the court these days, and I'd hate to be left out of the truly important trends."

"Ah," Dayja said. "I trust these rituals aren't done in public?"

"Oh, no, the sessions are quite private and secretive," d'Ashewl assured him. "But that's a good point. Unless we happen to meet up with others of my same lofty stature, there really wouldn't be any purpose." He considered. "At least not until we get back to Imperial Center. We may want to try it then."

"Speaking only for myself, I'd be content to put it off," Dayja said. "It *does* sound rather pointless."

"That's because you have a lower-class attitude," d'Ashewl chided. "It's a conspicuous-consumption sort of thing. A demonstration that one has such an over-abundance of servants and slaves that he can afford to put one out of commission for a few days merely on a whim."

"It still sounds pointless," Dayja said. "Ripping someone's flesh from his body is a great deal of work. I prefer to have a good reason if I'm going to go to that much effort." He nodded at the datapad. "Any luck?"

"Unfortunately, the chance cubes aren't falling in our favor," d'Ashewl said, tossing the instrument onto the couch beside him. "Our tip-off came just a bit too late. It looks like Qazadi is already here."

"You're sure?"

"There were only eight possibilities, and all eight have landed and their passengers dispersed."

Dayja turned back forward, eyeing the planet rushing up toward them and trying to estimate distances and times. If the yacht carrying their quarry had *just* landed, there might still be a chance of intercepting him before he went to ground.

"And the latest was over three hours ago," d'Ashewl added. "So you might as well ease back on the throttle and enjoy the ride."

Dayja suppressed a flicker of annoyance. "So in other words, we took the *Dominator* out of service for nothing."

"Not entirely," d'Ashewl said. "Captain Worhven had the opportunity to work on his patience level."

Despite his frustration, Dayja had to smile. "You *do* play the pompous-jay role very well."

"Thank you," d'Ashewl said. "I'm glad my talents are still of *some* use to the department. And don't be too annoyed that we missed him. It would have been nicely dramatic, snatching him out of the sky as we'd hoped. But such a triumph would have come with its own set of costs. For one thing, Captain Worhven would have had to be brought into your confidence, which would have cost you a perfectly good cover identity."

"And possibly yours?"

"Very likely," d'Ashewl agreed. "And while the Director has plenty of scoundrel and server identities to pass out, he can slip someone into the Imperial court only so often before the other members catch on. They may be arrogant and pompous, but they're not stupid. All things considered, it's probably just as well things have worked out this way."

"Perhaps," Dayja said, not entirely ready to concede the point. "Still, he's going to be harder to get out of Villachor's mansion than he would have been if we'd caught him along the way."

"Even so, it will be easier than digging him out of one of Black Sun's complexes on Imperial Center," d'Ashewl countered. "Assuming we could find him in that rat hole in the first place." He gestured toward the viewport. "And don't think it would have been *that* easy to pluck him out of space. Think Xizor's *Virago*, only scaled up fifty or a hundred times, and you'll get an idea what kind of nut it would have been to crack."

"All nuts can be cracked," Dayja said with a shrug. "All it takes is the right application of pressure."

"Provided the nutcracker itself doesn't break in the process," d'Ashewl said, his voice going suddenly dark. "You've never tangled with Black Sun at this level, Dayja. I have. Qazadi is one of the worst, with every bit of Xizor's craftiness and manipulation."

"But without the prince's charm?"

"Joke if you wish," d'Ashewl rumbled. "But be careful. If not for yourself, for me. I have the ghosts of far too many lost agents swirling through my memory as it is."

"I understand," Dayja said quietly. "I'll be careful."

"Good." D'Ashewl huffed out a short puff of air, an affectation Dayja guessed he'd picked up from others of Imperial Center's elite. "All right. We still don't know why Qazadi is here: whether he's on assignment, lying low, or in some kind of disfavor with Xizor and the rest of the upper echelon. If it's the third, we're out of luck."

"As is Qazadi," Dayja murmured.

"Indeed," d'Ashewl agreed. "But if it's one of the first two . . ." He shook his head. "Those files could rock Imperial Center straight out of orbit."

Which was enough reason all by itself for them to play this whole thing very carefully, Dayja knew. "But we're sure he'll be staying at Villachor's?"

"I can't see him coming to Wukkar and staying anywhere but the sector chief's mansion," d'Ashewl said. "But there may be other possibilities, and it wouldn't hurt for you to poke around a bit. I've downloaded everything we've got on Villachor, his people, and the Marblewood Estate for you. Unfortunately, there isn't much."

"I guess I'll have to get inside and see the place for myself," Dayja said. "I'm thinking the upcoming Festival of Four Honorings will be my best bet."

"*If* Villachor follows his usual pattern of hosting one of Iltarr City's celebrations at Marblewood," d'Ashewl warned. "It's possible that with Qazadi visiting he'll pass that role to someone else."

"I don't think so," Dayja said. "High-level Black Sun operatives like to use social celebrations as cover for meetings with offworld contacts and to set up future opportunities. In fact, given the timing of Qazadi's visit, it's possible he's here to observe or assist with some particularly troublesome problem."

"You've done your homework," d'Ashewl said. "Excellent. Do bear in mind, though, that the influx of people also means Marblewood's security force will be on heightened alert."

"Don't worry," Dayja said calmly. "You can get through any door if you know the proper way to knock. I'll just keep knocking until I find the pattern."

ACCORDING TO Wukkar's largest and most influential fashion magazines, all of which were delighted to run extensive stories on Avrak Villachor whenever he paid them to do so, Villachor's famed Marblewood Estate was one of the true showcases of the galaxy. It was essentially a country manor in the midst of Iltarr City: a walled-off expanse of landscaped grounds surrounding a former governor's mansion built in classic High Empress Teta style.

The more breathless of the commentators liked to remind their readers of Villachor's many business and philanthropic achievements and awards, and predicted that there would be more such honors in the future. Other commentators, the unpaid ones, countered with more ominous suggestions that Villachor's most likely achievement would be to suffer an early and violent death.

Both predictions were probably right; the thought flicked through Villachor's mind as he stood at the main entrance to his mansion and watched the line of five ordinary-looking landspeeders float through the gate and into his courtyard. In fact, there was every chance that he was about to face one or the other of those events right now.

The only question was which one.

Proper etiquette on Wukkar dictated that a host be waiting beside the landspeeder door when a distinguished guest emerged. In this case, though, that would be impossible. All five landspeeders had dark-tint windows, and there was no way to know which one his mysterious visitor was riding in. If Villachor guessed wrong, not only would he have violated prescribed manners, but he would also look like a fool.

And so he paused on the bottom step until the landspeeders came to a well-practiced simultaneous halt. The doors of all but the second vehicle opened and began discharging the passengers, most of them hardfaced human men who would have fit in seamlessly with Villachor's own cadre of guards and enforcers. They spread out into a loose and casual-looking circle around the vehicles, and one of them murmured something into the small comlink clip on his collar. The final landspeeder's doors opened—

Villachor felt his throat tighten as he caught his first glimpse of gray-green scales above a colorful beaded tunic. This was no human. This was a *Falleen*.

And not just one, but an entire landspeeder full of them. Even as Villachor started forward, two Falleen emerged from each side of the vehicle, their hands on their holstered blasters, their eyes flicking to and past Villachor to the mansion towering behind him. Special bodyguards, which could only be for an equally special guest. Villachor picked up his pace, trying to hurry without looking like it, his heart thudding with unpleasant anticipation. If it was Prince Xizor in that landspeeder, this day was likely to end very badly. Unannounced visits from Black Sun's chief nearly always did.

It was indeed another Falleen who stepped out into the sunlight as Villachor reached his proper place at the vehicle's side. But to his quiet relief, it wasn't Xizor. It was merely Qazadi, one of Black Sun's nine vigos.

It was only as Villachor dropped to one knee and bowed his head in reverence to his guest that the significance of that thought belatedly struck him. *Only* one of the nine most powerful beings in Black Sun?

Just because the Falleen standing in front of him wasn't Xizor didn't mean the day might not still end in death.

"I greet you, Your Excellency," Villachor said, bowing even lower. If he was in trouble, an extra show of humility probably wouldn't save him, but it might at least buy him a less painful death. "I'm Avrak Villachor, chief of this sector's operations, and your humble servant."

"I greet you in turn, Sector Chief Villachor," Qazadi said. His voice was smooth and melodious, very much like Xizor's, but with a darker edge of menace lurking beneath it. "You may rise."

"Thank you, Your Excellency," Villachor said, getting back to his feet. "How may I serve you?"

"You may take me to a guest suite," Qazadi said. His eyes seemed to glitter with private amusement. "And then you may relax."

Villachor frowned. "Excuse me, Your Excellency?" he asked carefully.

"You fear that I've come to exact judgment upon you," Qazadi said, his voice still dark yet at the same time oddly conversational. The gray-green scales of his face were changing, too, showing just a hint of pink on his upper cheeks. "And such thoughts should never be simply dismissed," the Falleen added, "for I don't leave Imperial Center without great cause."

"Yes, Your Excellency," Villachor said. The sense of dark uncertainty still hung over the group like an early morning fog, but to his mild surprise he could feel his heartbeat slowing and an unexpected calm beginning to flow through him. Something about the Falleen's voice was more soothing than he'd realized.

"But in this case, the cause has nothing to do with you," Qazadi continued. "With Lord Vader's absence from Imperial Center leaving his spies temporarily leaderless, Prince Xizor has decided it would be wise to shuffle the cards a bit." He gave Villachor a thin smile. "In this case, a most appropriate metaphor."

Villachor felt his mouth go suddenly dry. Was Qazadi actually talking about—? "My vault is at your complete disposal, Your Excellency," he managed.

"Thank you," Qazadi said, as if Villachor actually had a choice in the matter. "While my guards bring in my belongings and arrange my suite, we will go investigate the security of your vault."

The breeze that had been drifting across Villachor's face shifted direction, and suddenly the calmness that had settled comfortably across his mind vanished. It hadn't been Qazadi's voice at all, Villachor realized acidly, but just another of those cursed body-chemical tricks Falleen liked to pull on people. "As you wish, Your Excellency," he said, bowing again and gesturing to the mansion door. "Please, follow me."

THE HOTEL that d'Ashewl had arranged for was in the very center of Iltarr City's most exclusive district, and the Imperial Suite was the finest accommodation the hotel had to offer. More important, from Dayja's point of view, the humble servants' quarters tacked onto one edge of the suite had a private door that opened right beside one of the hotel's back stairwells.

An hour after d'Ashewl finished his grand midafternoon dinner and retired to his suite, Dayja had changed from servant's livery to more nondescript clothing and was on the streets. A few minutes' walk took him out of the enclave of the rich and powerful and into a poorer, nastier section of the city.

Modern Intelligence operations usually began at a field officer's desk, with a complete rundown of the target's communications, finances, and social webs. But in this case, Dayja knew, such an approach would be less than useless. Black Sun's top chiefs were exceptionally good at covering their tracks and burying all the connections and pings that could be used to ensnare lesser criminals. In addition, many of those hidden connections had built-in flags to alert the crime lord to the presence of an investigation. The last thing Dayja could afford would be to drive Qazadi deeper underground or, worse, send him scurrying back to Imperial Center, where he would once again be under the direct protection of Xizor and the vast Black Sun resources there.

And so Dayja would do this the old-fashioned way: poking and prodding at the edges of Black Sun's operations in Iltarr City, making a nuisance of himself until he drew the right person's attention.

He spent the rest of the evening just walking around,

observing the people and absorbing the feel and rhythms of the city. As the sky darkened toward evening he went back to one of the three clandestine dealers he'd spotted earlier and bought two cubes of Nyriaan spice, commenting casually about the higher quality of the drug that he was used to.

By the time he was ready to head back to the hotel he had bought samples from two more dealers, making similar disparaging observations each time. Black Sun dealt heavily in Nyriaan spice, and there was a good chance that all three dealers were connected at least peripherally to Villachor. With any luck, news of this contemptuous stranger would begin filtering up the command chain.

He was within sight of the upper-class enclave's private security station when he was jumped by three young toughs.

For the first hopeful moment he thought that perhaps Black Sun's local intel web was better than he'd expected. But it was quickly clear that the thugs weren't working for Villachor or anyone else, but merely wanted to steal the cubes of spice he was carrying. All three of the youths carried knives, and one of them had a small blaster, and there was a burning fire in their eyes that said they would have the spice no matter what the cost.

Unfortunately for them, Dayja had a knife, too, one he'd taken off the body of a criminal who'd had similar plans. Thirty seconds later, he was once again walking toward home, leaving the three bodies dribbling blood into the drainage gutter alongside the walkway.

Tomorrow, he decided, he would suggest that d'Ashewl make a show of visiting some of the local cultural centers, where Dayja would have a chance to better size up the city's ruling class. Then it would be another solo excursion into the fringes, and more of this same kind of subtle troublemaking. Between the high classes and the low, sooner or later Villachor or his people were bound to take notice.

He was well past the security station, with visions of a soft bed dancing before his eyes, before the police finally arrived to collect the bodies he'd left behind.

HAN SOLO had never been in Reggilio's Cantina before. But he'd been in hundreds just like it, and he knew the type well. It was reasonably quiet, though from wariness rather than good manners; slightly boisterous, though with the restraint that came of the need to keep a low profile; and decorated in dilapidated scruffiness, with no apologies offered or expected.

It was, in short, the perfect place for a trap.

A meter away on the other half of the booth's wraparound seat, Chewbacca growled unhappily.

"No kidding," Han growled back, tapping his fingertips restlessly against the mug of Corellian spiced ale that he still hadn't touched. "But if there's even a chance this is legit, we have to take it."

Chewbacca rumbled a suggestion.

"No," Han said flatly. "They're running a rebellion, remember? They haven't got anything extra to spare."

Chewbacca growled again.

"Sure we're worth it," Han agreed. "Shooting those TIEs off Luke alone should have doubled the reward. But you saw the look on Dodonna's face—he wasn't all that happy about giving us the first batch. If Her Royal Highness hadn't been standing right there saying goodbye, I'm pretty sure he would have tried to talk us down."

He glared into his mug. Besides, he didn't add, asking Princess Leia for replacement reward credits would mean he'd have to tell her how he'd lost the first batch. Not in gambling or bad investments or even drinking, but to a kriffing pirate.

And then she would give him one of those looks.

There were, he decided, worse things than being on Jabba's hit list.

On the other hand, if this offer of a job he'd picked up at the Ord Mantell drop was for real, there was a good chance Leia would never have to know.

"Hello there, Solo." The raspy voice came from Han's right. "Eyes front, hands flat on the table. You too, Wookiee."

Han set his teeth firmly together as he let go of his mug and laid his hands palms down on the table. So much for the job offer being legit. "That you, Falsta?"

"Hey, good memory," Falsta said approvingly as he sidled around into Han's view and sat down on the chair across the table. He was just as Han remembered him: short and scrawny, wearing a four-day stubble and his usual wraparound leather jacket over yet another from his collection of flame-bird shirts. His blaster was even uglier than his shirt: a heavily modified Clone Wars–era DT-57.

Falsta liked to claim the weapon had once been owned by General Grievous himself. Han didn't believe that any more than anyone else did.

"I hear Jabba's mad at you," Falsta continued, resting his elbow on the table and leveling the barrel of his blaster squarely at Han's face. "Again."

"I hear *you've* branched out into assassinations," Han countered, eyeing the blaster and carefully repositioning his leg underneath the table. He would have just one shot at this.

Falsta shrugged. "Hey, if that's what the customer wants, that's what the customer gets. I can tell you this much: Black Sun pays a whole lot better for a kill than

Jabba does for a grab." He wiggled the barrel of his blaster a little. "Not that I don't mind picking up a few free credits. As long as I just happen to be here anyway."

"Sure, why not?" Han agreed, frowning. That was a strange comment. Was Falsta saying that he *wasn't* the one who'd sent Han that message?

No—ridiculous. The galaxy was a huge place. There was no possible way that a bounty hunter could have just *happened* to drop in on a random cantina in a random city on a random world at the same time Han was there. No, Falsta was just being cute.

That was fine. Han could be cute, too. "So you're saying that if I gave you double what Jabba's offering, you'd get up and walk away?" he asked.

Falsta smiled evilly. "You got it on you?"

Han inclined his head toward Chewbacca. "Third power pack down from the shoulder."

Falsta's eyes flicked to Chewbacca's bandoleer—

And in a single contorted motion Han banged his knee up, slamming the table into Falsta's elbow and knocking his blaster out of line as he grabbed his mug and hurled the Corellian spiced ale into Falsta's eyes. There was a brief flash of heat as the bounty hunter's reflexive shot sizzled past Han's left ear.

One shot was all Falsta got. An instant later his blaster was pointed harmlessly at the ceiling, frozen in place by Chewbacca's iron grip around both the weapon and the hand holding it.

That should have been the end of it. Falsta should have conceded defeat, surrendered his blaster, and walked out of the cantina, a little humiliated but still alive.

But Falsta had never been the type to concede anything. Even as he blinked furiously at the ale still running down into his eyes, his left hand jabbed like a knife inside his jacket and emerged with a small hold-out blaster.

He was in the process of lining up the weapon when Han shot him under the table. Falsta fell forward, his right arm still raised in Chewbacca's grip, his hold-out blaster clattering across the tabletop before it came to a halt. Chewbacca held that pose another moment, then lowered Falsta's arm to the table, deftly removing the blaster from the dead man's hand as he did so.

For a half dozen seconds Han didn't move, gripping his blaster under the table, his eyes darting around the cantina. The place had gone quiet, with practically every eye now focused on him. As far as he could tell no one had drawn a weapon, but most of the patrons at the nearest tables had their hands on or near their holsters.

Chewbacca rumbled a warning. "You all saw it," Han called, though he doubted more than a few of them actually had. "He shot first."

There was another moment of silence. Then, almost casually, hands lifted from blasters, heads turned away, and the low conversation resumed.

Maybe this sort of thing happened all the time in Reggilio's. Or maybe they all knew Falsta well enough that no one was going to miss him.

Still, it was definitely time to move on. "Come on," Han muttered, holstering his blaster and sliding around the side of the table. They would go back to the spaceport area, he decided, poke around the cantinas there, and see if they could snag a pickup cargo. It almost certainly wouldn't net them enough to pay off Jabba, but it would at least get them off Wukkar. He stood up, giving the cantina one final check—

"Excuse me?"

Han spun around, reflexively dropping his hand back to the grip of his blaster. But it was just an ordinary human man hurrying toward him.

Or rather, *most* of a man. Half of his face was covered in a flesh-colored medseal that had been stretched across the skin and hair, with a prosthetic eye bobbing along at the spot where his right eye would normally be.

It wasn't just any eye, either. It was something alien-designed, glittering like a smaller version of an Arconian multifaceted eye. Even in the cantina's dim light the effect was striking, unsettling, and strangely hypnotic.

With a jolt, Han realized he'd been staring and forced his gaze away. Not only was it rude, but a visual grab like that was exactly the sort of trick a clever assassin might use to draw his victim's attention at a critical moment.

But the man's hands were empty, with no blaster or blade in sight. In fact, his right hand wouldn't have been of any use anyway. Twisted and misshapen, it was wrapped tightly in the same medseal as his face. Either it had been seriously damaged or else there was a prosthetic under there that had come from the same aliens who'd supplied him with that eye. "You might want to see about getting a different eye," Han suggested, relaxing a bit.

"I need to see about a great many things," the man said, stopping a couple of meters back. His remaining eye flicked to Han's blaster, then rose with an effort back to his face. "Allow me to introduce myself," he continued. "My name is Eanjer—well, my surname isn't important. What *is* important is that I've been robbed of a great deal of money."

"Sorry to hear it," Han said, backing toward the door. "You need to talk to the Iltarr City police."

"They can't help me," Eanjer said, taking one step forward with each backward one Han took. "I want my credits back, and I need someone who can handle himself and doesn't mind working outside law or custom. That's why I'm here. I was hoping I could find someone who fits both those criteria." His eye flicked to Falsta's body. "Having seen you in action, it's clear that you're exactly the type of person I'm looking for."

"It was self-defense," Han countered, picking up his pace. The man's problem was probably a petty gambling debt, and he had no intention of getting tangled up in something like that.

But whatever else Eanjer might be, the man was determined. He sped up to match Han's pace, staying right with him. "I don't want you to do it for free," he said. "I can pay. I can pay very, very well."

Han slowed to a reluctant halt. It was probably still something petty, and hearing the guy out would be a complete waste of time. But sitting around a spaceport cantina probably would be, too.

And if he *didn't* listen, there was a good chance the pest would follow him all the way to the spaceport. "How much are we talking about?" he asked.

"At a minimum, all your expenses," Eanjer said. "At a maximum—" He glanced around and lowered his voice to a whisper. "The criminals stole a hundred sixty-three million credits. If you get it back, I'll split it with you and whoever else you call in to help you."

Han felt his throat tighten. This could still be nothing. Eanjer might just be spinning cobwebs.

But if he was telling the truth . . .

"Fine," Han said. "Let's talk. But not here."

Eanjer looked back at Falsta's body, a shiver running through him. "No," he agreed softly. "Anyplace but here."

"THE THIEF'S name is Avrak Villachor," Eanjer said, his single eye darting around the diner Han had chosen, a more upscale place than the cantina and a prudent three blocks away. "More precisely, he's the leader of the particular group involved. I understand he's also affiliated with some larger criminal organization—I don't know which one."

Han looked across the table at Chewbacca and raised his eyebrows. The Wookiee gave a little shrug and shook his head. Apparently he'd never heard of Villachor, either. "Yeah, there are lots to choose from," he told Eanjer.

"Indeed." Eanjer looked down at his drink as if noticing it for the first time, then continued his nervous scanning of the room. "My father is—was—a very successful goods importer. Three weeks ago Villachor came to our home with a group of thugs and demanded he sign over his business to Villachor's organization. When he refused—" A shudder ran through his body. "They killed him," he said, his voice almost too low to hear. "They just . . . they didn't even use blasters. It was some kind of fragmentation grenade. It just tore him . . ." He trailed off.

"That what happened to your face?" Han asked.

Eanjer blinked and looked up. "What? Oh." He lifted his medsealed hand to gently touch his medsealed face. "Yes, I caught the edge of the blast. There was so much blood. They must have thought I was dead. . . ." He shivered, as if trying to shake away the memory. "Anyway, they took everything from his safe and left. All the corporate records, the data on our transport network, the lists of subcontractors—everything."

"Including a hundred sixty-three million credits?" Han asked. "Must have been a pretty big safe."

"Not really," Eanjer said. "Walk-in, but nothing special. The money was in credit tabs, one million per. A hip pouch would hold them all." He hitched his chair a little closer to the table. "But here's the thing. Credit tabs are keyed to the owner and the owner's designated agents. With my father now dead, I'm the only one who can get the full value out of them. For anyone else, they're worth no more than a quarter, maybe half a percent of the face value. And *that's* only if Villachor can find a slicer who can get through the security coding."

"That still leaves him eight hundred thousand," Han pointed out. "Not bad for a night's work."

"Which is why I have no doubt that he's currently hunting for a slicer to do the job." Eanjer took a deep breath. "Here's the thing. The business records Villachor stole don't matter. All the people who worked for us were there specifically and personally because of my father, and without him they're going to fade away into the mist. Especially since the credit tabs were on hand because we were preparing to pay out for services received. You don't pay a shipper, he doesn't work for you anymore."

Especially if that shipper was actually a smuggler, which was what Han strongly suspected was behind the family's so-called import business. He still wasn't sure if Eanjer himself knew that, suspected it, or was completely oblivious. "Let me get this straight," he said. "You want us to break into Villachor's place—you know where that is, by the way?"

"Oh, yes," Eanjer said, nodding. "It's right here in Iltarr City. It's an estate called Marblewood, nearly a square kilometer's worth of grounds surrounding a big mansion."

"Ah," Han said. Probably the big open space in the northern part of the city that he'd spotted as he was bringing the *Falcon* in. At the time, he'd guessed it was a park. "You want us to go there, break into wherever he's keeping the credit tabs, steal them, and get out again. That about cover it?"

"Yes," Eanjer said. "And I'm very grateful—"

"No."

Eanjer's single eye blinked. "Excuse me?"

"You've got the wrong man," Han told him. "We're

shippers, like your father. We don't know the first thing about breaking into vaults."

"But surely you know people who do," Eanjer said. "You could call them. I'll split the credits with them, too. Everyone can have an equal share."

"You can call them yourself."

"But I don't *know* any such people," Eanjer protested, his voice pleading now. "I can't just pick up a comlink and ask for the nearest thief. And without you—" He broke off, visibly forcing himself back under control. "I saw how you handled that man in the cantina," he said. "You think fast and you act decisively. More important, you didn't kill him until you had no choice. That means I can trust you to get the job done, and to deal fairly with me when it's over."

Han sighed. "Look—"

"No, *you* look," Eanjer bit out, a hint of anger peeking through the frustration. "I've been sitting in cantinas for two solid weeks. You're the first person I've found who gives me any hope at all. Villachor's already had three weeks to find a slicer for those credit tabs. If I don't get them out before he does, he'll win. He'll win everything."

Han looked at Chewbacca. But the Wookiee was sitting quietly, with no hint as to what he was thinking or feeling. Clearly, he was leaving this one up to Han. "Is it the credits you really want?" he asked Eanjer. "Or are you looking for vengeance?"

Eanjer looked down at his hand. "A little of both," he admitted.

Han lifted his mug and took a long swallow. He was right, of course. He and Chewbacca really weren't the ones for this job.

But Eanjer was also right. They knew plenty of people who were.

And with 163 million credits on the line . . .

"I need to make a call," he said, lowering his mug and pulling out his comlink.

Eanjer nodded, making no move to leave. "Right."

Han paused. "A *private* call."

For another second Eanjer still didn't move. Then, abruptly, his eye widened. "Oh," he said, getting hastily to his feet. "Right. I'll, uh, I'll be back."

Chewbacca warbled a question. "It can't hurt to ask around," Han told him, keying in a number and trying to keep his voice calm. A hundred sixty-three million. Even a small slice of that would pay off Jabba a dozen times over. And not just Jabba, but everyone else who wanted a piece of Han's head surrounded by onions on a serving dish. He could pay them all off his back, and still have enough for him and Chewie to run free and clear wherever they wanted. Maybe for the rest of their lives. "I just hope Rachele Ree's not off on a trip somewhere."

To his mild surprise, she was indeed home.

"Well, hello, Han," she said cheerfully when Han had identified himself. "Nice to hear from you, for a change. Are you on Wukkar? Oh, yes—I see you are. Iltarr City, eh? Best Corellian food on the planet."

Chewbacca rumbled a comment under his breath. Han nodded sourly. His comlink was supposedly set up to prevent location backtracks, but electronic safeguards never seemed to even slow Rachele down. "Got a question," he said. "Two questions. First, have you heard anything about a high-level break-in and murder over the last month or so? It would have been at an import company."

"You talking about Polestar Imports?" Rachele asked. "Sure—it was the talk of the lounges about three weeks ago. The owner was killed, and his son apparently went underground."

"Well, he's bobbed back up again," Han said. "Is the son's name Eanjer, and was he hurt in the attack?"

"Let me check . . . yes—Eanjer Kunarazti. As to whether he was hurt . . . the article doesn't say. Let me check one of my other sources . . . yes, looks like it. His blood was found at the scene, anyway."

"Good enough," Han said. He hadn't really thought Eanjer was pulling a scam, but it never hurt to check. "I mean, not *good*, but—"

"I know what you mean," Rachele said, with what Han could imagine was a sly smile. "Second question?"

"Can you run a few names and see if any of them is in spitting distance of Wukkar right now?" Han asked. "Eanjer's offered me the job of getting back the credits that were stolen."

"Really," Rachele said, sounding bemused. "You been branching out since I saw you last?"

"Not really," Han said. Fighting a battle or two for the Rebel Alliance didn't qualify as branching out, he told himself firmly. "He just likes the way I do things."

"Doesn't everybody?" Rachele countered dryly. "No problem. Who are you looking for?"

Han ran down all the names he could think of, people who were both competent and reasonably trustworthy. Considering how many years he'd spent swimming through the galaxy's fringe, it was a surprisingly short list. He added three more names at Chewbacca's suggestion, and pointedly ignored the Wookiee's fourth offering. "That's it," he told Rachele. "If I think of anyone else, I'll call you back."

"Sure," Rachele said. "Did your new friend mention the potential take? Some of these people will want to know that up front."

Han smiled tightly, wishing he were there to see her expression. "If we get it all, we'll be splitting a hundred sixty-three million."

There was a moment of stunned silence at the other end. "Really," Rachele said at last. "Wow. You could practically hire Jabba himself for that amount."

"Thanks, but we'll pass," Han said. "And that number assumes Eanjer lives through the whole thing. You should probably make *that* clear, too."

"I will," Rachele said. "So it's all in credit tabs, huh? Makes sense. Okay, I'll make some calls and get back to you. Does he have any idea where the credit tabs are?"

"He says they're with someone named Villachor," Han said. "You know him?"

There was another short pause. "Yes, I've heard of him," Rachele said, her voice subtly changed. "Okay, I'll get started on your list. Where are you staying?"

"Right now we're just bunking in the *Falcon*."

"Well, you'll eventually need something in town," Rachele said. "Of course, everything in sight's already been booked for the upcoming Festival. But I'll see what I can come up with."

"Thanks, Rachele," Han said. "I owe you."

"Bet on it. Catch you later."

Han keyed off the comlink and put it away.

Chewbacca warbled a question.

"Because I don't want him, that's why," Han said. "I doubt he'd show up even if I asked."

Chewbacca growled again.

"Because he said he never wanted to see me again, remember?" Han said. "Lando *does* occasionally mean what he says, you know."

A motion caught the edge of his eye, and he looked up to see Eanjer moving hesitantly toward them. "Is everything all right?" Eanjer asked, his eye flicking back and forth between them.

"Sure," Han said. "I've got someone looking into getting a team together."

"Wonderful," Eanjer said, coming the rest of the way

to the table and easing into his seat. He must have seen the end of that brief argument, Han decided, and probably thought it had been more serious than it actually had. "This person is someone you can trust?"

Han nodded. "She's a low-ranking member of the old Wukkar aristocracy. Knows everyone and everything, and isn't exactly thrilled with the people who are running the show right now."

"If you say so," Eanjer said. He didn't sound entirely convinced, but it was clear he wasn't ready to press the issue. "I think I've come up with a perfect time for the break-in. Two weeks from now is the Festival of Four Honorings."

Han looked at Chewbacca, got a shrug in return. "Never heard of it," he told Eanjer.

"It's Wukkar's version of Carnival Week," Eanjer said, his lip twisting. "Anything Imperial Center does, someone here has to do better. Anyway, it's a seven-day event with a day each devoted to stone, air, water, and fire, with a prep day in between each of the Honorings. It's the most important event on Wukkar, with people coming from as far away as Vuma and Imperial Center to attend."

"And probably pickpockets from as far away as Nal Hutta," Han murmured.

"I wouldn't know," Eanjer said. "My point is that Villachor hosts one of the city's biggest celebrations on his grounds."

Han sat up a little straighter. "On his *grounds*? You mean he lets people wander around right next to his house?"

"More a mansion than a house," Eanjer said. "Or perhaps more a fortress than a mansion. But yes, thousands of people come and go freely over those four days."

Chewbacca warbled the obvious point. "Of course he'll have beefed-up security," Han agreed. "But at least we won't have to get over any walls and through an outer sentry line. How do we get an invitation to this thing?"

"None needed," Eanjer said. "It's open to all." The half of his mouth that was visible curved upward in a bitter smile. "Villachor likes to style himself as a philanthropist and a friend of the city. He also likes to show off his wealth and style."

"That's okay," Han said. "Some of my best deals came from people who thought they were better and smarter than everyone else. This might actually work."

"Then you'll help me?" Eanjer asked hopefully.

"Let's first see what Rachele comes up with," Han said. "I've got some ideas, but like I said before, this isn't our specialty. But if we can get the people I need, we should at least have a shot."

"Make sure they know what's involved," Eanjer said. "A hundred and sixty-three million."

"Yeah, I got that part," Han said. "Give me your comlink number, and I'll call when we've got more to talk about."

"All right," Eanjer said a bit uncertainly as he dug out a data card and handed it over. "When will that be?"

"When," Han said with exaggerated patience, "we've got more to talk about."

THEY WERE back at the *Falcon* when Rachele's report came in.

As usual with life, the results were mixed. Many of the people Han had hoped to contact were out of touch, out of the immediate area, or temporarily out of circulation. Others who might otherwise have been possibilities would take too long to get hold of, especially with the two-week countdown to the Festival that Eanjer was looking at.

And there were a couple who were unavailable themselves but had people they could recommend. Mazzic, in particular, had already grabbed the initiative and informed Rachele that he would be sending two new recruits who matched the skills of the ones Han had asked about.

Chewbacca wasn't at all sure he liked that. "Yeah, me neither," Han agreed, frowning at the note Rachele had sent. Still, Han had known Mazzic for a number of years, and he and Chewbacca had occasionally run cargoes for him and his small smuggling organization. Mazzic had shown himself both trustworthy and competent.

More to the point, he was notorious for not trusting anyone himself until he'd thoroughly checked out the candidate. If he was okay with these recruits, they were probably safe enough.

Unless he was trying to get back at Han for something. But that was unlikely. Han hadn't done anything to Mazzic, not that he could remember. Certainly not lately.

Chewbacca grunted a question.

"I guess we go hunting," Han told him, levering himself to his feet. "Go fire up the *Falcon*. I'll see about getting us a liftoff slot."